THE COCK & OYSTER

A HISTORICAL COZY MYSTERY SERIES

ELYSABETH GRACE

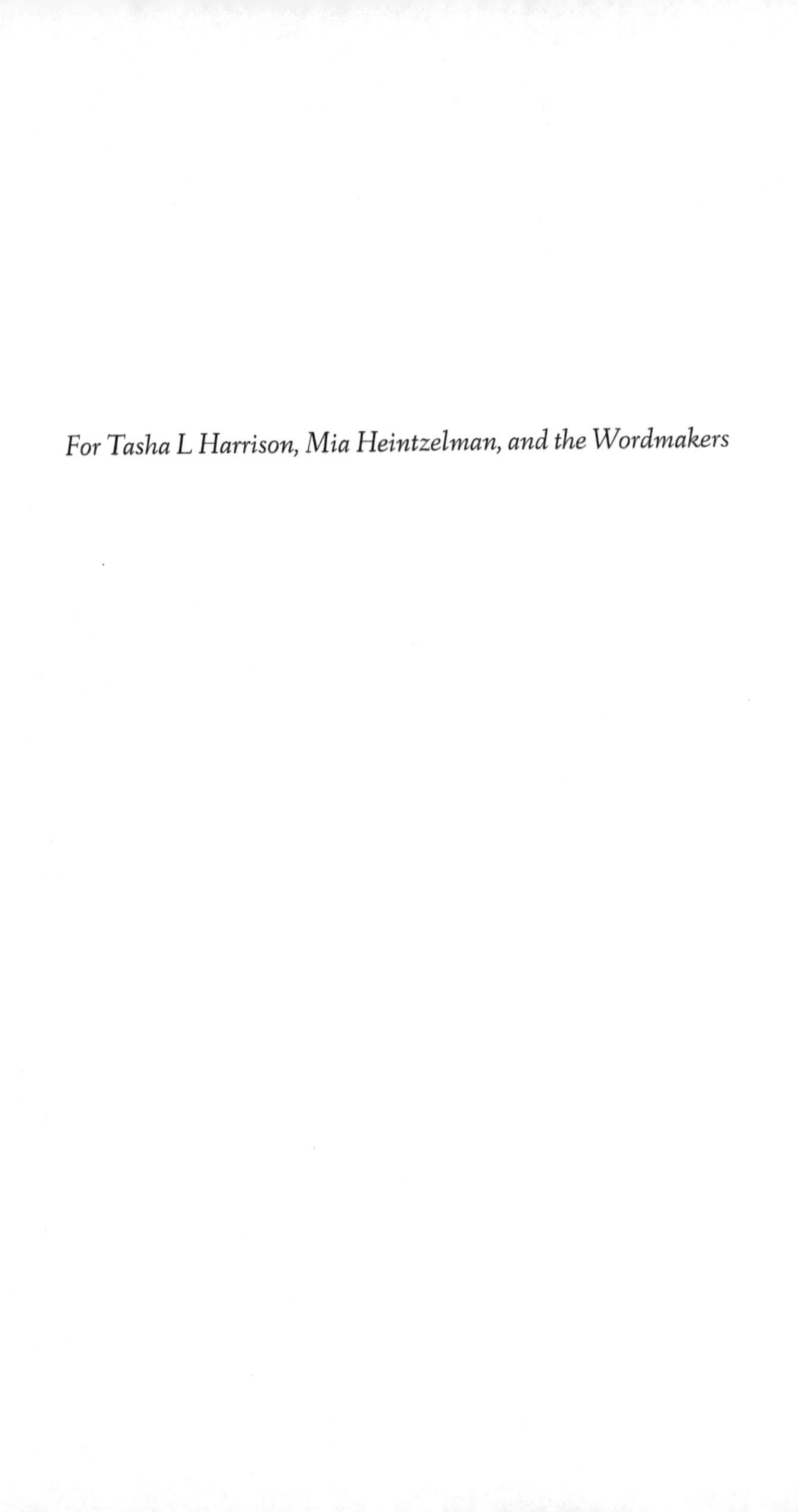

For Tasha L Harrison, Mia Heintzelman, and the Wordmakers

AUTHOR'S NOTES

Dear Reader,

If we shadows have offended,
Think but this, and all is mended,
That you have but slumber'd here
While these visions did appear. (*A Midsummer Night's Dream*)

The Cock & Oyster series has reached its end. A playful take on the cozy mystery genre and the film versions of Dashiell Hammett's *Thin Man* novels, my stories play fast and loose with Shakespeare's *Hamlet*, *A Midsummer Night's Dream*, *Macbeth*, *Othello*, *Much Ado about Nothing*, and *Antony and Cleopatra*. These tales are irreverent and in no way adhere to the idea of historical accuracy, although there is a wee bit of authenticity. My purpose has been nothing more than to craft a lascivious romp that hopefully readers find amusing and detracts from their daily cares.

What you'll find in these pages is the complete collection, slightly revised and edited and with new material. If typos occur, it's the fault of the author despite the exceptional care A.K Edits gives to my writing. It's always that last-minute tweak (IYKYK). Sydney Tricks designed the amazing covers for the first four novellas, while DotCovers designed the fabulous cover for this book. I could not have done this without these talented and forgiving individuals. Much love and appreciation to them. All faults are mine.

If you're new to the *Cock & Oyster Historical Cozy Mystery* series, know that each story involves a murder or crime and some violence (I am deeply indebted to Willie S for this). My world-building does reflect Elizabethan England's social landscape and a diverse population. The main characters are a former brothel owner, Aisha Resonne, who goes by the name of Ellen Chapman and is Black English, and Percy Howard, Lord Ross, who is white English and a spy for the Queen. Percy and Aisha are an older couple (40ish) and have an active sex life with added spice (BDSM). Like Nick and Nora Charles (*The Thin Man* films), Percy and Aisha imbibe. What this detective couple does differently is spend a lot of time making love whenever they can.

In writing these stories, I sought to avoid the racist, sexist, and homophobic language that pervaded the period as much as possible. However, it would be a historical lie to pretend Aisha's color or the issue of class weren't aspects of daily life in early modern England. Since any book dealing with history/ies should carry a content warning, I want to note that there may be references or depictions that can be triggers. Please exercise care when reading these mystery tales as they deal with murder, potential incest, kidnap, and child neglect.

I hope you enjoy *The Cock & Oyster Historical Cozy Mystery Series* with a dash of kink.

Elysabeth

HOW PERCY AND AISHA MET

"Well, fuck me," Percy Elwen Howard, Lord Ross and one of Queen Elizabeth's most capable spies, uttered as his gaze took in the best-looking arse in a gown he'd seen in years. "I do believe I've finally met my wife-to-be and the future Lady Ross."

A soft, throaty laugh floated across the room and wrapped itself around the nerve endings of Percy's hardening cock. Without a glance back at the man who spoke, the owner of the Cock & Oyster Brothel, where he presently stood, replied, "Fucking you is subject to conditions, diplomacy, and whether the voice and the man match."

Her hesitation was deliberate, filled with invitation and seduction, and Percy held his breath until she added, "However, since you are in a brothel, if your coin is plentiful and your cock well-formed and rigorous, all things are possible and negotiable."

Percy closed the door behind him. "Although I'm a stickler for negotiations and diplomacy in state matters, I doubt I'll have the will or the reason to do either when it comes to you, and I haven't even seen your lovely face. Nonetheless, my heart has been captured by your voice and arse, and I fear I've fallen in love."

Ellen Chapman's laughter brushed his senses like a slow-moving stream, languid and tempting at the same time. "So early in the day. Give it time, Lord Ross, give it time," she murmured as she turned to face her visitor. "Love and lust are two sides of the same coin. What matters is when the coin is tossed, which side lands face up."

Staring at the exquisite loveliness of Aisha Resonne, who owned the brothel under the name Ellen Chapman, Percy accepted he was done for. Hoisted. Ensorcelled. Bewitched. Done for. His days of wandering were over, for he'd found his home.

He held no prejudice when it came to a woman's beauty, for it was always in the eye of the beholder. Yet, to behold Aisha's dark eyes and luscious brown skin had his heart racing and his breath struggling to escape his lungs. His gaze slowly swept her, from the coiled braids framing an oval-shaped face to a nose neither flat nor straight but perfection in size and curve. However, it was her mouth that tangled his thoughts and made him want to capture her lips with his own. Full, lush, and an invitation to paradise.

His eyes trailed down her body. Aisha's blue satin gown was ordinary, not what he'd expect to find in a brothel, lacking the embellishments usually marking women of the trade. Her breasts teased the silken fabric of her bodice with the promise of a reveal, but it wasn't to be. Not to be deterred, he sauntered closer and inhaled, then hastily released the breath as the scent of her invaded his lungs and coursed through his blood. His lips parted, and his tongue whipped across his bottom lip. He wanted to taste Aisha's scent on her skin, especially between her thighs.

"You do realize you're staring," she observed, her voice steeped with amusement. "Have you not seen a Black woman before?"

"I...I...yes, I...of course. It's...they're everywhere in England...I mean..."

She chuckled at his awkwardness. "I suspect you are rarely at a loss for words, Lord Ross. Please sit and enjoy a glass of wine while you tell me your business with the Cock & Oyster since I'm sure you have no need of our services."

Percy stared at the chair she pointed to and, after a few seconds, walked over and sat. His words still hadn't found their way to his tongue, so when she handed him a glass of wine, he nodded his thanks and quickly took a sip. Ellen pulled a chair opposite him and raised her glass to her lips.

"Let me begin with a declaration, Mistress Chapman, or truthfully Aisha Resonne. I am in love with you, and one day, you will be my wife." He took another sip to hide his grin at her astonished face. "As to the business that brings me to your door, it involves a search for a young woman who eloped."

"If she eloped, why on earth would you visit a brothel in search of her?"

"It seems the elopement failed once the couple arrived in London."

"Presumably she's nobility, so I can assure you, Lord Ross, the Cock & Oyster hasn't taken on a noblewoman for some time," Ellen stated.

He peered at her. "You're going to ignore my declaration?"

She raked him with her eyes before she smiled. "No, but as I said, it's early in the day, Lord Ross, and although you know my names, we've just met. Shall we proceed to the matter that brought you to my door?"

Percy reached into his coat pocket and pulled out a miniature portrait. Handing it to Ellen, he asked, "Have you seen this young lady?"

She studied the portrait. "A lovely woman." Giving the portrait back to him, she shook her head. "Why do you believe she's in a brothel? Perhaps she is making her way home even as we speak."

"Not likely," Percy retorted. "The man abandoned her in London before he returned to the town where they resided. Her family wants to keep the matter private, without fanfare."

"Which is why they sought your aid."

He nodded. "I've interviewed several witnesses who swear they've seen her among the ladies of pleasure. Hence, my visitation to the likeliest houses to employ a noblewoman."

What is her name?"

"Alison Hathaway. She's eighteen years and, according to her maid servant, a bit flighty."

"Well, my lord, Alison Hathaway has not set foot in the Cock & Oyster. Have you tried Holland's League? Bess Holland is keen to add to her employees while I am not."

Percy smiled. "'Tis my next stop. Not that I mistrust you, but would you mind if I met the women of the Cock & Oyster?"

Ellen rose from her chair and walked over to a velvet rope. Tugging it, she turned to face him. "'Tis a common occurrence among men."

"What?"

"Mistrust. May I have the portrait please?" she asked, walking over to him.

He handed it to her, and she returned to the door she left ajar. Her voice was soft yet melodic with a hint of an accent he couldn't quite place as she gave instructions to whomever stood in the corridor. Several silent minutes passed before the women of the Cock & Oyster strolled into the parlor and seated themselves on the chairs and divans scattered about the room.

"Ladies, Lord Ross, one of Her Majesty's favorite employees, asked to be introduced to you. Sadly, it's not for your beauty or charm," Ellen stated drolly. "He is in search of a runaway who may be hiding in a brothel. Since birds of a feather are presumed to flock together, have any of you seen this young lady?"

She handed the portrait to the woman seated nearest her. "Please look carefully, and if you recognize her, speak up."

The courtesans passed the portrait among themselves and shook their heads. One of the women peered at Percy. "I know most of the courtesans working in brothels, and I've not seen this woman before. How recently did she arrive in London and start to work, my lord? What is her name?"

"Alison Hathaway. She ran away a month ago. The man she eloped with returned home, claiming she refused to return to her family and declared her intentions of becoming a courtesan."

"Have you checked Old Lady Holland? She's most likely to take the woman in."

"So true, Eleanor," one of the younger courtesans remarked. "Holland can't keep anyone longer than six months with her parsimonious ways. If this Alison went to work for her, she'll search new dwellings before the year is done. Do you recall Meg Carter? She didn't last two months and—"

"Thank you, Eveline," Ellen interrupted. "I'm certain Lord Ross isn't here for trade gossip."

Eveline tittered before she stood and followed the others out of the salon, shutting the door behind her. Ellen shifted her gaze to Percy. "Is there anything else I can do for you, my lord?"

Percy heard the teasing note in her voice, a lyrical sound that went straight to his cock. Rising from his chair, he approached her until only inches separated them. The sound of her quick inhalation triggered an instant semi-erection. *Lord, this woman is capable of destroying all of my self-control.*

"Yes, there is something else." He set his goblet on a nearby table, took her slender brown hand in his, and brought it to his lips. "I want you, Aisha Resonne, and yes, I know a number of your secrets."

He gently tugged her against him and wrapped his arms around her. "That is neither here nor there since I've taken an oath to make you Lady Ross. Don't frown. I'm only giving you fair warning."

"And if I choose to ignore your warning, reject your advances? What then, my lord?"

His fingers reached up and brushed a loose curl from her temple. "Kiss me, Aisha."

Her eyes darkened with an emotion he couldn't name but hoped it was passion since she didn't attempt to extricate herself from his hold. Instead, she peered into his eyes, studying him as if to decipher his reasoning. When he couldn't bear the uncertainty any longer and parted his lips, she smiled. "I believe I will, Percy Howard, Lord Ross."

Her head tilted slightly, and her pink tongue traced a wet path across her bottom lip before doing the same to the upper twin. The scent of mint invaded his nostrils when she softly exhaled and murmured, "Yes, I will kiss you."

Then her mouth brushed his, a feathery touch much like a butterfly's wing, and his stomach clenched. He dare not move for fear she'd change her mind, so desperate was he to know the taste and feel of the inside of her mouth. Ellen's lips were rose petal-soft against his, and he lost the battle to control his cock when her tongue flicked the corners of his mouth.

She leaned back and peered into his eyes, hers dancing with amusement. "Oh sweet Percy, thou dost please me."

With those words, she devoured his mouth with a kiss that curled his toes and had him praying she'd never stop. Her tongue danced atop his with a rhythm that nearly stripped him of breath. He was helpless to counter her movements, so deeply enmeshed in the wicked sensations she stirred inside him he wanted to beg for relief.

Her mouth was sorcery beyond imagination, a temptation he willingly pursued. Her kiss sent him soaring towards uncharted territory where every lick, stroke, and caress altered his perception of what desire should be. It was a heaven he longed for and feared he had no right to enter.

Percy's body shivered when slender fingers undid his breeches and wrapped around his hard flesh. Just one stroke and he'd be undone. "Aisha," he gasped.

"Yes, Percy?"

"Do you intend to fuck me?"

She licked the inside of his mouth before she pulled away, her hand still holding his prick. "I haven't decided. We will have to negotiate terms. I'm aware of your wealth, and your cock is definitely pleasing; thus what remains to be sorted are your expectations. I have no wish to marry, and therein lies the diplomatic rub."

He pressed his penis against the palm of her hand. "I surrender to whatever terms you devise for now. As we come to know each other, you will find I am a determined man, and when in pursuit, I'm quite successful."

She kissed him before she removed her hand and refastened his breeches, giving his prick a gentle pat. "I'm intrigued, and therefore, I will play."

Percy smiled and caressed her temple. "I promise, sweet puss, you'll have no regrets."

"I do hope so, since it was business that brought you to my door, and I don't mix business with pleasure, Lord Ross."

"As our business was concluded when the ladies departed, we are only about pleasure, Aisha Resonne."

"Ellen Chapman."

He bowed and strode to the door. "Good day, Mistress Chapman. Be warned, it is Aisha Resonne who I will make my wife."

MURDER MOST FOUL

ONE

"I must return to London, Percy," Aisha Resonne whispered, kissing his naked chest before she raised her head to peer at him.

Percy Howard had been her lover for six years, and she adored the man, which surprised her. She'd sworn never to give her heart to any man, to focus on the Cock & Oyster as she promised her Aunt Ahmara. While her resolve on the success of the exclusive brothel was unwavering, matters of the heart were less responsive to her will the day Percy Elwen Howard, Lord Ross sauntered into the exclusive house in search of a missing noblewoman who'd run off with a Cornish sailor. The sailor had seduced and abandoned the gullible woman, who was found working at Holland's Leaguer brothel, refusing to return to her family.

A light snore floated from Percy's lips, and Aisha studied his face in the early morning sunlight. Framed by thick silver and black hair, his visage was exactly the type white Englishwomen swooned over despite his forty-five years. A broad forehead, a nose not too thin or too long, and a firm jaw betrayed his stubborn nature. He wasn't a very handsome man, though he was quite pleasant to gaze upon. However, his wit was intoxicating and his manner deceptively seductive, and the man could love her into breathlessness.

Not even the Cock & Oyster's courtesans were immune to his wicked charms, becoming fluttery as hummingbirds whenever he had cause to visit. She wasn't sure whether it was the light brown eyes that twinkled with mischief or the slow, sensuous smile that curved his lips upward to draw attention to a pair of deep-set dimples. Whatever made the courtesans titter like sparrows, she herself wasn't unscathed.

Percy Howard had strolled into her office, self-assured and bordering on arrogance. His gaze swept her entire body slowly before he stated his business, and his personal intentions. Shivers went through her as his deep, sensual voice stripped naked her usual aplomb and trampled it. She'd assumed he was there to challenge her public vow to never become some man's mistress. In the minute of weighted silence floating between them, she was tempted to abandon her oath.

Instead, she'd forced a smile and said, "Be warned, my lord, I'm not for sale, and I don't mix business and pleasure."

Percy's rebuttal surfaced in her mind as she studied the man sleeping beside her. A faint giggle escaped at the memory. With the characteristic boldness he'd displayed over the course of their relationship, he had inhaled and replied, "I'm not looking to purchase, and I also don't mix business with pleasure. And for that reason, you will never be my business, Mistress Chapman. Only my pleasure once I conclude my current task."

She'd been intrigued, then seduced.

"What are you thinking, sweet Aisha?" Percy inquired, his voice thick with sleep. "Please don't disappoint me with words about the brothel's affairs. I'd prefer my proposal of marriage be the cause for your lack of slumber."

She sat up and glided her fingertips across his forehead. "Percy."

He reached up and gripped her hand, kissing the palm before placing it back on his forehead. "I've heard all your excuses, sweetheart. None of them mean shite to me."

"Percy Elwen Howard, watch your tongue."

He sat upright in the bed and tucked her into an embrace. "I'd much rather gaze upon your face while my tongue licks your sweet bud to convince you my intentions are honorable."

"Why can't matters remain as they are? There is no need to alter our arrangement."

He released her and rose from the bed, tension radiating across his naked back. Her gaze followed the tight muscles of his arse as he walked over to a table. She loved every delicious bit of the man and hated that her reluctance to marry frequently resulted in an argument. Watching him pour wine into a goblet and drink half, she resigned herself to another round.

"Percy, I'm neither noble nor white. Wasn't it enough your uncle gave up his title to marry my aunt?"

He slammed the goblet on the table and whipped around to face her. "I don't give a damn about your color or your birth, Aisha! As to my uncle, he has never been happier."

"Do you intend to give up the title, Lord Ross? To marry me, that is what you will have to do, and not just because of my common blood," she came back. "What will you say when your wife is called a bawd or a quean? Do you believe Ellen Chapman or even Aisha Resonne will be accepted in court as a Black noblewoman?"

She waited for him to flinch at her words. Instead, he came around the bed and sat beside her.

"Aisha, my uncle never wanted the title. He much preferred being a simple farmer, and your aunt has given him that life. He regrets nothing about his choice; he would have sacrificed the world for her. As to Aisha Resonne in court—I've yet to meet a woman more noble than you. Besides, I don't care what the court thinks."

His gaze swept her face. "Your color...I wish my pale skin was as beautiful. I want you, Aisha Resonne, as my wife. My uncle didn't sacrifice anything for love, and neither will I."

Her eyes became wet, and she shook her head. "I can't let you, Percy."

"It isn't your choice, Aisha. It's mine." He pressed a finger to the space just below her bottom left eyelid, halting a tear in its track. "Look at me."

When her eyes met his, he smiled. "One day soon, you will become my wife, and I don't need to make sacrifices to bring it about."

She opened her mouth to speak, and he placed a finger on her lips. "Hush, love. Let me bring you pleasure since I know you're in a hurry to return to London."

He then captured her mouth, and his tongue rendered her silent while his hand slid between her legs, teasing her into a familiar state of bliss.

THE CARRIAGE RUMBLED toward London and Percy smiled when Aisha snuggled closer. His gaze lingered on Aisha's hair, and his fingers instinctively stroked one of the coiled braids. Afternoon sunlight spiked through the parted leather curtains and illuminated the few threads of silver concealed among the sable strands—visible if you knew where to look. He adored the soft, silky texture, especially when she undid her braids and he toyed with a shoulder-length curl, which inevitably led to an erection.

Her exquisite brown skin was unblemished and petal-soft. When they first met, her dark eyes studied him before she asked whether his visit was one of pleasure or for another purpose. She was direct, even fierce in her protection of the women who practiced their trade in the Cock & Oyster, several of whom he suspected were daughters and widows of noble birth who'd rejected marriage. A suspicion he'd left unexamined.

He'd been enchanted by Aisha Resonne from the second he walked into her parlor. It had taken him several months to convince her to dine with him. She'd agreed but with a condition—they would dine at her Southwark house. It was late when he'd reluctantly departed with a quick brush of her lips across his cheek. As he made his way to his London house that night, Percy accepted he'd never find a woman like Aisha in several lifetimes and was determined to win her affections.

His arm tightened as she shifted. Everything about the woman asleep in his arms had him like a male cat in heat. Her mind was one of the sharpest he'd encountered, and her wit often reduced him to unfettered mirth. He'd tossed his vaunted self-restraint the first time he set eyes on her, vowing to make her his. The only obstacle was the lady herself.

The carriage bobbled, and his arm gripped her protectively. His coach was sturdy and Samuel was an excellent driver, yet Percy hated the roads between his home near Frome in Somerset and London. This trip was less arduous as they'd stopped overnight in Basingstoke to visit his mother's cousin Emery and his companion, both of whom dearly loved Aisha. He'd been happy to appease Emery's request since it meant another night with her. Once they arrived in London, she'd become the owner of a brothel and he Lord Ross, and he hated it.

"What has you so pensive, Percy?" Aisha queried before she sat upright in the coach.

Heavens, he loved her. Kissing her temple, he said, "You realize this is the sixth time you've refused me. If I weren't a determined man, I'd say my pride has taken a veritable beating."

Her laughter filled the inside of the carriage. "Determined? Obstinate, obdurate, pig-headed, mulish—"

"Determined," he insisted. "I wanted a life with you and I went after it, Aisha Resonne."

"Ellen," she snapped.

He sucked in his agitation and slowly released it. "Ellen Chapman. I will not be marrying Ellen, just so you know."

She reached up and kissed his bearded chin. "If—"

"When," he cut her off. "When you marry me. I'm at the point where abduction is under consideration."

"Should I agree to marry you, Percy," she corrected.

"*When*, Aisha," he gritted. "There are no conditionals."

"When I agree to accept your offer, dearest love, I promise to come to you as Aisha Resonne, not Ellen Chapman. Until that time, I suspect only your employer knows my true name, and I will do everything in my power to keep it so."

"Glad you've finally admitted defeat."

He lowered his head and kissed her, his tongue an invasion of her mouth. He licked, tasted, and moaned as she opened wide for him. He succumbed to the invitation, savoring the essence of the mint leaf she'd chewed. Her kisses incited and excited him, and he felt the painful grip of silk on his cock. His hand roughly shoved her gown upward to expose her thighs. A shiver went through her as his fingers stroked their way to her lower lips and two fingers pushed inside her wetness.

The sounds of her pleasure never made it past his lips as he brought her to a quick climax. When her body slowed its quaking, he gentled his kiss. Raising his head, his breathing ragged, he murmured, "If we weren't so close to Ross House, I'd halt this carriage and fuck you."

Aisha shuddered as his fingers left her, and he licked them clean before smoothing her gown back into place. A satisfied smile on his face, he stared into eyes glazed with pleasure. "Alas, there isn't time enough."

She brushed her lips across his mouth. "You will also need softer cushions and a wider seat before I permit such liberties, Lord Ross."

"I so love you, Aisha Resonne," he said with a chuckle. "So very much, and I will hold you to your word. And not just about the carriage."

"My lord, we've arrived." Samuel's voice penetrated the thick leather covering between the driver's seat and the carriage's interior.

Percy waited until Samuel opened the door and placed a stool near the coach. Climbing out, he assisted Aisha from the carriage and led her into his home. "I know you won't stay, but will you remain with me until night falls?"

After a footman removed her traveling cloak, she thanked him and turned to Percy. "Of course."

Taking her hand, Percy Howard led his future wife toward the parlor.

TWO

Aisha stared at the account book splayed open in front of her and frowned. This was the worst part of her week, and she wished she was back in Somerset, cuddling with Percy and being spoiled. The sonorous voice of St. Olav's priest resounded in her head: *Procrastination is a sin.*

"Oh shut up, you lecherous old fool. So are your weekly visits to Mary Cuthbert," Aisha muttered. "She should charge you more than ha'penny."

She picked up two letters, one from her aunt and the other from her brother Issac and his wife, Penelope. She read Issac and Penelope's missive first, smiling as they reminded her she'd not visited her nieces and nephew in some time. Setting the letter aside, she knew the reason she'd distanced herself from her family, even though they were aware of her trade.

Grabbing a clean sheet of paper, she penned a quick note to her brother with a promise to visit in spring. Sucking in a deep breath, she gritted her teeth and stared at the sealed letter from her aunt Ahmara. Aisha offered a quick prayer to her ancestors to care for her aunt before she slid the sharp letter opener beneath the wax seal and opened the folded paper. Relief flooded her as she read. Her aunt and her husband, Percy's uncle Robert, would arrive in London in a fortnight. They were to stay with Percy, and her aunt expected her presence. Aisha chuckled at the gently written command. If she didn't make an appearance, Ahmara would drag her from bed before dawn.

Aisha tucked the letter in a drawer and focused once more on her accounts. A smile creased her lips. After the weekly bribes to the local constable, the "tithes" to the village priest, the expenses for food and drink, and payments to the workers of the Cock & Oyster, her profit was quite good for the month. She recorded the courtesans' payments in a separate journal before she went to a tapestry on the wall behind her desk. Running her hand across the smooth brick, she pressed slightly and a portion of the wall opened. Aisha removed an iron chest and returned to her desk. It only took a few minutes to sort out the various coins needed to pay everyone, including herself. A small pile of leather bags grew on the desk top before she closed the chest, locked it, and returned it to its hiding place.

With wages taken care of, she tugged on a velvet rope beside the tapestry. Her back to the door, she glanced around the room. There were no windows, and she missed the natural light of the sun. Her aunt had explained the reason to her; since this was the accounting room, there should be no means for a robber to enter except through the door, which was always locked.

Three quick raps on the thick doorframe brought her to the door. "Good morning, Randall," she greeted when he strolled into the room.

"Miss Ellen, you've been busy this morning."

Shutting the door, she eyed the large Black man who served as confidant and protector of the women residing in the brothel. His lover and the house's cook, Matthew, was the only other man living in the Cock & Oyster. They'd fled the religious persecutions sweeping France, arriving in London and nearly imprisoned as foreign beggars. Her aunt, seeing their plight, employed them on the spot when she learned Matthew possessed a skill with food and that Randall had been a nobleman's guard.

"The deliveries are ready," Aisha said. "We turned a tidy profit this week, so there is a bit more in each lady's bag and yours and Matthew's. Will you see to the tithes and bribes?"

"Don't I always? What did Tante Ahmara have to say for herself?"

Aisha chuckled. "You'll find out yourself when she arrives in a fortnight. She's determined to visit her business to make certain we've not run it into the ground and," she added with a long-suffering groan, "to see me married."

Randall's booming laughter echoed in the room. "About time she stepped in. It will be good to see her and Lord Robert."

"We'll see," Aisha mumbled. "Any concerns I should put my mind to?"

He shook his head. "Mary wants to go to Holborn to visit the stalls. Once I've taken care of this matter, I'll escort her."

"What's wrong with Camden? Joan is the only herbalist we've used."

Randall sighed. "It seems one of the herb sellers in jealousy spread a few lies, and Joan's stall was taken away. She's returned to her mother's stall in Holborn."

Aisha sucked her teeth. "Do we know which seller?"

"Etta Peterson."

"That charlatan," Aisha spat. "I should have guessed. She preys on the weak-willed and those seeking a quick cure. Let Fate be unkind to her for her wickedness. Inform Joan, should she wish to return at any time, to send word and a stall will be waiting for her."

Randall nodded. "I also think Joan misses her ma and Harry. Etta probably did her a favor with her meanness, although it might not benefit her as much as Joan. Anyway, I'm off. I'll return before you leave for Lord Ross."

As he gathered the bags, Aisha stood and went to the door. She waited until he left the room, then locked it and followed him up the stairs to the brothel's main hallway. Randall turned toward the back of the house, and she laid her hand on his arm.

"Unless there's a murder or fire, I'm taking a bath and don't wish to be bothered."

He chuckled. "I don't understand why you don't employ a clerk to do your scribal work."

"As much as I hate keeping accounts," she huffed, "at least I won't have to worry about an embezzler. It wouldn't be a pretty sight should the ladies' wages come up missing."

Aisha went upstairs to her private room, where a bath waited. She'd sent word to Celeste, and the maidservant never failed her. Despite her shyness, Celeste was a gem. Although far too innocent to be a courtesan, her initial reason for coming to the Cock & Oyster, she'd accepted a maid's position with relief.

Scented steam rose from the tub, and Aisha quickly stripped, tossing her service gown on the floor near a chair. A silk robe and a linen bath sheet were neatly folded on a stool next to the large bathing tub. Climbing in, she lowered herself into the heated water, and thoughts of Percy filled her awareness.

Persistent Percy.

The man gave her no peace. Where was his head, thinking to marry a Black commoner, and a brothel keeper to boot? Her sigh was audible and filled with sadness. She loved the man, and if he came without a title and entailed estates, she'd wed him on the morrow. However, because of his position at court, marriage was unthinkable. They couldn't retire to the country as his uncle did. Marrying Percy meant she'd have to give up the Cock & Oyster, and a small part of her was reluctant to hand the reins over to Ahmara's heir, who had no inkling of her inheritance and was unprepared to take on the burden.

Aisha reflected on her mixed feelings about giving up the brothel. Since taking over the Cock & Oyster, she'd accumulated enough wealth to live comfortably. Why couldn't she acknowledge or speak the real reason for her reluctance to Percy? The answer was obvious—her fear of losing him.

She needed to confront her fears and talk to Percy about them. Maybe Ahmara's visit was an auspicious sign that it was time, and whether it involved marriage or not, Aisha knew her life would always be with Percy.

The tinkling sound of a bell brought her upright. She got out and dried, then smoothed scented oil over her skin. Celeste had placed her latest purchase, a new gown, on her bed. Percy had chosen the color—the green of early summer grass. Slipping it over her head, she loved the feel of the silky fabric against her skin.

Sitting in front of her mirror, she undid the braids she usually wore, brushing and combing her hair before redoing it in a single braid. Once she was satisfied with her appearance, she left the room and went down to the receiving parlor where the courtesans were gathered.

"Look at ya, Miss Ellen," one of the nine women in the room remarked. "Are ya working tonight?"

"Don't be silly, Sally," Ophelia Swinden chided. "Mistress Ellen doesn't sell her wares at the Cock & Oyster. The rest of us wouldn't have no clients."

Aisha blushed and joined in the laughter that followed Ophelia's declaration. Most of the women assumed she was only for private hire, and never at the brothel. Since Percy entered her life, the courtesans viewed her affair with Percy in such light, and she encouraged it. Her gaze swept the room. "Who are your clients tonight, ladies?"

Except for Sally Wooster, all the women practiced the trade. Once she heard the names, Aisha reminded them to look after each other and to make sure Randall, Mary, or Matthew escorted the men from the house once their business was done. She promised to dine with them the next day.

"Mistress Ellen, the sedan chair is here," Mary said as she popped her head inside the parlor.

Aisha nodded and looked at the women in the room. "Make them pay well, ladies. We can all use some new trinkets and gowns."

The laughter that followed her out of the room warmed Aisha's heart. There was a close bond between the women. Even the most recent additions, Ophelia Swinden and her servant Sally Wooster, had found a place among the courtesans —especially since Ophelia preferred working with the more difficult-to-please clients. As she climbed into the sedan chair, Aisha knew part of her reluctance to give up the brothel was because of the people who made it their home. Yet, in the quiet of early evening, she found herself longing for a simpler life. One empty of worry about the precarious nature of the business she ran. She tired of the constables' visitations, the drunken lords who thought she was for sale, and the priestly interference should a tithe be late. Nine years was a veritable lifetime to have survived in the trade.

The only time she knew joy and contentment was in Percy's arms.

THREE

Percy plucked apart the parlor's curtains and peered at the street in front of his London home. The street was empty, nary a soul walking on the cobblestone. Where was she? He'd sent the sedan chair some time ago, and Aisha should have arrived by now. He turned away from the window and rang for his butler, then returned to his vigil in front of the paned glass.

The door swung open and, without looking behind him, Percy said, "Silas, fetch my cloak, please. My guest hasn't arrived, and I'm worried."

"How exactly did you misplace your guest, Lord Ross?"

He swung around, a smile creasing his face as Aisha walked into the room and shut the door behind her. He strode to where she stood and pulled her into his arms. "I didn't misplace her; she didn't arrive when I expected."

Aisha kissed him. "Ah, therein lies your mistake, Percy. Never lay expectations on a woman and you will never be disappointed or worried. I was delayed doing the accounts."

"Then I should count myself blessed that you arrived at all."

"Smart ass."

He removed her cloak and tossed it on a chair. "Do I have your company for the night, Aisha? I have several new bottles of wine, and I'd like your opinion. The winemaker is newly settled near Sussex, having fled Burgundy some months past, bringing with him what he could to England."

"And how did you come by them since I don't recall you traveling to Sussex, Percy Howard?" She rolled her eyes and snorted. "Never mind, I assume said visitation was the reason my dildo was my only companion for a fortnight some months past."

He chuckled and squeezed her right breast. "As long as it *was* your only companion."

Aisha slid her hand down his belly and inside his breeches. "Jealous?"

"Only of you playing without me to watch." He groaned as her fingers squeezed his flesh. "Another man in your life—no, I trust you with my heart, my soul, and my life."

"Well said, Lord Ross. Feed me, and perhaps you can practice your observational skills tonight." Aisha removed her fingers and licked them. "Are we dining in here?"

He slid his arm across her shoulder. "Unfortunately not. Silas insists on waiting on you hand and foot, so it's the smaller dining room this evening. Were it just me, he'd place my bowl of gruel on the floor in here and tell me to enjoy it."

Aisha's throaty laugh echoed in the hallway as they walked to the dining room. "That's because you're English, my lord."

"So is he and Martha; they're Somerset-born," Percy retorted. "You're also English."

She halted and patted his chest. "English-born, Mauretanian-bred. Martha has come to appreciate the gifts of spices I send, which is why you eat well when I visit. Now, if you're done blaming others for your dull palate, I want to taste one of these wines rescued from Burgundy."

When they reached the dining room, Silas bowed to Aisha, then seated her. He flashed her a quick smile. "Martha is thrilled you're joining Lord Ross for dinner. She's prepared lamb for the meat, madam."

Percy's gaze whipped between Aisha and Silas before settling on her. "You've been conspiring with my staff?"

She shrugged. "Do sit, Percy. Someone must, or you'd live like that odious Lord Ashedon." When Percy grimaced, she chuckled. "Although we'd have you lodged in Bedlam before we permit you to descend to his peculiarities."

Silas's tittering earned a dark look from Percy as Silas placed their plates before them. After filling their wine goblets, he went to the door. "Enjoy your supper, my lady."

Before he closed the door quietly behind him, Silas muttered, "You too, my lord."

Aisha's laughter earned several grunts from Percy. "Oh sweetheart, wipe that frown from your face. If Silas and Martha didn't adore you as they do, you wouldn't be the man I love."

"You love me?"

"Of course, I do. Besides, no other woman—or man—would have your taciturn self," she teased. "Nor bear with the occasional disappearances for weeks only to show up muddy, exhausted, and wanting to fuck."

He sipped his wine, then said, "True. How do you put up with me, Isha?"

"Quite easily, Percy," she murmured. "Quite easily."

The rest of dinner was familiar as they conversed about the daily worries of living with an aged and dying sovereign, the recent capture of several French and Spanish spies in the court.

Percy stared at the woman he loved. "Is your family well, Isha? What does Issac or Simon report?"

She took a sip of wine. "They're worried but not overly much. Unless there is civil war in England, not much affects people's need for cloth or clothing. Issac begs me to visit."

Percy waited through her silence, then interrupted her thoughts. "Will you go?"

"I want to, but it means being away from the house for a month or so."

"Are you listening to yourself, Aisha? When did a brothel become more important than family? It's a business, and a very profitable one, but Issac is your brother, his children your blood, and his wife your closest friend. Stop running from those who love you, including me."

"We are not having this argument," she retorted.

"As you wish." Percy angrily pushed his chair away from the table. "If you want me, I'll be in my parlor. I've lost my appetite."

He strode out of the dining room and upstairs, needing to rein in his anger and hurt. The arguments over their relationship and her somewhat-strained relations with her family had increased over the past year, and he was reaching a breaking point—not certain whether the fight for Aisha Resonne would ever be won.

Silas was just leaving the parlor when he approached. "Thank you, Silas. Aisha is in the dining room."

His servant frowned and peered at him, then silently walked out and closed the door. Percy went to the table where Silas had left two glasses and an open bottle of wine. Pouring himself a drink, Percy went to the window and pushed aside the curtains. Below was a small garden, mostly flowers and herbs bathed in fading sunlight, and he stared down at it.

Lost in thought, he didn't hear the door open and close

until a hand gently pressed his back. His heart seized in panic. *Here it comes, she will end our love.* Steeling his spine, he turned and gazed at Aisha. "Would you care for a glass of wine?"

She studied his face for a second. "Please."

He watched her walk over to her favorite chair and sit. Filling a glass, he handed it to her and lowered himself on the chair opposite hers to see her face, read her expression, and prepare for the devastating blow of rejection.

"I'm so sorry, beloved," she began. Her fingers clenched her glass as she raised it to her lips and drank. "It's just that I'm afraid, Percy."

"Afraid of what, Isha? Has someone threatened you?"

She smiled. "No, nothing so drastic. It's a different kind of fear." Her eyelids lowered as she peered into the red liquid in her glass. "When Issac's ship was destroyed and he was a prisoner for a year, I watched Penelope suffer heartbreak each passing day. She held fast to her vow despite her father's insistence she marry another, but her despair was obvious."

"Yet Issac returned safely, and they married," Percy stated.

"What if he hadn't? It would have shattered Pen, my family..." She broke off. Sucking in air, Aisha continued, "Me. Issac has always been important in my life. He might be younger, but he understood my impetuous nature, my love of adventure, and never faulted me. He may not approve of what I do, but he's accepted my choices. Like my father, Issac would prefer that I marry."

"I agree you've done well with the Cock & Oyster, Isha. But you deserve a life, happiness, and love. You deserve me, and my name."

"I love you, Percy. So very much, and my greatest fear is losing you. I don't think I can be your wife and live with you serving the Crown as you do. The not knowing when you will disappear and where you've gone. If you'll come back the same man or return maimed...or dead. It's the latter I fear the most. That one day, you will not return to me."

Seeing the tears gather in her eyes, he pulled her onto his lap and held her. His mouth brushed her temple as he whispered how much he adored her, that she owned his heart. He tucked a knuckle beneath her chin and lifted her head until their gazes met. "Will you marry me if I give up spying, Isha?"

"Don't, Percy," she blurted out. "That is unfair. I don't want you to give up anything for me. I can't ask you to do that."

"Why not? I've asked you to give up the Cock & Oyster."

"They are very different matters. You serve Her Majesty and England. I profit off men's lusts, their inability to be satisfied with their wives, or who have unconventional desires."

"True, but I still believe it is the asking that we have in common. Will you become my wife if I give up spying? Would you retire to Somerset and live a quiet country life?"

She stared at him, searching his eyes. Finally, she said, "For you? Without question."

"Then you need to set a date, and preferably not years from now, my love. I've informed Cecil I am no longer available for clandestine work that takes me away from London or Somerset." He kissed her slowly and deeply. When he lifted his head, he peered at her. "I never want you to worry or fear for my return, Aisha."

She laid her palm against his cheek. "Before I arrived, I pondered what it would be like to be a country mouse. To tend a garden and bake bread, to prepare your porridge, mend your socks."

He chuckled. "I doubt Martha will allow that. You will have to find some other form of entertainment to keep you amused."

"What I'm trying to say, beloved, is I believe it's time for Bella to acquire her inheritance. I've been a caretaker long enough." She kissed his chin. "Would a spring wedding suit you?"

"I'd prefer next week." He faltered at her narrowed eyes. "However, I can be patient. Shall I speak to the priest at St. Olav's?"

She shook her head. "Would you agree to Issac's home? There is a priest who serves our people in the nearby village, and I'd like his blessing."

"I don't care where we marry, as long as you become my wife," he murmured before his mouth lowered to hers.

A rap on the door brought them apart. "What?" he barked.

The door swung open, and his Uncle Robert and Aisha's Aunt Ahmara entered. Aisha hastily rose and fastened her bodice before she looked at her aunt. "Aunt Ahmara. What are you doing here? Your letter indicated you and Uncle Robert wouldn't arrive for a fortnight."

Ahmara strolled over to her niece and kissed her forehead. "Forgive the interruption," she said cheekily. "We assumed you and Percy were dining and we wanted to join you. However, we can have Silas and Martha send something to our room."

Percy glanced at Aisha's face and ducked his head to hide his grin at her obvious discomfort at her aunt's subtle jibe. He rose from his chair and went to Ahmara. Kissing her cheek, he said, "Welcome, Aunt, Uncle. Sit, please, since I know you're not planning to leave. I'm sure Silas has already arranged for food. Would you like a glass of wine?"

Ahmara smiled at him before she sat on a divan. "No, thank you. Martha is sending up atay along with supper. However, I'm sure Robert would enjoy a glass."

Percy filled a glass and handed it to his uncle, who joined his wife on the divan. Taking a sip, Robert nodded. "This is quite good, nephew. Burgundy?"

"Yes," he replied. "The winemaker sadly lived long enough to see the French king grant Christians their freedom to worship, but the years took a toll. The vineyard was confiscated, but I managed to get several bottles of wine."

The men sat and talked wine for a few minutes before Ahmara looked pointedly at Percy but spoke to Aisha. "How are the ladies, Randall and Matthew, and any news on your pending retirement from the sex trade, Aisha?"

"Is that why you've traveled to London, Aunt?" she snipped. "To hurry on my retirement? Why should I retire? The house is profitable, the courtesans have no complaints, and the clients pay generously. Randall and Matthew are happy, to my knowledge."

Percy rose from his chair. "Come, Uncle, I have some papers I want to review with you."

Robert stood and walked with his nephew to the door. "Coward," Aisha hissed.

Percy turned and walked over to her, leaning down to kiss Aisha's forehead. "Ring for Silas if there's to be a duel. He knows where my swords are, and I suggest the rapier, much more delicate."

With this advice, he and Robert left the room.

Ahmara's laughter provoked Aisha's and, patting the space Robert had just abandoned, Ahmara said, "Come sit next to me, Isha. Tell me when you plan to train Isabelle to take over her inheritance. And when are you going to accept Percy's marriage offer?"

"Is that why you and Uncle Robert traveled from Wiltshire? To badger us into marriage?"

"No, he came to visit his nephew," Ahmara declared. "I'm here because I love my husband and being apart from him makes me unhappy."

Aisha smiled at her aunt's words. "I'm so happy for you, Aunt Ahmara. How is your health?"

"It is well. And," Ahmara intoned, "I am here to make sure you do right by Robert's nephew. You've dangled him on a string long enough."

Aisha rolled her eyes. "Not you too. First Issac, then Percy, and now you. Is there no peace to be allowed for a maiden's hesitancy? Perhaps I prefer Diana's path and would have you lay virginal bouquets on my marble bed."

"Useless shite, those romances, and you've not been a virgin since you took up with Percy." Ahmara spat. "What did Issac write? I assume Penelope and the children are well."

"They are all well, and he begs me to visit." Aisha sipped her wine. "He's of your mind about Percy and me."

"Good."

"I sent Issac word we will visit in spring. Will you and Uncle Robert travel...for a wedding?"

Ahmara's scream brought Percy and his uncle rushing into the room, followed by Silas. They halted when Ahmara said, "Finally!"

"I agree," Percy remarked, knowing what prompted Ahmara's screech. "It's time for Aisha Resonne to make a respectable man of me."

Aisha side-eyed him. "Impossible, Lord Ross. You do recall where we first met?"

"Aye. It was a sign, or I should say, the sign Fate had taken me in hand." He refilled their glasses. "Here's to the Cock & Oyster."

FOUR

AISHA LIFTED her gaze from the paper beneath her fingers to stare at the nervous servant explaining that Ophelia, usually one of Aisha's more reliable courtesans, wasn't in the house. Reassuring the lad, she sent him to fetch Sally Wooster. In the privacy of her study, Aisha let loose a string of curses that were utterly improper yet indicative of her increasing irritation with Ophelia. The courtesan had taken to occasionally disappearing over the past fortnight, and it had to stop.

Irate clients weren't a headache Aisha wanted, no matter how profitable they were. Sadly, no other woman in the brothel had Ophelia's gift for discipline and desire. The men who enjoyed Ophelia's particular talents with crops, silver beads, and dildos paid well and left the Cock & Oyster very satisfied.

She glanced at the clock on her desk. It was noon; she was meeting Percy, her aunt, and his uncle for dinner, and she hadn't even bathed. Rising from behind her desk, she strode toward the doorway, muttering to herself that a review of the Cock & Oyster's list of clients might be in order. Some of the noblemen who visited for Ophelia were becoming a veritable pain up the arse—and the only pain Aisha was willing to tolerate in that location was Percy's fingers.

As soon as her mind gives life to the thought, a rush of heat flooded her privates. What she wouldn't give for a quick fingerfuck before dealing with a missing courtesan.

Stepping into the corridor, she was nearly knocked over by Sally, a timid young woman training to the courtesan's life and entirely unsuited for it. Aisha buried her frustration at the obsequious apology, eyeing the flustered woman until she bobbed her head and backed away.

"What is the rush, Sally? Have you seen Ophelia? Robbie just informed me Lord Eglantine is faced down on the bed, the drunken sot, and crying for Ophelia to come beat his arse and then his cock."

"Beg pardon, Mistress Ellen," Sally stammered. "It's just Ophelia asked me to tell you she's gone to visit her sick mother in Clapham and will return tomorrow morning, but you couldn't be found, and I forgot to mention it to Randall."

"Damn, what am I to do with Eglantine?" The skin between Aisha's exquisitely plucked eyebrows puckered. "Ophelia's the only one who can handle the buffoon."

Sally ducked her chin, peeking up at Aisha. "Maybe I can help. She's been training me, Mistress Ellen."

So that's where Sally's been disappearing. Aisha thoughtfully eyed her. She'd always assumed the woman wasn't the brightest penny in London, but maybe she erred.

"Go prepare yourself to tend to my lord, Sally," Aisha said brusquely. "You'll earn the two shillings instead of Ophelia. Do you know where her tools are?" Sally shook her head. "Look inside the cabinet beside the bed, and Eglantine enjoys the smallest crop first."

Sally's pale blue eyes lit up, and a grin split her face. "Thank you, Mistress Ellen. I swear I won't let you down."

Aisha waved a dismissive hand. "Just make sure Eglantine's rod is flaccid before you strike or you'll be there until nightfall. Oh, and change your garment."

She watched Sally happily skip down the corridor before returning to her private parlor. Once inside, Aisha realized she needed to send a note to Percy that her arrival would be delayed. She tugged on the velvet rope pull before she began pacing the floor.

This was the third time Ophelia went missing just before Eglantine's appointed visit. The last time, he'd been serviced, but his dissatisfaction was quite evident. Gregory Tidwell, Lord Eglantine was a regular if boorish patron—she could ill-afford for him to turn against the Cock & Oyster.

Aisha's fingers massaged her brow. She'd heard rumors the courtesan was also entangled with Hamlet Tidwell, Eglantine's heir. Ophelia's foolishness with the uncle and his nephew might prove costly. Perhaps it was time to give Ophelia a warning, and some advice. It may also be time to consider a replacement, discreetly discourage Eglantine's visits, and send him to Evangeline, who would be grateful for the trade.

Aisha pursed her lips and walked over to her desk. She pulled a key from her pocket and opened a private drawer. Removing a sheet of paper, she started to scan the list of names on it. There were at least twelve persons begging to join the staff of the Cock & Oyster. One name caused her to arch an eyebrow. Why was Martine wanting to leave Holland's Leaguer? Elizabeth Holland could afford to protect Martine from those who would abuse her because her birth sex was not female.

Something must have changed. Aisha penned a quick note for Randall to discreetly investigate Martine's reasons before she reached out to the courtesan. A piercing scream sounded beyond the door. A second scream sucked the air from Aisha's lungs and sent her heart racing as she scrambled to the door. Flinging it open, she stepped into the corridor. "What in heavens was that noise?"

"Mistress Ellen, come quick!" a breathless Sally screeched, running toward her. "It's Lord Eglantine, he's...dead!"

"That useless sack of flesh better not have died in one of my beds. Are you sure he isn't sleeping off the wine?" Aisha grabbed Sally's wrist and dragged her down the hall to the room Eglantine reserved for his visits.

Sally balked at the door and jerked her hand from Aisha's fingers. "I'm not going back in there. He's pissed hisself, and he stinks, and there's blood everywhere."

Aisha glared at her. "Go tell Randall I need him immediately, but do not say a word to anyone else. To no one. If news gets out, that'll be the end of us, and since you were the last to see him, you'll end up in jail. Not one single word, Sally Wooster."

Sally bobbed her head and scurried away, leaving Aisha to enter the bedchamber. The man was arse-up, and Aisha swore. Eglantine wasn't the first client to die without paying—that distinction went to Clergyman Zepharia Wilton, who'd thought crossing the Thames for his pleasures was a secret.

Pah! The only secrets in London were the ones everyone thought they knew and therefore didn't bother to repeat.

What a nuisance Eglantine was going to be. She'd have to deal with the Chancery and Lord Cecil and—her gaze flicking to the bed, she groaned— all new furniture for the room. "Well, my lord," she growled, glaring at the dead man, "I didn't like you, but not enough to kill you. I wonder who hates you enough to end your life like this?"

Randall walked into the room and snorted. "Damn! That is the whitest arse I've ever seen. Are you sure there's blood on the bed?"

"Just help me turn him onto his back," Aisha hissed.

With much huffing and puffing, they got the dead nobleman face up. Randall's deep-throated laughter erupted a second time. "He's a mangey eunuch! How the hell did Ophelia or any one of the ladies manage to ride that...it's smaller than my little finger. Beshrew my eyes, it's a maggot."

Aisha rolled her eyes. "Are you done with the jests? We can discuss the man's insignificance later, but at the moment, I couldn't give two weasels about the size of Tidwell's cock. Please tell me there were no clients when Sally screamed."

"Fate really adores you, Mistress Ellen," Randall observed. "Eglantine was the only customer left, waiting for his sweet Ophelia. Hearing Sally's screeches about a dead man, I sent Castor to fetch Lord Ross."

"What message did you give him?"

"'Flights of angels sang him to his rest' and told Castor to tell him to hurry."

She shook her head as she stared at the newly deceased. "First Wilton, now this pompous fool. Why couldn't Eglantine die in his own bed or at some other brothel?"

Randall eyed her. "Because your house offers delights no other can. Besides, Wilton left here and died in his own bed, hoisting his petard, leaving a note in praise of the Cock & Oyster."

"I do not need to be reminded."

He grinned and continued with his salacious tale. "I heard his housekeeper found him and it was at least a half-hour before she called for help. One of the serving boys peeked in the bedroom and spied her riding Wilton's prick like a stallion. Rumor has it she and several of the clergyman's staff serviced themselves before reporting his death. Joseph, the clergyman's coal man, attended the funeral and said she was beside herself because Wilton's penis had to be cut off for him to fit in his coffin."

"Randall! Can we please focus on this situation? Help me look for the weapon, and if you see his purse—"

"Robbing the dead, Mistress Ellen?"

"No, claiming payment to replace the bed and lost income since we'll have to close tomorrow," she snapped.

Randall continued to make such rude comments about Eglantine and the size of his rod that Aisha couldn't prevent the laughter from bubbling up. "Let the dead rest, Randall."

It didn't take long to find the murder weapon—one of her letter openers, which meant someone had entered her parlor. "Any sign of the man's purse? Green silk, with his initials in bold lettering?" Randall shook his head, and she muttered, "Then we must add robbery to the crime."

They searched the room, finding no signs or clues to the identity of the murderer. "I'm afraid, Randall, this doesn't look very promising for the brothel. With Ophelia missing, this does make her appear guilty. Where the hell is Percy?"

The door swung open, and the man strolled into the room. His dimpled smile and adoring light brown eyes sent a spark of heat coursing through Aisha. She could definitely use a tumble, given the day so far. Her eyes studied his languid movement, his graying black hair brushing the dark linen of his cloak with each step, and her heart skipped a beat. At forty-five, he was fit, fastidious, energetic, and inventive in bed. Despite moments of doubt, she intended to wed him once she'd trained Isabelle to take over the Cock & Oyster.

When he reached her, he pulled her into his embrace. "I rode as fast as I could once I got your message." His tongue searched the inside of her mouth, tasting until she moaned softly. Raising his head, he peered at her. "Never a dull moment with you, Ellen Chapman. How are you, and when will you allow me to remove you from all of this nastiness?"

"One more dead body, Lord Ross, and I'm all yours." She stepped away from his arms, and her hand swept the scene of the crime. "Murder and robbery."

A glint in his eyes brought a smile to her face. Since they'd agreed to marry, Percy had gradually stepped away from the clandestine work that made him one of the best spies in England,

"Who was the last to see Eglantine alive?"

"I have no idea," she replied. "His favorite, Ophelia Swinden, couldn't be found, and to quiet him, I sent Sally, who Ophelia has been training in her particular arts. Apparently, she's done this before, and Sally assured me Eglantine wouldn't be troubled if she served him."

"Where's Sally now?"

Aisha glanced at Randall, who answered. "In her bedroom. Matthew stands guard."

Percy nodded. "Please see that she remains there, Randall, and the other women in their rooms as well. Also, make the necessary arrangements for the removal of the corpse and the soiled furniture."

Randall inclined his head and left. Percy pulled her back into his arms and drove his tongue between her lips, hungrily tasting her. When they finally parted to breathe, she ran her fingers along his strong jawline. "Not in front of Lord Eglantine."

"He's dead," Percy uttered, planting brief kisses on her cheeks and forehead. "Tidwell won't notice how firm your nipples are getting, nor the bewitching scent wafting upward from beneath your skirt."

"Percy," Aisha moaned as his fingers pushed up her skirt and stroked her wet flesh. Distracted, she let him finger her before she pulled away. Percy's deep sigh rumbled from his chest as he removed his hand from beneath her raised skirt and let it fall.

Putting herself beyond his reach, she said, "He was a braggart and a buffoon, but his death isn't a good advertisement for the business."

"No, it isn't. I'm more concerned about you facing charges for murder, which I can't allow since you've agreed to become my wife. Lady Ross, murderess...just not the thing. Come, let's go to your parlor so you can persuade me to take up your cause."

As they walked, Aisha gripped his hand. "I can't let you do that, Percy. I'll send for Constable Webster."

"And tell him what? 'By the way, Constable Webster, someone murdered Lord Eglantine in one of my courtesans' chambers, and I have no idea who committed the crime.' Of course, he'll understand."

He guided her inside the parlor, his booted foot tapping the door shut behind them. Percy faced her and ran his thumb across her lips. "Let me handle this, especially since the deceased is a nobleman. I need to protect you."

She stared into his eyes. This wasn't the first time Percy had come to her rescue, although most of her clients were easily managed. The exceptions were the few men like Sir Alistair Goodly, who'd wanted exclusive rights to her bed. Most accepted her answer—not Goodly. He'd gone into a rage and struck her. Randall intervened and immediately sent for Percy.

The deadly expression on Percy's face when he saw the bruises and demanded a name terrified her into a stammering silence. It was Randall who answered. As her bruises healed, she forgot about Goodly until she overheard two clients bemoaning his absence from London and the coins they'd lost from his gambling. Her discreet inquiry had given her joy and worry because she knew Percy was the reason for Goodly's permanent removal from London.

She knew Percy would intervene, no matter what she said. "What do you want me to do, love?"

His smile produced flutters inside her belly, and she knew whatever he was about to ask, she'd agree, except for his, "Marry me tomorrow." She moved back into his embrace.

His arm draped over her shoulder, and she leaned against his solid frame. From the first time she set eyes on him, Aisha knew she'd never marry nor bed another man. It was a vow she'd kept, much to her family's dismay, although they never shunned her as some families did with their daughters. If they had, she would have accepted banishment because Percy Howard was worth it.

"If you won't marry me tomorrow, then let me kiss your tickle button," he replied, his fingers bunching up her skirt.

"Tickle button? Lord Ross, stop making up words. My puss does not have buttons, though it is ticklish." Aisha moaned. "Percy, you do recall why you're here."

"Of course. By now, Eglantine is resting peacefully on a wagon and covered with a piece of linen—albeit the cloth is wasted, but it is the appropriate thing to do—and waiting for his family to come claim his body. All the bedding has been removed and taken to Rotherham for destruction. A quick fuck won't change anything, but if you insist, we'll save this for later."

"Thank you," she stammered. His finger had been busy the entire time he spoke, and she knew it was quite soaked.

Percy removed and sucked his finger before he said, "I'd like to question Sally. Do you have any idea where Ophelia might be? Or who might want to see Eglantine dead?"

Aisha walked over to the rope and tugged. When Robbie arrived, she said a few words, and he was off. She turned to face

Percy. "According to Sally, Ophelia is visiting her sick mother in Clapham, and before you inquire, I had no idea her mother lived. I've also heard rumors Ophelia was dangling both uncle and nephew on a string. About a fortnight ago, a drunken Hamlet Tidwell came and demanded to see her, vowing to marry her if she'd give up his uncle. I had Randall arrange for his transport home."

Her gaze flew to Percy's face. "Do you think he managed to slip in and murder his uncle? I was locked in the accounting room when Eglantine arrived, and I only learned he was in the house when Robbie came to tell me the man was making a fool of himself."

"How frequently did he visit? What was the pattern of his behavior once he was here?"

She chuckled. "Usually, he visited four times a week until a fortnight ago. Yesterday he sent word to reserve his chamber and inform Ophelia he'd arrive before noon, and that he was feeling feisty."

"When did you send Sally to him?"

"Half past noon."

Percy cut her off. "And you didn't hear a peep from him once he entered his room until Sally came to tell you he was dead?"

She shook her head. "I was in my accounts room when Tidwell arrived. Apparently, Ophelia wasn't in the bedchamber, and Eglantine was yelling for her to come whip his arse. He was quiet when I sent Sally to him."

Percy walked around the room, then returned to her. The hungry look on his face made her regret her interruption of his play earlier since her kitten hadn't calmed. He sensed her desire because he tugged her into his arms, and his tongue ravaged the inside of her mouth. "Percy."

"Shh," he murmured and continued setting her on fire.

By the time he released her, she was wet between her thighs and her puss was sated. Yet she needed a good fuck. She was about to drag him into her bedchamber when a knock occurred, and they hastily separated. Her voice was breathless and raspy when she said, "Enter."

Randall marched Sally into the room. "I think you need to hear this, Mistress Ellen."

The anger in Randall's voice sent a shiver through her, and her lust withered on the vine. "What do I need to hear?"

"Go ahead, Sally."

She glanced between Randall and Percy before she looked at her. "This was shoved under my door, Mistress Ellen," she stammered, handing her a sheet of paper.

Aisha cursed as she read.

Mistress Ellen, I beg your forgiveness, but I'm frightened. I didn't heed your advice and now I fear I may be jealousy's next victim. Upon my return from my ailing mother, I walked into Lord Eglantine's room and he was snoring so I went to my bedroom to make preparations. I heard Sally's scream and rushed out to see her coming from his room. I snuck to the open doorway and peeked in and saw all the blood. I'm sorry to leave my lord's murder on your head but no one will believe a courtesan innocent of murder. I've not included the note I received from Eglantine's nephew Hamlet because it may be the only proof of my innocence. Forgive me, Ophelia.

Percy held out his hand. "May I, Mistress Chapman?"

She gave Percy the letter and studied his face as he read. Percy lifted his gaze. "Sally, do you have any idea where Ophelia has gone? I assume she'd confide in you."

Sally ducked her head and refused to look at him when she answered. "No, my lord. She didn't tell me nothing about leaving other than going to her mother. I haven't seen her since yesterday morning."

Percy stared at her for a long moment before he nodded. "Randall, escort Sally to her room and see that no one leaves the brothel."

Sally gaped at Aisha. "You need to help Ophelia, especially if somebody's trying to kill her. Whoever killed my lord might be after her. You need to find her, Miss Ellen."

"We will," Percy spoke calmly. "You'll be safe in your chamber. Please don't leave without permission. You also may be in danger."

When it was just Aisha and Percy in the room, she stared at him. "Percy."

Adjusting his cloak, he leaned over to brush his lips against her cheek. "Don't worry, beloved. Everything will be just fine. Would you like to go to your aunt? I must go to Lord Cecil and apprise him of this situation."

She rubbed his chest. "No, the women need me here. I love you, Percy."

"I love you, Aisha. Don't fret."

She watched him walk out the room. Fretting was exactly what she'd do until the mystery of Eglantine's murder was solved.

FIVE

Percy rapped on the thick wood door to Cecil's private chamber in Richmond Palace. At the Lord Secretary's command, he strolled inside and locked the door behind him. Cecil studied his face and drawled, "Is it that serious, Ross?"

He drew up a chair and sat. "It is, Lord Secretary." Cecil's disgruntled exhalation provoked a chuckle. "I'll handle the matter, but I wanted to apprise Her Majesty Gregory Tidwell is dead."

Cecil shrugged. "I can't say I'm disappointed, although his nephew Hamlet isn't much of an improvement. How much time can a man spend in university and still not possess enough knowledge to fasten his breeches?"

"Eglantine's death, my lord," Percy intruded. "He was murdered. However, it wasn't in his bed but one at the Cock & Oyster. Stabbed. Rather messy, and unattractive."

"I don't want the details. I also know you intend to protect your mistress. Therefore, do what is necessary, Percy, to handle this matter. Her Majesty doesn't take kindly to brothels, and when one of her lords dies in one... Well, do what you must to solve this...mishap."

Percy nodded and stood. Cecil raised a hand to halt him. "I suggest you assist Ellen Chapman in finding another occupation. She is a remarkable woman and deserves more, much more."

"Once this mess is taken care of, I intend to do exactly that, my lord," Percy replied.

Cecil stared at him. "I suppose there's no way to stop a marriage?"

"Not even by Her Majesty's proclamation."

"Then it is a wise decision to retire to Somerset, Lord Ross. A very wise decision."

Making his way to the royal stables, Percy collected his horse and headed to Ross House. He needed to inform his uncle and Ahmara of the nasty situation before he returned to the brothel. There was no way he'd leave Aisha alone tonight, and he knew with certainty he couldn't convince her to leave the Cock & Oyster.

It was nearly dusk when he knocked on the brothel's door and heard the soft click of metal. When the door swung open, he stepped inside. "Evening, Randall."

Randall flashed him a tired smile. "I was wondering when you'd return."

"How is she?"

"Brave face and all that. She's in her sitting room, ignoring the meal Matthew prepared just for her."

Percy nodded. "No matter who arrives, I don't want her disturbed. I assume Eglantine's household has claimed the body."

"They have, my lord. His nephew sent a cart and retainers an hour after you departed. Lord Hamlet also sent word he intends to visit Mistress Ellen on the morrow." Randall took his cloak and draped it over his arm as they walked toward the stairs. "I worry he'll bring the constables."

"Good," Percy huffed. "It will save me the trouble of sending for them if Hamlet Tidwell actually pays a visit, although I doubt he will. Good night, Randall."

"Good night, my lord." As Percy turned down a passage, he heard, "I'm glad you're here. She needs you."

He continued until he reached the door to Aisha's parlor and knocked softly.

"Go away, I'm fine."

Percy's fingers gripped the handle and twisted. The door was unlocked, and he entered, locking it behind him. "Are you sure you want me to leave? And are you fine, beloved?"

"Percy?" She pushed herself from her chair, nearly knocking it over, and flung herself into his arms. He heard her half-hearted attempt to choke back a sob, then felt the first teardrop on his shirt.

"Oh, sweetheart, no tears. Did you think I'd leave you to sleep in a bed without me? Foolish woman," he murmured, kissing her forehead. "I love you, and I haven't played with your kitten enough today."

Her muffled laughter rumbled against his chest. When she lifted her chin, she shook her head, tear stains evident on her cheeks. "What am I to do with you, Percy Howard?"

He kissed her lips. "Feed me, let me lick your puss, and then fuck me senseless."

She released him and tugged him over to where covered dishes sat on a circular table. He held her chair while she sat, then lowered himself onto the chair beside her. She grinned at him. "I suppose it's the least I can do for all your help today. Wine?"

He glanced at the half-empty bottle. "I assume there's

another bottle in the room. I don't plan to leave until tomorrow, and after today's mess, I'll need more than a glass."

She filled a goblet and handed it to him. "Did you speak with the Lord Secretary, and will we be closed?"

He watched her prepare him a plate of her favorite comfort food, and he silently thanked Matthew for the gesture. Taking a piece of flatbread, Percy scooped up a mouthful of stew and ate it. When he finished chewing, he sipped some wine, then asked, "Do you think Matthew would like living in Somerset?"

"You realize he and Randall are a pair," she replied. "Besides, I intend for Bella to take over her inheritance, and she'll need them."

"Too bad. Do they know she's Ahmara's daughter?"

Aisha sipped her wine. "Yes, and I wish Aunt Ahmara would tell Bella the truth. About her father. About the choices Aunt Ahmara made, both with the brothel and not revealing she is Bella's mother."

Percy took her hand. "Her choices were well-founded. To hurt Ahmara, Joseph Glasden threatened to sell their infant daughter into slavery, or worse. What would you have done?"

"If you were the father—"

"We wouldn't be having this conversation," he cut her off.

Aisha turned her palm up and squeezed his fingers. "True. I am glad Aunt Ahmara sent Bella to my eamm and she was with our family. Perhaps once this is all over and Bella takes possession of her inheritance, my aunt will find a way to tell her the truth."

"Eat, Isha. You'll need your strength for our bed games later." She laughed and began to eat. Percy nodded his approval. "Cecil's given me permission to investigate Eglantine's murder."

"What do you think was the killer's motive, Percy? And why murder him in a courtesan's bed?"

Percy ate the remainder of his food and gently pushed the plate aside. Taking a long sip of his wine, he swallowed slowly before he gazed at Aisha. "Have you considered the murderer might be one of the women?"

"Of course not," she declared. "The Cock & Oyster women aren't criminals except in the church's eye, and the only problems are those stirred up by your species."

"How long has Ophelia serviced Eglantine? Who were the women that preceded her?"

"How dare you accuse any of the women here? We've never had a single mishap in all the time I've overseen this house."

Anger rode Aisha's face, and he reached for her hand. "I'm not accusing anyone, Isha. But if we're to unmask the killer and save the brothel's reputation, we can't exclude anyone from consideration."

"Not even me?" she retorted. "I was here, you know."

"Actually, it's quite easy to absolve you," Percy said with a smirk. "Were you so inclined, you'd murder Tidwell in his own bed since you're far too fastidious to kill someone here. Although..."

Aisha snatched her hand from his. "Percy Elwen Howard!"

He chuckled. "Answer my question, sweetling. Who serviced Tidwell before Ophelia?"

Aisha's finger tapped her chin, and he had an urge to take the slender brown digit into his mouth... *Focus, Percy.*

"Eleanor, Rose, and Christina. His visits were occasional, so any one of them would do. Ophelia had been in the house for two months when he arrived demanding attention. She offered and, despite my doubts, she proved adept at the task. Since then, Eglantine's visits have been more frequent, and the others were quite happy to be relieved of the duty."

"Were there any clandestine meetings between Ophelia

and Eglantine, to your knowledge?" At Aisha's quizzical expression, he said, "Your generosity is legendary, love. The women here can come and go as they please, which is why they're loyal to you."

"I don't own them. As long as they are available to our clients and inform Randall when they leave, I refuse to control their comings and goings."

He nodded. "I assumed as much, but I had to ask. I'll speak to Hamlet Tidwell in the morning since, frankly, he has the most to gain from his uncle's death. However, tonight my cock is crowing, and we are in a brothel."

Aisha's cackle brought joy to Percy's heart. He hated when she was unhappy. "Lord Ross, your puns are going to be the bane of my existence. Come, I'm in need a bath and an extra pair of hands."

He rose from his chair and assisted her. As they left the room, she tugged on a pull so the dishes would be removed. Percy draped his arm across her shoulder, pulling her closer to kiss her temple. "I'll be delighted to lend you my hands."

THE BATH SHEET felt exquisite against the palm of his hand as Percy dried Aisha's skin. His cock was rigid with desire. She was temptation in human form.

"Percy," Aisha crooned with a slight tremble to her voice. "I'm getting chilled."

"Spread your legs," he muttered gruffly. "I need to make sure puss is dry before I make her wet again. Which oil do you want?"

"Your preference, sweetheart," she breathed. "I don't care as long as you fuck me."

"Tsk," Percy came back. "Is that any way for the future Lady Ross to speak?"

"Get used to it, Lord Ross, and get on with it."

He kissed her bare skin, loving the smooth texture. When he first discovered Aisha had removed all the hair from her private parts, he was flabbergasted—until he licked her. That night was the one he swore off all other women, and not just because her privates were hairless. Aisha made him aware of his body, his mind, and his desires in ways he didn't know was possible.

Percy swept her up in his arms and carried her to her bed. The covers had been pulled back, and he laid her on the bed sheet before he went to the dressing table and studied the oils she kept there. They were the same ones to be found in her bedroom in Southwark and both his houses. "Ah, yes, I think this one will do."

The oil was a favorite. She refused to tell him what went into its making, but it often reduced him to a mewling bundle of nerves. Returning to the bed, he undid the stopper and poured oil onto his open palm before he set the bottle on the bedside table.

Holding his hand over Aisha's belly, he let droplets fall singly, creating a heart-shaped pattern on the brown skin he adored. Then he went to work, gently rubbing the oil into her flesh, avoiding the one place he was most desirous of touching. Her soft moans rose like wisps of smoke into the air before disappearing, her hips in motion as he smoothed the oil down her thighs and legs to caress her feet.

There was no place he didn't love, and he bent down to lick his favorite toe—the middle one on her left foot. It was just the right length and size, and the most sensitive. For several minutes he wallowed in the pleasure, tasting the spicy sweetness of the oil as he nibbled, teased, and sucked.

"Hmm, feels lovely," she murmured.

He kissed his way up her right thigh until he was able to straddle her. "I need recompense for my labors, Madam."

"What dost that entail, my lord?"

"A kiss."

"Pray tell, where wouldst thou claim thy boon?"

He leaned down and brushed his mouth across her forehead. "Perhaps here." He licked the space between her eyes and followed the length of her nose. The tip of his tongue traced the flare of her nostrils. "Or here."

He grazed the space between the bottom of her left nostril and her top lip. "Or here," he whispered as his tongue traced her lips.

Percy continued his tasting journey, taking a moment to kiss her before his mouth followed the trail leading to his favorite spot, savoring the effect it had on his senses—especially smell and hearing as her erotic sounds and her scent encouraged him.

"No, here is where I want to be." He planted a wet kiss on her naked mound.

Percy had no idea how long he toyed and loved Aisha's lower lips and the tiny bundle of flesh and nerves hidden inside. Only when her fingers gripped his head and tugged did he awaken from the luxurious stupor of bringing her to multiple climaxes.

"Percy," she moaned as her body slowly stopped quaking. "I want your cock. We can play tomorrow."

He shifted and gripped his prick, guiding it inside her, his hips pushing his erection deep. Her words spoke her need. Aisha wanted to be loved, not fucked. She needed the side of him few rarely saw. His thrusts were gentle strokes, languid and delicate, a motion intended to calm, to erase her troubled thoughts and worries.

When her fingers pressed into his buttocks, soft vises locking him in a particular spot, he responded. His hips followed her instructions, tapping the spot, then shifting a fraction to brush another place as he withdrew, then pushed forward. Percy was methodical in working her body into a frenzy, mapping each move and pause until she screamed his name.

"Now, Isha?"

A throaty mewl preceded her breathless "Now, Percy," and his groin pinned her to the mattress. The tip of his cock excited the spot it touched, and he slipped his hand between them to stroke her passion bud. Her body jerked, but his weight held her in place as the pressure of his penis and finger sent her into a series of climatic quakes.

Aisha's inner muscles tightened around his erection, and Percy grunted before his body jerked, then went rigid. He felt the uneven vibrations of her muscles work the release from him like a whirlpool claiming a sinking vessel.

"I love you, Aisha," he panted. "I'll always take care of and protect you."

There was a long silence before he heard her murmur, "I love you, Percy. I will always take care of and protect you."

SIX

PERCY GRIPPED the side of the wherry carrying him from Richmond Palace. The Thames apparently shared his mood as the river's waves were choppy and made the trip back to Holborn much longer than usual. He resented having to leave Aisha's bed so early in the morning, but when the Lord Secretary summoned, his top domestic spy had no choice but to attend. He'd prayed the matter was related to Tidwell's murder because, for the first time, he'd have to refuse Cecil.

Percy was surprised how quickly the news of Tidwell's death had spread. Before his early morning departure from the Cock & Oyster, he'd received a note from John Resonne informing him Asia Resonne waited for him near Holborn and would bring him to the Resonne dwellings. As he read Resonne's note, he wasn't sure which summons he dreaded more—Aisha's uncle or Cecil's. In the end, he chose the Lord Secretary, realizing if he needed Aisha's uncle on his side, the more he knew the better.

A rough wave bumped the boat, and Percy cursed. He ran a gloved hand down the back of his neck, frustration nipping at his calm. He had awakened to the noise of Aisha's muttering as she prepared to leave for Hamlet Tidwell's house. After a few kisses and some fingering, he'd dissuaded her from the visit, telling her it was better for him, as the Lord Secretary's agent, to visit Tidwell.

Before he left the brothel, Percy handed Aisha her uncle's note and begged her to go to her family, or at least to his London house until he finished his investigation. The woman was definitely stubborn, refusing to leave the Cock & Oyster although she did agree not to take matters into her own hands until he returned from meeting with Cecil. Percy glanced up as Asia docked the wherry. Once he was on the beach, he thanked and asked Asia to inform Resonne he'd visit after meeting with Hamlet Tidwell.

The boatman nodded and turned his boat back towards London Bridge. Percy walked up the steps and hailed a chair. By the time he reached the Cock & Oyster, it was nearly midday and, handing the men some coins, he walked into the courtyard behind the brothel. He'd nearly reached the door when a coach pulled up at the stable gate. Curious, he turned to look. It was his coach, and he masked his frown when his uncle and Ahmara climbed out. "What are you doing here?"

"Don't be daft, boy," his uncle retorted. He guided Ahmara past his nephew and into the house. "Where's Aisha?"

Percy followed them down the hall and into the brothel's parlor. "She's resting."

Ahmara gazed at him until he blushed. "In other words, you poked her until she was too exhausted to get involved."

"Aunt Ahmara," Aisha said frostily as she strolled into the room. "Percy does not poke me. He either makes love to me, swives me, fingers me, fucks me, or licks me into insensibility. Poking is what one does to a fire."

She went to her aunt and hugged her before she embraced

Robert. "What prompted you two to abandon your midday play time?"

"You," Ahmara declared. "Why are you still in this house?"

"Because the women need me here," Aisha replied with a shrug.

Ahmara waved her hand. "They don't need you. They have Randall, Matthew, and each other. You're thinking 'I'm the only one who can take care of this,' and you know that's a lie. Why do you have Percy about? Investigating murders and disappearances in brothels is his business. Isn't that how you two met?"

"Actually, Aunt Ahmara, most of what I do is unrelated to brothels," Percy offered. "The only brothel case was a favor to someone. This situation is personal."

She tutted. "Have you talked to the dead man's family yet?"

"I was just leaving to visit Lord Eglantine."

"Isn't Tidwell dead?" Uncle Robert queried.

Percy groaned. "The nephew, Uncle. Hamlet Tidwell is now Lord Eglantine." Going to Aisha, he brushed his mouth across her lips. "I'll return as soon as I can. We do need to visit your Uncle John."

"Why?" Ahmara demanded. "My brother is arrogant and authoritarian. Is he trying to make sure the Resonnes' good name remains unsullied? She's not going. I'll send him a message."

Percy kissed Aisha once more, then went to the door. "I shall return as soon as possible."

"Don't you worry about Isha, nephew," Robert said. "We'll take good care of her. Do you expect the constables to come round?"

"No, and if they do, please let Aisha engage them, Uncle Robert."

Percy was afraid to leave the three of them alone, but with a deep sigh, he retreated down the hall and outside to his waiting coach.

~

AS THE CARRIAGE rolled through the streets toward Tidwell House, Percy felt a surge of excitement. It had been several years since he faced a nobleman's mysterious death. While he didn't like that it touched Aisha, he welcomed the chance to test his skills one final time before he retired to the countryside.

His forehead wrinkled as he pondered the crime and why it took place at the Cock & Oyster. Predictability was a factor since Tidwell visited the house three to four days a week, always on the same days. Eglantine's recent visits were spent with Ophelia Swinden, and apparently Sally Wooster. Tidwell's penchant for the brothel was well-known, but in that, he was no different than any of the men who frequented the Cock & Oyster.

What he didn't have was motive.

Percy's hand stroked his chin as he compiled a list of suspects in his head. Who'd benefit the most from Eglantine's death? Gervase Markham, a disgruntled business partner topped the list. Eglantine's heir, Hamlet, and Hamlet's mother, Gertrude, who was bitter about the loss of her dowry were quickly added, as well as Hortense, Lady Eglantine and Tidwell's estranged wife.

While each may have motive, only Markham and Hamlet would venture into the brothel...unless Gertrude or Hortense bribed someone. Unlikely, since Aisha was very particular about who frequented the house. So if money exchanged hands, it could only happen with one of the newer additions to the brothel. Percy swore beneath his breath. He should have asked Aisha about Markham, whether the man had ever visited the house.

The ride was mercifully short on London's poorly kept streets, and Percy arranged for Samuel to return in an hour. Climbing the six steps to the entrance, he knocked. After a minute or two, he banged his fist on the wood until he heard approaching footsteps and the door cracked open.

"Lord Ross to see Lord Eglantine."

"Lord Eglantine's dead, and he don't live here. Or he didn't live here. This is his nephew's house."

"I'm here to see Hamlet Tidwell, the new Lord Eglantine," Percy explained drily.

The crack opened wide enough for him to enter, and a gaunt servant beckoned him inside. Percy's sharp eyes took in the shabby entrance as the man led him into a small parlor. "Beg pardon, I forgot. If you'll wait here, I'll fetch Master Hamlet...I mean, Lord Eglantine."

Once the servant left, Percy scanned the room. Dust had accumulated on the collection of books and cheap trinkets on the shelves. Glancing down at the carpet and then the threadbare divan and chairs, he winced at the wine and food stains that darkened the woolen rug and the tapestry-covered seating. Hamlet Tidwell's indebtedness was well-known, but to allow one's residence to descend into such filth was unconscionable.

Percy's gaze jerked to the door when it swept open and the servant rushed in, his mouth agape and his hands clenched together. "My lord, come quickly! It's Master Hamlet. He's dead," the man sputtered. "His throat's been cut, my lord, sliced like he was a chicken about to be plucked. I didn't kill him, I swear!"

"Take me to him," Percy ordered, striding out of the salon.

He followed the servant up the stairs and into a

bedchamber at the end of the corridor. The curtains had been drawn back, and sunlight fell on the bed, creating a halo effect around the man's body. Percy stared at Hamlet's unmoving chest for several seconds before he peered at the crimson-hued stain encircling the man's head. Hamlet Tidwell was thirty-three years old, and the man didn't deserve to die like this.

A quick scan of the bedroom indicated the only mess was on the bed. Striding over to the side of the bed, Percy touched Hamlet's cold, pale arm. *Dead as a doorknob.* He coughed slightly to conceal the chuckle threatening to break free.

"Send for the constables immediately and tell the other servants not to leave the house," he ordered. "What is your name?"

"Gerard, my lord."

"Gerard, do not allow anyone into this room until the constables arrive." Percy glanced around the room once more before he said, "Gerard?"

"Yes, my lord?"

"Do leave the door ajar," Percy admonished.

He waited until the servant left the room before he did a slow circuit around the bedroom when a flash of light caught his attention. He leaned down to pick up the shiny object—a woman's ear-bob. Hearing voices in the corridor, he slipped the trinket into a pocket and returned to where he stood when Gerard left.

The servant stuck his head in the doorway and announced, "My lord, here's Constable Tucker and Constable Brown. They were right close because of a scuffle down the lane."

"That'll be all," one of the constables stated as the officers walked into the room. He abruptly halted, seeing the blood-stained bed and Hamlet's naked body.

The second constable approached Percy, stared at his face, and broke into a wide grin. "Be you Percy Howard, Lord Ross?"

"I am."

"Well, I'll be a goose's gizzard! The name's Tucker, my lord, and it's an honor to make your acquaintance. Alice, that's me wife, isn't going to believe me when I tell her I met ye face to face. 'Twas a new constable I was, serving under Jack Piper when you solved the Hawkins murder right here in Camden."

Constable Brown was clearly less impressed as he looked askance at Percy and demanded, "What brings you here, my lord?"

Percy shifted his gaze to Brown. "My intent was to talk to Hamlet Tidwell, Lord Eglantine, about the murder of his uncle, but—"

"On whose authority?" Brown cut him off.

His smile frosty, Percy answered, "On the authority of Her Majesty's Lord Secretary. I must deliver this tragic news to Lord Cecil, Constable Tucker. When you've finished your investigation, please send word to Ross House."

"Of course, my lord."

"Good day, Constable Brown," Percy snapped, walking out of the bedroom and down the stairs.

Gerard hovered near the front door. At his nod, the servant opened the door, and Percy crossed the road to where his coach waited. Climbing inside, he said, "The Cock & Oyster, Samuel."

As the coach rumbled toward his destination, Percy stared at the leather-covered window separating him from his coachman in an attempt to unclutter his mind and consider who might want both Tidwells dead. Instead, Aisha's lovely brown thighs filled his imagination. His cock stiffened as he closed his eyes and thought about pushing into her from behind. Her muscles would clench his rod and they would tussle for dominance.

She'd win, as she always did. He had no idea how she

managed to strip him of self-control when he entered her from behind but she always did. The only time he proved victorious was after his tongue worked her into lethargy. It was his favorite position, his tongue deep inside her cunny, tasting her as she drenched his face. He could spend hours with his head buried between her thighs.

"We've arrived, my lord."

Brought back to his senses, Percy glanced down at the erection between his thighs. "One moment, Samuel."

It took several moments to rein in his lust since he wasn't ready for Aunt Ahmara's prickly jests. Climbing out of the coach, he instructed Samuel to join Matthew in the kitchen and get some food. Making his way towards the private rooms of the brothel, Percy could hear Aisha's agitated voice. As she talked, the faint lilt in her tone sent a chill down his spine. She was frustrated and angry, which meant Ahmara was attempting to badger her niece.

Percy halted outside the door to the parlor. As Aisha's loud sigh penetrated the thick wood, he briefly toyed with the idea of quietly retreating to the safety of the kitchen.

"Join us, Percy Elwen Howard, instead of skulking outside the door," Aisha ordered. "Cowardice does not become you, and you might as well report on your conversation with Hamlet Tidwell."

Percy squared his shoulders, sucked in air, and released it. He never understood how Aisha always knew he approached, no matter how silently he did so. With a deep sigh, he realized he'd better solve this mystery quickly. If not for Aisha's sake, then for his.

SEVEN

"Aunt Ahmara," Aisha asserted with as much patience as she could find, given the past two hours with her aunt. "The ladies need me. What would they think if I left them to whomever is the murderer? How do we know the victim wasn't supposed to be Ophelia instead of Lord Eglantine?"

She eyed Percy as he walked over to where she stood and kissed her cheek. With a nod, she asked, "What did Hamlet have to say for himself? Is he implicated in his uncle's demise?"

Robert Percy sipped his wine then observed, "Ol' Tiddlywinks was the victim, not that Ophelia person, make no doubts about it, Isha. I'm putting a wager on his nephew Hamlet as the culprit." He took another sip. "Or that wife of his, what's her name...Horatia? No, it's Hortense. Quite jealous, though can't see the reason. It's not like Tidwell was a catch. Anyway, most likely she hired someone to do in both Tiddly and your courtesan."

"Robert," Ahmara said crisply before eyeing Aisha. "Don't change the subject. Isha, you don't know who's responsible, and this murder most foul may be the first shot. I do wish you'd come to Percy's, at least until he solves the mystery."

"I'm quite safe here, Aunt," Aisha insisted. "Randall and Matthew are capable of dealing with any trouble that knocks at the door."

Three pairs of eyes focused on the doorknob when it turned and Randall entered, carrying a tray. "Matthew thought you might like a cup of atay, Tante Ahmara."

"So nephew, what does Hamlet have to say about his uncle's death? Did he feign sadness, shed a few tears?"

Percy walked over to the table where a bottle of wine sat, poured himself a glass, and drank nearly half. He looked at Aisha. "Hamlet Tidwell has gone the way of his uncle, except the killer neatly cut his throat, which, of course, means he didn't have much to say about his uncle's demise."

"Are you telling me he was naked and in his bed?" Aisha screeched. She shook her head. "What the hell is going on? Percy, there's more to this than a naked man being murdered in his bed. And why the Cock & Oyster? Is someone determined to destroy me?"

"Come sit with me, sweetheart," he said as he lowered himself on the divan. Once she was seated, he took Aisha's hand in his left and, with his right, raised his glass to her lips. She drank some of the wine, and he kissed her.

"There were differences," Percy explained. "Hamlet was on his back. It was obvious he'd just swived someone because his seed was dried on his right thigh. His killer carefully sorted his limbs and his prick because Hamlet's semi-erect cock rested on his left thigh, not between them as to be expected."

Randall seated himself and asked, "Was he better-endowed than his uncle, Lord Ross? Or did insignificance run in the family?"

"Randall," Aisha chided. "I don't think that matters since neither Tidwell will be using their cocks any time soon." She ducked her chin and groaned. "I can't believe I'm even responding to you."

"Well, Mistress Ellen, size may be a factor in their deaths. There are some ladies who feel betrayed, although..." Randall paused for a second. "I was once told you should always study a man's foot length to determine whether he will measure up."

At that point, the conversation veered into uncharted waters on whether such notions were capable of being tested and Randall queried Percy about Hamlet's foot size. Despite her efforts, Aisha couldn't turn the talk about the murders, so she sipped her wine until the discussion about the Tidwell men's lack of penile stature subsided and Percy returned to the matter of Hamlet's death. "I couldn't search the room thoroughly, but I do have a possible suspect in mind. However, a motive for the killings isn't obvious."

"Who?" his uncle demanded. "One of the cousins? Was it Beaufort Tidwell? He was always sneaky and envious his father wasn't firstborn."

"It wasn't a man," Percy replied, shaking his head. "I believe the murderer was a woman, a young woman, in fact, which exonerates his aunt. Sorry to disappoint you, Uncle Robert."

"Well, these murders can't all be like the Dawson one. Now that was a case, Percy." Robert shook his head ruefully. "Pecked to death by your own hens. Although, that was some clever thinking on the part of his son. Get the old man drunk before he goes off to feed the hens, bash his head, then cover him in honey and corn. If it weren't for the small cudgel you found under one of the hens' nests, Toby Dawson would have gotten away with murder."

Aisha sighed and refilled her wine glass while Ahmara

rolled her eyes at her husband and said, "Do go on, Percy. My only concern is why the Cock & Oyster, and how will these murders affect my niece and the women here? I don't give a rat's arse about the Tidwells, rising from ragpickers to a title and then believing they're better than everyone."

"Now, Mara dear, that's Hortense's side of the family. Tiddly married beneath himself, but he was desperate for money and his uncle Polonius—what kind of English name is that—anyway, Polonius wasn't willing to share. Tiddly told anyone who listened Hortense's family had set a trap for him. She used to be a pretty girl, but bitterness and the fact that Hamlet was the Eglantine heir turned her into a pickled pear."

A snigger brought Aisha's gaze to Randall's face. The man was clearly enjoying himself, having settled on a chair and holding a glass of wine. Percy, on the other hand, was toying with her fingers while smiling at his uncle's gossip. She closed her eyes and sighed. It was as if nothing untoward had happened. Just another day in the existence of the Cock & Oyster.

Lifting her eyelashes, she let her gaze drift over the others in the room until it settled on Percy. "Percy."

"Yes, my love?"

"Can we be serious for a moment? What happens now? Will we be able to open our doors soon? I need answers, any answers I can take to the ladies."

He leaned over and kissed her temple. "Cecil insists that the house remain closed until the matter is solved. I must visit the grieving widow and Hamlet's mother Gertrude, but given my suspicions, which I won't voice until I have more information, I'll ask Cecil for a boon."

"Lord, her mother must have disliked her to give her that name," Robert mumbled.

When Ahmara and Randall's tittering ceased, Percy asked, "Has Ophelia returned?"

"No, my lord," Randall answered. "Sally has been instructed to send for me the moment Ophelia arrives. Most likely, she'll send a message asking for her wages since tomorrow is when Mistress Ellen pays the women."

"Which is why I can't leave the house, Aunt," Aisha stated. "What if something has happened to Ophelia?"

Ahmara shrugged. "Randall can pay the women. He does it when you're in Eggford. Since I don't know Ophelia, tell me about her."

"She's new to the house—four months—but apparently not to the trade, according to our clients. Ophelia has a...a talent for giving her clients a certain type of pleasure," Aisha explained.

Randall interrupted. "She's quite handy with a whip and a dildo, along with other toys, Tante. Ophelia told us once she used an extra-large dildo up Tiddly's arse while she beat his widdly, and he spewed so hard it went all over his belly."

Aisha groaned as laughter erupted. Ahmara stammered breathlessly, "A bit unusual. Did he enjoy his prick being whipped?"

"Yes, indeed, and he claimed only Ophelia could peg him just right."

Ahmara's laughter returned before she remarked, "I always knew that man wasn't right, not right at all. Although, such predilections shouldn't surprise me since I once owned this business." Her gaze shifted to Aisha. "Is it usual for Ophelia to leave for some time?"

Percy squeezed Aisha's hand. "She left a note. Apparently, she received a missive from Hamlet, which we don't have. Ophelia said in her letter she believes her life might be in danger because she peeked into the room where Tidwell died after hearing noise. Afraid she'd be charged with murder, she fled. I doubt she'll return for her wages."

A brisk knock on the door had Randall rising from his chair. Opening it, he grinned when Matthew entered and said, "I've prepared a meal in the private dining room, Mistress Ellen." He paused and eyed Randall. "Have you been drinking?"

A tipsy Randall grinned and blew Matthew a kiss. "Just a glass, mon chéri. To calm my sensibilities with all the gruesome deaths."

"Or two or three glasses," Aisha muttered.

"Traitor," Randall hissed.

Matthew grabbed his hand and pulled him into his arms. "You naughty man, you know how wine affects you."

"It's been a trying two days, my love. The women are bored, some of the lords have attempted to sneak into the house. Two murders and a missing courtesan... I'm about to pull my hair out."

Matthew snorted. "First, you don't have any hair, my dear. Second, you've enjoyed the hubbub because it gives you a chance to fuss over Mistress Ellen and the ladies. Finally, remember I share your bed and your secrets. Have you voiced your suspicions to Lord Ross?"

Randall shook his head. "Couldn't get a word in with all the chatter."

"Liar," Aisha quipped.

"Anyway, Lord Ross, do you think these deaths and the missing Ophelia might be related to another brothel?" Matthew asked. Looking at Aisha, he said, "What about Bess Holland? Didn't she attempt to hire Ophelia away from the Cock & Oyster?"

"She did, the sea worm," Randall gritted. "As if those dried-up, over-used women of hers could ever compare. She's even tried to hire Matthew. That woman doesn't treat her courtesans well, and that's why the best ones leave or seek employment here."

Matthew sniffed majestically. "As if I'd work in that hovel of hers that passes for a brothel. Her cook has given her notice and says it's because she's a pinchpenny. Even asked if I needed help in my kitchen. No one stays with Holland's Leaguer beyond six months because they're treated so poorly."

Aisha stared openmouthed at Matthew. It was rare to see the quiet man so voluble. Shaking her head, she said, "Perhaps, we should sup now. Would you and Randall care to join us?" Looking at Randall, she added, "Only if we can discuss the murders without mention of the dead men's cock size."

"Lord Eglantine's was rather insignificant, Mistress Ellen," Matthew commented.

She groaned. "I'm not going to ask—"

"How do you know, Matthew?" Ahmara piped up. "Did you see it? Perhaps it was flaccid, and in an erect state it was larger."

Both Matthew and Randall spoke at once. "Oh no, Tante Ahmara." Matthew continued. "When Randall told me what happened, I had to see for myself. There was still a bit of hardness to it, and it couldn't have been more than four inches, and very wormlike in its girth."

"Please stop," Aisha pleaded. "Can we talk of something else besides a dead man's prick?"

Laughter sputtered, then erupted in the room. Percy wrapped an arm around her. "It was rather small and a bit crooked. Hamlet's rod appeared to be a normal size, perhaps six inches with a healthy girth."

"Percy!"

"In this type of investigation, attention to detail matters. It can mean the difference between a successful conclusion or a dismal failure." He rose from the divan and pulled her up. "Let's sup, Lady Ross."

She rolled her eyes at him. "Not yet, Lord Ross. Not yet."

He halted and tugged her into his arms. His eyes twinkling, he leaned down and kissed her, his tongue thorough yet quick in defusing her defenses. When he lifted his head, his soft pants an echo of hers, he whispered, "You will be, and soon," before he kissed her nose and walked her out the salon and into the dining room.

EIGHT

"Why can't I accompany you, Lord Ross?" Aisha pouted. "I've always wanted to beard Bess Holland in her den."

Percy kissed her and stroked her mound. "For that very reason, Isha. I don't wish to explain to Lord Cecil why the woman I intend to marry is in jail. Besides, Holland might be less forthcoming with you present."

"Percy..." she cooed.

"That sound only gets you one thing, Madam," he said as he dove beneath the bedcovers. His hands parted her thighs and his mouth latched onto her flesh. A quick stroke, then a long, slow combination of nibbles and flicks had her moaning in seconds.

"Percy Elwen Howard," Aisha breathed unevenly, "this is no way to conclude an argument."

Pushing the covers from his head, he lifted his mouth from her private parts and replied, "I beg to differ, this is a perfect way to end an argument."

Aisha was helpless as he sucked and bit the inside of her left thigh. He was nowhere near the tiny cell of flesh imprisoning her desire. She wiggled her hips in an effort to instruct him, but his hands gripped her and held her in place.

"Percy, she needs a bath," Aisha moaned.

He shook his head and continued to bite and suck everywhere but the fleshy bit she wanted. When her hands reached for his head, he abruptly rose and got out of bed. "Percy." He ignored her as he walked over to a cabinet and removed several silk ribbons.

When he returned to her, he gazed into her dark eyes. "With your permission, my love? You're distracting me from my duties."

A smile lit her eyes, and she dragged her tongue across her lips. "You always have my consent. It's been a while."

He leaned down and sucked her tongue into his mouth, then released it. "It has."

Percy threaded one of the four ribbons through a discreet hook on one of the bedposts, then tied the ribbon around her wrist. "Is it too firm?"

She shook her head. "A bit tighter, please."

"Of course."

Once her hands were bound, he brushed his palm across her breast before he secured her ankles. Strolling over to the window, he parted the curtains, and morning light poured into the room. He turned and stared at Aisha's beautiful body laying spread-eagle, a fucking glorious sight to behold.

There was nothing to compare to her skin. It was perfection in its smoothness and color. Isha's expressive brown eyes stared at him with expectancy; this was a game they both loved to play. Her full mouth glistened from the wetness a quick swipe of her tongue had left in its wake. His gaze drifted to her still-firm breasts and slightly rounded belly. In his youth, he might have desired to see both enlarged with his child, but wisdom had granted him another wish—to grow old with Aisha

Resonne. To know that her life wouldn't be endangered by childbirth. Although Ahmara was an excellent midwife and herbalist, he couldn't imagine a life without Aisha.

Perhaps it was selfish of him, but he was thrilled when he'd told her of his infertility and she'd smiled, telling him she had no wish to bear children and possessed the means to abort any mishaps. In the years of their love, there had been no pregnancies.

"What has you so preoccupied, Percy?"

"You, beloved. I wish I had the skill of an artist to capture your beauty."

She chuckled. "Why don't you come over here and practice with your hands and mouth?"

He laughed and climbed onto the bed to kneel between her thighs. "Oh my, what a feast I see laid before me."

He bent and bit her just above her knee. "'Tis a bit firm, not as tender as I like."

He dragged a specially designed short riding whip between her legs. The whip's leather was wrapped in silk and its tip bound with Cuddy duck feathers. She had taught him how to strike so the pain and pleasure were simultaneous. As his cock hardened, Percy decided that night would be spent in his bedroom.

AISHA SHUT her eyelids in anticipation, waiting for the first lash and touch of her favorite toy. She loved the feel of the whip and feathers against her sensitive flesh, but Percy was ignoring her body's wishes. Her hips had sent repeated messages for him to begin and he chose to delay, his mouth lingering on her skin, teasing with bites and kisses, ignoring the pleas her throat pushed past her lips. Her first climax should have been motivation enough for the man. Her body's gyrations had rocked the sturdy bed when the flood she'd been determined to hold back broke through. With nothing to clench, her muscles had vibrated inside her, and deep waves of pleasure moved through her puss to radiate across her flesh.

Once mind and body reconnected, she peered at him, and he grinned. "I'd planned to gag you, but I love the wicked sounds that come from your mouth, Mistress Ellen."

At his use of the word that signaled an end to this particular type of play—wicked—she flashed him a saucy smile. "If you want more, you'll have to earn them, Lord Ross."

Then she raised her chin and turned her head. Her breath locked in her lungs as she awaited the first strike, not knowing whether it would be tender or cruel, on a thigh or her mound, or perhaps even a breast. Her body pleaded for him to begin, to ease her uncertainty. Instead, he placed the feathers on her right breast and, with excruciating languidness, dragged them downward.

"Oh fuck, Percy," she squealed, her body writhing. "I'll release in seconds if you keep on this path."

"Will the bed sheet be drenched, Isha?"

The feathers had reached her mound and brushed the hooded bud, and she squealed. Percy repeated the gesture, sending her body into a tempestuous spiral. "Oh fuck, please strike me, beloved. Now!"

Instead, he lifted the feather and stared into her eyes. "I know you have more resolve, Mistress Ellen. You will not climax again until I ask for it. Must I silence your lips so I'm not disturbed? What is the proper gesture when you want me to stop?"

She smiled and answered. "Shake my head twice. It's been a while, so I don't think I'll be using it."

He nodded and waited until her body quieted its tremors. She peered at him. His expression was thoughtful, as if he were trying to solve a dilemma. He rose and went to the cabinet, returning to the bed with a silk cloth and gently tying it across her mouth.

"I need to concentrate," he explained as he laid her head tenderly on her pillow. He then tucked another pillow beneath the first one. "You are such a distraction, and I want you to watch but not speak."

He kissed her forehead. Retrieving his whip, he looked at her. "Fear not, my sweet tigress, I won't let your outburst go unpunished."

He trailed the feathers down her leg to the arch of her left foot. The silken restraint held it in place despite her twists and turns. He teased her for a few minutes then leisurely dragged the feathers up her right leg, lingering on her thigh then moving to her navel. As the feather moved in faint strokes, her hips jerked, and a half-smothered sob slipped past the silk tie.

"I see you enjoyed that," Percy observed as his fingers gripped the whip's handle. "Will you enjoy this as much?"

Slowly raising the whip, he brought it down on her belly, and she jerked. He traced the rising welt with the feathers and elicited another moan before delivering another lash. After a few minutes, Aisha watched him run his middle finger along her slit, then bring it to his exposed tongue. Had she not been deprived of speech, she would have screamed to have a taste of the wetness running down his finger.

She closed her eyes, praying that her mind ruled her body. If not...

The feel of the silken handle against her vulva caused her body to lurch against the ties. She knew exactly what was coming next, and the sting of pain brought tears to her eyes with the first stroke on her mound. Pleasure dispersed the ache when Percy's tongue licked the spot, and he glanced at her. She nodded, and he brought the whip down on her thigh. Her tears flowed even as his mouth soothed the lingering sting before he repeated the pattern, feeding her passion. She was dripping between her legs and wanted him to lap it up, but the gag hindered her plea.

Aisha knew that her resolve was weakened and her release was imminent. They'd gone beyond the time of their usual play and she needed him. The next stroke did her in, and she shook her head twice.

He went to her and removed the cloth, kissing her lips before he murmured, "Impressive, my sweet. Eight strokes and a very wet puss."

She watched him untie her ankles and waited for him to release her wrists. When he strode over to the cabinet and placed the ribbons and whip on a shelf, she said, "What are you doing, Percy? Aren't you going to untie my hands?"

He turned to her. "No."

For the next half-hour or so, Aisha cursed him, begged him, and praised him as he made her climax repeatedly. Only when her body was limp with satiety did he use his cock to send them both hurtling toward oblivion.

PERCY STROLLED into Holland's Leaguer and was immediately repulsed by the onslaught of courtesans seeking his business. The shabbiness of the entryway attested to the brothel's decline and showed the stark difference between the Cock & Oyster and Holland's Leaguer. It was no wonder Aisha was so successful. He noted enough flaws to provide both Aisha and Ahmara details. A woman strode briskly from the back of the house. Her face was heavily painted and her smile dripping with artifice, while ruthlessness in her eyes betrayed the genial demeanor of the woman. It could only be Bess Holland.

"Ladies, he's here to see me," Bess crooned.

Several groans and a few curses accompanied the women's departure. "Thank you, Mistress Holland."

Her eyes raked him, and she sucked her teeth. "I do believe you're wasted on that Black bawd."

He eyed her. "I'm here on the Lord Secretary's business. May we proceed?"

With a toss of her head, Holland led him into her private parlor and went to sit behind a desk. "Have a seat, Lord Ross."

He sat on a chair opposite the desk. "I won't detain you long. Several of the Cock & Oyster women report you've sought to hire them away from the establishment."

"I have—and failed. Ellen Chapman has tripled the brothel's profits since that old witch Abigail left, and, from what I hear, the courtesans are well-trained and rarely lose a client. Who wouldn't want to steal them?"

"Was Ophelia Swinden one of the women?"

Holland's eyes lit up. "Of course. Her skills with certain arts of Eros have caught my ear. She refused me but did promise to send word should she become unsatisfied with her treatment at Chapman's house."

"Are you aware she is missing?" Percy stated. "Since the deaths of both Tidwell men. In fact, she disappeared the day Gregory Tidwell, Lord Eglantine died."

Holland's eyes narrowed before she replied, "No, and if she were here, I'd turn her over to you. Are there any other questions? I need to prepare for our new clients. I suspect several of them are worried about being seen at the Cock & Oyster."

"I do have one final question. Was Hamlet Tidwell a client of yours?"

She rose from her chair and strolled around to where he sat.

"Lord Ross, my client's list is private for reasons that should be obvious to a man of your intelligence. Good day, my lord."

Percy stood and went to the door. He looked over his shoulder. "Should I discover your involvement in any fashion, Mistress Holland..."

He opened the door, leaving his words to hang in the room, and exited. Several of the women accosted him before he reached the front door. He shook his head and departed the brothel. Once matters with the Tidwell murders were solved, he'd have a word with the Lord Secretary about Holland's Leaguer. The brothel was a blight. It was obvious Bess Holland gave little attention to the health of the women working in the house, several appearing to suffer from the pox. Not even face paint covered some of the pitted skin or the lesions on the women, and they plied their trade unabated.

As he approached his coach, he watched several men stroll up the steps and into Holland's Leaguer. He recognized one of them; Jasper Dolittle, a distant cousin and current heir to Baron Snobey of Gloucestershire. Shaking his head, Percy climbed into his coach and instructed Samuel to take him to Ross House. While his words with Cecil would be too late to save the men who just entered Holland's den, perhaps some future good might be done with the closure. For now, all he cared about was a bath and then a conversation with Aisha's aunt.

NINE

Aisha tapped her fingers on the edge of her desk, then immediately stopped. It was a habit she was trying to end. If Percy were in the room, he'd take her hand and rub two fingers, but he wasn't there, and her patience was being sorely tested by not knowing what passed between him and Bess Holland and exacerbated by Ophelia's continued absence. Where was she? Was her disappearance and the death of Gregory Tidwell an attack on the Cock & Oyster? And by whom?

Bess Holland. The only choice. The woman hated the success the Cock & Oyster had achieved since Aunt Ahmara established the brothel. Before then, Holland's Leaguer was the fashionable place for gentlemen. Bess founded the Leaguer when she was nineteen and fresh from the country. Seduced by her suitor's cousin, she'd fled and settled in London.

That was twelve years ago, and until the Cock & Oyster rose to prominence, Holland's Leaguer was favored. However, what distinguished the Cock & Oyster was the promise of healthy women, a limited clientele, exotic foods, and delicious wines. Men paid more but the service was impeccable and discreet, well worth the cost. Demand led Ahmara and the courtesans to adopt a rule that each courtesan had no more than six clients. Few had expected the brothel to prosper, but it did.

Aisha grunted and started to push away from her desk when a rap on the door halted her. "Enter."

Sally walked in, followed by Randall. Aisha frowned as he closed the door behind them. Sally slouched toward her desk, then stopped. "I was about to go out, Mistress, but Randall wouldn't let me. Said I had to stay here until I talk with Lord Ross. Is that true?"

"Yes. He's speaking to all the women in the brothel, and you and Ophelia are the only ones remaining. Has she returned?"

"Nah, Mistress. I've not seen hide nor hair of her since old Eglantine turned his toes up." Sally squinted. "Well, down because he was on his belly. Anyhow, Ophelia was scared, as her letter said. I suspect that's why she's gone."

"Do you think Ophelia has gone to her mother's residence in Clapham? Is there any way we can send word to her?"

Sally's face clouded. "Our families don't want us, and when Ophelia goes to visit her ailing mama, she has to sneak into Clapham. I doubt she'd go back there, Miss Ellen. She mentioned a distant cousin somewhere in London, but I don't know where he lives."

Aisha sighed. "I do hope she returns or sends word that she's safe. Please don't leave the house until Lord Ross returns. You're closest to Ophelia, and we may need your help."

Sally pouted, then nodded her head. "Yes, ma'am."

Randall escorted her from the room and returned a few minutes later. "Mary is watching Sally's door, and there's no window for her to climb out. She reeks of falsehoods worse than a drunkard who shat himself. She knows where Ophelia is."

"Did you give Sally her wages?" Aisha asked.

"I did, and she said I could give Ophelia's to her so she can hold her coins safe until Ophelia returns. She must believe I'm lacking candles in the nave to think I'd fall for that."

"What did you tell her?"

"That the wages would remain with you until Ophelia returns. She didn't like that but laughed and said she didn't want to get me in trouble so forget she asked."

Aisha rose and paced the room. "Where the hell is Percy? I can't hold Sally against her will if she's determined to leave."

"He sent a note," Randall said. "And Tante has arrived."

Aisha rubbed her temples and groaned. "Where's my aunt? Never mind, I'll search her out. May I have Lord Ross's note, please?"

Randall handed her the note, and she read it. "If you need me, I'll be with my aunt. Thank you, Randall. Let the women know tomorrow is another day of rest."

Aisha waited until he left, then tore the note to shreds and flung the bits of paper on the floor. How dare Percy leave town in the midst of everything? What was she supposed to do with the brothel shuttered and the women not earning? "Damnation!"

Closing the window curtains, she walked out the room and locked the door. The house was silent when it should be filled with the chatter of men and women. She went past the dining room, normally well-lit with the play of Eros scenting the room. Now, it was dark, broodingly dark. And she missed Percy.

Strolling to the private room her Aunt Ahmara favored, she knocked. At the invitation to enter, Aisha walked in and plopped down on a chair. Her aunt peered at her, then got up from the divan and went to a table, coming back with a glass of wine and handing it to her.

"Percy thought you might like some company," Ahmara said, returning to her chair. "Don't you think it's time to leave this life, Isha? It's been nine years. When do you intend to train Isabelle to manage her inheritance? Once this intemperate murder is solved, she needs to be given the responsibility. What are you waiting for?"

Aisha stared into her glass. "I've agreed to marry Percy. I'd hoped to hand over the house and the trade by October, but with these murders and a missing courtesan...I don't know."

Ahmara sipped her wine. "Will you and Percy be able to marry in spring? Robert and I need to make plans."

"A wedding? I'm not certain what will happen beyond this day, so I'm not planning. When will you tell Bella the truth? She has a right to know that her mother lives and why she was raised by Uncle John and Aunt Maryam. That her father threatened her life if you didn't give her away. Bella should know all this; she should know you."

"Should I also tell her I murdered her father?"

Aisha stared at her aunt's agonized face. Getting up, she went to the older woman. "He was trying to kill you, Aunt Ahmara. You were defending yourself, and there were witnesses even before Robert intervened. Even the justice of the peace recognized your innocence."

Taking her aunt's hand, Aisha said, "Do you love Robert?"

"More than anything in this world. He has my heart," Ahmara said softly.

"Then heed his advice. Let Bella know who you are. She deserves the truth, and you and Robert deserve your daughter. Tell her."

Ahmara sighed. "Sit there, child."

Aisha smiled and sat at her aunt's feet, her back against

the chair's seat and positioned between Ahmara's open legs. Her aunt's fingers stroked her head, then undid the coil of braids. As she took apart each braid, Aisha felt the tension leave her body. It had been some time since they shared this bond.

"You take good care of your hair, Isha."

Aisha knew the minute her aunt got her brush and comb out of the cloth bag she always carried. A smile lit her face, and she said, "You taught me well."

As Ahmara began to brush the thick curls, she inhaled, then released. "It's why Robert and I are here. The man won't give me peace until I confess my sins."

"You haven't sinned, T."

Ahmara chuckled. "You haven't called me that since you were a child. Pride and shame. You know, among our people, we suffer those more than what the Christians preach. Despite being of the people, Joseph Glasden had demons no one saw and the English ways made them worse. He was handsome, intelligent, and before others, loving. In private, he was possessive and jealous."

She brushed Aisha's hair as she talked. "At first, it was exciting to be loved so. At the mention of children, his quiet rage should have been a sign, but I ignored it, newly married and believing I was in love. What I haven't shared with anyone but Robert is I became pregnant after a year. I lost the child within the first three months."

Her hand trembled, and Aisha stroked her aunt's leg. "Joseph gave me a tisane he'd gotten from the local midwife. After, I thought he would be saddened, but there was joy. He said he didn't want to lose me in childbirth and didn't want children. Begged me to protect myself. I did, yet Isabelle was determined to take her place in the world."

"Once she was born, small incidents began to happen when

it was clear she would grow healthy and strong, and I rarely left her alone."

Aisha reached up and wrapped her fingers around her aunt's hand. "You needn't talk about it, T. I know how painful the memories are."

"I need to talk, Isha," she insisted. "The night I knew I had to save her...he had taken Isabelle from her bed and stared at her with such hatred before he tossed her into my arms and said if I didn't get rid of her, he would. She was three years old and the happiest of babies. The next day, I took her to my brother and Maryam. Joseph waited outside the gate for my return, and two months of hell ensued."

Ahmara began to rebraid Aisha's hair. The effect was soothing, and Aisha closed her eyelids. "The Cock & Oyster was purchased with the bride price he paid my father and the selling of the house Joseph and I shared. To this day, I honor my mother for her wisdom for insisting that should I be left a widow and with children, I would return home with an equal share of the house's worth."

"Where did you go for the year before his death, T? We were worried he'd harmed you."

Ahmara laughed bitterly. "Somerset. I wanted to be as far away from Joseph as possible, and we knew no one in the county. I landed in Frome, where a Black seamstress took pity on me and let me stay in her home. I cared for her children and her house. One market day, I was strolling through the stalls when Joseph appeared."

Her fingers tightened in Aisha's hair, then relaxed. "I'm sorry, Isha. Did I hurt you?"

Aisha shook her head. "No, T, you know father always said my head was hard."

Ahmara chuckled, then sobered. "Joseph had a coach waiting and dragged me toward it. Robert stepped in to prevent him, and Joseph became enraged, accusing Robert of being my lover. In the midst of everything, Joseph fell, and I hit his head with a rock. He died a day later, which freed me, yet I'm still imprisoned."

"It's time to free myself," she added wearily.

Aisha looked up at her aunt's tear-stained face. "It's also time for Isabelle to learn the truth about who she is, Aunt Ahmara. It will be her decision to take on the Cock & Oyster, and she needs the truth about its beginnings."

Ahmara patted the top of Aisha's head. "Yes, it is."

A knock on the door had both women looking up. "Come."

The door swung open, and Matthew walked in, a tray in his hands. Randall followed him carrying a bottle of wine. "We've been instructed to care for you two while Lord Ross is wandering the countryside. Now, you two eat and leave the dishes and glasses here."

With those instructions, the two men left. Aisha got to her feet and went to the table. "Oh, my. A lamb stew and flatbread."

Ahmara came to her side and grinned. "The best thing I ever did was to employ those two. And teach Matthew how to use a tagine pot, although his stews far surpass mine."

Their supper passed in hilarity and memories. When the women were ready to seek their beds, Aisha hugged her aunt. "I'm happy you're here, T. With Percy out trying to solve the murders, I'm not sure what I'd do except sit here and fret."

Ahmara kissed Aisha's forehead. "When this distasteful situation is over, we'll dine at Ross House with Isabelle."

Aisha gaped at her aunt. "Are you sure, T? Perhaps you want to wait until—"

"No, I'm going to listen to wiser heads and do what is right for my daughter. She needs to know the truth, and I'd like to hold her in my arms again. I need my family."

Aisha walked her aunt to her bedroom and bade her goodnight. As she went to her room, she wondered what Isabelle's reaction would be. It was going to be a difficult moment, but the Resonnes were a strong, loving family. Aisha prayed that Isabelle could understand and forgive her mother's decision. She believed Bella would, but the hurt would need to be assuaged.

Entering her room, loneliness swept over Aisha. She missed Percy so much. He understood her spirits, and tonight he would bathe her, rub her with oil, and either cuddle or make exquisite love to her. As she undressed and performed her nightly bathing ritual, Aisha came to a decision that brought a smile to her lips. Blowing out the candles, she climbed into bed. The scent of Percy's favorite soap was deep in the pillow where he laid his head. She pulled it into her arms and hugged it, inhaling his essence, taking in his love, and easing her heart pain until sleep claimed her.

TEN

As much as he wanted to ride straight to the Cock & Oyster, Percy turned his horse toward his London house. Ten o'clock in the morning was no time to show up on Aisha's steps, and he was much in need of a bath. Entering his house through the back door, he greeted Martha and asked her to send one of the boys she fostered to prepare his bath. Once inside his study, Percy rang for Silas before he sat at his desk and took a sheet of paper from a drawer. With a quick dip of his pen in the ink pot, he wrote Aisha a note, finishing as Silas knocked and entered.

"Good morning, my lord. 'Tis good to see you've returned unharmed," Silas said. "In the future, should you go wandering off without a guard or two, I shall inform Madam Aisha. Your bath will be ready in a few minutes, and I shall have someone clean your chair. Would you like me to see your missive delivered?"

Silas's reprimand stung. Percy knew he shouldn't have gone off without a guard, but the possibility of locating Ophelia Swinden was an opportunity he couldn't afford to miss. "Yes, please, and accept my apology for my lack of foresight, and the chair. I trust we can keep this betwixt ourselves?"

"Of course, my lord. However," Silas intoned, "Lady Ahmara is visiting her niece, so your request might be moot. Did you find what you were looking for, my lord?"

"Not exactly. Where is my uncle?"

"Presently occupied in your garden and tasked with the onerous duty of waiting your return. Ah, your bath is ready," Silas said as he went to answer a knock on the door.

The boy entered and helped remove Percy's boots, then left with Silas. Percy walked into his bedroom and smiled. Steam rose from the tub and the scent of rosemary and mint filled the air. He stripped off his clothes and climbed in, his eyelids lowering as the heat seeped into his muscles.

"Bless you, Aisha, for this gift," he muttered.

She'd taught Martha and Silas the value of baths and a mixture of herbals to soothe whatever ails a person, whether a fever, sadness, or aching muscles. She took very good care of his body and his mind, and in spring, she would become his wife.

After his bath and neatly dressed, Percy went downstairs. Wandering into the kitchen, he grabbed one of Martha's delicious pasties and went in search of his uncle. He found him sitting on a bench, writing in a diary.

"Good morning, Uncle."

Robert looked up. "Ah, you've returned in one piece, I see. Aisha will be happy."

"I'm about to go reassure her," Percy said with a laugh. "Would you care to accompany me? I'm certain your wife will be happy to see you."

"Of course. Let me change my coat, and I shall be ready to depart."

The two men walked into the house, Percy watching his uncle ascend the stairs before heading to his study. He spent the next half-hour dispensing with the business of running his estates. He was about to ring for Silas when his uncle Robert strolled into the room.

"I'm ready to depart, nephew," Robert announced. "I've not given my Ahmara her morning kiss yet. If I don't, she tends to be short-tempered for the rest of the day."

Percy laughed. "I suspect the short-tempered one is you, but I will believe the lie."

SAMUEL PULLED up behind the Cock & Oyster, and once Percy and his uncle exited, the driver drove the carriage around to the brothel's stable. Percy strolled up to the back door and knocked. The click of a latch and the slide of metal on metal revealed a pair of eyes framed by a small rectangular opening.

"Good morning, my lords," Matthew greeted as he opened the door. "Mistress Ellen and Tante will be happy to see you. I'm preparing breakfast, will you join the ladies? They're in the dining room."

"All of them?" Robert inquired, a mischievous grin on his lips.

"Yes, my lord, every one of them."

Robert started for the dining room, mumbling about having some fun. Percy shook his head. "I pity the women."

Matthew chortled. "They enjoy his spirt whenever he visits, Lord Ross."

Percy strolled into the dining room and grinned. His uncle had swept Ahmara into his arms and was kissing her with great relish. As he approached the empty chair next to Aisha, Percy heard her mumble, "Don't even consider it, Percy Howard."

Sliding onto the chair, he leaned over and brushed a kiss

across her lips. "I wouldn't think of it, Mistress Ellen. Besides, these aren't the lips I'd wish to kiss at the moment."

Squeals and giggles echoed in the room, and Aisha glowered at him. Randall and Matthew entered and placed several platters with piping hot food on the large side table at the back of the room. Randall left and returned with cups of steaming atay on a silver platter. As everyone rose and went to the side table to get food, he placed a cup at each person's seat.

Once food and drink were served, Randall and Matthew excused themselves despite Ahmara's plea for them to join the group. For several minutes, quiet prevailed. Aisha picked up her atay cup and inhaled before she sipped. "Perfection."

She turned her gaze to Percy. "When can we return to our trade, Lord Ross?"

Silence moved around the table like a slow-building wave as the women's eyes focused on him. He sipped his atay and softly cleared his throat. "The Lord Secretary says you may resume your business whenever you wish, Mistress Chapman. With no conditions."

Shouts and squeals merged into happy laughter as the courtesans celebrated and returned to their breakfast. The talk was of new gowns, perfumes, and private notes to their clients. Percy surreptitiously studied Aisha's face, noting the relief that smoothed her forehead. He knew she had questions but would wait.

"Is there word of Ophelia, Lord Ross?" Hannah, one of the ladies asked.

Percy frowned. "I'd hoped Mistress Chapman or one of you had news. I assume she hasn't returned or sent a message."

Aisha responded. "Nothing."

"Is Sally here? She's not taking breakfast with you all," Percy observed.

"She went to visit the midwife. She should return soon," Hannah said.

Except for the faint tightness of her fingers around her cup, Aisha had no visible reaction. He realized she didn't know the girl had fled. Scooting his chair back, he rose and peered at Aisha. "Mistress Chapman, if you have time, I'd like to speak to you."

She stood. "Of course, my lord."

Robert and Ahmara rose from their chairs. "We're returning to Ross House. I'll send the carriage back for you, nephew."

Percy nodded and led Aisha from the dining room. "Where shall we talk?"

"My accounts room," she replied.

She led him down a corridor and through two doors until they ended up in her accounting room. She locked the door behind her once Percy entered but didn't move away. Her gaze focused on his face. "Thank you, beloved. If I had to read one more note from that vile Bess Holland, I intended to pay her a visit. The woman's a blight on the trade."

Percy went to Aisha and pulled her into his arms and kissed her deeply. "I missed you, Isha. My bed and I were both warm, and you know how much I hate that."

Her laugh sank into his chest. "I should send you home, Percy Elwen Howard. My feet aren't that cold."

He arched an eyebrow. "Sweetheart, there are so many things about you that are warm, even fiery. Your beautiful feet aren't one of them." He kissed her chin. "I didn't think it fair for the Cock & Oyster to suffer because of someone else's misdeed. I spoke to the Lord Secretary, and since your house is one of the few that has no complaints, he saw no reason to impede your prosperity."

"As you can tell," Aisha chuckled, "the women were

overjoyed. We'll send notice to their clients and plan a special evening."

"The men will be quite happy. Cecil received a few complaints about Bess Holland's brothel and intends to shut it down since Holland's protector is dying of the pox. Anyway, forgive me for leaving so abruptly and without word, beloved." Percy drew her over to the divan. "I received information about Ophelia Swinden and needed to investigate quickly."

"Have you found her whereabouts, Percy? Is she safe?"

Shaking his head, Percy said, "No, she is still hidden, and I suspect we won't find her lair. I also fear Sally Wooster has joined Ophelia."

"Why do I sense I'll need a glass of wine to hear this story?"

"You'll need more than one," he replied.

She muttered an obscenity as she filled two glasses and rejoined him on the divan. After taking a quick gulp from one of the glasses, she declared, "I'm ready."

"You've heard of the female insects who kill and consume their mates." Aisha nodded. "Think of Ophelia and Sally as a pair of those insects."

Aisha took another sip. "They marry then kill their husbands? Interesting." Her forehead knitted, and she said, "A clever way to accumulate wealth, though potentially devastating if caught. Hanging is a horrible way to die."

"True. Anyway, a relative of a Bedford squire murdered a year ago was determined to bring the killers to justice—the man's young wife and her servant. He spoke with Cecil, who sent for me to meet with the man. Based on his description of the two women, I'm quite certain Ophelia and Sally are the murderers."

Aisha stared at him, her mouth gaped. "Fuck! I gave employment to a pair of killers? I really do need to marry you, and the sooner the better."

He leaned back and peered at her. "I'm afraid to ask you to explain, Isha."

"No, it's not that," she insisted. "I've been lying to myself about why I need to remain. These murders and the likes of Bess Holland are exactly why I shouldn't."

"Alas, I should be crushed that it's not my thick cock or my devilish tongue that inspires your decision."

"Those are significant factors, Percy, but at the moment, we need to locate our murderesses. If the pair of them are together, how do we find them?"

"Do you still have their wages?"

Aisha sipped her wine. "Sally received hers, but Ophelia's wages remain locked in this room.

"Sally will return with some story and ask for both their money, or there will be a note. Either way, I want you to agree to make payment. I'll have someone follow Sally or the messenger, and they'll be arrested."

Aisha finished the rest of her wine and stood. Her body wobbled a bit, and she giggled. "I do believe I've had more than enough wine. Will you return to Ross House?"

Percy rose from the divan. He took both glasses and set them on her desk, then returned to her. "No."

She grinned. "'Tis a bit early, but would you care to join me in my bed, my lord?"

"No."

Her smile faded. "No? Then exactly what do you wish to do, my lord?"

"That is the question I want to ask you, my lady. What exactly is it you wish to do? In this room, now."

She smiled and began to unfasten her bodice. He watched as she stripped away her garments, one piece at a time. His penis thickened, his breeches suddenly feeling far too tight. She grabbed several of the divan's cushions and tossed them on the floor.

"I've not been ridden in a while, my lord. Shall we?" She purred. "A gallop would be beneficial to my well-being. A naked back or the saddle?"

By the time she'd finished her statement, Percy had removed his jacket and shirt. Excited about the use of a dildo, which they gave the nickname 'the saddle,' he sat on the nearest chair and snatched off his boots. Crossing over to where Aisha kneeled on all fours, he ran his hand from the base of her neck to her luscious arse. He removed his breeches and kneeled behind her. "I must see if what I'm to ride is prepared for me to mount her. If not, I must use the saddle," he murmured."

"She is quite ready, my lord, but it is always best to test before you mount. There are several saddles in the bottom drawer of my desk for your choosing should you have need."

He kissed her buttocks, then raised her hips to position her exactly as he wished. Leaning forward, he slowly licked until he reached the hooded flesh. She wiggled in his hands, and he lowered her back to her knees. Gripping his cock, he rubbed it against her split. "Most ready, my lady. I shall not need the saddle."

With a single thrust, he pushed deep inside her. "Do not play with me, Percy. I'm in no mood."

He leaned forward and kissed the small of her back. "Oh, sweet Aisha, I have no intentions of playing with you, and I intend to ride hard and fast."

ELEVEN

"Do stop glowering, Percy," Aisha whispered from behind the veil she wore as they approached the Hen's Nest tavern near St. Katherine's dock. Despite the somewhat reputable appearance of the tavern's exterior, the area was decidedly not a place she'd visit without an escort. "I could have traveled here with one of the lads."

"Not as long as I'm living, and I glare, madam, because I don't care for this situation one bit," he snapped. "Are you going to tell me whose ear-bob I found, and what was in the note you received? I assume the pair are connected."

She ran her hand along his arm. "Do you trust that you've trained your apprentice well, sweetheart?"

"Of course," Percy declared.

"Then trust me with this. The bob belongs to Sally because she wore them all the time. Although I know you believed it belongs to Ophelia because of her lineage, she purchased them for Sally within a month of their arrival. A fact you wouldn't have known, Lord Ross."

"Astute. Continue."

Aisha smiled at him. "As to the note, I recognized Ophelia's handwriting. She asked me to deliver her wages and promised to explain everything. She also professes her innocence and begs for my help."

"Where have I failed? You intend to blithely stroll into a murderer's den and do not suspect harm?" Percy glanced around them before he hissed, "Are you so credulous you can't see this is a trap? I won't let you go in alone, Isha."

She tugged him to a discreet corner where they couldn't be heard or seen from the tavern. "Your words hurt, Percy. Have I given you reason to believe I'm credulous? I am armed, I intend to remain near the door, and I assume you will be just outside should I have need of your brute strength."

She moved back into the lane and waited for him to join her. "Now, with your approval, Lord Ross, we will proceed and bring this matter to an end. However, once we return to Ross House and before we marry, we will discuss your words."

When they reached the tavern door, Aisha adjusted her veil so that her face was completely concealed, and they entered. Percy nodded to the rough-looking man behind the bar before he walked over and spoke a few words. The man grunted and answered.

Rejoining Aisha, Percy said, "Second door on the right, far end of the corridor."

They climbed the stairs, and Aisha halted. "If I don't come out in ten minutes, please feel free to exercise your masculine judgment and brute strength to stop me from stabbing one or both of them."

"Ah, my sweet Penthesilea." He pulled her into his arms and kissed her thoroughly. "You have my word, and do have a care."

Percy followed her, stopping just out of sight when she reached the designated room. Adjusting her veil so her face was revealed, Aisha patted her left hip, then her right. The two daggers were sharp and ready for use. She glanced in his direction, nodded, and, assured he was concealed, knocked twice, then once more.

A voice called out, "Do come inside, Mistress Ellen, and shut the door quickly, please."

Turning the handle, Aisha walked into the dimly lit room. "Please lock the door."

She did and then glanced between the knife in Ophelia's slender hand and the dangerous-looking pistol in Sally's grip. The pistol changed matters a bit. "Since you're both armed, do you mind if I maintain my distance? I'd hate to have this gown and veil ruined in a mishap."

Ophelia laughed. "I do adore you, Ellen Chapman. In another life, I would be happy to remain one of your ladies. As long as you make no sudden movements, where you're standing is fine."

"Is there a reason for us to meet here? Rather than the Cock & Oyster?" Aisha inquired with a grimace. "By the way Sally, this belongs to you."

Aisha opened her hand, and Sally walked over to get the ear-bob. "Please lower the pistol just a bit? Thank you."

"Where did you find that? Never mind. You're not even going to ask about the knife or the pistol?" Sally questioned. "If I were you, I'd worry less about the room and more about my skin."

Aisha smiled. "Worried? No. I am curious, though. I assume you have a demand to make, but before you issue it, please satisfy my curiosity."

"About Eglantine and Hamlet, I suppose," Ophelia moaned.

"Naturally. May I offer my hypothesis?" At Ophelia's nod,

Aisha said, "You and Sally have long been lovers, and together you fleece foolish men of their money."

Sally smiled. "You are a smart one, Mistress Ellen."

"Thank you, although I am puzzled why you chose a brothel, and mine in particular, to play your game."

Aisha tapped the tip of her nose and said, "I'd think playing a widow and her maid would be more effective. You have youth and beauty, and men like Eglantine would set you up in a cottage, allowing you two to love each other until the cows come home, as long as you practiced discretion."

Ophelia snorted. "The late Squire Melton didn't see it that way, especially when several gold and silver plates turned up missing. That old bat of a housekeeper searched my room and found a small bowl and took it to Melton. With the jig up, we needed to flee, and so we silenced him and his gossipy housekeeper."

Sally looked at the floor and sighed. "And that made four. Then the bodies grew until there were six."

"Six before Eglantine and Hamlet or including the Tidwells?" Aisha asked.

Sally raised her gaze to her. "Before, Mistress Ellen. Ophelia didn't want to, but I wouldn't let her get into trouble because I love her so."

"Hush, Sally sweeting. We swore not to speak about the others," Ophelia chided gently. "Far too distressing."

Aisha was getting tired of standing and eyed the dirty chairs in the room. Sitting was decidedly out of the question. "I remain confused on why you chose a brothel, although the Cock & Oyster makes sense."

"See, Phelia," Sally piped up. "I told you Mistress Ellen's was the best." She grinned at Aisha. "I asked around and some of the queans near King's Cross said if they could work for any bawd, it would be you."

Aisha blinked several times, then said, "I suppose I should be flattered by such high praise." She retrieved a small pocket clock from inside her cloak and peeked at it. "Lord Ross is to meet me downstairs in a few minutes, and I'd hate to keep him waiting. If you would kindly lower your weapons as I'm unarmed, I will tell you what happens next."

Sally lowered the pistol. "I wouldn't hurt you, Mistress Ellen. It's not even got powder in it, and I don't even know how to use it."

"I know, Sally. I'm familiar with pistols and that one is more decorative than useful. Your knife, Ophelia?"

Once Ophelia adjusted the knife, Aisha reached inside her cloak and withdrew a small bag, a pencil, and a sheet of paper. She offered the pencil and paper to Ophelia. "I will need a full confession, including all victims' names, signed by the two of you."

"What?! Are you mad?" Ophelia shrieked. "I'm not signing my own death warrant."

"I'm not asking you to do so. Your confession will prove my innocence in the murders of Eglantine and his nephew, and the worst I can be accused of is hiring two murderesses as courtesans. What I offer you in return is fifty pounds and two hours to arrange your departure from London. Perhaps you should make your way to France or Spain, better yet Denmark since it is farthest removed from England."

She glanced at the clock. "We have five minutes to come to an agreement. What is your decision, ladies?"

After a few seconds and several glances at Sally, who was nodding her head, Ophelia snatched the paper and pencil and stomped to the table. She laboriously penned a confession, then signed the paper. Beckoning Sally, she handed her the pencil and crossed the room to Aisha.

"Why? Why are you willing to help us?" Ophelia questioned, her befuddlement obvious.

Aisha waited until Sally handed her the paper and pencil. Giving the confession a quick scan, she folded and tucked it into her pocket and handed Sally a bag filled with coins. Adjusting her veil and unlocking the door, Aisha studied the pair of lovers. "I have been fortunate. Selling my body has never been a necessity. However, for several women I knew, family cruelty and necessity led them down that path, and worse."

She speared the pair with a look. "Listen well, Ophelia Swinden and Sally Wooster. Your plight as lovers has earned my pity. Your murderous ways are abhorrent, and should you remain in or return to London, you will be tried and hanged for murder. You two are fortunate I do pity you, very fortunate."

Opening the door, she turned and said, "By the way, there are better and far less messy ways to dispatch a life. I suggest studying with an apothecary or a midwife. So much more efficient."

Aisha walked out of the room. Her fingers patted the slender dagger on her left hip, and she was grateful she didn't have to resort to violence. It was obvious the moment she entered the room that she wasn't in any danger. Ophelia's hand trembled each time she spoke, while Sally needed lessons on the use of pistols and how to load the powder.

Gazing up to the ceiling, Aisha muttered, "Dear Lord, please look out for those two fools."

Percy stepped out of the shadows as she started toward the stairs. Taking her elbow and escorting her out of the tavern, he led her down the lane and into his waiting carriage. As Samuel put the horses in motion, Percy said, "You know I don't approve of the way you handled this matter, Aisha Resonne."

His voice was stern, and she couldn't see the brown eyes that usually twinkled with merriment when they were together. She suspected they were quite dark, probably black, and his eyelids narrowed into thin slits—a sure sign of his ire. She slid her fingers into the lining of her cloak and retrieved the women's confession.

"Why, because I had all the sport? No need to pout, sweet Percy. You've enjoyed years of such amusements without me. Now it's time to share."

"Not the same, Isha. Did they have weapons? Were you in any danger? Of course, you were," he groaned, slapping his palm against his forehead.

"If I didn't adore you, Percy, and need my piping cleansed," she drawled, handing him the piece of paper, "you'd receive a tongue lashing, and it would bring you no pleasure."

He slid closer to her and licked along her neck from the base to her ear. She shivered and shifted so she could peer into his eyes. "Before we proceed apace, take this. It's Ophelia and Sally's confession. You do know, sweet Percy, I was never in danger. In fact, it was rather comical to watch the pair. Sally had a pistol—"

"What?" he screeched. "Pistol? What the hell were you thinking, Aisha? You might have been killed, and for what, a sheet of paper? Once you suspected them and knew their whereabouts, why didn't you let me handle the matter? Madam, you are going to drive me to an early grave."

"Don't be silly," she tsked. "Now, are you going to finger me while we ride, or spend your time repeating a lyric much written and oft told but usually ignored?"

She reached up and untied the strings to her cloak before undoing one of two silver buttons on her bodice. "I would much prefer the feel of two, perhaps three fingers sending me to paradise for several minutes. Which do you prefer, Lord Ross?"

He pulled her into his arms and kissed her roughly, shoving two fingers into her wet channel. He began to move his fingers inside her.

"Well, this is unexpected pleasure," he murmured before he thrust his tongue back into her mouth.

Aided by the uneven motion of the coach, she climaxed quickly and, as the carriage came to a slow stop, she made repairs to her bodice and her rumpled skirt. Peeking through the dark curtains that shielded them from unwanted eyes, she muttered a tiny curse. They were entering the stables attached to Ross House.

"This is unacceptable, Percy Elwen Howard. Take me to the Cock & Oyster. I have business to attend and preparations to make for tomorrow evening's festivities."

Samuel came around to assist them out, and Aisha hissed, "Percy."

"No, beloved," he stated. "I will not spend another night without you in my house, and in my bed. I love you, Aisha Resonne. What needs to be done at the Cock & Oyster can be handled by Randall. I will escort you there in the morning. Besides, we have to settle on a wedding date."

"I will not marry you before spring, Percy Howard," she declared. "If we do wed, where will we live? I still have a house in Southwark."

"Somerset, and I think the Southwark house should go to Isabelle," he suggested. "As to our marriage date, I will abide by your wishes until I convince you a winter marriage has all the advantages."

She eyed him saucily. "And how do you plan to do that, Lord Ross?"

He flashed her a cocky grin and offered her his hand. "To uncover that mystery, you will need to enter my humble lair, Mistress Resonne."

Aisha laughed and clasped his hand. "I do love a good mystery, Lord Ross."

A TANGLED WEB

TWELVE

Aisha laid her head on Percy's shoulder. "I didn't realize how much I missed my family until they were gathered for our wedding."

He kissed her forehead. "If I'd known what awaited me, I would have kidnapped you, taken you to your brother's home, confessed that I debauched you, and insisted on marriage just for the meals." He sighed dreamily. "The food was amazing, sweetheart. I assume the dishes are native to Mauretania since there wasn't a sickly-looking sauce on the meats."

She giggled. "Not all of the dishes, and was it my mother's cooking that convinced you to wed me?"

"Of course not," he replied, rubbing his finger along her cheekbone. "The chance to bed you each night was the primary cause. However, the food makes the bargain priceless. I can't imagine eating English meats again. I understand why the Cock & Oyster is exalted."

"Did you think it was just the courtesans?" Aisha shook her head. "You men... Anyway, several of the wedding dishes were Moroccan. A woman from Rabat instructed mama and Aunt

Ahmara, who taught me and Penelope when we were young. By the way, Pen and I are gifting Martha a tagine pot. I'll have to show her how to use it."

He ran his tongue along the outside of her ear. "Does this mean you'll cook private meals for your husband?"

Aisha tutted and pushed him away. "You're proud of that name, aren't you, Percy Howard?"

"Most definitely. You have no idea how vexing it's been for five years not being able to call you Aisha Howard, Lady Ross."

"Only five?"

He slid his hand up her skirt. "The first years were about seduction and debauchery, and I must thank Ellen Chapman for your courtesan talents. They are exquisite."

"I will convey your words of praise to her, my lord." She groaned when they hit a rut in the road. "How much longer, Percy? As comfortable as your traveling coach is, my arse is getting sore."

He removed his pocket watch and checked the time. "An hour, Isha. I have a wedding game that will help to pass the time. Would you care to play?"

"Will it ease the soreness?"

His tongue flicked her ear. "No, more likely to worsen it, but you won't care. Here, place these two cushions behind your back."

She stared at him, puzzled by his instructions, but did as he asked, becoming even more confused when he moved to the bench opposite where she sat. He raised her skirt to her belly and spread her thighs before he got on his knees. Sliding his palms beneath her bottom, he moved her to the seat's edge and lifted her legs over his shoulders, his head positioned in close reach of her lower lips.

"Do you wish to play, Lady Ross?" he asked before pressing

a kiss on the inside of her thigh. "I promise not to cause any greater discomfort."

Aisha smiled. "I believe this type of discomfort is quite bearable. Yes, I definitely want to play."

She closed her eyelids at the press of Percy's lips on her mound before he adjusted her body so his tongue could find its way home. "Oh sweet Percy, you have no idea how difficult it was to refuse you for all these years."

"Yes, I do, madam, and I intend to extract recompense. Now, close your eyes and let me break my fast."

AISHA LAZILY LIFTED her eyelids as Percy's finger stroked her cheek. "We've reached the stables, Isha."

She abruptly sat up, then relaxed. He'd taken care of the disarray that ensued during the final hour of the coach ride. The door swung open, and Samuel peeked inside.

"Welcome to Howard Manor, Lady Ross."

As she took his hand to exit, she smiled at him. "Thank you, Samuel."

Once she was on solid ground, he released her hand. "If I may speak for the rest of the servants, we are thrilled you've finally agreed to marry my lord. With your gentle heart, perhaps he will stop wandering and settle into a country gentleman."

Percy snorted and muttered, "You might want to inform the staff about your toys, Lady Ross."

"I intend to see that he does, Samuel," Aisha said smoothly, ignoring her husband's jibe. "If not, he's taking me with him."

The driver's eyes widened, and he stared at Percy. "My lord? Is that wise after what transpired at the Cock & Oyster? We'd hoped you'd finally lead a quiet country life."

"That is my intent unless Lady Ross has other plans."

She waited until Percy took her arm and led her up the paved path to the front of the house. "My toys? Thou will payeth, Lord Ross," she mumbled just before the door opened.

Silas bowed to Percy, then to her. "Welcome home, Lord and Lady Ross. My lord agreed when the staff expressed their wishes to greet you personally, my lady."

Aisha side-eyed Percy and saw the twitch of his lips as he struggled to maintain a respectable visage. "You're definitely going to pay."

She took her time speaking to each member of the household, learning their names and positions. Martha Stone was the last of the servants to come forward, smiling broadly at Aisha before she embraced her.

"Lady Ross, it's good to finally have you and Lord Ross home," Martha gushed. "*Permanently.* When you're all rested, I'd like to show you the garden I planted. Lady Ahmara took me to Borough Street Market in London, and Lord have mercy on my soul, I thought I was in heaven. The seeds and plants were such a generous gift. I never expected it. My lord, when you must return to London, I'll send a list."

Aisha laughed along with the servants. "Penelope and I have a gift for you." Martha cooed and peeked behind her to see the gift. Aisha chuckled. "Patience, Martha. Samuel, may I have the gift?"

He came forward to hand her a linen-wrapped object which she gave to Martha. As the woman removed the cloth, Aisha's smile widened at the joyous expression on Martha's face. "Every woman in the Resonne family has a tagine pot. Welcome to my family."

"Will you teach me how to use it, Lady Ross?" Martha asked excitedly, tears filling her eyes.

"It would be a privilege."

Percy moved behind Aisha. "Where is yours?"

She half-turned and rolled her eyes at him. "In Southwark, dear husband. A house only needs one tagine pot. As the owner uses it, a bond is created between the pot and woman."

"So, no more private meals," he moaned with a deep sigh.

Aisha ignored him and thanked everyone for welcoming her so warmly. "As my family, I promise to care for you until I join my ancestors."

She waited while Silas dispersed the group and then walked with Percy up the staircase. She loved Howard Manor. It was the perfect size for her and Percy, and she especially loved that the upstairs apartments were very private. They'd agreed during their second year together to always share a bed, thus the lady's bedroom remained unused, though beautifully furnished.

Once they entered their bedroom and Percy shut the door, she turned on him. "Percy Elwen Howard, am I thy lady?"

He grinned. "Aye, and I must be thy lord. What's your point, Isha?"

"If I'm your lady, then you cannot expect me to prepare meals for you or clean house or tend to your mending. 'Tis not a lady's duty."

"Actually, the mending is part of your responsibility," he said. "Did you not read the marriage contract or hear the vicar's words? 'Thou shall care for thy husband as thy self.' I do believe that obligates you to perform the tasks you've just mentioned."

He sauntered over to a wide-backed chair and sat. "Come, Lady Ross, remove my boots." A whizzing sound had him flinching to one side as a dagger pierced the cloth-covered wood above his shoulder. "Aisha."

"Yes, my lord?"

He rose from the chair and tugged the knife from the back.

Walking to her, Percy handed her the dagger. "You're improving."

She accepted the knife and went up on her toes to kiss him. "Thanks, beloved. Now that I have your attention, shall we discuss my duties outside of your bed?"

He swept her off her feet and into his arms. "Wife, you have no duties outside of my bed; that is your only employment."

She relaxed in his arms as his mouth brushed her lips. "I do love you, Percy Howard."

"And I love you even more, Aisha Howard. Care to share my bath?"

"Only if you promise to wash my back," she purred.

He kissed her roughly. "I'll wash more than your back, kitten."

"Meow."

THIRTEEN

Othello Blackwood strolled out of his cottage, a smile on his face as he headed to his garden to gather fresh herbs for the stew he planned for supper. With the village's summer fair two months away, his husband Cassio left each sunrise to ensure plenty of time to craft the jewelry and tools he'd sell during the fair. Although Frome's Market Day and Summer Fair were much larger, visitors to Eggford preferred the villagers' friendly manner.

He needed to finish the small jewelry caskets in his barn by the start of the fair. Since making a desk for Bath's mayor, he'd received far more requests than he could fulfill, which bode well for his coffers but not for his time to be a proper wife to Cassio.

As he turned the corner of his house, Othello heard the squawking of his hens and hurried to the coop. Sunlight brightened the opening as a red-combed brown and orange rooster nonchalantly strode down the wooden steps of the henhouse.

Othello cursed and yelled, "Walter Howard, get out of my coop!"

Several seconds hung in the air before Walter strutted toward him, stopping a few feet shy of his shoes and eyeing him with disdain. Othello clucked his teeth. "Does Miss Martha know you're visiting?"

Walter tossed his head, his comb glistening like fire in the morning light, and walked to the gate. Othello unlatched the gate and followed the rooster, re-latching the gate behind them. "I don't know how you do it. Everard has ceded his domain to you without a fight."

As they went past his pasture, he heard Ermegarde mooing and saw she was near the fence. Walter halted and crowed loudly.

"Another conquest," Othello mumbled as he rolled his shoulders. It wasn't just his hens who were excited when Walter visited. Ermegarde instinctively knew when the rooster was nearby and never failed to acknowledge the cock. The cow lowered her head with a final moo before she turned and walked away. Walter watched her, then eyed Othello.

"I have nothing to say," Othello muttered. "Nothing at all."

Man and cock continued until they reached the juncture between the path and the main road leading into Eggford, and Walter scurried toward the bank that edged the River Frome.

"Walter, come back here!" Othello yelled. "There aren't any hens in that direction, and Miss Martha's going to toss you into a stew pot if you keep leaving her coop. Aren't there enough hens there for you? Why must you roam?"

When he reached the bank, Othello noticed Walter standing with one leg tucked beneath his feathery body—the other leg holding him upright—and peering at a reed-strewn area near the river's edge. A man's body lay among the reeds and rocks along the shore.

"Damnation! Come on, Walter, we need to go see Lord Ross."

Othello learned long ago that if Martha's name didn't provoke Walter into action, the mere mention of Lord Ross was motive enough for the rooster to scurry home. Man and rooster kept pace until Walter headed toward the coop behind the barn and disappeared around a corner while Othello raced to the kitchen door and knocked loudly. One of the cook's lads came rushing to open the door.

"Is Lord Ross in, Chester?" Othello asked breathlessly.

"Aye, come in and I'll get Silas to fetch him."

Othello followed him to the kitchen, and Martha looked up. "Good morning, Master Othello. Did Walter get into your henhouse again?" she queried, wiping her flour-dusted hands on her apron. "I'm so sorry, but that cock just can't seem to stay away from your yard."

"For once, I don't mind, Miss Martha. As I was escorting him home, and he went to the riverbank...there's a dead man among the grass."

Percy entered the kitchen just as Othello uttered his news. "A dead man? Inconvenient of him to die before I've eaten breakfast. Where is the body located, Othello? I hope it isn't one of the villagers."

"I don't think it is, my lord. The garments were too fine to be one of us. He's lying where the path and the main road cross, just on the other side of the bridge. The body isn't visible from the road because it's tucked beneath an overhang; you can only see the man's legs. I didn't go down to examine him. I came to you as soon as I saw him."

Percy looked at Silas. "Please let Lady Ross know what has transpired and that I'll return as soon as possible. We'll have to take the corpse to Frome. Chester, I'll need my traveling cloak."

"Yes, my lord."

Once Chester returned with the cloak, Percy and Othello went to the stables. Samuel came from one of the stalls when he heard Percy's voice. Fastening his cloak, Percy said, "Good morning, Samuel. Othello discovered a dead body near the river, and we'll need the wagon."

"Good morning. Death seems to follow in your wake, doesn't it, my lord?" Samuel mumbled dourly. "First the Tidwells, and now a dead man in the river. You know, my lord, I could go a year without seeing another corpse."

Having said his piece, he walked away to grab what he needed and harness a horse to the hay wagon. Tossing in a tarpaulin, he waited until Percy and Othello were seated, and they were on their way. It didn't take long to reach the spot, and the three men made their way to the riverbank to retrieve the body.

Percy studied the dead man. Othello was correct; the man's clothing confirmed the deceased was a gentleman. His riding boots also betrayed his status since very few men wore them to walk—which meant the man rode into Eggford before he ended up in the river. Despite the corpse's bloated features, the victim had to be between twenty-two and thirty years of age, more likely in his mid-twenties. A swollen nose and mottled skin suggested the time of death was the previous evening.

Instructing Othello and Samuel to wrap the lifeless body in the tarpaulin, Percy assisted them as they carried the corpse back to the wagon.

"My lord," Othello stammered, then swallowed nervously. "His face. I can't be certain, but he bears a remarkable resemblance to Jamie Fairbanks, Cassio's cousin."

Samuel flicked a glance at Percy. "My lord, I recall you promised Lady Ross to give up this form of employment. It's not too late to fulfill your vow by summoning the constable."

"Now, Samuel," Percy intoned. "This is different. What I

promised my lady was no more work for the Lord Secretary. A mysterious death in Eggford is an entirely different situation."

"If you say so, my lord," Samuel grumbled. "Dead is dead, no mystery about it. My lady'll be in a fester when we return."

"Lady Ross doesn't fester, Samuel. I may have to examine her for daggers, but festering...not her preferred way."

"Your funeral." After a second, Samuel cackled loudly. "Yes, indeed."

Percy ignored his driver as the wagon stopped at Othello's cottage, and he looked at the young man. "There is no need for you to travel with us, Othello. I'll return as soon as I can. When do you expect Cassio home?"

"Before sunset, my lord. I would like it if you could confirm my suspicions before I tell him. It will break his heart if it is Jamie. Do you think you'll learn the deceased's identity quickly?"

"I can't promise," Percy replied.

"Then I'll wait until you bring word. In the meantime, I've got to finish the bed for Desdemona Brabanzio. It's been one thing and another with that woman. I just wish she'd heed my no." Othello moaned dejectedly. "If I can get the frame done this morning, I vow to take no more projects from that family. There are other joiners in the county."

Percy chuckled. "Wishing you luck. She is a determined young woman. Have you explained your situation to her?"

Othello frowned. "No, and I don't intend to since I don't trust her or her brother Iago. Always up to mischief."

Samuel's harrumph evoked laughter from both men. Percy shook his head. "Good day, and good luck with the bed, Blackwood."

Othello nodded as Samuel put the horse in motion.

～

SAMUEL GUIDED the horse through the village and to the carpenter's shop. Stopping in front of a plain brick building, he held the horse steady while Percy got down and went in to talk with Swinton, who was also the village undertaker. Swinton and his apprentice came out to retrieve the corpse, and Percy followed them inside.

Percy exited the building half hour later. "I'll meet you at the Pig's Nip in an hour, Samuel. Shouldn't take me long to put the case in Edward Smyth's hands, have a tankard, and see what gossip is afoot. Perhaps someone noticed the man passing through."

He walked the short distance to Smyth's house. Smyth was recently appointed justice of the peace and was diligent about his duties. With a brisk knock on the door, Percy nodded when the servant who opened it gaped at him. "Good morning, Chevil."

"My lord. Do come inside. Is Master Smyth expecting you?"

"No, I'm here on unfortunate business," Percy answered as he entered the house and handed the man his cloak.

Chevil led him to the small parlor near the front of the house. "I shall fetch the justice quickly, my lord."

Minutes later, Justice Smyth strode into the room, a smile on his thin lips. Closing the door, he inclined his head. "Lord Ross, an unexpected pleasure. Felicitations on your marriage. Please have a seat."

"Thank you, Edward. My apologies for the unannounced visit, but we have a mysterious death on our hands. One of Eggford's villagers discovered a corpse among the reeds close to the river crossing near Howard Manor. The body is being kept by Swinton, and I've taken care of the cost since the dead man was found in Eggford. What we need to discuss, Edward, is why the man was murdered."

"Murder?" Smyth stammered. "Someone was murdered? We haven't had one in several years, and the last one was Mistress Pettigrew poisoning her husband because he was a bigamist."

Smyth's expression grew thoughtful. "Nasty work, that, though the women didn't blame her one bit."

Percy wrenched the conversation back and summarized what he'd gleaned from a quick examination of the man's head and hands, his garments, a search of his coat pockets, and the empty coin purse left beside his head. As he talked, Smyth had taken a seat at his desk and began to record the details and said, "Appears to be a robbery. Since he was found in Eggford, would you like jurisdiction, my lord?"

"Heavens, no," Percy replied with a shudder. "Lady Ross wouldn't be amused. I'll aid your efforts, but I won't be in charge. I'll ask around to see if one of the villagers or farmers expected a visitor. I suspect the man was passing through, and if he came through Frome—which is likely—a cutpurse spied him. If Eggford was his destination, I want to find out who he was meeting. With your permission, I'd like to keep the letter I found in his jacket."

Smyth looked askance at him. "Of course, my lord. However, if it's water-soaked, then it's useless."

"Perhaps. I'll send word if I learn anything else. Will you be able to travel to Howard Manor should I send for you?"

"Of course, of course."

Percy rose from his chair. "Then it's time I leave for home. My lady doesn't like it when I forego breakfast."

FOURTEEN

Percy parted the leather curtain between him and his driver as the coach turned onto the road leading to Howard Manor. "Stop at Othello's cottage, Samuel. I have a few questions to ask him. You may leave me, and I'll walk home."

"My lord," Samuel protested, "I don't think Lady Ross will be pleased with your decision. I should wait for you."

"Let her know I'll be home before supper and not to worry."

"But Lady Ross..." Samuel sputtered.

Percy chuckled. "Will punish me, not you, Samuel. She adores every one of you."

Samuel didn't argue further, stopping to let his employer off at the cottage. He waited until Othello opened the door and Percy waved him away.

"Do you have time to spare, Othello? I may have discovered a clue as to the dead man's identity."

"My lord, of course," Othello replied, stepping to one side to let him in. "Would you like a tankard of ale? Wine?"

Percy hesitated, then answered, "I think not. Lady Ross

will already be incensed with me, and if I return to the house reeking of ale, Walter and I shall share a cold bed in the stables."

Othello laughed and waved him to a chair at the dining table and then sat once Percy was seated. "What questions might I answer for you, my lord?"

"Did you see anything unusual on the way to Howard Manor?"

Before Othello could reply, Cassio entered the cottage. He halted on the threshold, seeing Percy seated at the table. "My lord," he said with a bow. "Felicitations on your marriage."

"Thank you, Cassio, and to you and Othello. Unfortunately, I'm here on sad business."

Cassio's eyes went to Othello's face before he walked over and placed a loving kiss on his temple, his fingers resting on his spouse's shoulder. "Is this about Desdemona? If so, Othello made no promises to her or her family."

"I have no idea what the Brabanzios are up to and do not wish to know. I'm here because Othello came upon a dead man near the river," Percy declared.

"What were you doing at the river, O?"

Othello caressed Cassio's hand. "Walter paid a visit to the henhouse and I wanted to make sure he got home safely."

"Apologies for my wandering cock," Percy said. "I'll speak to Martha about putting an end to his jaunts, although he pays no attention to any of us."

"No need, my lord. Our hens seem to prefer him over our rooster, and we're thinking about selling him to the Widow Johnson, who is in need of a cock. I must admit, since Walter's been coming round, we've gotten more eggs from our hens."

"What time did you discover Walter?"

"I'm not sure, my lord, but if I had to make a guess, it was between seven and half past. That's the time I usually go to collect eggs. The hens were awfully noisy, and I was a bit worried. Then I spied Walter coming from the coop, strutting as proud as a peacock before he marched over to our gate and waited for me to open it. I did have to threaten to report him to Miss Martha and you before he bade farewell to Ermegarde and started for home."

Othello scratched the tight curls on his head. "I had no idea he'd lead me to a body near the riverbank. There wasn't a horse in sight, but the man's riding boots indicated he'd ridden to Eggford. It was difficult to tell how long he'd been in the water, but he was obviously dead, so I hurried to inform you. Do you think the man was drunk and fell from his horse?"

"Perhaps, though it is puzzling," Percy replied. "Robbery appears to be the motive, although it's not clear why he was murdered when a good knock on the head would suffice. What I can't fathom is why he was riding through Eggford, and what happened to his horse. I did find a letter in his jacket. It's damp, and once it dries, I hope to have more information."

He rose from his chair. "I best take my leave before Samuel returns with Lady Ross. I suppose I should ask what is this business with Desdemona and her brother?"

Cassio cursed, then apologized. "She, or rather her brother Iago, is fixed on contracting a marriage between Othello and Desdemona even though Othello has rebuffed her. We fear a plot to entrap him since she often presents herself at our cottage without invitation."

"Have you spoken to her mother?"

"I believe she and Iago secretly encourage Desdemona, my lord," Othello spat. "My success is an enticement, as is this cottage and land I inherited. No matter, 'tis not worth your trouble, Lord Ross."

Percy glanced between the two men. "Perhaps not at the

moment, but if it escalates, and given Iago and his sister, I expect it to, please don't hesitate to send word."

He strolled to the door and opened it. "I wish I could promise no more visitations from Walter, but..."

Othello laughed. "I'd like to see that enforced. Your rooster is his own man." His face sobered. "Will you let us know what you discover about the dead man? I pity his family."

"I will," Percy replied as he left, knowing Othello wouldn't tell Cassio his suspicions until there was proof the murder victim was indeed Jamie Fairbanks.

Fortunately, the air was cool as he strolled toward the footpath leading to Howard Manor. It went past the riverbed, and there was enough daylight to perform a quick search of the area. Percy glanced at the still-damp earth. Walter's footprints were faint but visible, as were the imprints of Othello's thick-soled shoes. Following the edge of the road, Percy noticed hoof prints and strode over to them.

He studied them for several minutes before he scanned the area within ten to fifteen feet of him, smiling when he saw another set of prints near the middle of the road heading toward Cassio and Othello's cottage. Not far behind, he noticed additional hoof prints as well as the imprint of riding boots. He knew they weren't made by the dead man or his horse. There were three different sets of prints, which indicated at least two robbers, probably on horseback.

Returning to the place where the corpse was found, Percy peered at the flattened reeds. The body had been pushed or rolled down to the river, his momentum halted by several large rocks. "Doesn't make sense," he mumbled. "No signs of a struggle, yet the victim was definitely cudgeled and robbed. The robbers had to catch him by surprise."

Percy patted the letter in his cloak's pocket and walked to the bridge leading to his estate. His long-legged strides carried him across the wooden planks and onto the grassy path ending at an iron gate. He waved at several men wielding scythes to keep the grass neatly shorn before he passed through the gate.

It didn't take him long to reach the front door of the house, which swung open. Silas's brown eyes slowly swept him, his gaze lingering on Percy's boots before he sniffed his thorough displeasure. "My lord, perhaps you wish to enter through the kitchen?"

Percy peered down at his boots. They were filthy, but he was tired. "I'll apologize to Martha later," he said, entering the house.

"Of course, my lord."

Percy started for the staircase. Except for Aisha, no one could "of course, my lord" with such disdain quite like Silas Patchett. Percy sniffed his armpits and frowned. He hesitated and looked back at Silas. "I'll need a bath before I face my wife. Do you know Lady Ross's whereabouts?"

"Of course you will, Lord Ross. As to Lady Ross's location, she's with Martha in the kitchen."

Watching Silas's disapproving back as the retainer headed to the rear of the house, Percy sighed and continued up to his bedroom. He had no doubt Samuel had conveyed the day's events to Aisha, and she would deliver an earful of complaints.

With luck, he could distract his wife's attention from the dead man. With luck.

FIFTEEN

"Welcome back, Lord Howard. I assume you've settled the matter with the body discovered near the riverbank."

Aisha stood near the bathtub, her gaze following Percy's fingers as he lifted the cloth draped over his face. "Would you like your wife to wash your back, my lord?"

"Isha."

"If not, my lord, I will see you at supper in my sitting room."

She turned and left the bathing chamber, her melhfa swishing about her hips as she descended the stairs in search of Silas. He and Martha were in the kitchen and looked up when she entered.

"I suspect Lord Ross will be finished with his bath..." She removed her pocket watch and peered at it. "In approximately twenty minutes. We'll sup in my sitting room. Silas, will you please bring our meal?"

She turned and retraced her steps upstairs to her sitting room. Aisha knew her behavior was petty as fuck, but there was nothing to occupy her time or her mind and she wasn't going to sit idly while Percy had all the fun. Going to a side table, she filled a glass with wine and sipped. The Tidwell murders affected her business and Percy had no choice but to involve her. Such wasn't the case with this death.

Aisha began to pace, her fingers gripping her wine glass as she considered different ways to become involved. From what Samuel told her, the dead man had been robbed and pushed into the river where Othello Blackwood—guided by Walter—found the body.

"Think, Aisha Howard," she mumbled. "There has to be a way to persuade Percy to let me aid him."

"You can always ask," he observed, walking into her sitting room.

She squealed. "Don't do that!"

"I did knock, but you were so busy plotting you didn't hear me." He crossed over to where she stood and kissed her. "May I have a glass?"

She poured wine into a glass and handed it to him. "How was your bath, my lord?"

Percy took a sip and peered at her. "This is unlike you, Aisha."

She felt the heat of embarrassment race across her face, then relief at a knock on the door. "Come in, Silas."

Percy walked over to the table, standing behind a chair as Silas placed covered dishes on the tabletop. With an inward sigh, Aisha moved to the chair and sat, watching her husband walk around to sit opposite her.

"Thank you, Silas."

He flashed her a quick smile, then left the room. Percy served them, and she muttered her thanks to her ancestors before she began to eat. He waited until she'd chewed before he asked, "Why are you festering about this, Aisha?"

She knew exactly what "this" meant, and she sipped her

wine and sighed deeply. "I don't fester, and tell me about the murder since I'm certain the man's death was no accident."

Percy peered at her over the top of his wine glass. "There isn't much to tell. Englishman, between twenty-five to thirty years old, dark brown hair and mottled skin, most likely from resting in the Frome overnight."

"Who was he? Was he from Eggford?"

"No, Othello fears it might be Cassio's kinsman but couldn't be certain," Percy responded. "It seems to be a robbery gone awry. The man's empty purse lay beside him as if it'd been tossed from the road."

"But how did he get there?" She interrupted. "Surely he didn't stroll into Eggford on foot? How was he dressed? What was the manner of his clothing?"

Percy chuckled, and she glared at him. "What amuses you, my lord?"

"Forgive me, sweeting," he apologized. "I'd quite forgotten your fascination with my occupation."

"Curiosity, not fascination. Amorous toys fascinate me, which is why I have a collection. Dead bodies don't, which is the reason I do not collect them." She ate a bit more food. Once she swallowed, she waved her fork and urged, "Do go on."

"Othello...well, it was actually Walter who discovered the body and led Blackwood to it. From what I can detect, the victim was knocked from his horse and robbed before he was pushed down the bank. He is presently with the funeral undertaker in Frome. Wipe that spark from your eyes, Aisha Howard."

"What spark, my lord?"

The one glistening in your lovely brown orbs that tells me you intend to stick your pretty nose into this business, and don't 'my lord' me. This isn't like the Tidwell murders, Isha."

She sipped her wine before she said, "I assumed not. Since you prefer no questions, shall we discuss domestic matters? Martha tells me the hens have produced a rather large clutch of eggs and suggests we give some to the Widow Peatree and her eight children. Mr. Bishop stopped by and said Mistress Bishop is expecting her fourth child and is feeling a bit queasy. Unless you need the coach tomorrow, I believe I'll take her a restorative. Also, Mr. Andrews—"

"Enough, Isha," Percy groaned.

"Why can't I assist you? I'm as thoughtful and logical as you are and more so than most men. You know I'm not squeamish at the sight of a dead body. You do recall Tidwell died in the Cock & Oyster. Why are you opposed to me helping with this case?"

"The Tidwells' case was different. Two of the courtesans working for the Cock & Oyster were the actual killers. Gregory Tidwell died in your brothel and thus necessitated your involvement." Percy sipped from his glass. "Need I remind you that you strolled into a tavern's rent room where the killers were in hiding? Or, that matters might have turned out differently?"

Aisha licked her bottom lip. "Ophelia and Sally's victims were men, as you informed me. I wasn't worried because I am no man. Besides, all that is moot because the current victim's identity is a mystery, which is quite different."

"Yes, it is, and I'm not going to involve you, Lady Ross."

She stared at the stubborn set of Percy's jaw and sighed. "Will you at least share what you discover? Perhaps what puzzles you. Even if I can't be directly involved, at least I can help."

He rose and came around to her, taking her hand and tugging her from her seat. He pulled her against him and kissed her forehead. "Sweetheart, you are my life, my heart. If any danger befalls you, I'd never forgive myself nor whoever is responsible—and I'd make sure they paid dearly."

"Don't you understand I don't want to live as we did, Percy? You leaving and me not knowing where you are or when you'll return." She blinked back the tears threatening to spill over her lower eyelids. "If I am with you, at your side—"

His tongue silenced her words, slick against the walls of her mouth. She sucked his wet flesh before she nipped gently. The duel was intense, like a fugue but with a slight misstep that allowed them to taste and enjoy the passion that inevitably led to a night of bliss.

She put a small amount of distance between them and sucked in air, her voice breathless when she whispered, "You never fight fair."

A chuckle warmed her lips. "Not where you're concerned." He released her. "Where are your knives?"

She tilted her head and looked askance at him. "Why?"

"I have a request, but I'd rather not suffer Martha's stitching should you take umbrage."

Aisha stared at her husband for one second, then her laughter erupted. "You know me so well," she sputtered. "My daggers—they're not knives—are in our bedroom. What is your request?"

"Would you be willing to help me with another matter? It seems Iago and Desdemona Brabanzio are engaged in a plot to trap Othello Blackwood into marrying Desdemona."

"Aren't Othello and Cassio secretly wedded?" She frowned. "I distinctly remember Martha describing Othello's gown, and I do wish we could've attended. The pair have always been wonderful to me."

"You and I were busy, my love," he said against her ear before he licked the outside. "Negotiating the terms of your surrender."

She gently slapped his chest. "There was no surrender, Percy Elwen Howard. What is it you want me to do?"

"Find out what Iago and his sister are planning and put a stop to it. Pay a visit to Abigail Brabanzio. She's always been a magpie when it comes to her children and other people's secrets. It's time you wield your powers as the lady of the manor."

Aisha slid her hand inside his trousers and stroked his cock. "I'd much rather wield power as the woman who brought the inimitable Lord Ross to his knees."

Percy's moan provoked a smile, and she nibbled her bottom lip. He leaned his hips into her caress. "I'll be the first to admit it, and I'd love to be brought to my knees tonight, Lady Ross. Are you willing?"

She squeezed his semi-erect prick then released him, grinning at his pout. "I am always willing, Lord Ross."

Her fingers intertwined with his, she led him from the room and into their bedroom. "I'm still irritated with you, husband. You do know what that means?"

Percy opened the door and tugged her inside the room, using the heel of his shoe to close the door behind them. He slipped his fingers from hers and went to stoke the low-burning fire in the hearth. Turning to face her, he tucked his chin and began removing his garments.

Her gaze swept his body, and she tilted her head. "You need more sun. I believe I'll build a private solarium off my downstairs sitting room."

She strolled over to a chair and sat. Without a word, she watched him move silently about the room, collecting what they needed, humming a soft melody. She knew he was done when he placed several objects on the table beside her chair.

"Will these do, Mistress Ellen?"

She peered at him for a second. "You do not wish your wife?"

He dropped to his knees and bowed his head slightly. "Perhaps after. It has been some time."

"As you wish, my lord." She scanned the objects he'd laid on the table. "Are you certain you wish to be saddled? If so, you will need the mount, and place it beside the bed."

He rose to his feet, went to their closet, and retrieved the mount. It was specially made to offer balance and stability, and he placed it where she directed.

"Well done, my lord. You may lie on the bed, on your back."

Aisha picked up a small bottle of oil and removed the stopper. She'd blended the oil specially for Percy. As the scent filled the air, she set the bottle on the table and removed her gown but kept her shift on. Pouring some oil into her palm, she began to caress his shoulders. Her fingers pressed into his flesh as her palms moved across his chest, allowing the oil to sink into his heated skin.

She worked her way downward until she reached his nipples. They were hard knots, and her fingers pinched his flesh. "Open your eyes."

When he did, she rubbed the left nipple, then the right. "Will you permit the use of a gift I had crafted for you?"

"Yes," he breathed.

Walking over to the closet, she opened a chest and removed a small box. "Close your eyes, my lord. I want my words to fill your mind."

She flicked the clasp on the box and opened the lid, removing what appeared to be a silver chain with two small earring clamps at each end. Going to the bed, she ran her fingers down Percy's chest and belly before she leaned over and brushed her mouth across his lips. Her voice soothing, she explained what she was about to do and asked his permission.

When he consented, she rose upright and placed a clamp on his left nipple. A strangled moan punctured the air, and she kissed him softly before attaching the second clamp to his right nipple. Aisha murmured words of love and delight until he settled.

Retrieving a small, feathered crop, she brushed the feathers over his chest, and a tremor shook his limbs. "If my little toy becomes too much, how will you let me know, my lord?"

"*Fire*," Percy gritted.

"And that it is giving you pleasure?"

"*Air*."

"Well done. I will delay your desires no longer."

"I shall be eternally grateful, Mistress Ellen."

As he whispered the name associated with the Cock & Oyster, Aisha raised the crop and brought it down on a muscled thigh and began their night of passion.

SIXTEEN

Percy woke to a metallic click and the faint hiss of the bedroom door swinging open. His hands gripped Aisha's hips, tugging her backside against his groin and deeper into the bedcovers. His body was tender from the previous night's lovemaking, especially his nipples, and a pained moan escaped his lips. She'd surprised him with the new toy, and he'd struggled to contain the premature explosion of his seed. When she finally allowed his release, his mind and body had never felt such bliss, and to his surprise, he'd drifted into a dreamless sleep.

He leaned forward to kiss her naked shoulder when a sudden weight on his feet had him jerking upright. Aisha groggily lifted her head. "What's wrong, Percy?"

"Apparently, we have a visitor."

She opened her eyelids and stared at the foot of their bed. "Good morning, Walter Howard. What are you doing in my bedchamber, and how did you escape Martha's sharp gaze?"

Walter settled himself between their legs and eyed them.

"I'd appreciate your departure," Percy stated irritably. "My bedroom is not for the likes of you, and this hen belongs to me. Leave now, and close the door behind you, Walter."

Aisha smacked Percy's thigh. "*Hen?* I see marriage has made you bold, Lord Ross."

Walter rose to his feet, inhaled, then puffed out his chest before he shook the vivid red comb on his head and crowed. And crowed. And crowed.

"Percy!" Aisha screeched. "Do something with your cock!"

Percy leaned over and kissed her temple. "I had planned to, but it seems another cock thought differently."

He turned and swung his legs over the side of the bed to grab his robe and put it on. Walter sat in the now-empty space next to Aisha and, with a soft crow, extended a wing. She gently stroked his feathers. Percy watched with amazement. If ever a rooster was to learn to purr, it would be Walter.

A quick rap on the door and a breathless "My lord!" had him turning around to face a grinning Silas and a very flushed Martha. "Good morning, Silas. Good morning, Martha. Have you misplaced a member of our household?"

Martha rushed into the room and grabbed the rooster, who went into her arms without protest. "Forgive me, my lord. I don't know how he manages to enter your bedroom."

"He's been in here before?" Percy queried, a single eyebrow lifting as he considered her words.

Martha's chin lowered. "Aye, my lord. He's done it a few times, but he never engages in untoward behavior. I've taken to locking your bedchamber door since that's the only room he visits when you're away."

Percy's gaze shifted to Aisha, whose head was barely visible beneath the covers drawn over her face. Her muffled laughter registered, and he glowered at her. "You find his incursions amusing, my love?"

"Your cock missed you, Percy," she cooed.

We'll be taking our leave, my lord," Silas stated through tightly pursed lips, although the merriment in his eyes betrayed the contained laughter.

Percy watched them leave before he locked the door, and his gaze returned to Aisha. "Rise, madam, let's get our day started."

She flung the bedcovers away and got out of bed. Walking to him, she slid her arms around his waist. "Oh, my beloved Lord Ross, are you much put out? Shall I chastise the household?"

The final word came out on a giggle, and he shook his head. "You probably encouraged Walter behind my back."

"Don't be ill-natured, husband." She kissed his chest. "How do you feel?"

He lowered his mouth to hers and whispered, "Wonderful."

Brushing a kiss against her lips, he led her into the bathing room.

PERCY SET his cup of atay on the table. Aisha was finishing the last of her food, an expression of pure enjoyment on her lovely brown face. "I must stop by Othello and Cassio's cottage before we visit the Brabanzios."

"Is that an invitation to accompany you, my lord?"

"It is. I thought we'd pay Mistress Brabanzio and her ducklings a visit after leaving the cottage."

Aisha lifted her cup of atay and sipped. "Why do you need to pay a visit to Othello and Cassio?"

"The letter I found in the dead man's pocket was from Cassio's uncle, the one living in Bristol who entertained Cassio and Othello when they married."

"What did it say?"

Percy sighed. "Some of the words were smudged beyond reading, but it seems the uncle was sending a wedding gift to Cassio and his bride, five sovereign coins. Most of the words were faded or unreadable, but there are enough clues to prompt a visit to Cassio. I fear our dead man is Jamie Fairbanks, and I want to deliver the news personally."

Aisha rose from the table. "Then why are we sitting here? Come on, Percy. Time waits for no man."

"Nor apparently does a woman," he mumbled as she strode to the door.

An hour later, much to his chagrin, they rode out of the manor's stable, Samuel bringing up the rear. Percy glanced at Aisha. There hadn't been much reason for her to learn to ride before they met, but spending time in the countryside, she'd taken to horseback like a duck to water and eventually rejected a sidesaddle. Beneath her skirt and cloak, she wore a pair of leather trousers so she could ride astride.

As they approached the bridge to cross the Frome River, she turned to him. "Is this where the poor man was found?"

"On the other side. The rushes partially concealed his body. Had Walter not led Othello to the man, he might have lain there for days."

"He really should have a name," Aisha said as they trotted across the bridge. "I can't imagine what his family must be going through to have no news of him. To not even know he's dead."

Once they were on solid ground, Percy reached over to squeeze her hand. "Until I can confirm it's Jamie, we have nothing to go on. I'm hoping Cassio can provide the answer. Then I'll be closer to solving this mystery."

Aisha's soft snort didn't escape his notice, and he was grateful Othello and Cassio's cottage was in sight. When they reached the fence, he dismounted, then assisted Aisha from her horse. Tying the reins to an iron ring, they walked into the yard.

The cottage door swung open, and Cassio stood on the threshold. "Good morning, my lord, my lady. Please come inside."

He stepped aside and inclined his head as Percy guided Aisha into the small living room. "Good morning, Cassio. Do you and Othello have time to speak with me?"

"I do, my lord, but Othello isn't here. He's looking for Ermegarde. She's wandered from the pasture. You didn't happen to see her as you rode here?"

"No, why would she be among our fields?" Percy asked.

Aisha rolled her eyes and replied, "You really know nothing about your estate, do you, Lord Ross? According to Martha, besides the hens here, Walter has struck up a...a bond with Ermegarde, and she is apt to wander over for a visit."

He blinked several times. "Wander over for a visit? Aisha, we aren't talking about people. She's a cow, and he's a rooster, and animals don't visit each other."

"Umm, my lord, Lady Ross has the right of things. One of your herders has returned Ermegarde several times after she was found in your barn. We've locks on the pasture gates, but she still manages to leave through the one adjoining your land."

Cassio's face creased with bewilderment. "It's strange, though; the lock hasn't been broken, and each time we find the latch undone. I suspect Othello went to your house, my lord."

Aisha brushed her fingers along Percy's arm. "The reason we're here."

"Oh, yes. I believe the dead man may have a connection to you, Cassio. I found a letter that may be addressed to you in one of his pockets. Sadly, it's not quite legible, but I wonder if you might recognize the handwriting."

"I don't understand, my lord."

"Your name is mentioned, and what isn't smudged looks as if someone is just learning penmanship."

Cassio's cheeks paled, and Aisha rose to take his hand. "Come and sit. Percy, hand him the letter and stop scaring the poor man. May I get you a cup of water, Cassio?"

"No, my lady," he stammered. "I'm fine. I just can't imagine why the dead man would seek me out. May I see the letter?"

Percy handed him the paper and watched Cassio's face as he skimmed what was there. There were tears in the man's eyes when he looked up at Percy.

"The letter is from my uncle Andrew Fairchild," Cassio choked out. "He always said he did poorly with his lessons, and me and Jamie were the only ones who could read his handwriting. Apparently, he sent a wedding gift of five sovereigns entrusted to my cousin Jamie."

Cassio rose abruptly. "My lord, has the...the body been buried? Is it too late to identify Jamie? If I can see his face, I'll know."

"I asked the justice of the peace to delay burial. I'd intended to travel to Frome tomorrow, but it seems we better go today. Let me escort Lady Ross home, and Samuel and I—"

"No," Aisha snapped. "I will ride with you to Frome."

"Aisha."

Percy caught the faint smile on Cassio's lips before the young man said, "My lord, we have a horse, and it'll take a few minutes to saddle her."

Aisha crossed her arms and smirked. "There, it's all settled."

Percy waited until Cassio left the cottage before he glared at her. "Isha, I don't want you involved in this investigation."

She unfolded her arms and reached for his hands. "If you're going to engage in this business again, I'm going to be at your side. If it's dangerous for me, it's dangerous for my husband,

and what kind of wife would I be if I let you endanger yourself?"

He pulled her into his arms and kissed her. "You're not going to give me any peace, are you?"

Her palm rubbed his chest. "No."

Laughter spilled from his lips, and he walked her outside. Cassio had brought his horse around and was talking to Othello, who looked up as Percy and Aisha approached.

"Did you find Ermegarde, Othello?" Aisha inquired.

"Yes, my lady, where she usually goes when she wanders—your barn. She was sitting beside Walter in one of the stalls. My lord, I will repay you for the hay she's eaten. Your stablehand Jeremy has no idea how she got into the barn. He was certain it was barred."

Othello rubbed his chin. "Someone is engaged in mischief. I suspect it's the Widow Brabanzio's younger sons. Such foolishness isn't past them, although I didn't think they'd dare approach your stables, my lord."

"Perhaps we should be off before the day grows short," Aisha said. "Ermegarde is home and, I assume, safely locked in her barn."

Percy grunted before helping her mount her horse. Once he was seated on his, he asked, "Are you certain you want to ride to Frome?"

"Stop fretting, Percy," she chided irritably. "The sooner we start, the sooner we'll return home."

"Gray hairs, Lady Ross. Gray hairs."

SEVENTEEN

AISHA SHIVERED as they entered the cold brick building where the dead man's body was being kept. "Percy," she said softly, "why is there a special building to hold the dead? It's unusual."

"Several years ago, six bodies were recovered from the river. Foolish lads, two from Eggford, in a drunken state dared each other in a deadly game. There was nowhere to store the bodies for the families to reclaim them. The circuit justice agreed with my suggestion for a cold room behind the undertaker's establishment—as long as I paid for it."

He slipped his arm around her waist and pulled her close. "You don't have to go in, sweetheart. I suspect the body is somewhat decayed."

"You do recall Tidwell?" she replied. "I did see him in all his naked, pale glory. Another corpse isn't going to overset me."

Cassio's steps were hesitant as he approached the long wood table and pulled the tarp back from the dead man's face. A shudder nearly took him to his knees before he stiffened his spine and turned to the couple. "It's Jamie, my lord."

Aisha guided him from the room, her arm wrapped around his waist. "I'm so sorry, Cassio."

Once they were outside, he moved from her embrace to face her. "He was two years older and more like a brother. Who would do this?"

"Robbery, Cassio," Percy said as he joined them. "I've arranged for your cousin's body to be returned to your uncle, along with a letter from me. We will find the killer, I promise you."

Taking Aisha's hand, he said, "I must speak to Justice Smyth before we return to Eggford."

Silence accompanied their short ride to the Justice's home. Making certain the horses were stabled, Percy led Aisha up the steps to the front door, Cassio behind them.

The door swung open. "Lord Ross, Justice Smyth received notice of your arrival and is expecting you."

"Thank you, Chevil. Lady Ross and Cassio Fairbanks. The deceased is Cassio's kinsman."

Chevil's face remained impassive at Percy's introduction, although Aisha caught the slight lifting of an eyebrow as he bowed his head to her before he said, "This way, Lord and Lady Ross."

Aisha glanced around the entry, noting the ostentatious portraits and small statues placed in alcoves that covered the entry's walls. Must be Mistress Smyth's doing.

Chevil led them to the back of the house and into a library. "Justice Smyth, Lord and Lady Ross have arrived."

Aisha maintained a decorous face when Smyth's eyes widened as his gaze swept her. She didn't wait for Percy to do what was proper; instead, she approached the Justice and extended a gloved hand. "Justice Smyth. 'Tis pleasant to see you again. How fares Mistress Smyth?"

"Yes…yes, lovely to see you…Lady Ross. She is well and in her sitting room. Would you like Chevil to take you to her?"

"No thank you," Aisha said as she moved to a chair and sat.

Percy stood behind her as Smyth returned to his desk. "Edward, this is Cassio Fairbanks, cousin to the murder victim, Jamie Fairbanks. I've arranged for Swinton to return the body to Fairbanks's father post haste."

"'Tis kind of you, my lord," Smyth intoned. "Since we last spoke, I've learned details about the dead man, and he did stop in Frome the day he was found."

"Who provided the information?"

"Mabel Cuttlesworth. She owns the Pig's Nip tavern. It seems the victim—"

"Has a name," Aisha interrupted curtly. "His name is Jamie Fairbanks."

"My apology, Lady Ross. According to Mabel, Fairbanks arrived late morning and stopped in for a meal and tankard of ale. He left several hours later, riding in the direction of Eggford."

Percy rested his fingers on Aisha's shoulder, his thumb caressing her neck. She leaned into his touch. He'd sensed her irritation with Smyth from the moment they entered the library.

"Several hours in a tavern," she mused aloud. "I assume the Pig's Nip also serves other delicacies besides food and drink. Who was the person who delayed Jamie's journey?"

Smyth's mouth fell open, and he stared at Aisha. "Lady Ross, I do not speak of such matters in this house, especially in the presence of ladies."

"Why not, Justice? We should know whether Mr. Fairbanks ended up in someone's bed or not before he left Frome." She rose from her chair. "Husband, I think we need to speak with Mistress Cuttlesworth."

"Lord Ross, do something! It won't look well if Lady Ross struts in to question Mabel," Smyth hissed.

"I do not strut, Justice Smyth," Aisha retorted. "Roosters strut, peacocks strut, court popinjays strut. I may stroll, walk, meander, or saunter—I never strut. I leave that to the men."

Percy placed his palm on Aisha's back and gently rubbed her spine. "Perhaps you should just answer Lady Ross's question, Edward."

"Well, it's a sensitive matter, my lord. I'd prefer not to stir up rumors and the like. You have no idea how much trouble can arise."

"Justice Smyth, stammering doesn't become you," Aisha began. "It is common knowledge that Mabel's daughter Barbara practices the trade, and the rumors you're worried about reached Eggford long before Jamie Fairbanks lost his life, so your hesitation is wasted."

She glanced at Percy. "My lord, we should have a word with Barbara before we depart Frome. It's been an age since I've been in a tavern."

Turning her back to Smyth, she accepted Percy's arm, and they walked to the door just as it swung open. A woman of substance and obvious strict decorum strolled into the room, brushing past her before she spun to face Percy and Aisha. A haughty expression on her face, Mistress Smyth inclined her head to Percy and greeted him before her eyes focused on Aisha.

The woman's blue-eyed gaze filled with disdain as it encompassed her before Mistress Smyth patted several of her tight curls. "Good morn. I'm Tabitha Smyth, Justice Smyth's wife. I was visiting my mother when Justice Smyth was introduced to you."

Aisha nodded, not leaving the threshold as Percy and Cassio moved to stand behind her. "Lady Aisha Howard, Lord

Ross's wife. My apologies, but we can't linger, Mistress Smyth. We're here investigating the death of this young man's cousin, and my lord has pressing business with Mabel Cuttlesworth."

At the name, Tabitha Smyth's eyes narrowed, and she glanced at her husband. Smoothing a smile on her lips, she said, "I'm sure you don't want to be involved in that nasty business if it means a visit to that den of iniquity. Why not let the men handle it while you and I become acquainted, Aisha?"

Behind her, Aisha heard the smothered laughs of both Percy and Cassio. "Oh, my dear Tabitha, did you not know I was born to meddle in men's business? As to brothels and taverns, I have visited a few, and as yet, I've emerged unscathed."

As Tabitha's lips flopped open, Aisha added with a smirk, "Also, I much prefer the honesty of the ladies who practice the trade than the manners I've seen among women at court. Good day, Justice Smyth, Mistress Smyth."

As she exited the room, she mumbled, "Neither one of you better make a sound until we're away from this house."

As the door closed behind them, Percy took her hand and brought it to his lips. "You have no idea how much I adore you, Lady Ross. My only regret is that you didn't tell her your history."

"Tempted, Percy. Very tempted," she replied.

Assisting her onto her horse, he turned to Cassio. "If you prefer to return to Eggford, I'll understand."

"I think I'll remain, my lord. Despite the circumstances, I haven't been this entertained since Desdemona tried to climb through our bedroom window and got stuck. Othello and I were returning to the cottage from Bristol and heard Walter squawking loudly. We freed her, and he gave chase as she fled the yard."

The three rode to the Pig's Nip, Aisha struggling to contain her laughter as Cassio recounted more of Desdemona Brabanzio's antics. Percy halted in front of a well-maintained building. Only the Pig's Nip sign was weathered.

Aisha peered at her husband. "Since it's midday, shall we dine here, my lord?"

"Of course, my lady. Perhaps Mistress Cuttlesworth has a private room."

Aisha snorted. "I don't think so." She dismounted, not caring who might view her indecorous act. "We really must talk about your expectations, Percy. I remain the person you wooed and married."

He dismounted and took the reins to her horse, tying them to a post. "I'm quite aware of that fact, and it's often what causes me worry. How many?"

She ducked her chin briefly, then stared at him. "Two, in the usual places."

Percy noted the challenge in her brown eyes and said, "Thought so. Please restrain yourself should someone get out of hand."

"I'll try."

He kissed her cheek. "It's all I can ask, especially since the Rufus Beaulieu incident—"

"Percy, that man deserved it," she insisted, cutting off his words. "Drunk or no, he was wrong to insult you. Besides, it was only a smallish cut. The noise he made...imagine if I'd sliced off a cod."

"Restraint, Isha."

She sighed as he guided her into the tavern. The interior was well-lit, and the tables appeared to be clean, though worn. She gestured to one not far from the door with no obstacles in the way should they need to escape quickly. Percy led them to the table and seated her.

The woman who walked toward them was older than

her, probably in her fifties. She didn't fit the image Shakespeare and other writers often depicted of a widow tavern owner. Mabel Cuttlesworth was an attractive, if pale matron whose bearing suggested a gentlewoman's background.

"Lord Ross, 'tis a surprise to see you in here," she said. "I assume it's safe to welcome Lady Ross to the Pig's Nip."

Aisha extended a gloved hand. "Quite safe. Aisha Howard."

Mabel stared at the hand for a second, then gripped it. "A pleasure to meet you, Lady Ross."

"This is Master Cassio Fairbanks," Percy stated. "He is kinsman to the deceased man in Swinton's care. We'd like to ask—"

Aisha huffed and cut him off. "Mistress Cuttlesworth, might we get something to eat? I, for one, cannot think on an empty stomach when Lord Ross starts to ask questions."

"Of course, my lady. I have a good stew and freshly baked bread if you like."

"Perfect."

The woman left, and Aisha shot a dark glare at Percy. "Perhaps it would be better if I questioned Mistress Cuttlesworth. Your manner has gotten rather abrupt of late."

Before he could answer, Mabel returned, followed by a young woman carrying a tray with three tankards of ale. Mabel set three bowls of stew, a plate of bread, and eating utensils before them. "The ale is on me."

She nodded to the young woman, and they both pulled up chairs and sat. "This is my daughter, Barbara. We'll answer any questions you have."

An impatient Cassio was the first to speak. "It's been reported my cousin was here for over two hours."

Barbara flushed. "He was with me. Jamie, that was the

name he gave, said it'd been some time since he'd been serviced. So, I did. He paid me well."

"Do you have any notion what time Jamie departed the Pig's Nip?" Aisha asked.

"Aye," Barbara grinned. "He had a fancy pocket clock. Lord, it was so pretty, all shiny and whatnot. I've never seen anything like it except Justice Smyth's, and his isn't as fancy as the one Jamie carried."

"The time," Aisha pressed gently.

"Forgive me, sometimes I get beside meself. It was...half past four. He said he needed to leave if he was to get to Eggford before nightfall. He was a bit drunk, my lady. Offered him my room, but he said he had somewhere to stay once he got there."

Percy set his tankard on the table after taking a drink. "Were there others in the tavern, Barbara? Was it busy?"

"Aye, a bit, but mamma would know who."

Turning his gaze to Mabel, he nodded. "If you can recall your customers, I'd like their names."

She rattled off nearly a dozen names, and Aisha noticed they were mostly men, including Horace Chevil. Were Mabel and Horace lovers?

"I think that's all, my lord." Mabel frowned. "Wait, I forgot Iago Brabanzio came in for a tankard and left without paying. That pinchpenny! Thinks 'cause he's gentry that he's better than the rest of us."

"Do you know what time he left?"

"Of course, 'cause I sent my Barbara after him for coin. 'Twas half past four of the clock, by my reckoning." Mabel's face paled. "Oh my lord, you don't think he had something to do with the poor man's death? Oh, my dear lord."

"Let's not be too hasty, Mistress Cuttlesworth. Iago is given to larks and such, but I doubt he needs to engage in robbery and murder."

During the exchange between Percy and Mabel, Aisha focused on Barbara. The woman's expression went through a myriad of changes, the last one guilt. The daughter was dining at quite a few tables.

Retrieving a handkerchief, Aisha dabbed at the corners of her mouth once she finished her ale. "My lord, 'tis getting late in the day, and we should set off for Eggford. Martha will be worried if we don't arrive in time for supper."

Percy lifted his gaze to her eyes and, after a second, inclined his head. "Thank you, Mistress Cuttlesworth, and you, Barbara, for your help."

"Such a shame, my lord. He was so young and too lively a man to die such a horrible death. My condolences to you, Master Fairbanks, and to your family."

"Don't worry, we'll find the killer and make them pay," Cassio gritted, rising from his chair.

As the three walked out of the tavern and remounted their horses, Mabel turned to her daughter. "Wait until they've ridden from town, then take a message to Horace and let him know he's under suspicion for the Fairbanks death." Mabel rubbed the back of her neck. "Lord, it's all I need is for my private business to be bandied about Frome."

"I will, Mama."

EIGHTEEN

Percy draped a fine woolen blanket across Aisha's thighs. "Does this interior meet your expectations, Lady Ross? The carriage maker was taken aback by my instructions and, of course, demanded a higher price."

Aisha smiled as her gaze took in the new carriage. The seat they occupied was well-cushioned and had enough width for play. It was far more private than Percy's other coach. The small carriage window between driver and passenger was shuttered but easily opened if necessary. Most impressive was the comfort of the ride.

"Far better, my lord. Where are we headed?"

He adjusted the blanket so it covered them both. "The Widow Brabanzio."

"How much time do we have to christen your new carriage?" she purred, her fingers massaging his knee.

"Enough, kitten," he whispered as he leaned in to kiss her lips. "Shall I demonstrate its capabilities, sweet Isha?"

"If you wouldn't mind."

Percy shifted to the opposite seat. "In order to do that, I

must peruse what is hidden beneath the blanket." Aisha smiled and slowly raised the blanket and placed it beside her. "Now remove your skirt."

"I think not, my lord. 'Tis a bit cool still, and I fear I may take a chill." She raised her skirt until it was bundled around her waist and slowly parted her thighs. "You are free to undertake a closer inspection, should you choose."

Removing a small cushion from beneath the seat, Percy placed it on the floor and kneeled so he was between Aisha's legs. He tugged a hidden lever, and on each side of him, a leather stirrup dropped from beneath the bench. Taking Aisha's left foot, he slid it into the stirrup and tightened it. Once both her feet were secured, he glanced at her stunned expression.

"I had them designed so they're long enough to allow you some freedom of movement but not too long to impede my satisfaction."

"What other marvels have you equipped this coach with, husband?"

"In due time, sweet wife. For this short ride, I don't intend to spend my time in conversation."

He ran his hands up her smooth brown legs and spread her thighs as far apart as possible. One hand stroked her mound. She was already wet. Leaning forward, he placed his palms beneath her arse and lifted her lower lips to his mouth. His tongue darted inside to capture her liquid before he withdrew and licked the hooded flesh protecting what was concealed.

She tasted and smelled of roses from the scented oil she'd bathed in before they had breakfast. The tip of his tongue flicked the tiny bud, and a faint noise floated in the carriage. The sound was somewhere between a sob and a purr. He never got enough of tasting and licking her sweet flesh, and he wanted more.

Aisha's fingers clenched his hair as he sucked and nipped at her. She was fighting the desire rising so quickly inside her but to no avail. He knew exactly how to prolong her climax or to incite it. The twitching of her hips, the slight lift, and the tension of her thighs against his head—signs of instruction he ignored.

Percy thrust his tongue inside her, lapping the wetness as his finger teased the bud his lips had just abandoned. Her body stiffened, and her nails dug into his scalp just as rapture sent her reeling over the edge, her inner muscles pulsating with each stroke of his tongue. As her tremors slowed, he released her feet and adjusted their position so she was on her knees and he behind her.

Undoing his breeches, Percy waited until her hands were braced against the seat before gripping his cock and entering her. Initially, his thrusts were awkward before he duplicated the rhythm of the coach. Aisha moaned and pushed back against him, her inner muscles squeezing tightly with each withdrawal, his prick getting harder until self-control was beyond him.

"Such bliss," he whispered as he leaned down and kissed the back of her neck. "Extraordinary."

She mumbled something he couldn't grasp as her body trembled. The first pulse triggered an imminent release, and his fingers clenched her hips, pulling her tight against him as he drove deeply, then withdrew before he slammed into her.

"With me, Isha. Now," he gritted against her skin.

Her body tightened as the coach dipped slightly, then passion took them both over, drenching them in carnal delight as the carriage resumed its rhythm. Percy reached past her head to grab a linen cloth he'd placed beneath one of the small cushions on the seat. Easing himself from her, he cleansed the evidence of their lovemaking and returned to his original sitting place. He assisted her onto the space beside him, then into his arms.

Kissing her until she was breathless, he said, "Fuck, that was perfection. I love you, Aisha Howard. So very much."

Her hand caressed his cheek, and she gifted him with a sated smile. "You will always hold my heart, beloved." She reached over and refastened his breeches. "When next we travel, 'tis my turn. I might even have a few surprises hidden away now that I'm aware of the secret compartments."

"There are a few more," he answered, draping the blanket over her legs. "Let me show you."

"MY WORD," Aisha muttered as Percy assisted her from the carriage. "I'm beginning to reassess the terms of our wedlock and living in the countryside. That house violates all sense of order, and it reeks of Tabitha Smyth."

"Abigail and Tabitha are bosom companions, believing themselves the arbiters of social decorum. Smyth ignores his wife, making monthly escapes to Bath or Basingstoke. He favors the latter since his wife has no gossipy friends in Basingstoke to report on his time spent at the Wandering Eye brothel."

She glanced at the unkempt bushes arranged beneath the two bay windows facing them. "And mediocre gardeners. I would never place roses and honeysuckles alongside each other, and not just because I react badly to being stung by a bee. The odor would drive me from the house. What is Abigail Brabanzio's tale?"

Percy chuckled before he tucked a loose curl back into a braid. "It would be a delicate fragrance compared to the smells inside the house. There's a reason we didn't pay many visits to most of my neighbors before now. Abigail is a bitter person, abandoned by her husband and children's father. When he exhausted his monies, Lucio returned home a broken and sick man, dying within six months and leaving her impoverished with three sons and a daughter."

The door abruptly swung open, and a young woman stood on the threshold. She wasn't much older than twenty-two, but that didn't prevent her from flashing Percy a flirtatious smile before she inclined her head. "Lord Ross, what a pleasant surprise. Mother told me you intended a visit, but we didn't expect your company so soon."

"Good morning. Lady Ross and I are doing our visitations."

Desdemona eyed Aisha as if they were competing for the same prize and, with a quick bob of her chin, mumbled, "Lady Ross. Welcome to Brabanzio House."

Aisha acknowledged her before she and Percy followed her inside to a parlor in the west wing of the house. Just as they reached a door, Aisha gripped his wrist and leaned against him. He lowered his head to hear her words.

"Do none of them bathe?" she whispered. "I've smelled better in the stews near King's Cross. What is it with you English and bathing? This is the second visit where I want to toss people into the river."

"Mother is in here," Desdemona said, opening a door.

Aisha's mouth gaped slightly before she forced a smile to reappear. "Shit," she murmured in Arabic.

Percy squeezed her hand as he escorted her into the garishly furnished room. Her gaze slowly swept the haphazard mix of colors, fabrics, and furniture styles. Inconsistency was an inadequate word for the mess. Blues, yellows, and brown flowers had been embroidered on once-black but now faded linen cushions for the sofas and chairs.

Red curtains hung limply before closed windows, and the noxious smell that greeted her became more acute. Her mind wrestled with momentary indecision. Should she pretend a swoon and force the woman to open a window, or grit her teeth and endure the visit?

"Welcome, Lord and Lady Ross," a wisp of a woman said as she rose from one of the distasteful oversized chairs.

Aisha tensed as the woman approached. The mixture of perfume and an unwashed body rushed in with each step, and she struggled not to inhale. She stuck out a gloved hand. "Thank you, Mistress Brabanzio."

The gesture halted the woman, who clearly had other plans as she looked like a serial hugger. Aisha had endured brief encounters with a couple of Englishwomen who assumed such behavior—not to mention the touching of her braids—was acceptable.

After the widow gave her hand a limp shake, she glanced around the room and smiled. "What an interesting room."

"Thank you," Abigail preened. "I've been told I've a good eye for furnishing a room. Please sit, Aisha. Do call me Abigail."

Aisha searched for the cleanest cushion on a chair farthest from the woman and sat. She flicked Percy a look before she focused on Abigail. "In my culture, we never refer to the elders or someone of honor by their first name, and I must extend you that courtesy, Mistress Brabanzio. If not, my mother would pull my ear and chide me."

She ended her statement with a light chuckle, and the woman tittered in response before she instructed Desdemona to serve refreshments. "Our cook rivals Lord Howard's Martha for the excellence of her cakes and honeyed wine."

The door swung open, and a young man swaggered into the room. Aisha raised the cup to her lips and tasted the drink as she watched him saunter to the serving table. So, this was Iago Brabanzio. Although younger than Desdemona, he had the look of a shabby gentleman cutpurse and scoundrel, and Aisha suspected he was the mastermind behind the attempts to drag Othello to the altar.

Iago helped himself to a goblet of wine and draped his body on a chair beside his mother. "Lord Ross, 'tis good to see you again. How was your stay in London?"

Percy peered at Aisha. "More joyous than I expected. Lady Ross, this is Iago Brabanzio. Brabanzio, my wife, Lady Aisha Howard."

Iago sipped his wine, then eyed her with obvious appreciation. "No wonder the local gentlewomen never stood a chance. Well done, my lord."

"I assume your words are a youthful attempt at a pretty compliment. If so, thank you, but you do wrong the women you speak of, Master Brabanzio," Aisha commented.

She returned her attention to her hostess. "I understand there's talk of a pending marriage for your family, Mistress Brabanzio."

"Yes," Abigail gushed. "My Desdemona is nearly betrothed to Othello Blackwood. I don't know if my lord has told you, but they've been sweethearts since childhood. Why, she still has the love token he gave her when she was sixteen! Go get it, Desdemona, so Lady Ross can see."

"Mama, Lady Ross doesn't want to see something so childish," Desdemona whined.

"Go get it, Des," Iago ordered.

Aisha watched her rise and stomp from the room. "Mistress Brabanzio, there's no need."

"There's a reason, Lady Ross," Iago butted in. "I believe Blackwood is toying with my sister. She's nearly twenty-two, and he's played with her affections long enough."

His mother tutted, and Iago stopped talking when the door opened and Desdemona reentered. Iago rose from his seat, his goblet in his fingers. "My lord, might I have a word with you? It's about the open land abutting Jensen's farm. His sheep are encroaching, and I'd like permission to fence it."

"That land is common, Brabanzio," Percy said. "Your grandfather designated it so."

"I understand, but perhaps some arrangements can be made to correct my grandfather's lack of foresight."

Percy turned to Aisha. "I'm sure this won't take very long to resolve."

"Go, my lord. I'll be fine. Do recall we have a supper engagement," she replied sweetly.

PERCY FOLLOWED Iago from the room and down the hallway to a library. They entered, and Iago closed the door. Turning to face Percy, he consumed the wine in his goblet. "My lord, forgive the ruse. I must speak to you in your capacity as the Queen's representative and authority and ask you to overlook my bluntness. My sister is with child, and the father is Othello."

Percy tilted his head and studied Iago. "Othello is the father? Surprising."

"I'm aware of his deep...deep affection for Cassio, but," Iago hesitated, "while the cat's away..."

"Have you spoken to Othello? Or his father? Why bring this matter to me?"

"Othello swears he's never bedded my sister, even though I spied her, somewhat disheveled, leaving his cottage late one afternoon. Since then, he refuses all contact with my sister and fails to return my summons to resolve the matter."

Percy stared at the young man. Iago's move surprised him.

He hadn't approached Othello about Desdemona's condition—if it were true—or his father.

"Are you certain she is with child, Iago? Perhaps she—"

Iago arched a single eyebrow. "Are you questioning my sister's honor, my lord?"

"Don't be foolish, Brabanzio," Percy snapped. "It doesn't become you to take umbrage with the person you've asked to intervene. Before I approach Othello and his family, I need to be certain of the facts."

Iago strolled over to a table. Percy watched him refill his goblet before the wastrel faced him and said, "I understand, my lord. You must know how distressful this delicate matter is to my mother. The facts are Othello seduced my sister and she says she is with child. As her guardian, I must protect her reputation and insist he wed her and his relationship with Cassio end. Preferably within a fortnight."

"Why a fortnight?"

"Emily Townsend and I are betrothed. I've spoken to her father about posting the banns within a few days, and I'd like Desdemona's situation quietly settled before my wedding day."

"I see," Percy intoned. "Usually, I don't involve myself in such matters. However, I'm feeling quite magnanimous since Aisha became my wife. I make no promises except to speak to Othello."

"It is all I can ask, my lord." Iago sipped from his goblet. "I understand your lady hails from a prosperous Black London family of weavers, the Resonnes. Perchance there might be a younger sister or cousin looking to marry up in rank?"

"Are you seeking a bride for yourself or one of your brothers? I do believe Roland and Hubert are rather young to marry, being six and ten years of age, respectively."

"Given the beauty and wealth affixed to your wife, I'm willing to reconsider nuptials with Emily Townsend for something better. I'd only insist that she be as beautiful as your Aisha and fertile."

He's young, Percy. Expose him and bring him down a notch or two. Aisha's voice in his head, advising him, was enough to calm him so he could look at Iago and say, "I'll convey your wish to my lady. If our business is concluded, I will take my leave of you and your mother. Good day, Brabanzio."

Percy strode from the library, ignoring the man's insolence, and returned to the parlor. Within minutes, he and Aisha were settled in the carriage on their way home.

NINETEEN

Aɪsʜᴀ ᴘᴀᴄᴇᴅ ᴛʜᴇ ʟɪʙʀᴀʀʏ, her forehead wrinkled with irritation. Percy Howard was the bane of her existence at the moment. Abigail had written her about Iago's conversation with Percy, asking if the matter was concluded. He was presently in Bristol, conferring with Andrew Fairbanks. Meanwhile, she was left to wring her hands while all manner of mischief swirled around her.

You do not wring your hands, Isha, and the only real mischief committed was robbery and possibly murder—which is why I'm in Bristol.

She rubbed her forehead. "I can't believe I'm thinking in Percy's voice. Besides, in-my-head Percy Elwen, you may not consider Iago and Desdemona's heinous scheme a crime, but I do. And I'm going to do something about it."

A few more paces around the room and she'd devised a plan. She rushed out of the library and into the kitchen. Martha and Silas were sitting at the large table, chatting.

"Martha, Silas, I need your help! No, don't get up."

"What has you all flustered, my lady?" Martha asked, a worried look in her eyes.

Aisha plopped down on the bench next to Silas. "We need to expose the Brabanzios for their knavery. We can't let them cozen Othello."

"Absolutely," Martha agreed. "Cassio and Othello are the best neighbors and good men. What can we do to help?"

"Silas, I'd like to speak with Emily Townsend, tomorrow if possible. Do you think you can arrange for a visitation? Mid-morning would be best."

Silas nodded. "I'll send Jessup to the Townsend house. Do you want to send a note?" At her nod, he rose. "I'll get paper and pen."

"What can I do to help, my lady?" Martha inquired.

"Will you send Jeremy to Othello and Cassio with a message for me? I'd like to invite them to a mid-morning meal. We have so little time to set a trap for that conniving pair of Brabanzio siblings, and I thought it would be best to have Emily, Cassio, and Othello here to advise me."

"My lady, don't you think we should await Lord Ross's return? It seems to me that wicked Iago is willing to go to any length to achieve his aims—enriching his pockets. That family is as poor as a church mouse no matter how much they pretend." Martha sucked a deep breath, then released it. "Abigail don't have the wherewithal to give Desdemona a dowry, especially with Iago drinking, gambling, and wenching away his inheritance. I'm surprised the silly twit didn't turn up pregnant long ago, as much attention as her mama paid to her."

Aisha stared at Martha. It was rare for her to be so forthright, and she couldn't help but utter, "Martha Stone!"

"Well, it's all true, my lady. Ever since Lucio Brabanzio took off with that fake Spanish countess, things haven't been right over there. To make matters worse, before he departed, he declared Abigail didn't even know how to suck a man's yard, let alone swive him properly. I mean, Abigail didn't show her face for nearly six months."

Martha's expression shifted. "I did feel sorry for her in the beginning. To have your husband toss you aside like a sack of rotted barley isn't right. Then to have him come back begging her forgiveness and up and die... Well, it just made her bitter and calculating."

"Why Othello? Is there any truth to Iago's claim that he and Desdemona were childhood sweethearts? Like me, he's a commoner. I would think Cassio would be a better mark."

"There's truth in what you say, my lady. Othello and Cassio both left to apprentice in London because Cassio's father was the second son of a gentleman and married for love, not money. Since their return to Eggford, Othello has had greater success with his craft, with commissions and all. Cassio does alright for himself as a smith, but it's Othello who possesses the heavier purse."

Aisha peered at Martha. "So, it's not just Iago who is intriguing."

"No, indeed, it's the entire family. Right down to those two young sneak thieves Abigail lets run wild. They're all gentry cutpurses."

As Silas reentered the kitchen, Aisha grinned. "Well, I guess we'll have to teach them a proper lesson and cozen the cozeners."

~

"MY LADY," Emily Townsend stammered as Silas took her cloak and she entered Howard Manor. "I'm honored by your invitation. This is my sister, Anabelle."

Aisha, who stood beside Silas, smiled at Anabelle's nervous

curtsy. "Thank you, and welcome to you both. I'll admit I have a motive."

She led the sisters into the smaller dining room where Othello and Cassio were waiting. The four greeted each other before Emily turned to her and said, "I suspect I know the reason for this invitation."

Aisha chuckled. "Sit. We should enjoy Martha's food while we talk and plan."

The door opened, and a servant entered with a tray. He placed a bowl in front of each of them and then set a plate of flatbread in front of Aisha. He returned a minute or so later with a tray of steaming cups. Thanking him, she turned to her guests.

"Though I'm English-born, my family is Mauretanian. I have little love for sauces and even less for rotten meats. What's in your bowls is a stew made with onions, carrots, chicken, spices, and dried peas. We also eat it with this type of bread."

She took a piece of flatbread, then handed the plate to Cassio, who sat to her right. "The drink is called atay. It is made with honey and mint."

For a few minutes, the pings of spoons against porcelain bowls were the only sounds in the room. Aisha placed her spoon to one side and lifted the atay cup. She inhaled, then sipped before placing her cup next to her bowl.

"A few days ago, Lord Ross and I paid a visit to the Brabanzio household," she began. A collective groan prompted a laugh. "Aye, and I won't do so again, but that is neither here nor there. Before we talk, I must insist on everyone's discretion and promise not to repeat what is heard."

Each of her guests gave their solemn word, and she gazed at Othello. "Are you aware Desdemona claims to be with child—your child?"

Startled, he gasped. "That is a lie. I've never lain with her."

His gaze went to Cassio. "I am faithful to the one who holds my heart, and it isn't Desdemona Brabanzio."

"I suspected as much," Aisha reassured him. "She claims you and she made love while Cassio was away, visiting his uncle. I believe the month was April."

"Impossible," Othello uttered. "I was also in Bristol. My sister gave birth to my nephew, and I remained the entire month with her, my brother-in-law, and my parents."

Aisha recounted Percy and Iago's conversation, including Iago's claim he and Emily were betrothed. As she talked, she noted everyone's initial shock quickly gave way to anger. When she paused, Emily spoke.

"Iago is a fool if he believes I'll become his wife. I'd as sooner take an ass to husband," she declared. Her eyes bright with fury, she pressed on. "The man's a complete wastrel no matter his birth. My father's ambition and Iago's need for money...I won't do it! I love Roger, and he's the only man I'll wed. I'd sooner end—"

"That won't be necessary, Emily," Aisha stated.

"What do you advise, Lady Ross?" Othello queried. "I refuse to leave my home and village, and I will not be forced into an unwanted marriage."

"Will you be guided by me?" All four bobbed their heads. "Here's the plan. When Lord Ross returns, I will hold a reception. We will use the moment to expose the Brabanzios and put an end to this nonsense. What should I know about Roger, Emily?"

Anabelle sniggered as Emily's face brightened, and Emily glared at her younger sister. "He's handsome and kind. He's a commoner like we are, but that makes him not good enough to be my husband. It's silly because his farm is more prosperous than Iago's land. If it were merely wealth, my father would agree to Roger's suit. Instead, Father is obsessed with lineage."

"What does your mother have to say?" Aisha asked.

"She is sympathetic to my plight, but she will not challenge Father's decision."

Aisha drank the rest of her atay before it completely cooled. "What can you tell me about Iago? Please be candid. If we're to bring him to his knees, I'll need to know everything."

By the time Othello finished talking, she'd learned more than she anticipated. Even Anabelle was privy to Iago's knavery. "Thank you all. Emily and Anabelle, the coach is waiting outside. Rest assured, I'll make certain we won't fail."

She escorted the young women to the front door and watched as Silas assisted them into the carriage. With Silas at her back, she returned to the dining room.

"I know you both are aware of the reason for my husband's visit to your uncle, Cassio. Why?"

A quick exchange of glances confirmed her suspicion, and she tapped her foot. "Well?"

"Jamie's signet ring was missing when I viewed his body," Cassio said. "I mentioned it to Lord Ross, and he asked me to keep the information to myself. I crafted the ring based on one identical to my uncle's except for the two letters of Jamie's name. My lord believes Iago was in possession of Jamie's ring the day you and he visited the Brabanzios."

A stream of expletives poured from her mouth as Aisha stamped her foot. Infuriated, she momentarily forgot her guests as she mumbled invectives on her husband's head.

"Um, Lady Ross?" Othello said.

"What?" Her expression suddenly shifted. "My apologies for my tone, Othello. What is it?"

"We need to return to the cottage to tend to the hens and Ermegarde. If I might, perhaps Lord Ross wanted to be certain of his facts before he mentioned anything to you. He loves you and wants to protect you from danger."

Embarrassment clouded her face. "I know, but I prefer not to be held in ignorance. He may also be in peril since we don't know who is responsible for Jamie's death, and if it's Iago, the man is far more dangerous than we give him credit." Her eyes darkened. "If anyone harms so much as a hair on Percy's head, there is no place in England for them to hide."

Cassio came to her and took her hands. "No harm will come to Lord Ross, my lady."

Aisha nodded. "I know, but I still worry."

TWENTY

"WHAT DO YOU THINK, my lady?" Martha inquired.

Aisha glanced around the garden. Several wooden tables sat on the freshly mowed grass in an area of the lawn made square by symmetrically trimmed shrubs. Plates and cutlery were stacked neatly on each table. "It's perfect, although I hate to disturb our gardeners' beautiful work. However, with twenty or so guests, I couldn't have them in the great hall. The stench would be far too much to take for several hours."

Martha laughed. "Your candor is one of many reasons we love you, Lady Aisha. Not only have you brought happiness to Lord Percy, but you've also made our lives healthier and full of joy. Except for a cut or bruise, no one on the manor has been ill for some time."

"And we shall keep it that way," Aisha stated. "Do you need my assistance with the food?"

"Oh, no, Matthew has been a godsend in the kitchen, and Randall has taken charge of the lads. You just go rest, so you're bright as a penny by the time folk arrive."

Aisha hugged the housekeeper and returned to the house. She'd sent for Matthew and Randall to help the moment she decided to hold a social gathering. As it turned out, her aunt Ahmara and Percy's uncle Robert were visiting the Cock & Oyster and decided to accompany Matthew and Randall once they learned the pair were traveling to Eggford.

Even with her aunt's company, she missed her husband, and although it was late, she'd awaited his arrival from Bristol the previous evening. An exhausted Percy was grateful she'd kept a hot bath and food ready. His body cleansed and his belly sated, he climbed into bed, and the moment his head touched the pillow, he fell asleep. Kissing his cheek, she slid in beside him, draped her arm across his waist, and succumbed to Morpheus herself.

The next morning, she awakened early and eased out of their bed, leaving her husband to sleep longer. Quietly entering the bathing room, Aisha cleansed her face and teeth before she dressed and went in search of Martha. She should've known not to fret. With Matthew and Martha in charge of the preparations, there was no need to worry. The food was plentiful and delicious, and Silas had set several small casks of wine and ale on a long table opposite the one that would hold the food.

Aisha knew such gatherings were held indoors, but the mere thought of the stench in her home seeping into walls and furniture had left her determined to avoid such a fate. Thankfully, the day proved to be a lovely one, and with nothing to do except wait for the arrival of their guests, she climbed the stairs and returned to her bedroom, entering as quietly as possible.

"Good morning, Lady Ross." Percy sat upright against the bed's bolster, a faint smirk on his lips. "I assume Martha and

Matthew have matters completely under their control and shooed you from the kitchen."

Aisha strolled over to the wardrobe and took out the gown she intended to wear. "Good morning, Lord Ross. I assume you slept well after your secretive journey to Bristol. How was Master Fairbanks, and was his ring identical to the one Iago was wearing?"

Percy flung the bedcovers aside and climbed out. Before she could scamper away, he pulled her into his arms and gave her a mind-numbing kiss. When he lifted his mouth, he licked her lips. "You taste of atay."

"And you taste of mint, which means you cleaned your teeth," she said. "How long have you lain in wait?"

"I heard you sneak out."

She pushed against his chest. "I didn't sneak out. I left quietly so as not to awaken you."

"No matter, I'm awake now, and I need a taste of my wife's sweet nectar."

"Percy, we don't have time for that at the moment. We have a crime to solve."

"We always have time for me to lick your puss, Isha." He undid the ribbons to her bodice. "Time for me to suck your nipples, to run my fingers along your wet flesh—it is wet, isn't it?"

His tongue traced the outline of her lips before sliding inside her mouth and tangling with hers. It was a slow, seductive mingling of flesh, no one seeking mastery, just pure indulgence. The heat of his palms on her bare breasts burned a path to the slit between her thighs.

His hands followed the curves of her waist and hips until she felt a faint breeze on her stomach. He was so talented at undressing her. A finger brushed the hooded flesh, then followed the path between her thighs to her arsehole. She trembled against him. "Percy."

"I love when you speak my name that way, Isha, from the back of your throat. Soft and sultry with a dash of fire. It makes me want to do things to you that a religious man would deem dirty."

"Grateful you're not a religious man," she breathed.

He swept her into his arms and placed her on the bed. Bending down to kiss her mound, he replied, "Ah, dear Isha, but I am, and this is my favorite place of worship."

She moaned as he set about proving the truth of his words. He teased her outer lips mercilessly before dragging his tongue to the hard bud exposed by his caress. Her hips tensed slightly, then jerked as he bit her flesh just enough to send a wave of pleasure through her. Her body relaxed as he licked the pain away.

Aisha became lost in the sensation swirling around her hooded bud, gathering like a summer storm to unleash its power. She struggled to hold back the crumbling dam of her self-control and failed. With a quick thrust of his tongue between her fleshy lips and several swipes, he sent her careening over passion's edge. His hands held her tight as she rocked against his mouth, the sound of his throat swallowing her liquid heightening her pleasure.

As she calmed, he adjusted their position so he was on his back, and she straddled him. "This will be a quick one, my love —which is why you will ride. We'll have time to bathe before we face our guests."

Despite her wetness, his thick cock created a slight pressure as he buried his prick deep inside her, then the familiar ache fanned out across her body. She opened for him, his hips driving his erection into her. Time fled from her awareness as he plunged and withdrew repeatedly until her body quaked and her climax erupted. Her muscles gripped him, squeezing his rod, and he slammed into her, his body shuddering and his cock pulsating as ecstasy took over. Percy's groans rose from his throat like thunder, soft then louder as he emptied his seed inside her. She closed her eyes, the leisurely rocking of his hips a balm to her aroused flesh. Slowly, the weight of his prick inside her lessened, and she lowered herself until she lay lengthwise on him.

"Definitely how I want to awaken each morning," he murmured.

"BARON ASHEDON, Lady Ashedon, my wife Aisha Howard, Lady Ross."

"My lord, my lady," Lady Ashedon gushed, "'tis lovely that you've invited us into your home. Such a well-ordered garden, Lady Ross. I'm sure the interior of Howard Manor is equally lovely. I'm surprised you didn't hold your gathering inside the great hall."

Aisha's smile didn't reach her eyes. "Thank you, but the gardeners deserve all the praise for what you see." She felt Percy's hand run down her arse before he walked away. "Our intent is to spend more time in the country, and we decided to refurbish several of the rooms, including the hall and the parlors."

As Lady Ashedon shifted to avoid a servant, the scent of her wafted in Aisha's direction, and she pressed her lips tightly and avoided breathing until she managed to remove herself from the sphere of the woman's lack of cleanliness. "Enjoy yourself, Lady Ashedon," she said. "I shouldn't ignore our other guests."

Meandering through the small crowd, Aisha felt the

stiffness in her jaws from holding a smile—and her breath. Nature took pity on her and stirred a faint breeze. Pleading a need to speak to Martha, she escaped the drunken clergyman seeking Percy's sponsorship for his chapel and hurried into the kitchen.

Matthew and Randall took one look at her face and erupted into guffaws. Matthew fetched her a cup of atay. "Your aunt just left, mumbling she'd had enough of foul-smelling English folk. I assume you're in here for the same reason."

Aisha accepted the cup, inhaled, and sipped slowly. "Ahh. Thank you, Matthew. I feel like I'm back in London among the wealthy. Why don't these people bathe? The women are bold about wanting to make a social call. Not without a bath. We're also going to have to pay extra wages to the gardeners to return the pissing area back to habitability." She frowned. "I'll talk to the joiners about making a privy shed for future use. These people are such heathens."

Silas popped his head into the kitchen. "Lady Ross, my lord requests your company."

"How much longer until they go away?" she asked irritably.

Silas chuckled. "'Tis why he wants your company. The ones who live at some distance wish to take their leave of you."

She handed Matthew the cup and followed Silas from the kitchen. Percy's eyes twinkled with undisguised mirth as she approached. When he took her hand, she leaned in and said, "I will exact my revenge, Percy Elwen Howard."

His thumb brushed her cheek. "I know you will, sweetheart."

As they walked to the gate, he informed her the Brabanzios were remaining behind to discuss the matter of Desdemona and Othello. The garden finally empty, she and Percy returned to the house.

"They await us in the small salon," he said. "And the window is ajar."

"So, you do love me?"

Percy laughed. "More than you imagine, Aisha. However, I don't think I can stomach five minutes in their company without open windows. Here are the bit players."

Othello and his parents, Cassio with his uncle, and Ahmara and Robert strolled from the library and joined the couple to continue to the salon. Aisha placed her hand on Percy's arm, arresting his entrance. "I'll enter behind you so I don't have to smell these people."

The sniggering behind her had Aisha rolling her eyes. "Don't worry, my love," Percy consoled. "I had Silas strategically place flowers in the room to mitigate the problem."

"I do love you, husband," she said as he opened the door.

She stifled her smirk at the amazement on the Brabanzios' faces. Only Desdemona appeared a bit confused. Aisha noticed they'd remained standing and was grateful for the significant favor. Percy squeezed her fingers before he spoke to the family.

"You asked me to resolve a thorny problem when Lady Ross and I visited your home, Iago. I'm happy to say we've done just that, thanks to my wife's skills at ferreting out—"

"I do not ferret out, Lord Ross," Aisha huffed. "I seek information and facts as a reasonable person would do."

He kissed her cheek. "My pardon, sweet puss. You may judge and punish my misstep later."

"I will."

Percy returned his attention to the Brabanzios, who stood watching the exchange. "Before we engage the delicate matter of your sister's state, Iago, I noticed your signet ring. It is unusual."

His belly filled with Lord Ross's excellent wine, Iago preened. "Thank you, my lord. It was my father's and his father's before him. Now, if we may discuss the matter of my sister—"

"In time, Brabanzio," Percy stated. "Were you in the vicinity of the Eggford bridge when Jamie Fairbanks was riding to visit his kinsman, Cassio Fairbanks?"

"Of course not. I have no idea who this Jamie Fairbanks is, my lord," Iago stated. "I was home, which my mother can vouch. A kinsman of Cassio's, you say. Was he the poor man found by the riverbank? "

"And if I declare you a liar, Brabanzio? If I tell you the ring isn't your father's but once belonged to Jamie?"

Iago paled, then puffed out his chest, although when he answered, his voice quavered. "Then I must seek satisfaction for the insult, Lord Ross."

"There is no insult, only a fact," Percy declared smoothly. "Master Fairbanks, would you care to take a closer look at the ring Brabanzio is wearing?"

Andrew Fairbanks shook his head. "No need, my lord. I observed Brabanzio while in the garden, and it is my Jamie's ring. His cousin Cassio made it for him at my behest. The letters of Jamie's name are on the outside of the ring."

Iago's color dipped even more. "I will not stand here and be accused of theft."

"Will you accept an accusation of murder?" Percy inquired. "You need to choose your companions better, Brabanzio. Your accomplice, Peter Bigley, has given a sworn statement about the events of that night. He said you and he split the coins stolen from Jamie Fairbanks and the profit from the sale of his horse in Bath."

As he finished, Percy nodded at Randall, standing silently beside the door, who left the room. As fascinated as Aisha was by her husband's revelations, her stomach was queasy at the unwashed odor overpowering the flowers' scent, and she moved closer to the open window.

"As to the matter of your sister Desdemona's condition, Lady Ross can best explain what she's uncovered."

Aisha moved slightly and faced Iago. "You are a fucking scoundrel!"

Several gasps rolled through the air. After a brief lull, Aunt Ahmara released a throaty cackle, and Percy shook his head. "Aisha."

"Apologies, my lord, but it needs to be said. When my lord called you a liar, Iago Brabanzio, he spoke the truth. It is also a lie your sister is with child by Othello."

"I am so!" Desdemona screeched loudly. "Othello is the father. I will not give birth to an illegitimate child in six months." She turned to Othello's father. "Master Blackwood, your son promised to wed me when we were children, and he won my heart. I gave him my virginity and shared his bed on several occasions."

Desdemona returned her angry gaze to Aisha. "In fact, we last laid together two months ago, but you wouldn't know because you weren't Lady Ross or at the manor."

Aisha waved her hand at Othello, who was about to speak and fell silent at her gesture. "Two months ago, you say? You're correct, my lord and I were in London in April. However, we weren't the only ones absent from Eggford during that month. Othello, I do believe you were away."

"Yes, my lady," he agreed. "All of April. I visited with my sister and our family in Bristol. She'd just given birth to my nephew, and my father and mother arrived from Bath for the naming. I returned to Eggford the fourth day of May."

"Desdemona Brabanzio, you are no more pregnant than I am," Aisha said with a snort.

As if on cue, Abigail Brabanzio fainted, and Desdemona rushed to her side. Iago eyed them. "So, you had me besmirch my honor for a lie, Desdemona? I will deal with you when we get home." He glowered at his mother, whose eyelashes fluttered open. "Get up, Mother. Everyone sees through your pretense."

"Not yet, Iago," Aisha cautioned. "I've made inquiries, and it seems you and Desdemona have much in common besides shared parentage."

At that moment, a knock sounded, and Percy said, "Enter."

TWENTY-ONE

Aisha and her aunt Ahmara exchanged a look, then grinned when an elegantly dressed white woman strolled into the room, followed by Eggford's local constable. The woman's face was expressionless as she gazed at the people in the salon before she made her way to Ahmara.

"Well, well, Abigail Chapman. Forgive me, it's Lady Howard now. My lady, 'tis good to see you after all these years. I've heard the Cock & Oyster is doing well."

"Happily, it is, and I'm no longer Lady Howard, Patience," Ahmara stated. "That title belongs to my niece, Aisha Howard."

Patience Delbrey turned to Aisha and inclined her head. "My lady, thank you for the invitation, and my apologies for arriving late."

Aisha smiled. "Your timing is impeccable, Mistress Delbrey. I was about to share information with the Brabanzios."

Iago moved from his spot near his sister and mother, his face flushed—whether from embarrassment or wine, Aisha wasn't certain as he cleared his throat and began to speak in a rush.

"A man has needs, and I'd rather not have rumors float about," Iago declared. "After all, Master Townsend and I are in negotiations about a marriage between Emily and myself. I would never shame her by taking a mistress so close to home, and Delbrey's Wandering Eye has a reputation for clean women."

"Thank you," Patience responded. "I'm happy to provide such services. However, were you or your mother aware Desdemona works for me under the name Marie? In fact, she is one of the Wandering Eye's most profitable courtesans."

When her mother and brother gaped at her, Desdemona snorted. "I'm tired of being poor. I wanted new gowns and real jewels. How else was I to trap Othello?"

She stomped over to the fireplace. "Besides, I always wore a mask and spoke French. No man saw my face because I refuse to service them except in darkness. And no, brother, you didn't commit incest. Patience immediately recognized the resemblance when I walked in. Only she knew my secret."

Desdemona glanced at Othello. "Besides, Othello is besotted with Cassio, and they act like an old married couple. You and mama couldn't see that and expected this trickery to succeed. Mistress Delbrey, if you're returning to the Wandering Eye tonight, may I ride along?"

Percy's uncle Robert, whose wine glass had been refilled several times, chuckled. "Ahmara, my love, perhaps we need to return to Eggford now that my nephew and Aisha have settled here. I've not been so entertained since Tiddly was found arse-up and naked."

Shaking his head at his uncle, Percy turned his steely-eyed gaze to Iago. "As the Queen's representative, I'm ordering your arrest for theft and homicide."

"We didn't mean to kill the man!" Iago screeched. "It was an accident, a drunken lark that went awry. He refused to give up his purse and fought with Peter. I had to defend my friend. Fairbanks's death was accidental."

"Constable Warren, please arrest Iago Brabanzio for the death and robbery of Jamie Fairbanks."

Before the constable could act, Iago grabbed Aisha by her neck and dragged her against him. "If you want your wife to remain unharmed, you'll provide me a horse and an escape. I'm not about to lose my life over a commoner's death. It was an accident. I assume your wife's life is far more valuable than a signet ring, a few coins, and a mishap that went wrong, Lord Ross."

Percy's jaw tightened, and he waved his arm when the other men in the room started to move. Looking into Aisha's eyes, he noticed the angry glint in them before her gaze dipped slightly. She slid her hands along her hips and into her skirt's pockets.

"Percy!" Ahmara shouted. "Do something! She's having difficulty breathing and losing her color. Randall, go order Samuel to saddle a horse."

"Wise decision. For added security, I'll release Lady Ross near the bridge," Iago stated. "All of you, over by the fireplace."

Once everyone stood in a cluster near the hearth, Iago walked backwards to the door, dragging Aisha in front of him. He squeezed her throat. "Please don't be foolish, my lady."

His free hand reached for the handle and Aisha acted. She pulled her hands from her skirt's pockets, a dagger in each fist, and twisted her body, bringing one blade down across Iago's thigh. His scream reverberated in her ears as he shoved her from him.

"You stabbed me," he roared, falling to his knees, his palm pressed against the wound. "You stabbed me!"

"Actually, it's a shallow cut, and you'll live," Aisha explained with a shrug. "It might have been worse. What is it with you white English and touching people you don't know? The only white Englishman who has that right is Lord Ross, my husband."

She flourished both knives and glared at Iago. "I really should remove your cods since you probably left bruises on my throat."

Iago looked up at Percy and Constable Warren. "You've got to save me. Please don't let her near me. Please!"

Percy reached for Aisha. "I think he's cowed, beloved. Also, his mother *has* fainted this time, and we need to send for Martha because your aunt Ahmara and Mistress Delbrey refuse to tend to Mistress Brabanzio."

Aisha leaned forward and wiped the flat side of her dagger on Iago's coat. With a sigh, she let Percy guide her to her aunt. "I really wish Constable Warren wasn't in the room, Percy."

Percy kissed her temple. "Removing a man's cods is messy, Isha. I'd much prefer not having to drag Cecil into it. I also think sucking a man's cods—mine specifically—is a far better use of your skills and time."

"Percy Elwen Howard, you're incorrigible."

PERCY LEANED BACK AGAINST A CHAIR, watching Aisha brush and rebraid her hair. A few more gray threads mingled with her dark curls. Her robe was splayed open, and his gaze went to her throat. The imprint of Iago's fingers had disappeared, replaced by purplish bruises. Anger swept over him once more, tinted with fear.

While he knew Aisha had her daggers and was never in

harm's way, the tightness in his chest and the shiver that raced down his back—he never wanted to experience that again.

"Stop, Percy. He would've been a dead man if I thought I was actually in danger." She finished the last braid and gazed at him. "Now you understand how I felt when you worked for Cecil."

"It's different, Isha. I should have anticipated his move, not let him get close to you."

She rose from the pillow in front of the fireplace. "It wasn't your place to prevent him. It was mine. I wasn't paying attention. I promise it will never happen again, but know you may not always be around when someone decides to use me for vengeance. Iago's foolishness was born of the moment—it wasn't planned."

"Damn, Aisha! I don't need to think about that right now," Percy grumbled.

She came to stand before him. Her robe fell from her shoulders and floated to the floor. "Shall I give you something else to think about, Lord Ross?"

He stared at her still-firm breasts, her stomach's gentle bump, and the naked brown skin below her navel. The sight stirred a heat in his belly that snaked to his groin. "Perhaps you can take my mind off today's events, Lady Ross."

"Lady Ross," Aisha said huskily. "Pray tell, who is Lady Ross? Are you wedded, my lord?"

A slow smile swept across his face. "Aye, Mistress Ellen. Will that pose a problem? I have been faithful to you and my wife since meeting you."

Aisha arched an eyebrow. "Do you think your wife will approve of what I'm about to ask of you? What I will do to you, Lord Ross?"

Percy glanced at his thickening prick before he answered.

"I cannot answer for my wife, but I grant you my consent and approval."

Aisha lowered herself to her knees and placed her palms on his thighs. "I accept your consent and leave you to explain to your lady."

She moved her hands to the inside of his knees and spread them apart until they pressed against the chair's arms. Her braids fell over her breasts as she leaned forward and kissed the slit of his prick. He flinched, and her fingernails dug into his thighs. "Do not move, my lord."

Aisha used only the tip of her tongue to tease his cock, caressing his skin before she flicked the head, then tenderly inserting the tip partially into the slit. He'd forgotten how skilled she was in bringing him to the point of ejaculation without ever taking him inside her mouth. His fingers clutched her braids, and she murmured fiercely, "Release me, Lord Ross. You do not have my permission to touch me or move again until I say so."

"Forgive me, Mistress Ellen."

"Forgiven, but you must pay the forfeit," she said. "You will not release until I give you the word."

"I understand, Mistress Ellen."

Percy leaned back against the chair and closed his eyes. It would take every ounce of will to stave off his release as Aisha resumed her tantalizing play. With every lick, she took him further along the cliff's edge, allowing him to dangle in a delicious yet torturous state of arousal. The strain on his muscles to remain immobile fed his expectation of the exquisite sensations and what they'd feel like once she set him free.

His mind sank into a state of semi-oblivion, half waking yet not fully conscious—he had no idea how long she kept him on edge. Then he heard it. The soft command.

"Release, my lord. I wish to taste your essence."

A tremor in his toes startled him as relief curled its way up his legs, loosening tense cords of muscles. His heart thumped heavily in his chest, a stark vibration of anticipation. Aisha kissed the tip of his cock, one of her loose braids brushing his flesh as she moved her head back. It was the spark that ignited the conflagration.

He jerked uncontrollably as his semen spurted in a thick stream over his thighs and Aisha's breasts, coating her smooth brown skin. His climax seemed to go on forever, yet he knew only seconds had passed.

"Look at me, Lord Ross."

Percy fought the lethargic weight of satiety to lift his eyelids and peer at his wife. Her fingertips were covered with his release, and she slowly sucked each finger one by one. By the time she cleansed the last one, his prick was hard.

Aisha rose and straddled him. The chair made for a tight fit, her knees pressing against his hips with no room to move. Her fingers guided him past her lower lips, and she slid down until flesh met flesh. Her body remained taut, only her inner muscles in motion as she squeezed his penis then relaxed.

The pattern continued, a lulling caress that stripped him of the ability to do naught but accept his fate. A fate controlled by the woman whose body was slowly draining and replenishing him with each breath. He floated, nothing above or below to bear the burden of his desire—the heaviness in his testes and a painful tightness gripping his cock.

"You may release, Percy," she breathed. "I cannot hold mine back any longer."

As the final word faded, she clenched and her muscles began to pulse. The heat of her climax drenched his erection, and he shuddered violently, swept away by his passion. Aisha's forehead touched his, the warmth of her breath an ethereal kiss on his skin.

"I love you so much, Percy Elwen Howard," she murmured in a breathless rush.

He lifted his face so his mouth brushed her chin. "I love you, Aisha Resonne Howard. However, my love is being sorely tested by the painful numbness in my arms."

Her laughter swept across his face, and she lifted her body from his. His cock, suddenly free, slapped his thigh as she detached herself from him and the chair. He studied her arse when she walked over to a bowl filled with water and dipped her finger in it.

"The water is cold."

"I don't care."

She took a cloth and soaked it before squeezing the water from it. Returning to Percy, she cleansed his cock and thigh. He rose from the chair and stiffly walked to the bed while Aisha rinsed the cloth and wiped her private parts before dropping it into the bowl.

Percy's gaze followed her as she moved about the room, extinguishing candles. When she climbed into bed, the only light was from the dying embers in the hearth. She snuggled against him, laying her head on his chest.

"What do you think will happen to Desdemona?"

He tugged the bed cover over Aisha's naked shoulder. "With no prospects of marriage, at least locally, I suspect she'll either take up the trade or leave in search of a husband."

She stroked his stomach. "I'm happy Emily's father finally approved Roger's suit, although he had no choice after Emily told a white lie that she was with child. It wasn't just lineage that had Townsend's breeches in a twist—it was Roger's parentage. His mother is from Tunis, and his father is Portuguese and Ethiopian."

Shifting so her arm was free of the bedcover, she ran her fingers across Percy's chest. "Townsend is such a fool. Although he grudgingly accepted Roger, the man banished Anabelle from his house and disowned her because she dared to side with her sister. I am so happy I'm not a white English woman. Had I been saddled with a father like Townsend, my mother would be a widow."

Stroking her jawline, Percy chuckled. "So am I, Isha. Now, if you are done with today's excitement and adding to my gray hairs, I'd like to make love to my wife."

She planted a kiss on his chest, then dragged her tongue over his nipple. "Your wife would love that just as much. And dearest Percy, she will adore each gray hair."

MUCH ADO ABOUT NOTHING

TWENTY-TWO

PERCY HOWARD STUDIED the woman sitting across the table. Aisha Resonne Howard was an extraordinary beauty. Her earthy brown skin was flawless, and he loved that she made no attempt, as many women did, to hide her color beneath white face paint. Aisha gazed back at him, her dark eyes bright with a quizzical amusement that bordered on teasing. She'd wait until he could bear the silence no longer and spoke. She often won the game simply because he wanted to hear her sensuous voice. Her full lips pursed, and she speared him with a narrow look.

"I ask—"

"Do not ask, Percy," Aisha interrupted. "I remain undecided. You know my feelings on Lord Cecil's requests and mingling with people who fear water so intensely it borders on a national horror. Besides, we just had those people here six weeks ago."

Percy lifted his crystal goblet and sipped his wine before placing the glass on the table. "I hadn't expected Cecil's latest move, and I am curious how he got wind of the Fairbanks case.

Alas, as the newly appointed Lord Adjudicator for the area, I'm forced to suffer visitations when there's a matter affecting the gentry or nobility."

Frowning, he sighed. "I do wish he'd spoken to me before he had the Queen sign an edict. Sadly, that's not how the Lord Secretary works when he wants his way."

"I still don't understand why we have to make visits to these people," she grumbled. "You can make a visitation and I will happily remain at Howard Manor. I do promise a welcome beyond your wildest imagination."

"I wish I could agree, Isha. However, the invitation is addressed to Lord and Lady Ross. For us not to accept...Well, it's just not done unless we are away from the area. Sadly, we're in residence."

"You do realize, Lord Ross, I'll be stuck in a house that isn't mine, everyone will probably be stinking to high heaven, and I'll be forced to eat poorly prepared or rancid English food? Intolerable. Insufferable. Don't you dare laugh at me!"

He shook his head and struggled to swallow his chuckle. "Forgive me, sweetheart. I tend to forget how histrionic you can be on occasion. I can't make promises about the conditions of Ashedon House, but I promise we will stay a single night."

At her arched eyebrow, he smiled. "I do recall you declaring to be my helpmeet, and I'm going to have to invoke that promise when I'm forced to engage in visitations. Have you finished with your meal?"

Aisha rose from the table and walked around to where he sat, taking his head between her hands. She leaned down and kissed him, her tongue slowly snaking in and out of his mouth. At his faint groan, she ceased. "I'd expect nothing less from you, Lord Ross. Yes, I am sated with food, and I'd like to walk in the garden for a bit."

He stood, taking her hand to escort her from the small dining room and guiding her out into the corridor. Silas Patchett, his butler, stood a few feet from the door.

"We're going for a stroll in the garden. We'll retire upon our return. Please inform the staff their service isn't needed this evening since my wife has decided to prepare supper for me."

Silas flicked a glance at Aisha's stunned face and grinned before he inclined his head. "Thank you, my lord. I'll let Martha know."

"Silas, if your lord goes missing, be sure to check the stables or the barn," Aisha said with a smile.

"I shall, my lady, although I hope measures don't come to such an extreme," he intoned, the seriousness of his words belied by the twinkle in his eyes. "It's been a joy to witness Lord Ross's gentling. We once feared his adventurous spirit would get the better of him."

"Et tu, Silas?" Percy uttered. "You do realize Lady Ross has become something of a spy herself since the Brabanzio incident? More likely, I'll need the household's aid in tempering her enthusiasm."

Silas looked at Aisha with concern, and her laughter erupted. "Rest assured, Silas, since my lord's appointment as Her Majesty's judicial representative for the county, there is not much mischief that requires long absences from home. Except for the occasional travel to London or my brother's home, we expect our days to be mundane. As to cooking for my lord, we are in negotiations, and as you know, these diplomatic matters take time."

"I have no doubt Lord Ross will not only be generous with his offer of compensation for the visit to Ashedon House but also benefit from the exercise. I have noticed a sharpness in his thinking after time spent in your company, Lady Ross."

"Were you listening at the door as usual, Silas?" Percy asked irritably.

"If I were, my lord, I'm not foolish enough to admit eavesdropping," he deadpanned before turning his gaze to Aisha. "Sadly, these country visits are necessary. I also believe you have much to teach the wives about good housekeeping. Know that the Howard staff will do everything to make your visit to Ashedon as pleasant as possible, given the circumstances. Please reconsider your reluctance, my lady. If not for poor Master Howard's sake, then for mine."

Aisha's laughter filled the hall, and Percy took her arm, giving her a soft pinch on her buttock. "Don't encourage his impertinence, Isha."

She kissed Percy's cheek. "That man's impertinence doesn't need encouraging. He's known you far too long, my love. You need to be less prickly."

"Come, my sweet," he said. "Let's see if you can pluck my thorns as we walk."

They exited the house and strolled over to the garden. Aisha paused, her gaze sweeping the green expanse. "I'm glad we decided to build a pavilion for future gatherings. I know 'tis wrong of me, but the mere thought of the unwashed sitting on our chairs and divans leaves me nauseous. Do they believe that bathing hastens illness?"

"Some do. Others probably assume it's fashionable."

"When did stench become fashionable?" she demanded before she huffed. "And you English consider Africans and Americans uncivilized."

He kissed her temple. "No one ever said the English are always possessed of common sense, Isha. And I'm not like them thanks to your loving care. Now, if you're finished heaping maledictions on the English nation for their smell, I have another, more important matter to discuss with you."

"What is it, Percy?" she inquired, a worried expression on her face.

He stopped and pulled her into his arms. "Would you be willing to let me fuck you in the maze? I've the perfect spot for a tryst with my lady. I promise to woo you with the finest wines, freshest strawberries, and the most delicate sweetmeats. What say you, Lady Ross?"

Aisha tilted her head before she stepped from his grasp and peered at him. "Before I agree to any attempt to compromise my honor, I will need to ensure absolute privacy and comfort. Show me this spot. If it meets my approval, I shall set a day and time."

"'Tis all I can ask," he said with an elegant bow.

STARING down at the naked mound between Aisha's thick thighs, Percy smiled at the play of light on her skin from the fire burning in the hearth. She was lying on a thick bedcover close enough to remain warm but not in range of the occasional spark seeking to escape the grate. His eyes followed the erratic movement of firelight, ensorcelled by the shadows briefly imprinted on her flesh.

Impulsively, he pressed a kiss on one of the flickers sliding across her skin into nothingness, and the scent of frangipane slipped past his guard. He needed to taste her, to feel the soft flutter that accompanied her climax when his tongue was deep inside her. He lightly touched his lips to her belly before he straightened.

"Supper was wonderful, Isha. Would you like to rise and go to bed?"

She reached up and stroked his cheek. "No, I want you to make love to me here."

Percy ran his fingers along the side of her neck. "With pleasure. Do you need another cushion or perhaps a bedcover?"

She shook her head. "What I need is to see you naked."

He kissed the slick space between Aisha's thighs before he licked her sensitive flesh. Her hips twitched, forcing him to grip them and hold her in place. "Tasting your cunny is one of my favorite things to do before retiring to sleep, Aisha."

His hands parted her thighs a bit more, so his head fitted perfectly in the V-shaped space. Soft, husky moans floated down her belly and into his ears. His tongue swiped the length of her slit, causing her arse to lift off the bedcover. "Be still, wife."

"Impossible when you do that, husband," she panted.

"Try, sweetling. Try."

He teased the outside of her cunny and her hooded bud until she was writhing and wet. Then, with no warning, he thrust a finger inside her. The noises she made spurred him on, and his tongue and finger kept pace until she screamed as her womanly juices streamed over his finger. He captured the essence, purring at the spicy taste in his mouth. When her body settled into a less frantic motion, he positioned himself over her and gripped his cock.

"I do love you, Aisha Howard," he murmured. "So very much."

He guided himself into her slickness, then pushed deeper until her muscles constricted. The sensation was so exquisite he felt a sharp pinch in his testes as they seized. One stroke or squeeze of her muscles and he was done for, so he froze, letting himself still between her lush thighs while he fought for self-control.

"Percy?"

"Yes, sweetheart?"

"I do insist you perform some type of motion. It's not fair to leave me dangling like an unpaired earring."

"If I move, my love, my pleasure will be great," he breathed. "However, yours will not, and I cannot bear to face such a day. So, beloved, if you will permit a man a moment's respite—"

"Move, Percy Howard," she hissed. "Now!"

His chuckle earned him a slap on his naked arse. "As you wish, my love."

TWENTY-THREE

"Who holds a masquerade in the middle of August to announce a betrothal?" Aisha grumbled as she fanned herself. "A houseful of unbathed people in stifling heat is beyond my tolerance, Percy Howard. Why couldn't you attend without me?"

Percy took her ungloved hand and brought it to his lips. "Because you're my wife, and if I must suffer...a biblical rule for spouses."

"There's no such rule," she snapped. "I really don't appreciate the lengths you go to press me into public service."

He chuckled. "If I left you at Howard Manor, you'll be bored silly. At least this way, you can complain to a captive audience."

"I will not sleep on unclean sheets."

"I've taken care of that," he reassured her. "Cecily and Chester were dispatched to see to our chamber and keep you from stabbing our host, and we will be here just the one night."

Aisha sighed, and he kissed her hand again. "The times I will ask this of you, my lady, will be infrequent. Be aware, your fortitude in dealing with the local gentry shall be rewarded, if not in heaven then by me. Although I have no desire to sleep anywhere other than our bed, Ashedon's relation to Cecil..."

"I realize we can't completely escape court life," she muttered. "However, we will minimize its place in ours. So, what disease should I choose to avoid eating Maude Ashedon's food? A sensitive belly or the plague?"

Percy roared with laughter. "If it were the plague, we would be ostracized, and that's a battle I'd rather not fight at the moment, sweetheart. Save the plague for later. I think a sensitive stomach will be sufficient, although some might think you're breeding. Anyway, Martha made certain Cecily can prepare our food while we're there."

"We'll have to increase Cecily and Chester's pay when we return home. Drat! I'll have to discard my clothing upon our return home. You'll owe me a new gown, husband."

"I'll happily purchase you any number of gowns, although I much prefer you without."

Aisha glanced at her hands. "Tell me about Ashedon's daughters. Henrietta and Beatrice are their names, correct? How old are they, and are they cut from the same cloth as Desdemona?"

"No one is like Desdemona Brabanzio, my love. Beatrice at twenty-one is the elder by two years and rather outspoken. They're both intelligent, though her sister is a bit shy. So far, they've refused every suitor Ashedon has brought home. I suspect he's finally decided to play tyrant and force them into wedlock."

"Why?"

"Harvey Ashedon's mother despised the woman he married, and for good reason. Maude Hopplewink seduced Harvey and, within months, was with child, a son who did not survive his second year. Beatrice and Henrietta are Ashedon's only children, so a distant cousin will inherit the title, and Harvey's mother never forgave her son or his wife."

"Is this one of those 'wicked cousin inherits everything and boots the widow and children from their only home' stories, Percy?"

"Of course not, it's actually fairly simple. The cousin has his own wealth and estates, just no title. No, the story is the late Dowager Lady Ashedon arranged a match for her son and his affair with Maude put an end to that. Harvey's mother rewrote her will and left most of her wealth and properties to Beatrice and Henrietta with the stipulation if they're not married by the age of twenty-three, then the fortune goes to a charity for fallen women. If they are wed, Harvey receives one thousand pounds."

"I hate that term," Aisha hissed. "*Fallen women.* No one ever says, 'fallen men.'"

"Lady Ashedon the elder was enamored of nuns as a young child and wished to join a convent. However, her father had political ambitions and married her off, twice. Both her husbands died."

"Mysteriously, I suppose?"

"No. Husband one went riding naked and quite drunk one evening, and I don't think his mount appreciated the feel of the man's balls and tossed him. He died instantly and wasn't discovered until morning. One of his herders found him. Husband two, Rollins Ashedon, died a less exciting death. He choked on an oyster, and by the time someone realized it, he was in death's arms. Did I mention he was with some friends in a hunting lodge?"

Aisha stared at him, her lips parted, then she shook her head. "I cannot believe you wish me to associate with these people. I swear, Percy Elwen Howard, some people shouldn't have children."

"Agreed. Anyway, the rush to the altar means Ashedon can receive his inheritance."

"Ah, the marital intrigue," Aisha mumbled. "I suppose the daughters have other plans in mind."

Percy shrugged. "I've no idea. Rumors do abound, but..."

As his voice dropped, Aisha patted his thigh. "You can't stop now, husband. What are the rumors? I'll need something to make the next hours bearable."

"The most viable one is the sisters are secretly enamored of a clerk and a stablehand. I suspect there might be an elopement during the masquerade."

Aisha clapped her hands. "I do hope so. It would befit Lady Ashedon for stinking to high heaven and believing she is superior to other women."

"As long as no one is murdered, I can bear a day of stench," Percy muttered.

Samuel tapped the small window between his seat and the interior of the carriage. Percy leaned across to unlatch and open the window. "We've arrived, my lord. Let me apologize in advance, my lady, for the failings of the English nation excepting Lord Ross."

Aisha stared at Percy before her laughter erupted. Tears of amusement clouded her vision, and after a hiccup or two, she said, "Thank you, Samuel, but I can't accept your apology, for you aren't at fault. You, Silas, and Martha and all of the Howard staff are the reason I agreed to marry Percy, and you are English. Lord Ross knows his employment with Lord Cecil was the hindrance."

"Now, Isha, I'd pretty much given up the wandering life when we met."

She eyed him and snorted. "Shall I remind you of the time in our third year when you arrived at my door in the middle of the night reeking of sweat, sewers, and rotten fish?"

"No, but I did have an excuse. Chasing one of the Spanish king's spies through the docks will have that effect, and I did capture the arse." He grinned at her. "The past, sweeting, the past. At present, I am a changed man, all because of your love."

"You are so full of shit, Percy Howard," she retorted as she took Samuel's hand when he opened the door to assist her from the carriage.

"See how my lady wounds me, Samuel? Harsh words, and I used the privy before we departed from home." Percy's face twisted with disgust. "I refuse to relieve my arse while at the Ashedons."

Samuel waited until he stepped from the carriage and closed the door. "My lord, my lady. Enjoy your visit."

"Where will you be, Samuel?" Aisha questioned.

"My cousin, twice removed on my father's side, has a small farm a mile or two south, my lady. I plan to visit him and his wife since they are getting on in age."

"Take me with you!"

Samuel's soft laugh was followed by, "My lord will need you by his side if he isn't to run some buffoon through. I shall return promptly early morning to rescue the pair of you. Please, my lady, keep my lord out of trouble."

Aisha giggled as Percy humphed. A footman came out to carry their luggage, and with a wave to their driver, they entered the Ashedons' house.

CECILY MOVED about the bedchamber placing small jars of dried lavender and rosemary where Aisha directed. When the final jar was placed, Aisha smiled. "Thank you for airing out the room before we arrived, Cecily."

"I had to, my lady. When Chester and I walked in, he

turned a funny color and rushed over to open the window. Once we could breathe, I sent him to fetch two of Lady Ashedon's servants and had them thoroughly clean the room. The dust and webs... I don't think this room's been used in a long time, Lady Aisha."

Looking around the room, Aisha concurred with the maid's assessment. The furniture was sturdy but worn, probably crafted before Elizabeth became queen. One night, she reminded herself. And she was doing it for Percy.

She smiled inwardly. She was still Ellen Chapman in spirit, but becoming Percy's wife had its outside-the-bedchamber benefits. "What shall I wear to dinner, Cecily?"

"The yellow gown you're wearing will do, the blue one for the masquerade."

"Why the blue gown?" she quizzed. "I'd like to wear the red one."

"Several of the women are wearing blue, and if you want to flee the circus, no one will know it's you," Cecily stated.

"Clever."

Percy entered the room, a haggard expression on his face. Aisha swallowed the laugh about to emerge and went to hug him, then abruptly backed away. "Cecily, please have Chester arrange for hot water while I fetch my soaps. Come, my lord, there's a bathing tub in the anteroom. Not much in size, but we'll use what we have."

"Thank you, beloved. I fled as soon as possible, but..." Percy's sigh was long-suffering as he followed her to where the tub had been placed.

Cecily and Chester returned with buckets of hot and cold water. Once the tub was filled, Aisha sent them from the room. Percy was partially undressed when she came around the screen, carrying one of the soaps and a cloth she'd packed.

"In you go, husband," she said. "The evening will be long."

He stepped into the water and kneeled. Aisha used the cloth to wet his body and then soaped him and his hair. Chester had left a bucket of warm water beside the tub, and she used the water to rinse Percy.

"There," she declared, "now you smell like my husband."

He laughed and accepted the drying cloth she held out. Her eyes followed the movement of his hands, wishing they were on her breasts.

"Don't stare at me like that, puss," he said. "I'm not above ravishing you."

"Perhaps I'll be the ravisher," she teased before she strolled into the bedchamber where Cecily waited to help her dress.

"My lady, I've set your supper on the table. I didn't think you and my lord wanted to eat what was being prepared." Cecily sniffed derisively. "It took some doing, but I convinced the cook to let me prepare your food when I told her you had a very sensitive stomach, and she didn't want to be the one who gave you an ailment. This way you can join the others for dinner but not eat the food. Chester and I will sup while you eat."

Percy walked in and heard Cecily's words. "Thank you. I'm starved. Come, Isha. Let's dine."

TWENTY-FOUR

Beatrice stared at her cousin, Hope Fortnoy. Hope's light brown curls drooped alongside her delicate jawline. In many ways, Hope was the epitome of the poet's ideal beauty. Her hair, though not quite blond, glistened in the sunlight. Hope's complexion was pale, nearly pasty—only the soft smudge of cheek paint giving her the blush believed desirable. At the moment, her pretty features were marred by a worried frown.

"Hope Fortnoy, you sly chick. Confess all, how did you meet Benedick Bottomore?"

Hope flounced on Beatrice's bed. "Lady Morton's garden party six weeks ago. You know mother is determined to parade us before the courtiers. Claude Swineborne is Lady Morton's godson, and he and Benedick are childhood friends."

Charity Fortnoy blushed and dipped her chin. "Claude is quite handsome and not at all bristly the way Benedick is."

"You're just a child, Charity," Hope declared. "Has Claude even kissed you?"

The red in Charity's cheeks darkened, and her sister

chuckled. "I thought so. So, will you help us, cousin? Mother says Uncle Harvey is determined to marry you and Henrietta to the men we love. You can't! It would break our hearts."

Hope pushed off the bed and stomped over to the window. "It's not fair. Benedick and Claude will agree to the betrothals for the money, not because they love you."

Henrietta glanced at her sister before she went to Charity, who was getting rather teary-eyed. "Sweet Charity, don't weep. I have no intentions of marrying Claude, who I've never met. My heart belongs to another. We'll find a way to aid Cupid."

"And you, Beatrice? Will you do as your father insists, or is your heart closed to love?" Hope inquired, a slight quaver in her voice. "It is not like you to be sheepishly obedient, but if you have feelings for Benedick, I will step aside."

Beatrice studied her cousin's back. "No, Hope, Benedick Bottomore is nothing to me. I'd never attach my feelings to a man whose character and temperament is unknown to me. What do you need Etta and me to do? Have you a plan? If not, I may be able to come up with one."

Hope turned away from the window, a smile on her lips. "Elopement. I can see your amazement, cousin; however, desperate times require extreme measures."

"I agree," Beatrice said. "I just didn't expect you to propose the option, especially because it would be expected of me. Well done, cousin."

Hope smiled. "I suspect we are more alike in our boldness, cousin Beatrice, than our families realize. Where I need your cunning is how to proceed. I have an inkling of an idea and I need your thoughts." She lowered her voice conspiratorially. "We can use the masquerade as a foil to our parents' oversight. Since we four are of similar shape and size, we can exchange gowns and masks and our parents will assume that I am you and Charity is Henrietta. Before the unmasking, Charity and I will flee with Claude and Benedick. With love and luck on our side, we can be miles away."

Beatrice's forehead squinched in thought. "Aha! I have a slight refinement if you're willing. How do you feel about being compromised?"

Charity frowned. "I don't understand. If we elope, aren't we compromised?"

"I mean compromised in the loss of your virginity without leaving the house." Beatrice flopped on her bed in a most unladylike fashion, and Henrietta followed suit. "Hope, Charity, you need to be compromised in front of witnesses, that way Aunt Millicent and Uncle Clarence can't prevent a marriage."

Hope climbed on the bed and patted the space beside her. Once Charity sat, Hope said, "While I haven't given Benedick my virginity, and I don't think Charity has either—"

Charity ducked her head. "Um, Claude and I..."

Hope rolled her eyes. "It's always the one who seems the most innocent. What is your plan, Beatrice?"

"A bed trick."

Both Henrietta and Charity stared at her in confusion.

Hope cackled. "Brilliant, cousin! How do we pull it off?"

"We start with your plan and pretend to be each other. Since Bottomore and Swineborne have never met my sister or me, only seen portraits, they won't easily recognize us. Father intends to introduce us at dinner and announce the betrothal tomorrow. Since our voices are somewhat alike, Hope, you'll only have to speak with the candor I'm castigated for during the masquerade. Our aim, dear ladies, is to see that the brides will be you and Charity."

Beatrice leaned in and suggested a variety of ways to get Bottomore and Swineborne into Hope and Charity's beds. Once the details were sorted, Beatrice summoned her maid

Evie and asked her to bring Hope and Charity's gowns to her room. Evie returned and hung the gowns in the wardrobe. While Evie didn't ask the question evident in her eyes, Beatrice took her into their confidence. She explained the plan and asked for Evie's help. In love herself, Evie readily agreed and promised to aid in any way she could.

After Evie's departure, Beatrice had each of them put on the gowns, grateful she and Hope were of a similar shape. Eyeing her sister in Charity's gown, she grinned at the likeness. Hope clapped her hands and giggled, "My word, Henrietta. If I didn't know it was you, I'd swear you were Charity."

Henrietta twirled and laughing said, "Beatrice, this is the best idea you've had in a while."

"It's Hope's, and you all look amazing. Now let's change before mother pays us a visit, heaven forfend."

They'd just hung the gowns in Beatrice's wardrobe when the door swung open, and Lady Ashedon strode into the bedroom. "Good, you're all here. Hope, Charity, I shall speak on behalf of my sister, your mother. Sit, the four of you."

She waited as her daughters and nieces scrambled to sit on the bed. Drawing in a deep breath, Lady Ashedon eyed each one before she slowly exhaled. "As you know, Beatrice, Henrietta, your father is in negotiations with Sir Benedick Bottomore and Claude Swineborne. If matters fall out as I...we wish, your betrothal announcement will be made before our guests depart tomorrow."

She directed a steely gaze to her nieces. "Hope, Charity, without larger dowries, your chances of snagging a husband are limited. However, there will be several unmarried and widowed men attending the masquerade. Your mother and I assume you will be ladylike yet diligent in pursuit of a husband. Several are prosperous farmers, although commoners."

Lady Ashedon's eyes narrowed like those of a famished

eagle about to swoop. "All of you should have been married long before now. I don't know what is happening to young ladies of good breeding these days. No matter, I've instructed Evie to bring supper to you so there's no need to join my guests. I will send a footman to retrieve you for the masquerade, and please be attired, Beatrice. Your father often overlooks your wanton manner, but tonight, please refrain from disputes with the gentlemen. Try to be more like your sister."

"Yes, mother." "Yes, Aunt Maude."

Satisfied she'd done her duty, Lady Ashedon swept out of the room as Evie avoided a collision that would see her fired. Entering the bedroom, she placed the food tray on a table and bowed to Beatrice. "I'll return in a moment with Miss Hope and Miss Charity's supper."

The four sat in silence until Evie returned and set a second tray on the table. "I've snuck in some of Cook's bread," she murmured, with a wink. "Don't want you swooning in the middle of a dance."

Evie left, and Henrietta hurriedly locked the door before strolling over to the table to get a plate of food. "I'm counting on you to be argumentative, sister. Otherwise, the night will be tedious. Sir Pomfrey will be spouting platitudes about the mark of a good housewife, all the while treading on your slippers. If you dance with him first, it'll save me the tragedy."

Beatrice joined her sister at the table. "Only if you distract Farmer Kentworth. His breath is foul, and his fingers calloused. I don't understand why he doesn't wear gloves, 'tis not like he can't afford them. However, tonight Kentworth and Pomfrey will be Hope and Charity's problems."

For the rest of the afternoon, the cousins traded accounts of their worst suitors and how they managed to deter the most persistent.

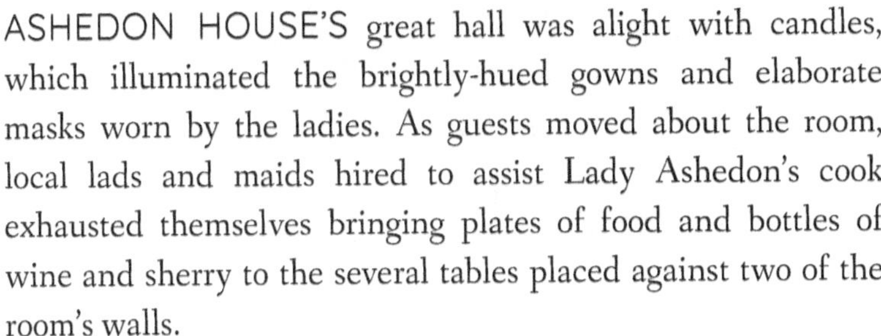

ASHEDON HOUSE'S great hall was alight with candles, which illuminated the brightly-hued gowns and elaborate masks worn by the ladies. As guests moved about the room, local lads and maids hired to assist Lady Ashedon's cook exhausted themselves bringing plates of food and bottles of wine and sherry to the several tables placed against two of the room's walls.

Beatrice glanced around the room in search of her parents before she turned to her cousins and, in a soft voice, gave final instructions to her sister and cousins. "Remember, avoid our mothers at all costs, which shouldn't be too difficult with the crowd in this room. Hope, be forthright since it's expected of me. Etta and Charity...just be yourselves, that'll do."

Her gaze lighted on a couple who entered the room, and she smiled. Adjusting her mask, Beatrice uttered, "Our first test. Wish me success."

She left the group and squeezed past several ladies until she neared Percy and Aisha Howard. When one of the guests moved on, she stepped into the space. "Good evening, Lord and Lady Ross," Beatrice said as she curtsied. "Felicitations on your marriage. Lady Ross, your gown is quite beautiful. Is it London-made?"

"Thank you, it is," Aisha replied, a curious gaze focused on the young lady standing before her. "I'm not certain we've been properly introduced."

"Hope Fortnoy, Lady Ashedon's niece. My aunt has talked of nothing else but Lord Ross's marriage."

"I'm sure she has," Percy mumbled. He waved at a servant burdened with a tray of wine glasses. When the servant approached, he took two glasses and handed one to Aisha. "How is your father managing, Hope?"

After a short pause, Beatrice answered, "Well, my lord. He doesn't speak much of his concerns. Shall I convey your question to him?"

Percy eyed her. "No need, Miss Fortnoy. I'll speak to him when our paths cross tonight. Enjoy the masquerade."

"Thank you, my lord."

Once she scurried away, he leaned into Aisha and whispered, "Something is afoot, sweet wife. That was not Hope Fortnoy. I've known Beatrice Ashedon since she was a child, and that was her. I wonder what game she's playing."

"Perhaps she wants to meet her potential suitor without prejudice. A disguise works if no one suspects, and because you've known her since childhood, it makes sense to test the disguise. Shall we stroll? Perhaps towards the open windows?"

"As you wish, my lady."

TWENTY-FIVE

"Hmm, that's the way, Marie," Benedick groaned. "Just like that. My prick is such a happy boy."

Marie Stewart knew exactly when to make a man spend his seed based on payment, and since Benedick Bottomore had paid a paltry shilling, his time was up. Her fingers gripped the base of his cock and squeezed as her lips moved rapidly up and down his rod.

"Yes, make me give it to you, wench," Benedick moaned as he thrust his hips forward. "Ah, fuck!"

Marie jerked away and directed his release toward the floor. "Ya didn't pay me enough to swallow, my lord."

"How much to bed you?" he panted.

She stood and stepped over the wet spot on the stone floor. "I've another client in a few minutes, and I needs to refresh meself. Enjoy yourself, and why don't you try one of the young ladies in the great hall? They'll probably give you a tussle after enough wine is poured down their throats."

Marie walked away as Benedick refastened his breeches. He cursed when he realized she'd taken the candlestick with her. His hand on the wall, he slowly made his way through the corridor until there was enough light to guide him back to the great hall. Entering the hall, he spied Claude and sauntered to where he stood amid a trio of masked women. He recognized the women despite their masks, thanks to Lady Ashedon's description of what her daughters would be wearing. The odd one had to be one of the Fortnoys.

"May I entice you to dance with me, Lady Beatrice?" Benedick asked.

Hope peered at him, allowing her eyes to take in his black garments. "We've not been properly introduced."

"Forgive me. Benedick Bottomore, at your command."

"Ah, the friend of Sir Swineborne," she intoned. Offering Benedick her gloved hand, she nodded. "Delighted."

Claude led Charity to the open space beside Benedick and Hope, where the two couples joined others in a pavane.

Beatrice stood beside her sister and watched their cousins charm the two men. As the music ended, Bottomore and Swineborne escorted Hope and Charity to a table laden with wine and food before the couples started back toward them.

"Ah, you must be Lady Beatrice's cousin Miss Fortnoy," a middle-aged man said as he stepped directly into Beatrice's view. "I'm Timothy Kentworth, a neighbor to Lord Ashedon. Your mother encouraged my approach. Might we have a word of conversation?"

Beatrice dipped her chin to keep from sniggering. It took a few seconds to master her self-control. "Sir Kentworth?"

He shook his head. "A simple farmer who's looking for a wife. I do have a tidy income, however. I figure that should matter more than a title."

"My apologies, Master Kentworth. I meant no insult," Beatrice simpered. "I just assumed...and there is nothing inelegant about farming. 'Tis how we eat so well."

Kentworth preened. "Well said, Miss Fortnoy. Well said."

With a deep inhalation, Kentworth launched into a disputation on the failings of gentleman farmers, who were often too busy wasting their time and coin in the cesspool of London courtly life. With another inhalation, he began to preach the merits of proper crop rotation and the proper mixture of dung and ash to ensure the soil's good health.

When he said his late wife used to mix a bit of both in her face creams, Beatrice was ready to scream. If there was any doubt that the late Mistress Kentworth was as foolish as her husband, this terrifying bit of nonsense confirmed it.

"How long have you been a widower, Farmer Kentworth?"

"Ten years ago dear Eldwitha left this world. She's with her maker, and it's time for me to consider the disposition of my property. She gave me no sons. I'm still in my prime, not yet forty-six years of age."

Beatrice tittered. "My word, I wouldn't have guessed."

Kentworth grinned beneath his mask and rubbed her bare forearm. "I'm still frisky as a colt. You may call me Timothy."

Beatrice gasped and put distance between them. "I...I'm certain you are, Farmer Kentworth...Timothy."

Her voice trailed off. He'd never been this bold with her, and she was about to give him the vicious side of her tongue before recalling he believed he was speaking to Hope.

Before he could say another word, Henrietta rushed to her side and whispered in her ear, "Is it time to rescue you, sister?"

"What? Oh dear, I best hurry." Beatrice turned to Kentworth. "Forgive me, Timothy, but there's a matter I must attend to. Will you save a dance for me? My business will only take a few minutes, and I'll return directly to you."

Kentworth took her hand and brought it to his lips. Kissing her gloved fingers, he said, "Of course, Miss Fortnoy. I won't move a step; that way, you'll find me amongst the crowd."

"Of course," Beatrice replied as she walked away.

When she and her sister had put distance between her and the farmer, she muttered, "Thank you, Etta. I had to remind myself I was playing Hope. Were you aware Farmer Kentworth is as frisky as a colt even at the ancient age of forty-five and his wife buried ten years ago?"

Henrietta stumbled as laughter sputtered through her. "Judging by his breeches, I can quite believe it. If he'd said a stallion, I'd have my doubts."

"I question the colt analogy, Etta."

The sisters made their way to the meeting place where Hope and Charity waited, an unused corridor with an alcove that afforded them privacy. Beatrice saw her cousins standing in the shadows, Hope's foot tapping nervously.

"Cease, Hope, unless you want to draw attention," she warned. "Did matters turn out as we intended?"

"Yes," Hope replied. "I sent word to mother that I'm suffering a megrim, and Charity is aiding me."

"Well done. I'll speak to Aunt Millicent about Farmer Kentworth and ease her mind since she sent him in search of you."

"I saw him conversing with you, Beatrice," Hope stated. "He's ancient!"

"In his mind, forty-six and frisky as a colt are still youthful. Now to our next step. Do you have your notes ready?" When Hope nodded, Beatrice grinned. "Good. Etta and I will deliver them to Bottomore and Swineborne. Expect them shortly. Are you and Charity certain you wish to proceed? We can end this now—"

"No," Charity hissed. "If this is the only way I can have Claude, I will do it."

"I feel the same," Hope added. "I'll wed Benedick or no one."

The cousins hugged each other and parted, Beatrice and Henrietta slipping back into the great hall while Hope and Charity went up the servants' stairs to their cousins' bedchambers.

"Claude and Benedick are feeding themselves, Etta. Shall we replenish our bellies? Do you have Charity's note handy?"

"I do, and I hope we succeed, sister. I will not marry Swineborne."

Beatrice took her sister's fingers and gave them a squeeze. "Our success is assured as long as we play our parts."

"Miss Fortnoy," Benedick greeted. "Are you enjoying the masquerade? May I get you a glass of wine?"

Please," Beatrice said coyly.

As he reached for the wine glass, she palmed Hope's note and slipped it to Benedick as he handed her the glass. His hand jerked a bit, and he stared at her.

"I understand a betrothal is pending between you and my cousin."

"The details have yet to be finalized, but I'm hopeful."

"And you, Mr. Swineborne?" Henrietta asked, palming him a note.

He gripped the paper and replied, "Ever hopeful. I do find your cousin enchanting and look forward to an announcement."

Beatrice was the first to move. "I've promised Farmer Kentworth a dance. Come, Charity, Mother wouldn't care to see you near the food tables as she's worried about your complexion, especially when you consume the Spanish olives."

The pair went to where Farmer Kentworth stood, talking to Sir Archibald Pomfrey. In minutes, the sisters were among a group of dancers and struggling to maintain a ladylike decorum as the two men pranced decidedly out of step with the music.

BEATRICE AND HENRIETTA left the great hall in search of Evie. When they found her, Beatrice sent the servant to her mother with the news that Beatrice and Henrietta had disappeared from the masquerade and Evie had found a note outside Beatrice's bedroom door when she went to prepare her bed.

Within minutes, Maude Ashedon and Millicent Fortnoy hurried from the hall and raced upstairs, followed by their husbands and several guests. Beatrice and Henrietta trailed the group, turning off to slip into Hope and Charity's bedchamber. Quickly stripping off their masks and ball gowns, they donned their earlier garments and left the room.

Inching their way past the curious guests, the sisters positioned themselves to have clear sight into Beatrice's room. Maude flung open the door to the bedchamber and gasped. From where she stood, Beatrice could see a man's arse, a pair of legs around his hips and stocking feet gripping his buttocks.

"Damn, Beatrice, you're so tight," Benedick grunted. "Yes, squeeze my prick just like that!"

Lord Ashedon strode over to Henrietta's room and flung open the door. A garbled sound drew Beatrice and Henrietta along the wall to get a better view. Beatrice slammed her hand over her mouth while Henrietta gasped and grabbed her sister's other hand.

A completely naked—except for her mask—Charity and Claude were entwined, Charity's head bobbing up and down as she sucked his prick. "That's the way, Etta. Yes! Oh Jesu, damn, I'm about to spew! Squeeze my balls hard."

"What the hell is going on? Henrietta Ashedon, you get off that man immediately and dress yourself!" Lord Ashedon ordered.

His wife, fanning herself furiously, strolled into Beatrice's room, grabbed Benedick's hair, and jerked. "Get off my daughter, you lecher!"

"Oh my god!" Millicent Fortnoy screeched from behind her sister. "That's not Beatrice! It's Hope! I'd know her birthmark anywhere. Where's Charity?"

Millicent stomped over to Henrietta's room and gasped. Charity's head was between Claude's thighs, her lips wrapped around his penis, her hand moving up and down his flesh. Her bottom was in the air, Claude's fingers gripping it as he licked her cunny. Charity raised her head and peered at her mother. "Hello, Mother."

"Charity Fortnoy, you stop that immediately!"

"Just a minute, Mother," Charity panted as her climax struck at the same time as Claude's. Her body trembling, she collapsed on Claude.

When one of the female guests fainted, Ashedon screamed for everyone to leave. It took several men to carry the woman downstairs and for Clarence Fortnoy to clear the corridor.

Beatrice and Henrietta sniggered as the men struggled with the unconscious woman before returning their attention to the unfolding of their master plan. Bottomore and Swineborne were the first to emerge, disheveled but happy smiles on their faces. Lord Ashedon and Sir Fortnoy trailed the two men. Not long after, Hope and Charity walked out, their shoulders drooping as their mother and aunt berated them. When Lady Ashedon spied her daughters, she beckoned them to her side.

"I know you are involved, Beatrice Ashedon," she accused. "You will join us in your father's library. You as well, Henrietta."

TWENTY-SIX

Henry Fortnoy smothered a laugh as he listened from the other side of the library door. He hadn't thought Hope and Charity possessed a courageous bone in their bodies when it came to their parents. Yet, in one night, they'd outdone his years of debauchery and mayhem.

"Oh, well, not my affair," he mumbled beneath his breath and returned to his bedchamber.

It was after midnight, and the house was silent as a tomb when Henry stepped from his room and noiselessly closed the door behind him before secretly making his way to the servants' stairs and following them until he reached his uncle's library.

Entering the room, he walked over to a paneled wall and pressed a lever. A door swung open, and two people emerged from the darkened tunnel. "What was the racket, Harry?" a woman's voice asked as she stepped into the library.

"Lower your voice." Henry released the laugh he'd held. "My sisters were caught fucking their cousins' suitors, Marie."

"Which one fucked Benedick?"

"Hope."

Marie chuckled. "You might want to tell her to squeeze his cods if she wants to end things quickly given the size of his cock. Hmph, she gave it up for free because he's a pinchpenny."

"They're looking to marry," Henry retorted. "You're only interested in money."

The man who followed Marie from the tunnel snorted. "Since her plot to trap Othello Blackwood failed, there isn't much chance Desdemona—sorry, Marie Stewart will find a wealthy husband."

"May you grow blisters on your arse, Tom," she shot back.

"Enough bickering, you two, " Henry hissed. "Let's get this over with, and quietly. Follow me. We need to go through the tunnel to the servants' entrance to the dining room."

The usually bickering Tom and Marie were quiet as church mice as they trailed behind him. Once they reached the servants' entrance, Henry had Tom light the candle he carried. After Tom's muttered curses about the flint, the light flickered into existence, and the trio entered the room.

Henry took the candle and walked over to the large cabinet where his aunt Maude kept her silver plates and cups. "Hist, Marie, do your magic."

Marie pulled a hairpin from beneath her cap and hip-bumped Henry to one side. "Adjust the light a bit. Good."

She fiddled with the lock for a few seconds, then stepped back. "All yours, monsieur."

Henry motioned for Tom to bring him the linen sack he held. "Guard the door."

Once Tom was in place, Henry removed items and placed them in the sack. When he finished, Henry rearranged the remaining cups and plates. "No need to be greedy. Besides, some of these are fakes and we wouldn't get a copper penny for them. Never understood why Aunt Maude keeps worthless trinkets in here."

He closed the door to the cabinet and started for the servants' entrance. Footsteps echoed outside the main door to the dining room, and Tom blew out the candle. The door creaked as a hand pushed it open and a candle was thrust inside the room. Henry motioned the others to the wall behind the door. Marie's knife made a soft whoosh as she unsheathed it. He placed a hand on her thigh—she was far too hot-headed, and they didn't need any bloodshed if it could be helped.

"Who's in there?"

Henry swore silently. What was Burnley doing up? The old fart should have taken his withered arse to bed an hour ago. *Go back to bed, old man.*

The room darkened as the candle was withdrawn, and he breathed a sigh of relief. Relief was short-lived when the door was pushed ajar further, and Burnley shuffled into the room.

Ashedon's steward walked past the intruders and toward the dining room's windows. He checked each one, never hearing the trio as they moved behind the door.

"Right and tight," Burnley mumbled before he turned back to leave. "What's this?"

He hurried to the cabinet. "Who left the door ajar?" He pulled it open and looked inside. "Lord have mercy. We been rob—"

Burnley fell to the floor, a pained groan his last sound as Marie hit him with a candlestick several more times. Henry closed the door to the room and raced to where she stood over Burnley.

"Once would have been sufficient, Marie," he hissed as he kneeled and checked the man's neck for a pulse. Finding none, he rose and strode to the door. "Let's go in case someone heard him. Marie, we'll need to talk about your habit of taking extra. I suppose you snatched the pair."

"What good is a candlestick without its mate?" she whispered as they stole their way through the servants' entrance and back to the priest hole.

"HELP, MURDER! HELP!" One of the maids shrieked from the bottom of the staircase. "Murder, I say! Wake Lord Ashedon!"

The woman's voice was shrill and loud enough to awaken Percy and Aisha. Aisha yawned. "What now? Did Lord Ashedon run Benedick and Claude through for jilting Beatrice and Henrietta?"

"Unlikely, sweeting," Percy said as he got out of bed. "Harvey would wait, like any civilized father, until Swineborne and Bottomore married his nieces before doing that. It's not like Harvey Ashedon to make much ado about nothing, and the compromising of Hope and Charity was a deliberate plan by the young women. No, someone else has been murdered."

Aisha flung the bed covers back and climbed out of bed. "Then let's see who it is. A murder case will make this visitation even more interesting. I must ask, Percy, is this type of behavior common among gentry folk?"

She joined her husband at the twin bowls placed for their use and cleansed her face and teeth. Within a few minutes, the rumble of footsteps and a cacophony of voices swept past their room and trailed off. The couple dressed quickly and went to investigate.

They followed the sounds of crying and raised voices until

they reached the Ashedons' dining room. Lord Ashedon was kneeling beside an unmoving body, his wife keening behind him.

"What has happened, Ashedon?" Percy asked.

"Murder, Ross. A heinous murder. Burnley has been bludgeoned to death."

"Ay me!" Lady Ashedon wailed. "The stains! The stains won't ever come out of the carpet. It cost me six sovereigns! They won't ever come out."

Aisha and Percy exchanged a glance, and she shook her head as they walked past the wailing woman to where the dead man lay.

"Who found him, Harvey? And when?"

Ashedon rose from his knees and faced Percy. "Matilda came in to clean and saw him lying on the floor. She screamed and fainted. Chloe heard her scream and rushed in to find both Matilda and Burnley on the floor, dried blood around his head. It was her screeching that woke the house. They're over there with Cook."

"I'll see to them," Aisha volunteered quickly. "I'm sure the poor girls are distraught."

With that, she walked over and inquired which one was Matilda. Signaling to one of the footmen to bring her a chair, Aisha took the maid's hand and sat.

Percy scanned the dead man's colorless face before he glanced around the room. "Is it common for the cabinet for plates and silver to be unlocked?"

"What?" Ashedon hurried over to the cabinet. "We've been robbed! Maude, order all the servants and guests to come here immediately."

Percy's gaze swept the room. "Harvey, I do believe everyone is here...except your daughters."

Ashedon searched the room and roared for Beatrice and

Henrietta. When the pair didn't arrive, he screeched for Evie and went back to where Burnley lay and Percy stood.

Evie approached cautiously, knowing her master's temper. She trembled when he shook his finger in her face and shouted, "Where are my daughters?!"

Tears flooded down Evie's face as she mumbled an answer.

"What, girl? What did you say?"

"They've eloped," Aisha said from where she sat. The entire room went silent.

Maude wailed louder, then demanded, "With whom?"

"Obviously not Bottomore and Swineborne since they're in the room," Aisha offered. "Evie, do you have any idea who Henrietta and Beatrice ran away with?"

"Aye, my lady."

Ashedon reached for Evie's arm, and she evaded his fingers. Aisha moved swiftly across the room and put herself between Evie and the man. "I think you should tell us, Evie. If they're responsible for Burnley's death, they'll be hanged."

Evie's eyes widened, and more tears flowed. "'T'weren't them, my lady. 'Twas someone else."

"How can you be so certain?"

Evie pressed her lips together, then swiped her cheeks. "Because I helped them escape. Lady Beatrice is in love with Ralph Fitzgerald, and Lady Henrietta gave her heart to Egbert Simpson, Master Ashedon's stableman."

A shrill noise and a loud thump announced Lady Ashedon's faint. Ashedon ignored his unconscious wife and glared at Evie. "When did this elopement take place? And don't lie."

"Last night," Evie said. "While everyone was sorting out the Misses Charity and Hope, the young ladies snuck out to meet their loves and fled to Eggford to be married."

"Lord Ashedon, you may wish to see to your wife," Aisha observed. "She's still unconscious."

"Hang her, let her sleep," Ashedon retorted. "If she'd give me a proper son, I wouldn't give a donkey's arse who those empty-headed girls married."

At his words, Maude groaned in response to the foul-smelling tincture Cook waved beneath the woman's nose. Cook and a footman assisted Lady Ashedon to her feet.

"Did she say my daughters eloped with a stablehand and a common clerk?" Maude demanded.

"Yes," Ashedon grunted.

"Go after them, Harvey. They can't have gotten too far. Evie, where did they go?"

"Eggford, my lady. To marry."

Lady Ashedon blanched. "Marry? Impossible. They don't have our consent!"

Evie wisely put more distance between her and her employers. "Special license. I suspect they're being married even now."

Turning to Percy, Lady Ashedon waved a finger at him. "My lord, send your coachman to fetch them back. We'll have any marriages annulled."

Aisha laughed loudly. "I suspect it's far too late, Maude. Besides, there is the matter of Burnley's murder."

Maude waved her hand. "That can wait, he's not going anywhere." She frowned, then uttered, "Aha! Fitzgerald and Simpson are the murderers."

A servant walked over to Percy and handed him a glass of wine, then gave one to Aisha. "Thank you." Taking a sip, Percy stared at Lady Ashedon. "Might I ask how you came to that conclusion? Were the men in attendance last evening?"

She sniffed. "Of course not. I'd never invite a stablehand into my house."

"It was a masquerade," Aisha remarked. "It's not difficult to disguise one's appearance and achieve one's goal—as your daughters and nieces proved."

Lady Ashedon's cheeks reddened beneath the white powder she wore. "I cannot appreciate your tone, Lady Ross. My daughters—"

"Eloped with a pair of commoners, and your nieces were caught fucking two men they'd supposedly just met. Shall I tell you what happened, Lady Ashedon?"

Aisha sipped her wine, then handed it to Percy. "Hope and Charity Fortnoy were already involved with Bottomore and Swineborne, while Beatrice and Henrietta haven't been virgins since you and Lord Ashedon decided to marry them off to Bottomore and Swineborne."

"How would you know this, Lady Ross?" Millicent Fortnoy demanded.

"Evie."

Millicent turned her anger on the young servant. "Were you aware of my daughters' charade?"

"It was more than a charade," Percy muttered.

Evie looked at Aisha, who nodded. "Yes, Mistress Fortnoy," the maid replied. "I overheard them devising the entire trick, including getting Master Swineborne and Sir Bottomore into bed with your daughters."

"Who, by the way, quite enjoyed the men's cocks, given what I could see and hear from the corridor. If I'm not mistaken, I believe it was Charity who asked you to wait while she climaxed?" Aisha hid her grin by sipping her wine.

Millicent sputtered for several seconds, then stomped away from the group. Aisha tilted her head and peered at Maude, who pursed her lips as if to speak but wisely chose silence.

Percy finished the last of his wine. "I'd really like to get back to the dead man lying at our boots, if you don't mind."

He handed his glass to a nearby servant. "It does look rather suspicious, Lady Ross, that Beatrice and Henrietta Ashedon eloped at the same time a robbery and murder occurred."

"Hallo, what's this about a murder and elopement?" Henry Fortnoy strolled into the dining room, a glass of wine raised to his lips.

TWENTY-SEVEN

Percy watched the younger Fortnoy strut into the dining room. When he reached the group standing over Burnley's body, Henry asked, "I say, who's been murdered?"

"Burnley," Lord Ashedon said. "Robbery."

"I thought I heard elopement and murder. Who eloped?" He glanced around, spied his sisters and Bottomore and Swineborne, and grinned. "Ah, Cousin Beatrice has fled the nest."

"And Henrietta's ran off with Harvey's stablehand," Millicent declared. "At least Beatrice had the intelligence to choose a lawyer's clerk."

"Must you remind me, Millie?" Maude groaned.

Henry shook his head. "Do you think they had a hand in Burnley's death?"

"My daughters? Of course not, it's those commoners who robbed us and killed Burnley." Lady Ashedon inhaled and blew the air out in an angry huff. "I suspect they kidnapped Beatrice and Henrietta."

"Don't be foolish, Maude," her husband snorted. "They ran

off with those men and took our good plates and silver with them. Lord Ross, I want them all arrested."

"Harvey, think about what people will say! Our daughters...you can't. We'll quietly send them to my aunt in Scotland. She can find good husbands for them. Think of the embarrassment to our reputation if Beatrice and Henrietta are taken up as thieves."

"Do not leave Hope, Charity, Claude, and Benedick," Aisha said when the couples headed toward the door. "I'm sure Lord Ross will have questions for everyone who slept in Ashedon House last night."

She peered at Percy. "I instructed a servant to send for the local constable. I suggest we cover poor Burnley with a tarp or blanket until the man arrives."

"Well done, Lady Ross. Might I ask that everyone move to the great hall? I do have a few questions that need answering."

One of the servants left and returned with a tablecloth. "'Tis the handiest, Lady Ross."

"It will do," she replied.

Once Burnley was beneath the cloth, the group filed out and down the corridor to the hall. Percy and Aisha were the last to enter. The tables had been cleared of food but not the wine and sherry. "If you need a drink, please do so now. I'd like the men on that side of the room and the women over there. Lady Ross will speak with the women while I question the men."

Several chairs were pulled up for Lady Ashedon, Millicent and her daughters, and Aisha. Aisha stood behind her chair. "Lady Ashedon, is it customary to lock the plate cabinet at night?"

"It's always locked except when I host a small dinner or supper," she said. "Only two people have the key, myself and Burnley. Harvey, send one of the footmen to check Burnley's pockets for the cabinet key. If it's missing..."

Aisha asked each servant their whereabouts between midnight and the time Burnley was found. It was as she expected—most were exhausted and in bed. Since the women shared rooms, it wasn't possible for them to be the murderer. However, an accomplice was a different story. Well, she'd leave the men to Percy.

"I need to know whether any of you are involved with any of the male staff, taken them as lovers?"

Maude Ashedon huffed. "Of course not! I won't tolerate fornication in my house. Anyone who does will be immediately dismissed."

"Then you'll have to get rid of the lot of us," Cook mumbled.

"What did you say?" Maude demanded, her gaze whipping to the older woman's face. "Speak up, Cook. You know my right ear has more difficulty than my left."

"Forgive me for mumbling, my lady," Cook replied. "I'm still stunned by Burnley's murder. If I may speak for the others, we wouldn't want to lose our employment."

While Cook was appeasing Lady Ashedon, Aisha noted all eight women standing behind the woman's chair had raised their hands a fraction, grins on their faces. They were young and had no intentions of withering their lives away without pleasure.

"What ho! I hear there's a murder afoot."

Aisha looked in the direction of the voice. "Oh lord, who in the fuck is that? Or should I say what is that?"

Titters and giggles rippled behind her, and she realized she'd spoken aloud. Thankfully, the source of her amazement didn't hear her words. She peered over her shoulder to the group of women. "Who is that?"

"Constable Costard Dogberry," Cook stated.

Aisha's eyes focused once more on the man who stood on

the hall's threshold. His woolen jacket was a pattern of different shades of brown where he'd obviously had tears and rips patched and, given the degree of food-stained blots, hadn't been cleaned in a month of Sundays. His dark trousers were also patched, though with light brown squares whose stitching betrayed a bad seamster.

As he strutted into the room with the importance of a peacock, Dogberry's unkempt beard and felted constable's hat, crowned with a crow's feather and a curious medallion, nearly triggered a bout of laughter in Aisha. "I say again, what ho! I was commandeered from my meal with a hue and cry of murder. Lo and behold, I was shown a dead body in the dining room. Who is the villain, and where is the weapon? I say, as the duly appointed officer for the village of Seacole, I shall have an answer out of you."

Aisha peered at her husband and pressed her lips together until they ached. She'd never seen Percy at a loss for words until this day. Finally, his wits appeared to return and he waved Dogberry into the room.

"Good day, Constable. I'm Percy Howard, Lord Ross, and a guest in Lord Ashedon's home."

"Constable Costard Dogberry at your service, my Lord Ross, a servant to Her Majesty's Secretary. I've heard as good exclamation on your worship as of any man in the city, and though I be but a poor village constable, I am glad to aspire to your worship's egress."

Percy had tented his fingers and pressed them against his lips as the man talked, struggling to contain his amusement. When Dogberry whipped off his hat and bowed, a choked sound followed by a cough pushed through Percy's fingers.

"Pardon me, a dryness in my throat."

"A bit of vinegar, honey, and asafetida is just the thing for the dryness." Dogberry glanced behind him at the door. "Farnsworth, you must take notes."

A slender man of indeterminate age and temperament shuffled into the room, his shoulders hunched, most likely, Percy thought, from too much time spent in the constable's company.

"I'm here, Costard. Got me paper and me pencil ready."

"Good man, Farnsworth. My lord Ashedon, has a murder occurred today?"

Ashedon rolled his eyes. "You claimed you saw the body."

"I did, but I need you to confirm the facts for Farnsworth. What is the murderer's name?"

"I have no idea," Ashedon retorted. "The dead man in the dining room is my steward, Samuel Burnley. Apparently, he was killed last night or this morning during a robbery."

"What ho!" Dogberry exclaimed. "There was no mention of a robbery. Murder and robbery. There was no mention of robbery. Murder the man cried, murder I say."

Ashedon's exasperation provoked a chuckle from Percy, who interrupted. "Will you permit me to speak, Constable Dogberry?"

"Aye, my lord. Perhaps you can make sense of Lord Ashedon's refutations of his man's accusations."

Aisha hurried to the table and poured two glasses of wine and went to stand beside her husband. She handed one to Percy, then offered the other to Dogberry. "A glass of wine, Constable?"

Dogberry eyed her suspiciously, then nodded. "You are a comely wench. Are you wed?"

"Constable Dogberry, my wife Aisha Howard, Lady Ross."

"Ah, I thought her too florescent to bloom locally," Dogberry said before he sipped the wine. "Thank you, Lady Ross. 'Tis a balm for a parched throat."

"You're welcome, Constable Dogberry."

Percy cleared his throat. "Constable, here's what we know so far. Between midnight last evening and this morning, a robbery took place, and Burnley was cudgeled several times and died of his wounds."

"Did you get that, Farnsworth?"

"Yes, Costard. Cudgeled several times and died of his wounds."

"The robbery, man. You must record the robbery." Dogberry sipped more wine. "Please continue, my lord."

"A servant roused the household, and that's when we discovered the robbery, Burnley, and Lord Ashedon's daughters had eloped."

"An elopement, ye say? Well, not much I can do about that. This is a drinkable wine. Is there more?"

Aisha, enjoying the growing frustration on Lord Ashedon's face, signaled a servant to bring another glass. Dogberry pompously thanked the servant as he handed him the empty glass. "Please continue, my lord."

"Beatrice and Henrietta Ashedon have eloped with..."

"Ralph Fitzgerald and Edgar Simpson," Aisha supplied, noting that Lord Ashedon had left them and was at the table filling a glass with wine.

"Where was Lady Ashedon? To allow her daughters to run away...tsk, tsk."

"A masquerade was held last night in honor of the proposed betrothal between Beatrice and Henrietta Ashedon and Sir Claude Swineborne and Sir Benedick Bottomore. Although that's moot since Clarence and Millicent Fortnoy's daughters are now betrothed to Swineborne and Bottomore."

Dogberry gaped at Aisha before focusing his wine-glazed eyes to Percy. "Perhaps we best stick to murder and robbery."

"Well, it's possible that the runaways may have undertaken

the robbery to fund their elopement and inadvertently murdered Burnley in their escape," Percy explained.

"So you know the killers? Well, that should make the solving of this case easy. Where are they? The elopers?"

Ashedon sighed and drank half of his wine. "Do you comprehend what elopement means, Dogberry? It means they've run away, got married, and don't intend to return. It means—"

"It means we married the men we love and now return to ask our parents' blessings."

TWENTY-EIGHT

Beatrice, Henrietta! You're back!" Charity screamed and raced to hug her cousins. "Are you married? Are these your husbands? Oh my, they're quite handsome."

"Charity Fortnoy, you come away from them this minute!" Millicent yelled. "They're murderers, and we will not associate with murderers."

"Murder? Who's been murdered?" Beatrice asked.

"Burnley was codged on his head and died while someone robbed Aunt Maude's finest silver plates and cups. Because you eloped with commoners, everyone believes it was you and Henrietta," Hope explained.

All of this came out in a breathless rush, which was exhausting to Aisha and she signaled the man who had become a favorite wine bearer. He brought her a glass filled to the brim and a chair. "Thank you," she murmured.

"This family can be tiresome, my lady," he said softly. "You wouldn't happen to have need of another servant at Howard Manor? My cousin Royce Tanner and his family reside in Eggford, and it would be a boon to be near my kinsman."

"Is one of the maids included in this request? And your name?"

"Aye, Evie Russell, and my name is William. William Spears."

Aisha sipped her wine. "We shall talk after Lord Ross solves this case."

Beatrice strode to where her father stood, Ralph Fitzgerald, her sister Henrietta, and Egbert Simpson at her heels. A frosty glare in her eyes, she said, "Is this true, father? You believe Etta and I are capable of theft and murder?"

He flushed and gulped some wine, swallowing hard before he spoke. "What else were we supposed to think? We rise from bed, and there's a dead man in the dining room. The door to your mother's silver cabinet is ajar, and valuables are missing. We find out you and your sister have eloped with men we know nothing about."

"That isn't true, my lord," she interrupted. "Egbert has worked in your stables since he was a young boy, and Ralph is clerk and nephew to your rival. Also, you knew very little about Bottomore and Swineborne before you and mother sought to marry us to them. Did you believe we would be dutiful daughters and marry men we hadn't met? Men who swore their dying love to our cousins without a word to you or mother?"

"I—"

Beatrice shook a finger in his face. "Fie, fie on you. That is not the worst of your crimes. How dare you accuse Henrietta and I of murder? Burnley? He was the nearest we had to a kindly grandfather. Shame on you for listening to our mother."

Dogberry, completely in his cups, pulled out a whistle and blew it loudly. "What ho! That is no way to pontificate to your father, young lady. And if you didn't cudgel Burnley, who did?"

"How am I supposed to know the answer to such a foolish question? I was on my way to Eggford to be married this morning. We departed not long after Hope and Charity were discovered swiving Swineborne and Bottomore. We've only returned to retrieve our clothing, then we will depart from this house."

"Then I'm quite confused," Dogberry slurred. "If you didn't murder Burnley, who is the conspirator?"

Aisha's smothered laughter earned a look from Percy. He leaned down and whispered, "If you have any clue as to who the culprit is, Isha, please speak so we may depart. Cecily and Chester have our things packed, and I need to fuck you, my beautiful wife."

"Prettily said, my lord," she murmured. "I shall take pity on you." She rose from her chair. "Constable Dogberry, I may be able to resolve your dilemma. Will you ask everyone to return to the dining hall?"

She handed William her glass and accepted Percy's arm. They strolled out of the hall and returned to the dining room.

"You're not sharing your thoughts, are you, puss?"

"No, although I'm surprised you didn't fathom the murderer before now." She halted and kissed his chin before they entered the room.

After everyone was gathered again in the dining room, Burnley's body neatly wrapped in a blanket and tucked in a corner, Aisha nodded to Farnsworth. "Please close the door, Mr. Farnsworth."

"Yes, my lady, and it's just Farnsworth. No Mister to it. Not even a first name 'cause I was an orphan left on the church steps in Basingstoke. So it's just Farnsworth."

Aisha swallowed, then walked over to the cabinet. "According to Lady Ashedon, there are only two keys to unlock this cabinet—one she held and the other kept by Burnley. Lady Ashedon, do you have the key in your possession?"

"Of course," she snipped. "I keep it on a chain about my neck. See?"

"The other key, the one belonging to Burnley, was retrieved from his pocket. Is that correct, Lord Ross?"

Percy lightly sucked his teeth. "Damn, I know where you're leading with this. Well done, Lady Ross. Yes, the key was found in Burnley's pocket, and Harvey has it."

"Thus, if the only keys that can open the cabinet are in the possession of the two people solely responsible for them, and Burnley is dead, then there appears to be only one logical conclusion," Aisha observed. "Lady Ashedon is the murderer and a thief."

Lady Ashedon's outraged screech was so loud no one heard Percy's roar of laughter. All eyes focused on her, and she screeched a second time. "How dare you accuse me? I'd never rob myself or kill Burnley. How dare you, you...you London baggage!"

"I'm not accusing you, Lady Ashedon. Based on the facts, I indicated what logic would dictate. However, since your amorous relations with Burnley are well-known among your servants, there's no reason for you to murder him except jealousy, which is neither here nor there. Let's return to the unlocked cabinet, shall we?"

Aisha closed the cabinet door and, having taken possession of Burnley's key, locked it. "Constable Dogberry, will you come and confirm the door is quite secure?"

An inebriated Dogberry stepped on several pairs of feet as he made his way to her side. He tugged on the handle.

"'Tis locked right and tight, my lady."

"Good."

Removing a hairpin from one of her braids, Aisha asked him to step aside. She then used the hairpin to unlock the door before she returned it to her braid. In response to Percy's arched eyebrow and questioning look, she grinned. "A Southwark bawd taught me that."

He came to her and kissed her cheek. "You are full of tricks, aren't you, Lady Ross?"

She smiled wickedly at him. "You have no idea, Lord Ross."

Dogberry approached the couple. "Well, my lord and lady, you've taught me a lesson today. If you do take a thief, is to let him show himself what he is and steal out of your company. In the Queen's name, I must comprehend your aspicious person, Lady Ross, for robbery and murder. My Lord Ross, I would have you examine her before your worship."

"Oh, shut the fuck up, Dogberry," Ashedon hissed. "You're not fit to clean the shit from my stables let alone investigate this case. Lady Ross, I assume you know the culprit behind Burnley's death and the robbery."

"Culprits," she said. "William, please open the door to the servants' entrance."

Her request was greeted by puzzled faces before William went to the door and opened it. Two bodies were shoved into the room, their hands tied behind their backs and their faces masked. Chester ducked his head and stepped into the dining room, two of Ashedon's footmen at his back.

"Your thieves and killers," Aisha said. "Constable Dogberry, please remove their masks." As he did so, Aisha cackled. "Well, well, if it isn't Desdemona Brabanzio. Left the trade, have you?"

"My name is Marie Stewart. I have no idea who this Desdemona person is."

Percy's derisive snigger earned a tight-lipped glare. "Then you will hang as Marie Stewart. Would you care to confess now and return what was stolen? Perhaps you can escape hanging and spend a few years in prison."

Desdemona's gaze flicked between Henry Fortnoy and the

man beside her. Her face had become ashen at the mention of hanging. "I'll admit to opening the cabinet, but that's all."

"Who removed the plates?"

She remained silent, her eyes downcast. Percy shook his head. "Then both you and your partner will face the hangman's noose."

"I'm not dying for them!" the bound man shouted. "I'll tell you what you want to know if you'll put in a word to the judge."

Percy eyed him. "That will be up to Lord Ashedon. What is your name?"

"Thomas Kemp. Everything was planned by him," Thomas said, tilting his head toward Henry. "He and me been thieving together for a year. We was doing fine until he took with her, and Marie Stewart isn't her real name. She was one of the Wandering Eye ladies and got greedy, so Mistress Delbrey kicked her out 'cause Marie—her name *is* Desdemona—was stealing from her clients."

A sudden crash drew everyone's focus toward the door. Henry lay on the floor, moaning about a hurt knee. Beatrice stood over him. "Yes, I stuck my foot in your path, you filthy piece of muck. You devised this comedy, dear cousin, and you absolutely must stay for act five."

Several servants grabbed him and dragged him over to where Dogberry stood. "What ho!" the constable slurred.

Percy sighed. "Let me end this quickly so Lady Ross and I may depart. Who cudgeled Burnley?"

Thomas and Henry said simultaneously, "Marie."

Henry continued, "He came in as we were about to leave. Marie pilfered a pair of candlesticks even after I told her not to remove anything. She also carries a knife, but I warned her off using it. We hid behind the door, thinking the old fool would go away, but he came inside the room. So Marie whacked him."

"Several times," Thomas added. "I'll admit robbery but not murder. No one was supposed to die."

"Well, there you have it, Constable Dogberry," Percy intoned, offering his hand to Aisha. "Come, my lady. It is time for us to depart. I'm in need of a bath and require your assistance."

He led her to the door. "Constable, Farnsworth, Lord Ashedon, I leave the matter in your hands. Good day."

EPILOGUE

"I'm curious, Lady Ross," Percy said as he assisted her into their carriage.

Aisha settled herself on the seat before she looked at him. "Curious about what, my lord?"

"Many things about the Ashedons, but two matters perplex me most," he replied, climbing in beside her. Once the carriage set off, he continued. "I'd assume our intrepid thieves would want distance between them and their victims. What made you suspect they hadn't left Ashedon House?"

Aisha smiled at him. "I'm surprised I came up with the answer before you, Percy. It was something Evie said as she told how Beatrice and Henrietta managed to slip out of the house. Women's intuition is so much more effective than a man's direct questioning."

"I'll accept the insult from you and no other," he said, pulling her into his arms and kissing her. When he was done, he murmured, "I'm familiar with your sensitive places, madam, so answer my question."

She giggled and placed her fingers over the hand resting on

her thigh. "Evie said Beatrice and Henrietta left the house through a priest hole and tunnel that eventually led to the Ashedons' stables. There are two entrances inside the house connected to the priest hole, one is in the library and—"

"The other entrance was in the dining room," Percy interjected. "I assume there are different corridors leading to the exit."

"Percy Howard," she said with mock exasperation, "must I school you on your nation's hysteria about Catholic priests?"

"Proceed, madam."

Shifting into a more comfortable position in Percy's arms, she rubbed his ungloved hand. "According to Evie, only the house servants and Ashedon knew about the priest hole's connection to the dining room. The entrance is concealed by the tall cabinet where the Dowager Ashedon's remains are kept, along with her husband's and his father and mother. Apparently, the Dowager's fury at both her late husband and her son knew no bounds. Not even Maude Ashedon dares go near the cabinet. What no one knew was the cabinet was a false front and easily moved. I do have to say, the Catholics are far more interesting than your lot."

"I'm a heathen, my lady."

Aisha giggled. "Once I knew about the entrance's existence, I deduced the logical action on the part of the thieves was to be inside the house, waiting for everyone to depart, then leave among the crowd. But where, oh where could they hide?"

"You're enjoying the telling, aren't you, wife?"

"Yes I am," she admitted. "Once Evie mentioned the priest hole, it was obvious there had to be a guest who knew the house as well as its owners and the servants. The only possibility, besides the Ashedon sisters, are the Fortnoys. Since Hope and Charity were quite busy getting their pussies stroked, that left Henry Fortnoy."

Her forehead furrowed for a second. "I had a niggling recollection of Henry's face when he strutted into the dining room. After he spoke, I knew who he was—a complete charlatan. About a year and a half ago, he thought to make use of the Cock & Oyster. A discreet investigation kept him out since he is indebted up to his balls, with no expectations of steady income. Not a client I'd entertain."

Percy pulled out a flask and removed the top. Offering it to his wife, he remarked, "I'm not very familiar with the Fortnoys since they reside in another county. My only dealings with Clarence Fortnoy came about when he approached Cecil for a favor. While not impoverished, the family struggles to maintain their position."

"Anyway, once I deduced the household spy was Henry, it was easy to device a trap," Aisha declared. "I spoke to Cecily and Evie and arranged for Evie to direct Chester to the priest hole's exit. Fortune favors the fair of heart, and Maude's swoon was a perfect distraction. Chester and two of Ashedon's burliest footmen entered the tunnel and went to the room where Desdemona and Tom were sequestered. Apparently, it was coitus interruptus for Desdemona."

She stroked Percy's thigh. "You'll have to quiz Chester on the subduing of the culprits. I understand Tom was the easiest to capture since he was already coitus completus."

"Aisha Howard, don't make up words."

She shrugged, then her expression became thoughtful. "If I were still in the trade, I'd like the challenge of educating Desdemona. Alas, 'tis far too late for my wisdom."

"One more question before I satisfy my lust on you, Lady Ross," Percy said, his hand pushing her skirt up her leg.

Her fingers busily undoing the ties to Percy's breeches, Aisha mumbled, "Ask away, Lord Ross."

"How did you discover Lady Ashedon's secret?"

She squeezed his prick, and Percy moaned before he began to slowly move in and out of her clenched fingers. "Evie was quite forthcoming. The priest hole was equipped with a bed and beddings. Maude and Burnley's trysts took place there as the lovers were less likely to be caught. Most of the household servants knew Burnley was bedding the mistress whenever Ashedon was away and doing it in the priest hole. The male servants also made use of the room, and Evie informed me that they referred to it as the 'prick hole.'"

Aisha shook her head. "Even Ashedon occasionally used the room, swiving the cook and several of the older female servants—all of whom were also fucking Burnley." She chuckled. "If you could have seen the women's faces when Maude declared there was no fornication allowed in Ashedon House. Apparently, the only ones fooled were the master and mistress, and they believed their peccadilloes were a secret."

"You've hired Evie and William, haven't you?"

"They're too virtuous for that household, and William has a kinsman living in Eggford. Besides, Maude Ashedon fired Evie for her involvement in Beatrice and Henrietta's elopements. William resigned, and they are unemployed. You do know how this nation treats the unemployed," Aisha stated caustically.

"Well, Lady Ross, now that you've solved the mystery of Ashedon House, I've a bit of employment I'd like to offer you."

She stroked his hard cock and parted her thighs. "If you're willing to meet my terms, I'm happy to listen to your offer, my lord."

"Oh, sweet puss," he moaned, "I'm always willing to meet your terms."

AN ASP IN TIME

TWENTY-NINE

IT WAS a warm September evening that had settled over London, yet the unseasonable air was definitely not a boon to Aisha Howard's mood. Since receiving the Earl of Euston's invitation along with Robert Cecil, Lord Salisbury's missive insisting on Percy's acceptance, she'd devised various plots to return to Eggford and Howard Manor. She and Percy were in London to visit her family and the Cock & Oyster, not attend court functions. Cecil's spies were remarkably efficient, which explained Salisbury's note. However, the puzzle was Euston. How did he learn they were in residence, and who was he? With a soft snort, she answered her own question: the court. Percy had to make his presence known to Her Majesty, and therein lay the rub.

"Do you intend to make me suffer the entire evening, Lady Ross?"

Aisha eyed her husband. "No, I'm saving my polite disdain for Cecil, assuming he's present."

"Good," Percy murmured. "I have plans for when we return home."

"Please lace me up, Lord Ross," Aisha said as she turned her back to her husband. "You would order the most complicated gown for me to wear to a masquerade. I'm certain not even Cleopatra herself would have entertained this costume. Although," she mused, "I do love the color. 'Tis striking and suits me. I guess my complaint is, I don't mind showing flesh, but why weren't the laces at the front of the gown so I can tie them?"

"Because, my sweet Cleo, I wanted the pleasure of having you at my mercy when we return home. You will need Antony's assistance to remove the gown, and I'll have the pleasure of seeing your naked back." Percy positioned himself behind his wife and quickly laced the ribbons so the strings couldn't be easily undone. "It's rather simple if you consider it."

"Ha! You do realize I have other gowns I might wear? None as revealing but easily removed if I choose to cuckold you."

"The least of my worries, sweet puss," he replied, kissing her bare shoulder. "My prick is the only one you desire, and there is not a match for my tongue to be found in England, Scotland, Wales, or even Ireland."

"France? Spain?"

"Perhaps in Spain since, from what I've been told, there is little substance to that nation's collective instruments of pleasure, which is why their tongues arc somewhat enlarged."

"Percy Elwen Howard!" Aisha screeched. "You're making all this up. You know there's no inherent differences between nations. A man's length and girth is only as important as he wields his rod." She frowned. "Since I've only known your prick, I may be wrong."

She moaned when Percy's teeth nibbled her shoulder. "I do recall Tidwell. Neither length nor girth were attributes of his."

Percy bit the place he'd just nibbled, and she moved beyond

his reach. "You will not be engaged in an experiment to test my hypothesis, my lady. Your pussy belongs to me."

Turning to face him, she smiled. "Ooh, I adore it when you become territorial. Are you getting into character, my love? Is that why you chose Shakespeare's *Antony and Cleopatra*? Do know, Lord Ross, I shall not take to the asp because of you."

He reached for her hand, bringing it to his lips. "I would never ask you to, sweet Isha. By the by, that gown incites me to want to ravish you. However, the ladies of the Cock & Oyster desire our presence at dinner. It seems Matthew has something special planned for our meal."

A soft sigh escaped her lips, and Aisha grabbed her fur-lined cloak. When she returned to Percy, he stroked her cheek with his knuckle before using it to lift her chin. "What's amiss, Isha?"

She flashed him a smile. "Nothing, really."

"Nothing, really? Recall, Lady Ross, it's me, and I know when something is amiss with my wife."

"An unease, Percy. We've not spent time in London since the Tidwell cases. Although we solved who was responsible, I feel as if my decision to let Ophelia and Sally flee England will come back to haunt me." She raised her eyes to his face. "What do you know about Lord Euston? All I've heard is that he is a reclusive Scotsman living the existence of a monk after his wife died in a carriage accident. Of course, if he's seeking sainthood, I have no use for him unless he wants to make use of the Cock & Oyster."

Percy grabbed her and roughly jerked her into his embrace. "God, I love you. Do you think the ladies would miss us if we fucked for an hour or so? We aren't due to arrive at Allen House for another two hours. We can have an early supper—"

"No." She laughed and shook her head at the sheer disappointment on his face. "Your habit of letting Lord Cecil talk you into things is why we're attending a masquerade this evening in honor of Lord Euston's elevation. Now, who is this man?"

Aisha wrapped her arm around Percy's back, and they left the bedchamber she'd once claimed. Now it remained unused since she was most often at the manor house in Eggford. As they descended the staircase, Percy admitted he knew very little about the man beyond what she'd uncovered, except that his name was Alastair Farquhar, and he was the nearest male relative to the dead Earl of Euston. Since the Queen required all peers of the realm to travel to London to pay obeisance to the throne, Farquhar had made the trip.

Aisha halted. "Whose idea was it to hold a masquerade ball for the man?"

"I suppose the Queen's. With James set to become her heir, Cecil most likely encouraged her to entertain the new Earl of Euston. Of course, Her Majesty won't be present at the ball, but she made certain Euston would bear the cost."

"Is the unmasking at midnight as usual?" Percy nodded. "Shall we depart five minutes before the hour? Perhaps we can quench your thirst for conquest, Lord Antony."

Percy's laughter brought a smile to Randall's brown face as he stood guard at the dining room door.

"Given your evening plans, my lord, 'tis good to see you in a festive mood. Oh, my word, Lady Ross!" Randall grinned wickedly. "Those frisky lords will want to snatch you up like a thief running amok in the Queen's jewelry closet. My, my."

"Et tu, Brutus?" she retorted.

"As you can see, Randall, Lady Ross's beauty and humor haven't yet resolved themselves. Aisha gives me joy every day, but I do sleep with an eyelid lifted when she's forced to attend me in my courtly duties."

Randall's snort rumbled from his chest, and he chuckled.

"Lady Ross goes nowhere she doesn't wish to go, my Lord. However, the noise emanating from her belly does tell me she's beside herself to dine."

Aisha mumbled an insult beneath her breath and strode into the dining room when Randall opened the door. Percy winked at the man as he followed his lady into the room. The number of courtesans seated at the table was smaller than usual as several of the women were away from London visiting family.

Good evening, ladies," Percy said with an elegant bow.

Eveline Jordan rose from her chair and swished to where Aisha and Percy stood. She pecked his cheek before wrapping her arms around Aisha. "Ellen! I'm so happy you're joining us. Come, sit next to me, and tell me how country life is boring you to shite. I do hope Lord Ross has satisfied your every whim."

Aisha returned Eveline's embrace and responded with a blush. "Percy is...well, he's himself, and I want for nothing."

Percy sat across from her and raised his glass of wine to Aisha. "Well said, my lady. Just so you know, ladies, without being called a braggart, I've not heard one word of complaint from her."

Once the laughter settled, Aisha began to regale the women with the events that occurred while she and Percy were in Eggford. When she finished the tale of Desdemona Brabanzio and the Ashedons, Hannah Crawford, one of the first Cock & Oyster courtesans, rolled her eyes. "She could've just come to London and let us train her to empty men's pockets without fear."

"Sadly, that family has little in the way of sense and far too much hubris to think clearly. How have matters been with all of you?"

Aisha listened as the women talked. They'd fallen in love with Isabelle, who they knew as Belle Chapman, and were teaching her the trade. A quick learner, Isabelle had made some innovative changes to the brothel, and Aisha knew her cousin would do well once the Cock & Oyster officially became hers.

Percy rose from his chair. "It's time for us to depart, my lady. Thank you for a lovely repast, ladies. My wife and I are in your debt."

"I'd like you to pay now, Lord Ross," Eveline teased. "Show us what keeps Mistress Ellen happy."

Percy's red-faced embarrassment triggered Aisha's laughter. "Sorry, Eveline, that will remain betwixt my lord and me."

Hannah lifted her glass. "A toast. To the only man who could win and deserve Ellen Chapman's heart. To love!"

Wine was drunk, and cheers sounded in the room. Aisha smiled at the women as Percy escorted her to the front door, grabbed her cloak from the console table, and draped it over her shoulders. They left the brothel and climbed into their carriage. Initially, she wanted to take a sedan chair, but he reminded her they'd face difficulty leaving when they wanted since the chair had to be summoned.

Once they were settled in the coach, Percy pulled her into his arms and kissed her. Their tongues tangled like silken threads beneath less-than-nimble fingers. He licked her bottom lip when he lifted his mouth. "I'd love to fuck you right now, but I'll damp down my lust."

"Why is that, my lord? You've never hesitated before."

"We wouldn't make it to Farquhar's ball," he said huskily.

Her tongue glided across his generous and compromising chin, and she savored the faint saltiness of his skin. "I wouldn't mind at all."

He leaned away from her to look into her eyes. "Still troubled?"

Aisha sighed. "I don't know what it is, Percy. Something

about this night doesn't sit well with me. I fear we may be involved in another case. I can't explain it, but my spine is tingling."

He pulled her head against his shoulder. "We'll be fine, love. I promise, if something dreadful occurs, I won't get involved."

"I'll hold you to your word, Percy Howard."

THIRTY

Allen House was nestled in a wooded area northwest of London's St. James' Park. The entrance was alight with torches set some distance from the wood and brick building. It was obvious the new earl was determined to display the stately home, and the brightness of the flames danced eerily against the night sky, giving the house a sense of mystery and foreboding.

Grooms stood ready to assist with horses and carriages as the earl's guests slowly made their way to the house's entrance. Henry Jessup guided his horses to a halt and braked the vehicle. He slid open the small wood panel between him and the coach's interior. "We're here, my lord, my lady. I'll return just before midnight to fetch you to Ross House."

"Where will you be, Henry?" Aisha queried.

"Just over there, near the stone wall," he answered. "I think it's wise for you to depart before the nonsense starts up. These city lords are frisky as colts in an open meadow, especially when they're drowning in sack. My lord, you keep an eye on my lady. Don't want to face Martha's wrath should anything go amiss."

"She will never be beyond my touch, Henry." Percy climbed out of the carriage when a groom opened the door. After aiding Aisha, he leaned into the carriage. "Stay alert, Jessup."

"Of course, my lord."

Percy led her up the steps to the door, where a bewigged footman bowed and waved them inside. "Shall I take your cloaks?"

Aisha shivered as Percy removed hers first, then his. Her costume was provocative given courtly standards; however, as the footman led them to the ballroom, she felt quite modest compared to a number of the women moving about the room. She turned to Percy and said softly in Arabic, "I fear an orgy will transpire before long, given the state of dress, or should I say undress, in this room. I believe I'm rather overdressed compared to some."

Percy chuckled. "I much prefer you that way, Cleo. Come, I see Cecil holding court. I assume the man beside him is Lord Farquhar."

They made their way to where Cecil stood. Several men stepped to one side when Cecil's eyes settled on Percy, and a flicker of a smile formed on the man's thin lips. "Ross, pleased that you and Lady Ross have joined us in London. I've missed your skills."

Aisha forced a smile on her face when Cecil, who was several inches shorter and had to look up to meet her gaze, turned to address her. Although the Queen nicknamed him "Pygmy," the man was a cunning fox, right down to his poorly dyed wig and beard. *Bella could do better, she thought.*

"Lady Ross, enchanted to see your beauty and grace among

us again. I, for one, have missed your witty charm. Your husband has kept you far too long in the countryside."

"You are gracious and far too kind in your praise, Lord Salisbury. I, for one, much prefer country life to the bustling fervor of London, and knowing when I awake my husband is beside me."

His lips curved sardonically. "Your husband will tell you, there is nothing gracious or kind within me. At this moment, I speak only the truth. Not many English wives can make such a boast in these troubled times." He turned to the earl. "Euston, permit me to introduce you to Percy Howard, Lord Ross, and his wife, Aisha Howard, Lady Ross. They have earned Her Majesty's regard and affection."

With those words, Cecil strolled away, leaving the earl to converse with her and Percy. At first, she thought the earl was very much English, albeit from one of the border counties; his speech was carefully moderated and gave no hint of the man's Scottish birthplace. He also avoided her eyes when he spoke to her. She was accustomed to English lords looking past her or the disdain in their gaze as they attempted to negotiate the Cock & Oyster's prices, but Euston's behavior was different. The nagging sensation that had troubled her since the morning returned, and the urge to flee nearly choked her.

"Lady Ross," Euston said, speaking to her left ear. "I've heard much about your beauty since my arrival in London. To meet you and see the truth of the claims...well, I'm amazed. Would you honor me with a dance, your husband permitting?"

Aisha swallowed the temptation to sneer and proclaim, "You're full of shite, my lord, and I'd dance with Octavius Augustus in hell first." Instead, she looked at Percy for salvation, but he merely nodded, so she accepted the hand held out to her. Euston guided her out to where the other dancers were moving in time to the music.

He'd chosen a pavane, which meant he intended to talk.

"Tell me, Lady Ross," he said. "How is it you managed to entrap Lord Ross?"

She momentarily halted and peered at Euston before she resumed the dance. "How do you know it wasn't the other way around, my lord? Perhaps it was I who was entrapped. Are you enjoying your time in London?"

"No. Were it not for the Queen's summons and an unfinished matter to attend, I wouldn't have left Scotland. Having done my duty to Her Majesty, I've only to see justice is done, and then I should be on my way home in a few days."

The music ended, and Euston escorted her back to Percy. With a soulless bow, he left them. Aisha placed her fingers on Percy's forearm. "A bit too somber for my taste," she quipped. "Hmm, I wonder if a night at the Cock & Oyster would improve his humor?"

"What did he say to you, Aisha?"

She smiled at Percy. "It's what he didn't say that has me curious. Shall we find the wine, imbibe, and make insipid conversations with others so we can depart?"

"As you wish, my lady."

His arm slipped around her waist as they strolled to one of the tables laden with food and drink. Aisha eyed the food and sniffed derisively. "Not eating any of that," she huffed in Arabic. "And don't you dare touch the marzipan. It's undercooked."

Percy sighed. She knew the sweets were the only foods he'd eat when attending such events. He poured a glass of wine for each of them, then guided her toward the only open window in the room.

"I so love you, Lord Ross."

He glanced at her and winked. "It was affecting me, Lady Ross. I'm no longer accustomed to the aromatic flavors of a court gathering."

Her husky laugh earned her a few looks, and she ignored the censorious glances of the masked women. Before they reached the open window, a young man sauntered up to Percy.

"Lord Ross?"

"Yes," Percy replied somewhat curiously.

"My name is Ambrose Allen, a distant cousin to the Earl of Euston—I mean the late Earl of Euston. Don't know too much about the new head of the family, but that's neither here nor there. I was wondering if you would be kind enough to listen to a complaint I have about encroachments in Somerset. I own a small property in the county."

Aisha smiled at Percy, ignoring the man's rudeness. "I shall wait for you near the window, my lord."

Percy's tight-lipped smile betrayed his irritation as he said, "This will not take long, my lady."

She nodded and continued toward the window.

PERCY COULDN'T RECALL MEETING A MORE insipid lackwit than Ambrose Allen. Clearly, the late earl had reasons for avoiding distant relatives. He interrupted Allen's speech. "I have left my wife to her own devices long enough. Perhaps we can continue this conversation another time?"

"Forgive me, my lord. I didn't mean to detain you so long. Please give my apologies to your lady. Enjoy the masquerade."

"Of course," Percy grunted as he pivoted to find Aisha.

His eyes searched the area near the window, but he didn't see her. Refusing to give in to the unsettling feeling in his gut, he scanned the ballroom. Aisha was the only Black woman in attendance and not easily missed. He strode over to the window only to realize what they'd thought a window was a pair of doors opening to an enclosed garden.

Percy hurried outside. It wasn't like Aisha to wander away. A quick search revealed a pair of lovers seated on a stone bench but no sign of his wife. Worry seeped away, and panic began to set in. Returning to the ballroom, he didn't bother apologizing for his rough movements through the crowd. She wasn't in the room.

"Lord Ross?"

He halted and gazed at the servant who spoke his name. "Yes?"

"I was asked to deliver a message from Lady Ross. She asked me to inform you she was suffering a painful headache and would take a sedan chair to Ross House. If you need nothing else, I will go about my duties, my lord."

The messenger walked away, leaving a confused Percy behind. It wasn't like Aisha to up and depart without sending for him; something else must have happened. Percy strode toward the front door, and a footman opened it. Heading toward one of the grooms, he asked, "Did you call for a sedan chair?"

"Yes, my lord. Some time ago for one of the ladies."

"Did you overhear where she wanted to be taken?"

The groom shook his head. "Once she was inside the chair, I returned to my duties. Is something amiss?"

"Did you happen to notice what she was wearing?"

"The woman?" The groom scrunched his nose and said, "A black cloak. I believe her gown was blue, but I only caught a glimpse of the hem when she climbed into the chair. Couldn't see her face as her hood was pulled down and she was masked."

Percy swore and searched for his carriage. Without another word to the groom, he raced over to where Jessup waited. He wrenched the door open and climbed inside, issuing orders as he slammed the door behind him. The carriage jerked as Jessup set the horses in motion.

"If you left without me, Aisha Howard, we will have words. I promise."

The ride to Ross House was interminable, and he blistered the coach's interior, using language he'd never say in his beloved wife's hearing. Frustration and fear ate at him. It wasn't like her to leave without telling him, and his panic grew with each turn of the carriage wheel.

He didn't wait for Jessup to brake the coach as Percy flung open the door and leaped out. Racing up the steps, he banged on the door until Silas stood before him with an alarmed expression.

"Where is she?"

"Where is whom, my lord?"

Percy pushed past him. "My wife, Lady Ross, Aisha Resonne Howard."

Silas stared at his employer's back for a few seconds. "She isn't here because she left with you, my lord."

All Percy heard was, "She isn't here." His heart seized, and he whipped around to face his butler. "What do you mean, she isn't here? She left the masquerade. Took a sedan chair."

With those final two words, he knew it was all a ruse. Aisha had been taken.

THIRTY-ONE

THE HEADACHE WAS POUNDING, and Aisha reached up to massage her temples before the sharp pull of a rope stopped her. Her eyelids flew up, and she stared at her wrists. "Damnation!"

"Not really," a cold voice uttered. "That will come much later, after your husband is dead. By the by, he's probably at Ross House, aggravated that you're not there."

She turned toward the voice, and the pull of more ropes confirmed her capture. Opposite her, the Earl of Euston sat stiffly upright on a chair. Candlelight did nothing to soften the man's angular, thin face, and a shiver raced down her spine.

The painful headache lessened, and she glanced around her. She was in a bedchamber, which likely hadn't seen a good cleaning in months. A small window looked out of place as if an afterthought. "Why would you want my husband dead?"

He tilted his head, a thoughtful expression on his face. "I don't think I'll answer that question just yet, Lady Ross, also known as Aisha Resonne, who played the bawd Ellen Chapman."

Her face must have revealed her amazement because Euston continued with his taunt. "Oh, yes, Ellen, I know so much about you. Sadly, you have no idea who I am, but over the next few days, you will come to understand your plight and why I intend to kill your husband."

He rose from the chair to stand over the bed. Thick, short fingers traced a curious pattern on her temple and cheek, and Aisha flinched beneath the man's rough touch. "Keep your fucking hands off me," she hissed.

"I suppose you prefer the caress of an Englishman," he said. "Alas, mine will be the last you'll ever experience, Ellen. Not yet, though, not until you watch Percy Howard die painfully before your lovely brown eyes. Since you're a married woman and I respect the laws of God, you have not suffered my touch except for me to remove the daggers from your cloak. Ingenious, really."

Euston strolled to the door, unlocked it, and waved someone inside. It was a young girl, not much older than eleven or twelve. She was perhaps far too thin for her age, and Aisha wondered if she was also a captive.

"Allow me to introduce you to Roslyn, who will play the servant's part while you are my guest, Mistress Chapman. She will bring you food and water. In the wardrobe, you'll find clothing suitable to one of your trade. A chamber pot is behind that screen for your needs. Untie her."

Once the ropes were removed, Aisha slowly sat up. Her head swam a bit, and she was tempted to lie down again. Instead, she took several deep breaths. "I'll need a bathing tub and plenty of hot water."

Euston stared at her as if she'd asked for the moon. "A bathing tub?"

"You can't expect me to remain here for a few days and not bathe." She snorted. "You've heard that cleanliness is divine, haven't you? I rarely go a day without a bath. Also, is there someone to clean this room? It's filthy. Cobwebs and dust have taken root here, which means it hasn't been attended to in months, maybe even years. If this is the last place I'll see, I'd prefer it to be clean."

Euston's befuddled face cleared, and he motioned to Roslyn. "Go. Get Andrew to aid you."

"Don't forget the drying sheet and soap without lye. 'Tis very harsh on the skin. Also, clean bed covers and sheets, please."

Roslyn bobbed her head and left the room. Euston inhaled, then released the air. "This room has no escape, Mistress Chapman. I need to see to other matters. The door will be locked, and I possess the only key."

Aisha watched him depart before she climbed off the bed and walked around the small chamber. The window was too small to squeeze through, and the room lacked an antechamber. Besides the bed, there was one chair, a table, and a sleeping pallet. Either Euston intended the girl Roslyn to make her bed in the room, or this was where she usually slept.

A curse escaped Aisha's lips. Her favorite daggers were gone. Alastair Farquhar would pay dearly if she didn't get them back when Percy arrived. At the thought of her beloved Percy, her chest tightened, and she struggled to breathe. He must be frantic with worry. Well, frantic wasn't a word that described Percy's usual reaction—worried, yes, frantic never.

She had no sense of time. Was it day or night? Had the ball ended? If not, was Percy searching for her? Did he return to Ross House believing she'd left without him? What message had Euston sent to him? "Oh, my sweet Lord Ross, your plans for the evening are completely ruined."

Well, until Euston revealed his hand, there was little she

could do but speculate and make her prison as comfortable as possible until Percy arrived.

First things first, clean the room. It was intolerable, and she'd not sleep a wink for fear of creatures skittering about. A small hearth was the only means of warmth. The ashes and blackened grate indicated use, confirming her hypothesis that Roslyn was the room's usual occupant.

The metal slide of a key in the lock alerted her to Euston's return. She hurried back to where she was sitting when he left. The door swung open, and two men carried in buckets of water and placed them near the hearth. They left and returned with a tub just large enough for her to kneel in, setting it near the buckets. Roslyn entered the room, carrying a large basket filled with pieces of cloth and a broom.

"Your bath, my lady," Euston sneered. "Roslyn, start a fire. I'd hate for Lady Ross to expire from the cold before my little interlude is completed."

He headed to the door and looked over his shoulder at her. "Since this chamber does not meet your standards, you and Roslyn can clean the room before supper."

Aisha cursed him and his ancestors in Arabic once the door was closed. With an explosive huff, she stood and went to examine the pieces of cloth in the basket. They looked clean. "If you start the fire, I'll sweep the floors before we replace the bed sheets."

"Yes, my lady."

They worked in silence; Aisha had questions but refused to ask in case a guard stood outside the door. While she couldn't reach the corners of the ceiling, she did manage to remove most of the cobwebs and the thick dust from the walls. Without a word, Roslyn took the broom and continued to clear the room's corners.

Aisha searched for a bowl to fill with water to wash her hands. "Is there a pitcher or bowl for washing?"

"I put one in the basket beneath the cloth, my lady."

"Thank you."

She retrieved it, taking care not to get dust or dirt on the clean sheets and washing cloths. Once she had taken care of her dirty hands, Aisha went to the wardrobe and opened it. Several skirts and bodices hung on hooks. A serviceable nightgown and robe occupied the remaining hook. At least they appeared clean.

"I washed them myself, my lady. Lord Euston didn't want anyone to know they were here," Roslyn said softly.

She turned to the young girl. "Thank you, Roslyn, and for your help in cleaning this chamber."

Roslyn nodded. "I try to keep it tidy, but with me having to help Cook and the housekeeper, Mistress Elspeth, the dirt got beyond me. You should've let me do it, my lady. 'Tis not fit for you to be doing a servant's work."

Aisha shrugged. "It gave me a chance to release my anger at Lord Euston."

The sound of the key turning the lock drew her gaze to the door. Euston stepped inside the room and stood on the threshold while an older woman bustled in, a tray held tight in her hands. She placed the tray on the table and departed.

"Enjoy your supper, and please don't worry about having the tray removed. I'll have Roslyn return it to the kitchen when she goes to do her duties after I pay you a visit in the morning. Sleep well, Ellen."

He remained standing as if waiting for her to reply. Aisha stared at him, her lips pursed until he turned and slammed the door. Her gaze never left the doorframe until she heard the lock click. Only then did she relax her shoulders and cross over to the table to see what lay beneath the covers.

As she lifted one of the covers, she felt somewhat relieved. The dish looked fresh, the meat not overly cooked nor floating in a thick sauce. Peas and carrots were plenty, and the bread was freshly baked, though not warm. Aisha raised the second cover and saw a second bowl. "Come, Roslyn. There is enough for the two of us. It appears you are to share my prison."

Handing Roslyn a bowl and a spoon, Aisha watched her sit on a stool and greedily begin to eat. "Take your time, or you'll have a stomachache. If you need more, I will share."

Embarrassment colored the girl's pale face, but she did slow her eating. Once she felt it was safe to eat, Aisha spooned some of the stew into her mouth, tasting the parsley and rosemary that made it flavorful. Sitting on the sole chair in the room, she ate and offered a silent prayer to the ancestors that it wasn't poisoned. She had no reason to trust Euston, but the hatred in his blue eyes when he spoke Percy's name indicated the man played a deep game. Although she couldn't explain her reasoning, she was certain Euston wouldn't harm her unless Percy were there to witness.

A jug of water and two tin cups were on the tray, and she filled both, offering one to Roslyn, who stammered her thanks and placed it near her feet. "How old are you, Roslyn?"

"Thirteen years, my lady. My birthday is in two months, and I'll be fourteen."

"Is this your bedchamber?"

Roslyn dipped her chin. "Aye, since my lord arrived in London. He fetched me from where I slept with the scullery maids and placed me in here. I was scared for a bit, but now I don't have to worry much."

Aisha understood what wasn't spoken and, with a nervous swallow, asked another question. "Why do you call me 'my lady?'"

"Am I not supposed to? I mean, I heard my lord call you

Lady Ross as well as those other names and mentioned your husband's name, so I just assumed, I mean..."

"You were doing what any servant would do," Aisha said with a chuckle. "Listening at closed doors, eh? Good for you; that way, you'll know what to expect when you walk in. I think I'll bathe now."

Although she had no problem preparing her bath, Aisha let Roslyn do the work. It was obvious the girl was terrified on several counts, the worst being her fear of Euston, and that meant she had to rely on herself to get free. "Here, let me help with the water."

While Roslyn poured heated water into the small tub, Aisha emptied one of the buckets. Once the water was warm enough, she moved the screen into place for privacy before placing a drying sheet, along with the nightgown and robe, over the top of the screen.

A faint chuckle accompanied her awkwardly positioning herself in the tub. *This tub isn't big enough for an infant.* It didn't take long for her to cleanse most of her body as the water cooled rapidly.

Stepping out, she grabbed the drying sheet. The room wasn't warm enough to linger, so she dried, slipped on the gown and robe, and went to the hearth to warm up.

"If I may, my lady," Roslyn stammered, "might I use the bath? Sarah the Cook won't let me bathe like I want, says it causes ague and attracts insects."

"Sometimes these silly English people work my sensibilities," Aisha muttered. "Of course. Is there somewhere to empty the water?"

"Aye, the privy. I'll do it. Sarah the Cook isn't English. Lord Euston won't have them in his employ."

Aisha tied the robe's sash around her waist and rolled up the edges of the sleeves. "It'll take both our strengths."

By the time they tipped the tub over the privy hole, Aisha felt she needed another bath. While Roslyn heated more water, she poured one of the last two buckets into the tub. "Do you have a nightgown?"

"No, but I'll sleep in my shift."

Aisha searched the wardrobe until she found several linen shifts in a drawer. Snatching one, she strode over to where Roslyn stood, taking off her gown. "Here, this is clean. Wear it tonight."

She pursed her lips thoughtfully, then smiled. *Oh, my Lord Euston, you have no idea what you've gotten yourself into.* Climbing into bed, she polished her plan of attack.

"Thank you, my lady."

"No need to thank me, Roslyn. A warm bath always makes one feel better." As Roslyn settled on the pallet beside the foot of the bed, Aisha huffed. "Take one of the bedcovers so you'll be warm. Good night."

"Thank you," Roslyn happily answered as she grabbed one of the folded covers.

Another item on Lord Euston's must-do list—a trundle bed for Roslyn. With that thought, Aisha whispered her love for Percy and drifted into sleep.

THIRTY-TWO

Percy leaned against the bedpost, staring at his unmade
bed. The only impression on the mattress was his, reminding
him Aisha hadn't slept nestled beside him. "Where the fuck is
she?"

A sleepless night that seemed endless had him reliving his
mistake. He shouldn't have let her out of sight, should have kept
her at his side until they left the masquerade ball. Instead, his
wife had been taken, and he had no idea where or by whom.

A rap on his door broke his thoughts. "Come in, Silas."

The butler entered, his face carved with sadness. "My lord,
Lord Salisbury is in the small parlor. As is Master John
Resonne and his son Simon."

Percy nodded and followed him downstairs. When they
reached the salon door, Silas hesitated before opening it.
Clearing his throat, he gazed at Percy. "My lady is resourceful,
so I've no fear we'll find her safe. The entire household is ready
to do whatever is necessary to bring her home."

"Thank you, Silas," Percy said, humbled by the man's
obvious affection for Aisha. "So am I."

"One last thing, my lord." Percy peered at him as a tight-lipped smile formed on Silas's mouth. "Mistress Stone asks that you deliver the villain's head on a wooden plate since they don't deserve silver."

Percy's laughter provoked a soft chuckle from his butler. "That I will, Silas. Although Lady Ross may achieve the deed before me."

"Too true, too true. Was my lady armed as usual?"

"She was, but I suspect the kidnapper found her daggers since they were in her cloak, and we'd be visiting the jail if she remained in possession of them. Now, let me tend to my visitors so we can get her home quickly as possible."

Percy entered the salon to find Cecil and John Resonne in quiet conversation. John's son Simon stood near the glass-plated door leading out to the garden. The man's back was rigid as tension had taken hold and refused to release him. Shutting the door behind him, Percy strode into the room.

"Good morning and thank you for attending me so quickly."

With the impetuousness of youth, Simon whirled and demanded, "How did my cousin come to be kidnapped?"

"Simon," his father said, a warning in his voice. "Good morning, Percy. You have the appearance of an old, tattered rug a hound would drag into the house as a gift. I take it you've had no word from my niece or her kidnapper?"

Percy flinched at the gentle tone of the older man. He'd expected him to be enraged, especially since John had worried about the effect of their marriage on Aisha. They hadn't been married a full year, and now she was in danger. "No, not yet. I have spoken to a few people I've worked with before, and they are investigating avenues I can't."

He turned to Cecil. "Good morning, Lord Salisbury. Thank you for coming. Please, everyone, shall we sit?"

Silas knocked on the door and entered the room. "Mistress

Stone said you need to eat, my lord. Said she won't have you wasting away and Lady Ross thinking you wasn't being properly fed. If you value your ears, you and your guests will accompany me to the small dining room."

Cecil's hearty laughter eased some of the tension in the parlor, and the men followed Silas to the dining room. Percy smiled when he spied the table. Martha had prepared a simple breakfast just as she would if Aisha were there. Steam rose from the atay cups placed before each of them. Once everyone was seated and food served, Silas and the footman departed.

Lifting his cup to his nostrils, Percy slowly inhaled and begged Aisha's ancestors to keep her safe until he brought her home. He relinquished the breath and brought the cup to his lips to sip before he set the exquisitely painted cup on the table.

"My Lord Secretary," he said to Cecil. "What can you tell me about Alastair Farquhar? Why was my presence—and my wife's—required?"

A flush briefly colored Cecil's face. He set his cup on the table and stared at Percy. "I was about to ask you the same question, Percy. Why would Euston specifically request your presence, claiming to Her Majesty you were acquainted?"

"I have no idea what you're talking about, my lord," he snapped. "Until last night when you introduced us, I'd never met Euston."

For all the time he'd worked with Robert Cecil, Percy hadn't seen him flustered, yet the man sitting opposite him was that and more. Tension radiated across the table as John and Simon leaned forward. Before Percy could press the Lord Secretary, John Resonne gently set his cup down and focused his piercing brown eyes on Cecil's face.

"My lord, do you believe this man, this Euston, has my niece? And if so, why? Clearly, it has something to do with Percy's service to you and Her Majesty."

"'Tis a fair question, Resonne, and I have no answer."

"Tell me about the man's lineage," Percy demanded.

Cecil didn't flinch at the abrupt tone. "He was a great nephew to Gregory Allen, Earl of Euston, by way of Allen's sister Maude who was Farquhar's grandmother. Maude fell in love with Hugh Campbell, a minor Scottish lord, and eloped with the man. The late earl disowned her, and nothing was heard of her or her children. Alastair Farquhar's father was the son of Maude and her second husband James Farquhar and, until his elevation, Alastair had never set foot in England."

"How long has the man been in England, my lord?" Simon inquired. "Has he visited a tailor while here?"

Cecil shrugged. "I have no idea." He rubbed his forehead. "Quite frankly, I've been busy ferreting out those who plot against the Queen's rule. Given the man's dour manner, I doubt he's done much beyond court appearances and speaking with lawyers. The late earl's extravagance may prove costly to the young man."

"What is his mother's name? Is he wed? What do you know about Ambrose Allen, who tied me up in pointless conversation while someone kidnapped my wife?"

The Lord Secretary pulled out a packet from inside his coat and handed it to Percy. "Understand, Ross, I've not had much time to gather information, so that task will fall into your lap. It details the Allens; nothing about the Farquhar line. Scots, you know."

Cecil rose from his chair. "I'm sorry I can't be of more aid at the moment. I ask that you be discreet should Euston be connected to Lady Ross's disappearance. I'd prefer not to answer Her Majesty's questions or the King of Scotland's."

With those parting words, he strode out of the dining room. Percy opened the packet and studied the papers. His eyes widened when he spied a name long forgotten. Emeline Farquhar died in a carriage accident nearly twelve years ago.

"What is it, Percy?" John asked. "You have the oddest look on your face."

He raised his eyes to Aisha's uncle. "I'm not certain, John. There's a name among the ones listed I hadn't thought about in a long time. A woman my cousin Rupert and I once helped escape a horrific marriage. Sadly, she and Rupert died in a carriage accident. What I can't fathom is what connects her to Euston unless she is a relative of his."

Simon's fingers tapped the table. "What do you intend to do, Percy?"

"I promised my wife I'd give up my spying activities, but the situation demands otherwise. I'm certain she'll forgive me...in time, and once she's back in Eggford."

"Forgive you for what, nephew?"

The door swung open. Robert and Ahmara Howard strolled into the room, and the men rose from their chairs. "What will the lovely Aisha forgive you for, and where is she when a cabal of men are eating at her table?"

John was the first to move, going to his sister and embracing her. "Come sit, Mara."

"I don't like the looks of things," she grumbled. "You're being awfully nice, brother."

Once she was seated, everyone else sat. Percy sucked in a breath and then forcibly blew it out. There was no other way than direct. "Someone kidnapped Aisha, Ahmara."

Ahmara's gasp, followed by a litany of Arabic insults and threats, had her brother and nephew cringing. "Al'okht," John said, seeking to calm her. "You cannot behead people who might be innocent of this crime. Also, I believe al'ab would frown on your immodest language."

Smothered chuckles only exacerbated Ahmara's vitriol

before she speared Percy with a familiar look. He ducked his chin and peered at her. She was Aisha's aunt in all manner of ways.

"What are you doing to return my niece to her home, Percy Elwen Howard? Besides enjoying your breakfast and the atay she lovingly brought into your English life!" Ahmara demanded. "And you, akhi, with all your wealth and power, have you instituted a search for Isha?"

Robert Howard placed an arm around his wife. "Mara, sweet love, perhaps we should hear the details before we set fire to London, which I don't think is a very good idea, but if it's what you wish, I will light the first torch."

Silas walked into the room and placed a cup of atay before Ahmara. "Martha thought you might need this once Lord Ross informed you of the horrid circumstances affecting us."

Ahmara patted Silas's hand. "Thank you, Silas, and thank Martha. 'Tis exactly what I need. To arrive in London for a visit and discover my sweet Isha has been taken by a murderous assassin...'tis too much, too much."

"I don't have much information to share, Ahmara," Percy began. "Isha and I attended a masquerade ball last evening at the invitation of the Earl of Euston."

Robert's face creased in thought, and Percy suppressed a pained sigh. "Percy, my boy. Edgar Allen died several months ago. I attended the man's burial since he was a neighbor. Not a very friendly one. I think he was bled far too many times and became naturally bilious and prickly from the bleedings. I've rarely met a more disagreeable old fart."

Percy's gaze swept the table, noting the struggle on both John's and Simon's faces. "Uncle, Edgar Allen is quite dead. I'm referring to his heir, Alastair Farquhar."

"A Scot?" Robert's bark of laughter nearly fractured the Resonnes' fragile hold on their amusement. "Allen must be turning in his coffin. He hated that nation ever since his sister Maude eloped with that Campbell lad. Farquhar, you say? Let me think."

Accustomed to his uncle's tangents, Percy waited patiently for the collection of odd bits and memories to coalesce into useful information. Had Robert Howard been blessed to be a woman, he would be the keeper of histories.

"Aha! I have it." Robert sipped his atay and cleared his throat. "Maude Allen refused to marry where Edgar wanted. She'd fallen in love with Hugh Campbell, a second son. Edgar rejected Campbell's suit, so the pair eloped. Nothing was heard of Maude after that, although Edgar was quite pleased when her ward Emeline Farquhar fled an abusive marriage and traveled to Carlisle to seek his protection. Sadly, Emeline perished in a carriage accident on her way to London."

"Did you say Emeline Farquhar?"

Robert nodded. "I believe that was her married name, although Edgar referred to her as Emeline Thompson. Must've been her maiden name."

"Damnation," Percy muttered. "It's all my fault."

He pushed back his chair and started for the door before looking back at everyone. "Forgive me, but I need to send riders north posthaste. Uncle, Ahmara, I do hope you plan to remain here."

Ahmara snorted. "I'm not leaving this house or London until I see my niece in the flesh. Does Bella know?"

John shook his head. "We haven't had a chance to tell the rest of the family."

She stood and went to her brother. "Come, akhi. We'll do so together."

THIRTY-THREE

THE KNOCK CAME JUST as Aisha slipped her feet into her shoes. She knew the solid whack wasn't born of respect but a deliberate reminder of her imprisoned state, especially when the lock clicked and the handle moved down. The door swung open and the same woman, Sarah the Cook, who'd brought supper the previous night, entered, carrying a tray.

"What is it?" Aisha asked.

"Porridge and bacon with warm bread. Ale to wash it down your throat."

"Thank you."

Farquhar stepped into the chamber. "Good morning, Cleo."

Immaculately dressed in somber black garments, he appeared evil incarnate, Aisha thought before chiding herself for such theatrics. He was a man like any nobleman she'd engaged as Ellen Chapman. "Good morning."

He waited until the woman departed before he shut the door. "I trust your sleep was untroubled."

"It was."

"Please eat lest your meal gets cold; cold porridge is difficult to digest. I hope you don't mind if I sit on the bed while you dine?"

He sat in the very spot she'd abandoned to go to the table. Lifting the covers, she frowned and tore the large piece of bread in two. She beckoned to Roslyn, who was standing silently in a corner.

"Come eat. I don't relish bacon, so it's yours. I'll save you a portion of the porridge."

Aisha sat at the table and ate half of the porridge before giving what was left to Roslyn, along with the ale. Raising a cup to her lips, she sipped water to wash the bread down. "Lord Euston."

"Yes?"

"Since I'm your hostage—"

"My guest."

"Whatever," Aisha grunted. "I have a few requests for my comfort."

Farquhar's eyebrow lifted in surprise before he tented his fingers and leaned forward. "I'm listening."

"Have you paper and pen? My requests are very specific."

He eyed her before he sent Roslyn to fetch what she needed. "What are you up to, Lady Ross?"

"Seeing to my comfort. I'm not used to living like English people," she said. "I bathe regularly, I'm disgusted by poorly prepared foods, and I don't care to starve the people who make my life pleasant."

Roslyn returned with the paper and a pencil. "I got them from your scribe, my lord."

"Fine, just give them to her."

"Thank you. First, I'll need better soap—the one I used last evening was quite drying to my skin—as well as some oils and a packet of atay. I've noted the shop where I purchase these. Second, I'll need fresh water delivered in the morning and evening. Also, I prefer wine; the best ones are from Burgundy. Since you've assigned Roslyn to be my companion, we will require enough water for both of us to bathe."

She paused, tapping the pencil against her chin. "I'd like to speak to your cook about my meals. We will need warmer garments for Roslyn, and lastly, I'd like a trundle bed for her. She can't be a good companion if she falls ill."

Farquhar had sat listening to her, his mouth gaping. Aisha grinned inwardly. He had no idea how difficult she would make his life until he released her. He blinked several times before he asked, "Is there anything else?"

She scrunched up her lips before she smiled. "No, I believe that's sufficient for the moment. It really depends on how long you intend to play this petty game."

"This isn't a game," he hissed. "Your husband has cost me dearly, far more than you can imagine. I intend to exact my revenge, and you're the key to achieving my plan."

"Which is my husband's death," she retorted. "What I do not understand is why. What did he do to you that was so vile you'd seek his death?"

Farquhar rose from the bed and motioned for Roslyn to remove the tray. Once she'd left the room, he stared at Aisha, and her blood chilled. The hostility she saw in his blue eyes threatened her show of calm. Such hatred for one man was difficult to fathom.

"You have no idea what spurns my animus toward Percy Howard."

"Didn't I just make that statement, my lord?" she declared. "Make me understand why you went through this ruse to entrap him. Why am I being held against my will, and how long do you plan to keep me caged?"

"In due time, Lady Ross. In due time." A faint tap at the door drew his attention from her before his eyes focused once more on her face. For a brief moment, he studied her, his face impassioned, then he tilted his head and said, "'Under a compelling occasion, let women die; it were a pity to cast them away for nothing...between them and a great cause, they should be esteemed nothing.'

"I'm sure you recognize the lines from William Shakespeare's infamous tragedy. If Mark Antony had returned to Rome as he should have, he might have become Caesar. Alas, he loved a tawny Queen who cost him his life." He opened the door and let Roslyn back into the room. "It was fitting for you and your husband to attend costumed as Antony and Cleopatra, my dusky queen. Quite fitting. I shall see that your requests are taken care of and leave you with this parting thought: Fulvia is dead."

The door closed behind him, and the lock noisily engaged. Aisha's shoulders shed the tight knots of tension that kept her upright as she slumped on the chair. Her show of strength had taken something out of her.

"Would you like some water, my lady?"

She looked up and saw the compassion in Roslyn's brown eyes. "No, thank you. Sit and tell me about yourself. It will help to pass time."

"There isn't much to tell, my lady," Roslyn said with sadness. "My lord tells me I was a foundling and given to a parish home for orphans in Carlisle."

"What happened to your mother? Your father?"

"I've no idea, except I was told my mother was an adulteress and died escaping with her lover. I assume he was my father."

Intrigued, Aisha encouraged the girl to share her memories and past, hoping it would give some clues behind Euston's actions. "How did you come into Lord Euston's service?"

"The parish sent me to work as a scullery maid in a house that belonged to the previous earl. I was fearful I'd be turned out because none of the other girls cared for me, and I got pinched and slapped when Sarah the Cook wasn't looking."

A wan smile surfaced on Roslyn's thin face. "My lord came to visit that house, 'twas in Carlisle, and the housekeeper, Mistress Bennett, sent me to scrub the fireplace in the master's bedchamber. I was leaving the room when the new earl saw me. Before he left the house, he ordered me and a few others to make this house ready for his visit to London, including two of the girls who'd mistreated me."

"Why haven't you complained to the housekeeper here? Is she the same Mistress Bennett?"

"No, Mistress Bennett is kind, and Lord Euston left her at the Carlisle house. 'Tis Mistress Elspeth who runs this house, and one of the cruel girls is her niece, Sadie. Molly is kind except when Sadie is around. It's Sadie who pinches and hits me."

Aisha had been listening with one ear, the other paying attention to sounds in the corridor. She pressed a finger to her lips, silencing Roslyn. The door creaked open, and a young woman about eighteen years of age came into the room. Behind her was a footman carrying a large basket. He set it inside the door and left, returning with another basket.

The young woman set a tray of food on the table, and Aisha realized she was hungry. Her eyes followed the man who struggled to bring two buckets of water into the room and set them near the tub. The footman inclined his head. "Where do ye wish the trundle?"

"The foot of the bed."

She watched with decided amusement as the bedchamber was transformed into something livable, although she was curious why Euston played her game. Once the servants left, the earl walked in. He stopped on the threshold and, with the left corner of his mouth slightly curled, asked whether she was satisfied with her accommodations.

"I am, Lord Euston. I would give you my thanks, but it would be a lie since I'm your prisoner."

He sucked his teeth. "My *guest*. Your husband will be my prisoner when the time comes."

"How long do you intend to keep me here?" Aisha snapped.

Euston's smile reformed, cruelty laced across his thin lips. "Did I forget to mention, my dear Queen? This will be your home for the unforeseeable future. 'Tis why I humored your troublesome demands. By the by, I received a request to meet with Lord Ross. I'm certain it's to discuss your disappearance. Alas, I know very little since I was attending to my guests. Enjoy your new home, Aisha Howard."

THIRTY-FOUR

The heavily cloaked figure stepped from behind a large crate. Jamie Sewell spied Percy and walked over. "Here ye are, Octavius. Now, pay your Hector what you owe."

Percy took the packet the man held out and tucked it inside a secret pocket in his cloak before handing him a coin-filled purse. "Is there a reason for us meeting in a dockside alley?"

"I figured it was better snooping eyes didn't see you 'cause there are some who still have an itch to carve their initials on yer arse."

"Good observation, Hector. I'll send word if I need your services again."

"Any time, Octavius. Hope you find what yer looking for."

"Have you ever known me to fail?"

"Nah," Jamie replied with a rumble of laughter. "But don't strut too much and forget what's at stake."

In the harsh light of day, it would be easy to see his face, but the approach of evening revealed nothing, and Percy's voice was sharp when he said, "I haven't. I promise a head will roll for this."

"Good, 'cause I kinda like what was taken. Too bad you got there first. Don't go losing such a priceless work of art, or I'll find it and claim it for meself."

Percy shook his head and laughed softly. "I'll keep that in mind. Fare thee well."

Leaving the alley, he slipped into the Fool's Head tavern, where he'd often meet his agents, and seated himself in a darkened corner. It provided a view of the door and obscurity at the same time. The tavern maid brought his ale, and he paid her before he drank slowly.

He'd been followed but wasn't worried. Jamie had little tolerance for incompetence. Percy suspected the man lay in the same alley, his throat slit and his pockets inside out. The door swung open, and someone yelled for it to be closed while a few customers complained of the dripping water from the man's cloak.

Asia Resonne nodded to the tavern maid and motioned for a tankard before he claimed the chair opposite Percy. Once the maid delivered his ale and left, Asia took a long sip then set the tankard on the table. "Evening, Octavius. I was told you need a ride. Let me see your coin."

Percy grinned and laid two shillings on the table.

"That's for the ale; where are the coins for my boat?"

"Thief," Percy retorted. "Here. Finish your drink so I can get home before dawn."

The two men drank their ale in quiet solidarity, Percy musing on the packet of papers inside his cloak. He wouldn't read them until he was in his study, where he could make sense of his suspicions, but without certainty he couldn't make a move. He drained the last of his ale.

Asia stood. "My thirst is quenched. Let's go."

Percy rose and followed the man outside, stopping long enough to leave another coin for the tavern maid. They walked until they reached the quay where Asia's wherry was tied. In minutes, the river was carrying them north to Westminster Bridge.

"What did you discover, Lord Ross?"

Used to Asia's directness, Percy sighed. "Nothing yet. I'm hoping the papers Jamie just delivered will have information. Once I verify my suspicions, I'll send word to John."

"And the Lord Secretary?"

"He wants no knowledge, and I intend to grant him his wish."

"Good. Well, here you are, and there's Samuel with the coach. Peace go with you, Lord Ross," Asia said as he steered as close to the steps as possible.

Percy climbed out. "And with you, Asia. Also, I believe that's our coachman, Jessup."

"Jessup. Samuel." Asia shrugged nonchalantly. "You know it's difficult to tell your kind apart."

Asia put the boat in motion, heading toward Southwark, and Percy climbed the steps to where his coach sat. Jessup jumped down and opened the door. Once inside, Percy felt the familiar jerk as the horses started for Ross House. He leaned back and closed his eyes, praying the papers confirmed who took Aisha and where she was held captive.

ROSS HOUSE WAS QUIET, the bustle of the day finally subsiding. Percy sat in his sitting room, a glass of wine in his hand and the papers Jamie gave him splayed across his thighs. There was no longer any doubt Alastair Farquhar had taken Aisha and the reason for her abduction. A knock on the door had him saying, "I'm fine, Silas. I don't need anything else tonight."

The door opened, and his uncle and Ahmara walked in. "Except someone to talk to," Ahmara stated.

She crossed over to the divan and sat while her husband poured himself a glass of wine and plopped beside her. "No use drinking alone, nephew. Now, tell us what is in those papers on your lap."

Percy stared into the flames burning in the hearth. "It seems the woman I helped my cousin Rupert rescue was Emeline Farquhar, the present Lord Euston's late wife."

"Percy, no," Ahmara gasped.

"Rupert sent word he needed my aid. When I arrived in Carlisle, he said he'd fallen in love and intended to elope to France. I didn't ask, believing it was better to not know much. I arranged for him and Emeline to travel in a coach I'd often use in my employment."

He raised the glass to his lips and finished his wine. "We were to meet at St. Katherine's dock. I wasn't overly worried when they didn't arrive at the appointed time. A storm had left the roads in poor condition, and I assumed they'd sheltered in an inn or tavern, but an agent sent word that the carriage never made it to the meeting place, and he'd retrieved the dead and taken them to Rupert's family."

"The secrecy was because Rupert was traveling with her, I take it," Robert stated.

Percy nodded. "No one but me knew Emeline was with him, and that she was pregnant. They were buried in the same grave as man and wife, Emma and Rupert Grey. I sent word to Edgar Allen since my cousin wanted him notified should matters go awry."

Ahmara went to him and kissed the top of his head. "You did nothing wrong, Percy. You stood by your cousin. If anyone is to blame, it is this Farquhar beast, and he shall pay. Now, how do we find out where he's holding Isha?"

"Farquhar denies holding her, and without the Queen's warrant, I can't have his house searched. I've set watchers at Euston's three estates nearest London. I should have word of any unusual activity by tomorrow or the next day, and then I can plan."

He rose from his chair. "In the meantime, we should retire. Good night, Ahmara, Uncle."

THIRTY-FIVE

Elspeth Reid stomped into Euston's library after he said, "Enter." Her eyes flashing with irritation, she slammed the door and marched over to his desk. "My lord, you have to do something with That Woman."

Farquhar glanced at his housekeeper before he sighed wearily. "What has she done now?"

Elspeth sucked in a generous breath and heaved it from her chest. "What has she done? She's completely disrupted my orderly house. She bathes daily, and you know that's dangerous. I'm surprised she hasn't suffered an ague as much time as she spends in water. It's gotten so none of the footmen are around when I have need of them."

"I'll have a word with her."

"That's not the worst of her sins," Elspeth huffed. "She's corrupting Molly. As soon as the girl finishes her chores, she races down to that woman's chamber and remains there until I have to send someone to fetch her."

"I'll speak to Mistress Chapman," he reiterated. "I'm sure 'tis nothing."

"Son, I'm a good Christian woman, baptized in the kirk, and I know wickedness when I see it. She's a temptress, like that Salome or that wicked Egyptian...what's her name...aye, Cleopatra! Beware, she'll corrupt you as she's corrupting Molly and Roslyn, though given Roslyn's birth, there's not far for her to fall."

"Must I remind you to use my title?" Euston warned. "Your loose tongue will cost me all."

"Forgive me," Elspeth mumbled. "It's just—"

He rose from his chair. "No more needs to be said. I will handle Lady Ross."

With this pronouncement, Elspeth whirled and left the library. Farquhar reached for the whisky bottle and cup he kept in a desk drawer. Pouring himself a drink, he drank the whisky and refilled his cup. Aisha Howard was fast becoming a pain in his Scotsman's arse.

Though he wasn't worried his servants would help her escape, he found she'd charmed everyone who came in contact with her except Elspeth Reid. What cooked his goose was that her prison had become a luxurious haven. Lady Ross wasn't suffering, in fact, behaving much like Shakespeare's tawny Egyptian. If anyone was overset by her captivity, it was him. He wasn't certain how she'd managed to turn his household upside down in a matter of days, although he had to admit he was quite amused by Lady Ross's antics. Despite his threats, she went about as if she were settled in her residence, unperturbed by the fact that both she and her husband would die soon.

Farquhar replayed their last conversation in his mind, and a tinge of regret briefly tightened his chest. He'd taunted her with the idea of watching Percy Howard's life leach slowly from his body through a thousand cuts. The horror in Aisha Howard's dark brown eyes had pleased him, for it meant he'd finally pierced the barrier she'd erected from the first day. Her courage was slipping.

It was a fleeting moment, and he found himself engaging a side of her he hadn't expected. Most likely, he thought, it was how Ellen Chapman made the Cock & Oyster one of the finest brothels in London.

A brisk rap on the door had him cursing. "What is it?"

"My lord, you must do something!" Elspeth gasped and slammed the door behind her. "No work is getting done, and you need to do something immediately. If she's being held, then you need to treat her like the sinner she is."

He rose from his chair. "I said I'll see to the matter."

"Forgive me." Elspeth sighed. "I've raised you since you were a babe and stood by you when that woman broke your heart. I'll not stand by and watch you grow weak because of that tawny witch's charms. Once we've taken care of Howard and his besmirched wife, we can return home."

She turned to leave, then hesitated. "Don't forget who you are, Alastair Evan Farquhar. Percy Howard and Rupert Grey stole your wife and your unborn heir."

Farquhar sneered. "Are you certain it was mine? After all, Emeline came to me pregnant with another man's seed."

Elspeth's smile was icy. "Of this second child, I am certain. Do what you vowed, Alastair. Percy Howard must suffer."

"I will. You needn't worry, he will suffer."

With a nod, she left the room.

AISHA SHIVERED as she watched Molly and Roslyn practice a pavane. Closing her eyes, she fought the choking sensation of dread. A giggle brought her back from the edge, and she grinned as Molly broke into a jig, singing a bawdy tune about a country lad and his foolish love. The two girls had put aside their initial animosity and found a bit of joy whenever they were in the chamber. Their presence broke the monotony of her imprisonment and staved off her fears until Euston paid his ritual visit to torment her.

The door abruptly swung open, and she swore in Arabic. She hadn't heard the familiar cue—the turn of the lock—that presaged Euston's appearance. Molly's voice froze mid-song while a startled Roslyn clapped her hands over her mouth.

"Your visit is unexpected, Lord Euston," Aisha declared. "Had I known, we would have prepared you a cup of atay."

"Leave, the both of you," he hissed at Molly and Roslyn.

"Roslyn, stay," Aisha snapped. Her eyes raked Euston. "It is not appropriate for me to be in your presence without a chaperone, Lord Euston."

His voice was shrill when he shouted, "I said leave!"

Both girls rushed from the room, and he slammed the door, locking it. With a feral look, he took a step toward Aisha. "You will never countermand my orders again, Lady Ross. You've acted as if your time here is a frivolous lark, but I promise you that changes now."

He flung a package at her, narrowly missing her head. It landed on the floor. "Pick it up."

Aisha half-turned her back to him. "Lord Euston, I am not an inferior you can order about. Might I suggest you retrieve your package and hand it to me like a civilized nobleman?"

"Do not test me, Lady Ross. My patience is a worn thread. Now pick it up." Once Aisha held the package, his voice lost its feral tone. "You will join me for supper this evening, and I expect you to adorn yourself with what is contained inside. Antony's sojourn in your arms and court has come to an end."

Aisha's eyes widened. "What do you mean?"

"Tonight, I'm holding a supper masquerade for you, Lord

Ross, and myself. Wherein, my wanton Cleopatra, you will learn what sins your lord Antony has committed, what ignoble deeds he has basely done. And at his death, I will offer you, tawny Queen, a choice of ending your life, including the one by which your namesake died."

"You've lost all reason!" She flung the package on the bed and stood defiantly before Euston. "You won't win. You've held me captive nearly a week and yet you're no closer to breaking my spirit than the first day. I have no idea what compels you, what caused such hatred in you against my husband—"

Spittle formed at the corners of Euston's lips as he gnashed his teeth before snarling, "You want to know the cause of my hatred? Why your precious Lord Ross, Lord Salisbury's favorite spy and the man who cost me what no man should take from another, must die? Sit, Cleo. Sit while I tell you a tale of a seductress who led a noble lord astray."

Aisha sat on the chair. "Is this going to be a five-act tragedy as written by Kit Marlowe or a comedy of errors as penned by Will Shakespeare? If it's the former, would you mind sending for some wine?"

Euston blinked several times before he roared with laughter. "If you weren't beyond the age of bearing children, Aisha Howard, I'd take you to wife just to break your will."

He strolled to the door, flung it open, and bellowed for wine. Aisha heard the rush of footsteps and gasps from the footman, who arrived a few minutes later with a bottle and goblets. Euston snatched the tray from the man and shut the door. "Come fetch your wine."

Aisha smiled sweetly. "Of course, Lord Euston."

She rose to take the tray from him and placed it on the table. "Shall I pour?"

A growl rumbled from his chest, and he turned to lock the door. Aisha swallowed the chuckle that threatened to break free and filled the goblets with wine. "I'm going to assume the wine isn't poisoned since my part is to play the audience."

She handed him one and returned to the chair. He swallowed half of the wine. "Do you know the name Rupert Grey?" Aisha shook her head. "He was your husband's kinsman, a cousin on Ross's mother's side. Emeline Thompson was the goddaughter of my grandmother, Maude Allen."

Aisha sipped her wine. "I recognize none of these names except my husband's, so I assume this isn't a comedy."

"Your wit is waning thin, Lady Ross," Euston warned. "Bloodline is important to my family. We never marry willy-nilly nor out of our race."

"And yet you remarked on taking me to wife. I do believe I'm outside your race," she commented.

"True, but I'm beginning to understand Ross's fascination with you," he replied thoughtfully. "Anyway, my grandmother contracted a union between Emeline and myself when we were five and eight years of age, respectively."

"Are you always so correct in your speech, Lord Euston?" Aisha queried. "Wouldn't it be just as meaningful to say, 'Emeline was five and I was eight'?"

"Because of her birth," he continued as if Aisha hadn't interrupted, "she was presented to the King's court where she met Rupert Grey, a second son who made his wealth in trade."

"Isn't that expected of the spare sons of noble families?" She took another sip. "You know, Euston, I've always thought that particular snobbery was quite misguided. Embarrassed by a family member in trade, tush! What if the heir needed funds to make repairs to the estate? If his brother is wealthy, he could turn to him rather than a moneylender or a lawyer. It really is a silly rule."

She tilted her head and then righted it. "And what your kind does to women, tsk, tsk. Marry them off when they're far too young, shame them if some scoundrel seduces them with promises of marriage, turn them out when they don't obey."

"We aren't discussing society, and there's nothing wrong with my speech."

"Have you ever uttered a curse, Lord Euston?"

He sniffed his disdain. "Of course."

"Let me hear it. Your most offensive lashing out."

"Not in a lady's presence," he said, taken aback.

She grinned. "But you've made it clear that I'm not quite the lady you would associate with. You've labeled me a temptress, among other names. So I'd like to hear the worst curse you've uttered."

"Are you drunk?"

"No, quite far from it. Swear for me, Lord Euston. If you strolled into Ellen Chapman's Cock & Oyster and found yourself in bed with a courtesan who loves to hear the vilest language while sucking your prick, what would you murmur in her ear?"

She laughed when he choked on his wine and gaped at her. It took Euston a minute or two to regain control. "We are not discussing something so personal, Lady Ross."

She shrugged. "Forgive me, Lord Euston. If I'm to join you for supper, I will need to bathe. Please finish your story."

Completely baffled, Farquhar drained his glass. "I married Emeline when she was eighteen. I didn't know she'd a lover and was with child by him. When I discovered the truth, I sent the child to an orphanage in Carlisle. As much as I wanted to repudiate Emeline, I had to maintain face and keep her locked away until I seeded a child inside her. Then her father died, and she begged me to let her attend his burial. I did, sending outriders and a maidservant along."

He muttered what sounded like 'fuck,' but Aisha couldn't be sure. Before she could extend the man a smidge of pity, he lumbered on. "It was a ruse, although her father did die not long after. Emeline snuck out of her father's house and ran away with Rupert Grey, aided and abetted by your husband, who provided his cousin the carriage. My wife's adulterous elopement ended in tragedy as she and Grey perished in a carriage accident. Percy Howard, your husband, is the only guilty party to escape punishment for his crimes."

Euston set the glass on the tray. "If you'll excuse me, Lady Ross, I have arrangements to make for tonight's festivities. To paraphrase your Shakespeare, 'All's but naught and patience is a Scot's blood. Impatience, on the other hand, does become a dog that's mad: then is it sin.' I've been patient long enough, Lady Ross. Long enough. 'Tis time to become like a dog that's mad and embrace a momentary impatience to see vengeance is done. Once that is achieved, my blood will cleanse the sin."

Aisha watched him walk from the room, his back rigid and his fists clenched. Once the door was shut and locked, she set her wine glass on the tray.

"I may not be a Scotswoman, but I have patience you've not touched, Lord Euston. Now that I know the reason you've threatened what is mine, I will make certain the game ends tonight," she said softly. "If anyone is to punish Percy Elwen Howard, it will be me."

THIRTY-SIX

"I've been summoned," Percy gritted out.

Robert Howard lifted his gaze to his nephew while Ahmara sipped from her atay and said, "Cecil can't be serious. Doesn't he understand the precariousness of the situation?"

"It's not Cecil. When I called on Euston, he lied when he said he knew nothing of Aisha's whereabouts. Now he admits she is his captive, and," Percy looked down at the note in his hand, "if I wish to see my wife again, I'll need to be at Allen House St. James for a supper masquerade this evening. I'm also to arrive costumed as Antony."

"Antony? Who is Antony?" Robert demanded.

"Mark Antony of Cleopatra fame, uncle. Aisha and I attended Euston's masquerade attired as the Roman general and the Egyptian queen the night she went missing."

"Ah, I see. Actually, I don't, Percy, my boy. Why would he want you to do something foolish like that?"

"I shall have to find out. Will you excuse me while I make arrangements for the evening?"

Ahmara rose and went to him. "Bring her home, Percy. No matter what it takes, bring my niece home."

"I will, Ahmara," he vowed. "You have my word."

Ahmara watched him walk out before she returned to her husband. "Robert, he's in such pain."

Robert pulled her onto his lap and ran his hand down her spine. "He'll be fine once Isha is back in his arms, Mara. He's just been feeling helpless, that's all. Now give your husband his morning kiss."

She giggled. "Robert Howard, it's past noon."

"Somewhere in the world, it's morning, and a husband needs a kiss, and a wife should be accommodating."

"Just this once," she murmured, lowering her lips to his. "I wouldn't want to acquire a reputation for being too free with my kisses."

"Never, my love, never."

"MY LORD, I can't say I like the idea of you going in alone."

"It won't be a problem, Jessup," Percy replied as his carriage rolled through the streets of London toward St. James' Park. "I'll have my lady to see to my rear as she usually does."

"Jesting aside, Lord Ross, this man is dangerous, and you need to take his game seriously."

"Oh, I do, believe me. I have no illusions about what I face and what the outcome will be. He kidnapped my wife, and I suspect he intends to end my life along with hers. It would've been better if he'd just taken mine that night. I swear he will not see the morning light."

"Just be careful, my lord. We've gotten used to you being in one place and settled. I don't want to face Samuel should anything go wrong. Besides, I'm too old to train another employer."

Percy laughed. "I'll bear that in mind, Jessup. We can stop here; I'll take a sedan chair the rest of the way. I'll either see you before sunrise, or the Queen's guards will be knocking on the door, escorting Lady Ross home."

Jessup tutted. "Both of you better return safely, my lord."

Percy climbed out of the carriage when it halted before St. Martin-in-the-Fields Church. Waving his coachman on, he walked until he reached a tavern across the lane and entered. He searched the room until he spied an empty table in a darkened corner and made his way to it. "Forgive me. I didn't realize this table was occupied."

"Join me. Sometimes it's a pain to sit, drinking alone, with only one's wicked thoughts and memories of days gone by to occupy your mind."

The tavern maid sashayed up to Percy and flashed him a crooked smile. "What can I get you?"

"Ale."

"Anything else"?" she queried, running her fingers along Percy's arm.

"Nothing else except another tankard for my friend here."

A noisy pout trailed behind her. The two men waited until she left the drinks, collected the coins Percy laid out, and strutted away. He raised his tankard to the other man. "Here's to wicked thoughts and days gone by."

"Aye."

"So, what is it you're drinking into oblivion, my friend?" Percy asked.

"Business is slow, and I still owe the joiner six shillings for my chair. Perhaps you are in need of transportation?"

"Is your chair sturdy?"

"'Tis. I have faith in the joiner."

Percy sipped his ale. "I'll have need in fifteen minutes. What is the charge, and will you wait?"

"Six shillings."

Percy laughed. "Very well, you've a passenger."

They sat drinking and making small talk until the tankards were empty. Percy rose and headed toward the door, followed by the stranger. They walked for several minutes before turning to a lane leading toward St. James. A sedan chair stood several feet from them, and when they reached it, they climbed in.

"Evening, Charles, Jake."

The two men nodded and started walking. "Thanks, Jamie," Percy said to the man who accompanied him. "I owe you an enormous debt."

"Nah, my lord. Just kill the arsehole. He did his wife and Rupert's daughter wrong, so he deserves a slow death."

"Once I know my wife is unharmed, he will."

The rest of the journey to Allen House was done in silence, and Percy appreciated Jamie's taciturn nature. Despite all their preparations, things could go wrong. The situation could be a trap, or Aisha wasn't at the house. It was a cruel game and he hated it.

"Here you are, my lord. We'll see you inside in an hour's time," Jamie said when the sedan chair halted before Allen House.

Percy nodded and climbed out of the chair and paid the men. Strolling up to the door, he lifted the knocker and let it fall.

THIRTY-SEVEN

"Welcome, Lord Ross," Elspeth Reid greeted, opening the door. "Lord Euston is waiting for you in the supper room. Follow me. May I take your cloak?"

"I'd rather keep it," he said. "I've been a bit chilled lately."

She nodded and walked toward the rear of the house, halting before a closed door. "Everything is arranged, Lord Ross. Enjoy your evening," she said, opening the door.

"Good evening, husband," Aisha said, her eyes slowly raking him. "Has Martha not been feeding you?"

Percy walked over to her, his gaze scanning her body, looking for any marks or bruises. "Good evening, wife. You are well? Unharmed?"

She flashed a smile. "Unharmed? I am, but I must admit my captivity has been quite boring. I thought Englishmen were a species unique for their ability to leach the life out of life; however, I believe I've met their match in Lord Euston. He's been quite tedious, although he does foam a bit when your name arises."

"I see you're still costumed as Cleopatra. Is there a reason?"

"His Scot's humor. I assume there is a purpose since, until this evening, I've worn simple garments he thought befitting Ellen Chapman, rather modest and plain. Do you care for this shade of red? I'm not so certain it becomes my coloring."

Percy strolled over and took her into his arms. "I don't care what you wear; you in a sackcloth stirs my cock and my heart."

She kissed him deeply. "I'll take care of the former once we return to Ross House. I've missed you, Percy Elwen Howard."

"I've missed you, Aisha Resonne Howard."

"I assume you have a plan to get us out of here?"

"None."

Aisha tutted. "Then I'll have to rescue the both of us. Be warned, he's obsessed with Shakespeare's *Antony and Cleopatra* for unknown reasons. Also, he is excessively enraged because you aided his late wife to escape. I must admit, after being in his company for the past week, I fully applaud her decision."

"Enough!" Farquhar strode into the room and slammed the door.

"Did I mention he suffers from a choleric humor, especially when his wit falters?" Aisha stated.

"How in heavens have you remained wedded to this woman? She's lacking in all modesty and knows not when to be silent," Farquhar declared.

"It's a measure of her charm." Percy released her and stared at Euston. "I've missed my wife, and we haven't fucked for nearly a week. Shall we forego the pleasantries, and you tell me what you want in exchange for her release?"

"Will you sup with me while we discuss the conditions?"

Percy inclined his head. "Thank you, but no. I dined before I left home."

"Then humor me and sit at the table and at least partake of a glass of wine. I'm sure your wife is famished."

Percy escorted Aisha to the table and seated her before taking the chair beside her. His hand stroked her thigh, and a tiny sigh slipped past her lips. Farquhar picked up a small bell and shook it. The door opened, and Percy watched a thin girl bearing a heavy tray shuffle into the room.

As she approached, he studied her face and masked his reactive expression—or so he thought.

"You recognize her," Farquhar said smugly. "You should, since she is your kin."

The girl placed the tray on a side table before looking to Euston for instructions. He nodded, and she served the dishes and silently left. "I would've introduced you to your cousin's daughter, but since all is naught, I'll tell you about her life."

As Farquhar talked, Percy glanced at Aisha, whose anger mounted. He continued to stroke her thigh as the man droned on. When he fell silent, Percy laced his fingers with Aisha's.

"So all this—the masquerade, the kidnap, and this game you're playing—is about Rupert running off with your wife?"

He brought Aisha's fingers to his lips and kissed them. "Rather a long time to carry a grudge against a dead man, don't you think, Euston?"

"Not really, Ross," he replied smoothly. "Not when your wife is carrying your heir and dies with her lover. And, since neither of them are here to suffer for their actions, you will be the scapegoat."

"And my wife?"

"Sadly, a wife for a wife." Euston sipped from a glass of wine. "No grave upon the earth shall clip in it a pair so famous."

Percy squinted at him. "You do realize that we aren't Mark Antony and Cleopatra? Lacking their fame, if you end our lives, none will write such lofty lines about the Howards."

Aisha snorted. "Speak for yourself, Percy." She glanced at

Euston. "If you manage to end my life, I insist that the world know you brought to end the life of Ellen Chapman, owner of the Cock & Oyster brothel. I refuse to die as Cleopatra."

Percy eyed her. "You're attired as Cleopatra, and when your corpse is taken away, that's what will be written as your epitaph. Lady Ross died as Cleopatra."

"Do you really want to live in infamy as Antony? Seduced by a tawny queen? Led by the nose until a righteous Roman whose nose is equally as long arrives to put an end to your days of luxury, Percy? Tethered in chains silken and taut?"

He tapped his chin thoughtfully. "The image is enticing, Isha. I could be persuaded."

She leaned into him. "Imagine, dear Antony, your brown-skinned Cleopatra standing over you, a silk-wrapped riding crop in one hand and a soft goose feather in the other. Her lips wet with dew from the kisses you've exchanged, your cock dripping its precious juice, and your fingers incapable of bringing you release. What would you have her do?"

Percy's cock stiffened at Aisha's words. "If I were unbound, I would plead my case with gentle kisses to her nipples, a loving stroke here, a tender nip there. I would beg for her kindness, then plead to be buggered, and being the merciful queen she is, Cleopatra would bring me to the heights of joy and rapture."

His finger traced a slow path up her thigh until he touched her lower lips. One flick sent a delicious shiver through her, evoking Percy's smile. "If bound, my eyes would trap your gaze, and you would see my desire for the untold pleasures you promise. My body would beg for the pain of the crop and the ecstasy of the feather, my prick longing for the feeling of the slick silk along its length."

Leaning to kiss her, he murmured, "I would beg you to whip me until my release came jutting forth like a fountain of liquid ivory."

"Fuck, Percy," Aisha breathed unevenly. "I think we need to recall where we are."

She glanced at Farquhar, whose face was strained, eyes nearly shut, his fingers gripping his wine glass. "Since my husband is excessively lascivious tonight, would you care to begin your final act so we can proceed apace?"

Aisha peered at him and smiled. "Or would you prefer Ellen Chapman to offer her services? I rarely make such an offer, but Lord Euston, you appear in desperate need. Of course, I must seek my lord's permission, but I'm certain he will not withhold it, given the circumstances."

Percy shrugged. "I've never seen Ellen in action; it would be something to behold. If Lady Ross doesn't mind my observing, I'd grant Ellen such a boon."

"Lady Ross doesn't mind."

Farquhar slapped his nearly empty wine glass on the table, spilling the residue but not breaking the goblet. His mouth flapped open, then closed, then open, until he pressed his lips together and pushed his chair back from the table.

"Oh, my goodness, beloved," Aisha said when she spied the wet stain on his crotch. "He's released his seed already."

Farquhar's head whipped back and forth, his eyes wild with embarrassment, and his face mottled red with rage before he whirled and left the room.

Percy chuckled and kissed Aisha. "Are you certain you're unharmed?"

"Stop fretting, Percy," she scolded. "I believe Euston has had enough of me. The question is what end he plans for the two of us."

"I can answer that, Lady Ross."

She looked at Euston, who reentered the room a moment later. He'd apparently collected himself enough to continue with his game. Shutting the door behind him, Farquhar strode to where they sat and placed two small baskets on the table. "I've had enough of your games, Lady Ross. You and your beloved husband have a choice of death. Unlike Antony, Ross, you don't get the use of the sword."

Aisha rose from her chair, exasperation riding her face. "Please don't tell me you've brought a snake into the room."

Farquhar chuckled. "You sought 'the pretty worm of Nilus, that kills and pains not,' and I brought it thee, dear Queen."

"This is getting out of hand, Alastair," she declared. "I'd call you foolish, but even fools have some wit."

She turned to Percy. "Please take me away from this silly boy. Also, he has my daggers, and I want them back."

Percy removed his cloak and draped it over Aisha. "Happily, sweetheart."

"Halt!" Euston screeched, drawing a sword. "One step further, and I will run you through, Ross. Then I will have my way with your wife and slit her throat."

"Has he been this way the entire time you've been here, puss?

"He has. I do think it's pent-up frustration due to lack of marital congress and his peculiar relationship with Elspeth, the housekeeper who actually is his mother. It seems Farquhar senior's wife was incapable of bearing children, and he and Elspeth had long been lovers. When Elspeth became pregnant with Alastair, she got rid of Farquhar's wife, and he secretly married Elspeth."

"Who told you this?" Farquhar demanded angrily.

"I'm also interested in how you discovered this bit of information," Percy remarked.

"Jonas, the footman, and Molly, the scullery maid, who learned the truth from their parents who served the senior Farquhar. Euston thrust me into a disgustingly filthy chamber, and I insisted it be cleaned." Her forehead wrinkled thoughtfully. "I admit I also insisted on the purchase of soap, oil for my skin, and atay."

"'Tis why you smell of spring roses, and how my spy knew where to find you," Percy murmured, brushing his nose against her temple.

"That's another story. Jonas and Molly are in love, and Elspeth resents them, so they were happy to share what they'd learned about their employers. Percy, my love, do you think we can pay for their return to Scotland? They have family who will help them."

"Of course, Isha."

Euston banged his sword on the back of the chair. "You'll not be paying anyone except the devil his entry fee into hell!"

"I do believe you mean Charon," Percy corrected.

"Shut the fuck up!"

"There it is!" Aisha screeched happily. "I knew you could do it, Octavius Caesar!"

The door flung open, and Elspeth raced into the room. "My lord, my lord, there are men who've entered the house to rescue Lord Ross! Quickly, kill them before his men arrive!"

Startled, Farquhar swung his sword about wildly, knocking over both baskets. Shattered glass released the poison he'd placed in one while a linen bag wiggled frantically toward his feet. As two men rushed into the room, he never saw the deadly bite coming.

Percy grabbed Aisha and gingerly moved toward the door where Jamie and Charles stood, watching Euston's body seize before it began to shake violently, and he collapsed onto the floor. Elspeth screamed for someone to do something before she dropped to her knees beside him.

Turning Euston onto his back, she brushed bits of glass from his forehead. When a sliver pierced her skin, she winced but ignored it, crying, "Alastair, my son!"

She cradled his head in her lap. "This is not how it was supposed to end! You were to avenge your honor, not die in disgrace."

Spittle began to collect at the corners of Elspeth's mouth, and her face turned a curious shade of purple. One hand slammed against her belly. "Oh dear, I do believe I'm dying."

"Sadly, yes," Aisha said. "Your son is...was rather clumsy with his sword and released both the snake and the poison. We'll have the constables sent for immediately."

"Peace, peace! Dost thou not see my baby at my breast, that sucks the nurse asleep?" Elspeth whispered hoarsely.

Aisha shook her head and walked from the room, Percy's arm wrapped around her waist. "I love you, Percy Howard."

He kissed her temple. "I love you, Aisha Howard."

EPILOGUE

AISHA SMILED when Percy strolled into the private parlor of the lady's bedchamber in Ross House. "What's in the basket, Percy?"

He grinned. "You shall see, Lady Ross, and do not open it."

She watched him set the basket on a table before he left. As tempted as she was, she wanted to see what game Percy intended to play. She'd already selected her favorite tools to show him how much she missed him while they were apart. *What's in the basket, Percy Howard?*

Walking slowly around the table, she reached out her hand. "I said do not open the basket, Aisha Howard."

She jerked her hand back. "I wasn't going to open it, merely touch it."

Percy shook his head. "Impatient Isha. Let me finish, then you can explore."

Her sigh evoked more laughter as he busied himself lighting candles and strewing dried rose petals about the room. He went to the closet near the fireplace and removed a large rug, placing it in front of the hearth. He sprinkled a few more petals on top of the carpet.

"Come sit, Ellen," he urged. "We need to sup before we play."

"As you wish, my lord."

She sat cross-legged on the rug as he brought the basket over and began to unpack its contents. First, he handed Aisha her daggers. "I believe you asked me to retrieve these for you."

"Oh husband, I do love you so!" she cried happily. "These belonged to my grandfather, and I couldn't bear the thought of not possessing them."

Percy smiled and continued to unpack the basket, placing a bowl of berries on the table, along with cheese, bread, and roasted chicken. Aisha's eyes widened. "Percy Howard, where did you get strawberries? 'Tis far too late in the season."

"There is an advantage to being one of the Queen's best spies." He prepared a plate of berries, her favorite cheese, bits of chicken, and flatbread and brought it over to where she sat on the rug. "Besides, I need to make certain you have strength for the evening's games, sweet puss. I suspect you were poorly fed while in captivity."

"Euston's cook wasn't as talented as Martha, but the food was simple, fresh, and well prepared once I explained matters to her. I didn't suffer overmuch, especially after Euston realized I'm not easily intimidated nor ashamed of Ellen Chapman. He underestimated us, but I do think it's because he wasn't the brightest ha'penny to be coined."

"Enough about Euston. Tell me how you plan to woo your husband into your arms, Lady Ross."

She smiled. "I thought it was Ellen you wanted tonight—to bugger you."

"I've changed my mind. I want my wife, best friend, lover, and muse to peg me."

"Have you eaten your fill, my lord?" At his nod, she rose from the carpet and cleared away the remnants of their supper. Walking over to the door, she made sure it was locked and turned to face him. "Remove your garments, Percy."

He stood and hurriedly stripped off his breeches and shirt. Aisha returned and slowly circled him, inspecting every inch of his body, before she reversed direction. "I believe I will use the leather instead of the silk tonight. Go get it, and the goose feather. You may choose the oil and the ties."

Collecting the objects, he returned to where she stood. "Place them on the table there and fetch the wooden horse. Tonight, Lord Ross, you will ride and be ridden."

He moved an odd-looking device onto the rug. The 'wooden horse' had been an early gift from Aisha. Instead of triangular, the top was a flattened board cushioned for comfort. Slats extended on each side of the board to hold arms and legs apart with cloth-lined leather wrist and ankle fetters.

Percy's mouth gaped, and his breathing became erratic when she undid the ribbons to her gown and let it fall to the floor. A leather belt bound her waist. Attached to the belt was a strip that covered her lower lips, stopping at her hole. A dildo protruded, obscuring her feminine bud, and he shivered, his eyes alight with desire.

"Oh no, my lord," Aisha murmured, moving a small table next to her. "You must be punished before you are pleasured. Please mount."

He noticed the small jars of oil next to a water-filled bowl where Aisha had placed several pieces of cloth beside them. Turning to the wooden horse, he positioned himself flat on the mount designed to provide comfort and support for his body. There was a cushioned extension where he laid his head, and he slid his hands through the leather-bound openings while Aisha tended to his feet. "Are you comfortable, Lord Ross?"

"Quite, Lady Ross."

She laid the crop across his arse. "I cannot permit any movement."

Impatience scored through him as he waited for Aisha to bind him the way he preferred. Once she finished, she moved away. Percy knew what she was doing when mint and rosemary scented the air. Her hands were soft as she rubbed his body with oil. His eyelids drifted down, and his mind embraced the sensations her fingers were creating.

Such bliss. His heart eased as tension flowed from his muscles, his cells, and his thoughts, and he had no idea how long his wife caressed him to a boneless state. "Will you consent to my ministrations, Percy Elwen Howard?"

He mumbled his assent.

"I'm unable to hear the words, Lord Ross. I will need your consent before I can see to your needs."

It was a struggle; his body was in an exquisite state of relaxation, but he managed to lift his head. "You have my consent, Aisha Resonne Howard. Always and forever."

He felt her mouth on the cheek of his buttocks—first a soft kiss, then a painful nip that caused him to flinch. The soft leather ties, as did the ankle and wrist fetters, kept him motionless. Percy had no idea how long she toyed with him in this manner, each bite growing in intensity, sending waves of desire straight to his cock.

The moans echoing around his head were his, and he clamped his lips together to silence the noise. It was the one thing he could control. It also spurred Aisha to deepen her bite.

She kissed where she'd bitten his shoulder. Seconds passed before her hand smoothed along his spine, his arse, his thighs. Percy wasn't certain, but he sensed the strike was coming even though the weight of the crop remained on his flesh. Instead, she dragged the feather down his spine, between his arse cheeks, against his balls.

Aisha then positioned herself between his open thighs, and he felt the dildo's tip against his hole. He wiggled his arse when he noted the crop's weight was gone. Sucking in a breath, he waited...and waited. "Please, Isha."

The crop landed on his left buttock the moment her name passed his lips. The pain stripped him of air, causing his body to jerk. "Again," he stammered.

The pattern was set—he begged, and she gave. His prick throbbed, the pleasure pushing him toward a familiar edge until he couldn't stop the wet explosion. His grunts filled the air as his seed sprayed the carpet beneath him. The blows continued, though softer and infrequent, prolonging his release until he went limp.

Percy shifted his head so his cheek pressed the pillowed headrest. A contented sigh and a smile were all he could manage.

"Will you be ridden now, Lord Ross?"

His voice was thick with lust when he replied, "I will, Lady Ross."

"I have your consent?"

"You have my consent."

Aisha stroked his reddened arse before fetching the special oil blend she needed. Pouring a small amount in her palm, she caressed the dildo until it was covered. "I am ready, my love. If it becomes hurtful, you know what to say."

"I do," he replied. "Please, Isha. Don't make me beg."

She chuckled and positioned her dildo against the tight, wrinkled hole of his arse before she backed away and stroked with her finger. She slipped one inside and wiggled it. As he relaxed, she slid in another finger and then a third, stretching him as she stoked his desire.

Slowly withdrawing, she felt him clench as if to keep her in place. She reached for a small cloth and wiped her hand, then poured more oil into her palm, smoothing it over his arsehole and the dildo before gripping her toy and slowly entering him.

The silk-covered leather held a small protrusion that rubbed against her bud, and her desire quickly built as it always did when she fucked Percy's arse. When he was completely relaxed and she could go no further, Aisha moved the dildo inside him with short gentle strokes to ensure no discomfort.

Percy's moans were such a spur she gyrated her hips in rhythm with his sounds. "Faster, Isha, please."

She responded by driving deeply into him, her hands squeezing his buttocks, nails digging into flesh. She loved to peg him, knowing that it was one of the desires he hadn't satisfied until they became lovers.

"I can't stop it, Isha."

"Let it come, sweetheart," she murmured. "Let him come."

He stiffened, a muffled scream pouring from Percy's mouth as he ejaculated. The jerking of his body triggered Aisha's release, and she pounded him until bliss overcame them.

Once their tremors ceased, she eased from him and unstrapped the dildo. She grabbed a small cloth, dipped it into the water bowl, and began to cleanse the oil and soil from his buttocks. When she'd finished, she released his ties.

"Do you need my aid to rise, husband?"

He grinned. "I'm as weak as an infant, so yes."

She helped him to his feet and the divan before she returned to where the mount stood. Walking over to a screen, she tugged it forward to conceal the mount from view before ringing for Silas.

"I've arranged for a private supper, my lord. Tomorrow, we'll dine with our family. Tonight is just for you and me." She went to a cabinet and removed a Venetian glass bottle filled with wine. Aisha poured two glasses and handed one to him. "I love you, Percy Elwen Howard. If I were to become any man's Cleopatra, it is you."

Percy patted the space next to him. Once she was seated, he said, "I adore you, Aisha Howard. I will forever be your general and your lover," before he pulled her into his arms for a kiss. "Forever."

A SPOT OF MIDSUMMER TROUBLE

"No, Georgie, the plank doesn't go there," Othello Blackwood said. "It's part of the trapdoor, and it goes next to the pale oak one."

"Sorry, Master Blackwood, I forgot."

Othello walked over to where Georgie Hinton stood and placed his hand on the lad's shoulder. The thirteen-year-old didn't flinch as he did with others. "Come, let's place it so we can finish the stage. Would you like to see how it's going to work?"

Georgie's face lit up. "Oh, yes. I've never been beneath a trapdoor before."

"Well, once we finish nailing all this wood together, you'll be the first to test the new stage."

"He is so patient with the lad," Aisha Howard, Lady Ross, remarked to her husband as they watched Othello and Georgie work on the stage. "I also can't believe they've built an elevated stage and tiring house."

Percy Howard, Lord Ross, pressed a soft kiss against his wife's temple. "This is the first year. The Eggford players wanted a proper stage to compete with Frome and paid for the construction, and Ned Tanner volunteered a small plot of land near his tannery."

Watching Othello and Georgie, he continued. "They have a bond because Othello was there the day Georgie was born, delivering eggs and cheese to the Widow Hinton. Othello heard her cries for help and helped birth the baby."

Aisha leaned against Percy. "Our neighbors are very special. I never thought to hear these words from my lips, but I don't miss London, though I do miss my family and the Cock & Oyster ladies."

"Whenever you wish to visit, I am happy to accompany you. I do love our new carriage," he murmured, running his hand down her spine before he pinched the left cheek of her buttocks.

"Percy Howard!" she shrieked.

"You're far too beguiling, puss. Just being near you makes me want to toss you on the grass, raise your skirt, and fuck both of us senseless." He placed her hand on his forearm. "Instead, shall we continue to stroll the green and see what progress has been made?"

Lord and Lady Ross meandered among the busy villagers erecting stalls and helping to build the maypole. Several of the local players were rehearsing some distance from the noise. The Eggford players had chosen "the most lamentable Comedy and Most cruel death of Pyramus and Thisbe" from William Shakespeare's *A Midsummer Night's Dream*.

"Oh my," Aisha muttered. "I do wish the ladies could be here to witness this performance. *A Midsummer Night's Dream* is a favorite of Hannah and Eveline's."

"Lord Ross," a booming voice rang out, and a burly man strode over to the pair. "My lord, my lady. I can't express my sincerest gratitude for your excellent generosity in provisioning the garments for our performance."

Aisha smiled at Andrew Willoughby, the village's master brewer, constable, and one of five actors who would perform the silly bit of Shakespeare's comedy. "Good morning, Master Willoughby. How goes the rehearsals?"

"Well, Lady Ross," he inhaled. "We've had a mishap or two. Jack Kyd, who was to play the part of Thisbe, became drunk and fell off his horse. I thought to play both parts, as Pyramus bespeaks in Shakespeare's script, but Ned Tanner insisted on finding another to perform the role of Thisbe."

Willoughby's sigh barreled from his broad chest before he uttered, "Young Michael Todberry is to play the part."

Aisha frowned slightly before she recollected Todberry's face. "Ah, he was in the Christmas pageant, one of the wise men. He did perform credibly well, with his lines and all."

"True, true. I wrote them."

"I had no idea you penned the words, Master Willoughby. Well done. Have you made alterations to Shakespeare's play?"

Willoughby bobbed his head. "I have, my lady, as you will see. 'Tis some of my finest work." He bowed to Aisha and Percy. "I won't detain you longer, my lord and lady. I must make certain the others ken their lines."

The brewer rushed off toward the players. Within minutes, a fierce shouting match erupted between Willoughby and Tanner, and Percy took Aisha's hand. "Come, Isha, I don't intend to play judge at the moment."

"Has there long been animosity between the brewer and Tanner?"

"Sadly, yes. Over the Widow Preston, who jilted both and left with Rafe Winters for Herefordshire. Tanner and Willoughby blame each other for betraying a confidence and their friendship. Any mention of Helena Preston and the men have words."

Percy assisted Aisha mounting her horse and, with a wave to the men and women busily working, the couple rode back to Howard Manor. Ermegarde mooed as they went past her pasture. "Any idea where that wandering cock of yours might be?" Aisha inquired. "Ermegarde's lowing seemed especially tragic this morning."

"Most likely servicing Othello's hens," Percy offered. "Walter's relationship with Ermegarde does not preclude him from visiting henhouses."

Aisha gently tapped Percy's arm with her crop. "Poor Ermegarde to give her heart to such a fickle creature."

As they rode into the yard, she noticed a flurry of activity and an additional carriage. One she didn't recognize. "Visitors, Lord Ross?"

"It appears so, Lady Ross," he replied as he dismounted and helped her to the ground. "Shall we go roust them out of our home so we can fuck?"

"No, Percy, we shall do no such thing—unless it's Salisbury, then you can do what you want."

Percy sighed and escorted her into the house past the kitchen and toward the staircase leading to their bedroom. Before they reached the bottom of the stairs, Silas's voice magisterially sounded. "My lord, my lady, your presence is requested in the small salon."

"Can it wait, Silas? I need to bathe," Aisha said somewhat tersely.

"No, my lady, 'tis your aunt Ahmara."

With a deep sigh, Aisha grabbed Percy's hand and dragged him to the salon. "Your family, my lord."

Silas pressed his lips together to squelch his chuckle as he opened the door and the couple entered the room. Aisha's squeal of joy echoed in the hall as he closed the door once she hurried into the salon.

She went to the group and hugged everyone. "I didn't expect to see the ladies and gentlemen of the Cock & Oyster in Eggford. What drove you from London?"

"The plague," Randall said, sipping from a glass of wine. "And an invitation from Lord Ross with a promise we'll be entertained."

"Where's Matthew?"

Randall snorted. "Silly query, Ellen."

Percy chuckled. "When will you refer to Lady Ross as Aisha?"

"When you're no longer smiling, Lord Ross," Hannah quipped. "It's Ellen Chapman what put that spark in your eyes and a grin on your face. Though we were ready to gut you like a lamprey when you let yourself be tricked into losing her to Farquhar."

Percy flushed. "Not one of my finest moments, I'll admit."

"No matter, his end was deliciously well-deserved." Eveline grinned. "I'd have paid several crowns to witness the pair of them getting their comeuppance."

Aisha smiled at Eveline. "It was rather comical, though tragic to die as they did. No matter, we shall leave you to your devices, ladies and Randall. I'm in need of a bath."

It was a couple of hours later when Aisha and Percy descended the stairs and made their way into the salon. Aisha stopped before the door and kissed Percy's cheek. "You have ever been one to surprise me, Percy Howard."

"I plan to continue, Aisha Howard," he said, tucking her arm in his before he opened the door.

She'd just crossed the threshold when a young woman came flying at her and flung her arms around Aisha's neck. "Isha!"

Aisha released Percy, whose arm kept her from tipping over, and embraced the woman. "Bella! Oh my goodness, it's wonderful to see you. What are you doing in Eggford?" She turned to Percy. "If I wasn't so happy, I'd make you suffer."

"Later, sweet puss," he murmured. "Later.

Isabelle Resonne laughed. "I couldn't let the ladies have all the pleasures. I also need to speak with you about selling my shop."

"How long do you plan to stay?" Aisha inquired, managing not to reveal her surprise at Bella's words.

"A fortnight."

Kissing her cousin's cheek, Aisha grinned. "Percy Howard, you do realize that Mistress Simply will raise a hue and cry when she discovers the ladies are in residence?"

"Of course, Lady Ross. 'Twas done with the knowledge the Eggford Village Fair will be a miserable day for her and her kind. I haven't forgiven her remarks to Lady Ashedon about not being invited into our home."

Aisha shuddered. "She is the worst of her kind. Martha shared with me that, according to Mistress Simply's maid, the woman hasn't fully bathed in two years. Apparently, she believes using a warm, moist cloth on her privies is sufficient."

"My sweet Isha," Percy grimaced. "That information is far more than your husband wishes to know. Consider my delicate sensibilities and aversion to being forced to imagine what would happen if the wind were to whip her skirt up past her knees."

Bella cackled. "Imagine what monstrosities would be set alight into the world should that happen."

Ahmara, who was seated on a divan, observing her husband basking in the attention of the Cock & Oyster's ladies, glanced at her daughter. "Isabelle, I'm certain your aunt Maryam would chide your scandalous tongue."

"She would, then retreat to her bedchamber to have a good laugh, Mama."

Ahmara chuckled. "She would at that. Come sit with us, Isha, and tell us how what will surely be a comedy of errors is progressing. Have Willoughby and Tanner come to blows yet? What tragedy will they give us this year?"

Percy pulled up a chair for his wife and handed her a glass of wine before he sauntered over to where his Uncle Robert was holding court with several of the courtesans. Aisha took a sip and then shook her head. "Pyramus and Thisbe from Shakespeare's comedy. Tanner and Willoughby, despite their caustic relations, agree that Tanner should play the lion's part and Willoughby the role of Pyramus."

Robert peered askance at his nephew. "Percy lad, are those the two who came to blows over the Widow Preston some years back?" Tapping his chin, he grinned. "Yes, I remember. They didn't know they were both tupping her until she dismissed them both with the knowledge they were sharing her petals. Along with that charlatan from Basingstoke she ran away with, leaving the poor lads high and dry."

He sipped his wine. "I suppose neither one married."

"No, uncle, and the widow is still a bone of contention between them even though they're the best of friends. No one dares mention her name for fear of a cuff about the head, except Willard Tuberson when he's had a few too many tankards."

Aisha glanced at Hannah and narrowed her eyes. "Do not start mischief, Hannah. I see that glint in your eyes."

Silas entered the room and announced dinner. As everyone filed out, Aisha tapped Bella's wrist. "Shall we talk in the morning?"

"I'd like that, cousin."

THIRTY-NINE

"A plague upon your house!"

Andrew Willoughby drew in such a breath his chest expanded to twice its size before he exhaled loudly. "Ned Tanner, that is not a line in our play."

Ned glared at Willoughby. "Is this not a tragedy?" At Willoughby's puzzled nod, Ned pressed forward. "Are the families at war?"

"Yes, Pyramus and Thisbe's fathers are enemies," Andrew answered. "What is your purpose with these questions?"

"As Thisbe's father, upon discovering her bloodied corpse and Pyramus nearby, wouldn't he curse Pyramus's house?"

Willoughby stroked his chin. "Aye, I see your intent and 'tis true. Thisbe's father would curse his enemy. You shall do it! Do you have a sword, Ned?"

Ned's shoulders drooped. "Nay, Andrew."

Andrew patted Ned's shoulder. "I shall speak to Master Blackwood and have him make you a wooden one, for it would not do for you to use Pyramus's blade."

With the matter settled, the rehearsal continued with no

one forgetting their lines or their marks. Willoughby and Tanner dismissed the company and headed to the tavern for a tankard. Before they reached the door, they heard a woman's voice call out their names. Ned was the first to respond once they turned to look in the direction of the voice.

"It's the Widow Preston," he hissed.

Willoughby's body stiffened. "Pray tell, what is she doing here? Has the devil sent her to torment us a second time? I will not have it."

Helena Preston strolled over to the two men and inclined her head. "Good day, Andrew, Ned. You are both looking well."

"Widow Preston," Andrew replied curtly, though the lust filling his blue eyes betrayed his disdain. "Forgive me, I don't recall the name of your latest husband."

She seductively ran her fingers along his arm. "'Tis no matter since I am once again a widow."

The two men eyed each other before Ned observed, "'Tis husband three, if I mistake not."

Helena pressed her hand against her breast, and both men inhaled. What had drawn them to the widow beside her winsome looks were her ample breasts. When she dragged her fingers up to her throat, Andrew released a soft sigh.

"I was married young to old men, too impotent to breed yet desirous of heirs," she lamented. "Stuart McDuff, for that was the name of my recently departed husband, though youngish, succumbed to a mysterious ailment, one the physician said may have been caused by a predilection for eels."

"What brings you to Eggford, Mistress McDuff? Have you come to enjoy the fair?"

She smiled at Andrew. "I have, and perhaps to settle once more in the village once I find a cottage where I can ply my trade as a seamstress. Mistress Simply has rented me a room for now, though I may have to look further afield."

Ned tugged Andrew's sleeve. "Come, Andrew, the others are waiting in the tavern." He stared at Helena. "Do not assume you can reclaim my affections, Mistress McDuff, for that ship has sailed. The scar you inflicted on my heart when you fled Eggford remains. Good day."

Andrew watched his friend and rival stride toward the tavern before he peered at Helena. "I must be off; we've just finished our rehearsal, and I have a singular thirst."

"What play, Andrew?"

"Pyramus and Thisbe, from Shakespeare's *A Midsummer Night's Dream*." He beamed as he added, "Our players earned ten shillings each last year's performance, and we expect to earn even more. Now I must be off."

Helena watched the men enter the tavern and her eyes narrowed. While she didn't have a preference for either man, she decided Andrew Willoughby was the easier gull despite Ned's better fortune. She would have to exercise care since the small village had been her home from the time her mother moved to Eggford to wed Jack Wilton.

A smile formed on Helena's lips at the thought of her dead mother. Jack had been Marjorie Douglas's seventh husband, and the sixth who died by mysterious circumstances. Helena had followed in her mother's footsteps. Stuart McDuff had proven a bit difficult, but in the end, he'd joined Banquo McBain, Seamus MacBeth, and Oliver Preston to sing before the heavenly gates.

"Aye," she murmured, strolling to Mistress Simply's house, "Andrew Willoughby it is."

∾

"WHAT CAN I GET YE?" Betsy asked the stranger who approached the bar.

"A tankard, and if ye have one, a room."

Betsy filled a tankard and handed it to the gruff-voiced man. "I'll get the tavern's owner. Might not be nothing available, what with the Eggford Village Fair beginning tomorrow."

The stranger nodded and made his way to a table. A minute later, a portly man walked over to him. "You be needing a room?"

"Aye."

"Name's Abe. How long you be needing it for?"

The stranger peered at Abe. "Name's Duncan, maybe three nights. My horse needs tending, and I left him at the stables."

"Two pence a night. It's the last room because of the fair."

"I'll take it," Duncan said quickly. He removed a leather bag from his cloak and pulled out several coins. Draining his tankard, he stood. Handing Abe the coins, he asked, "Do many visitors come to Eggford for the fair?"

"Aye," Abe replied, leading Duncan up a staircase. "We've got some excellent crafters living in the area. People come from as far as Basingstoke or Frome to buy Cassio Fairbanks's jewelry and plates or Mistress Braddock's linen, which is some of the finest in the county. Proud to say the Eggford Village Fair is famous about the county."

Abe unlocked a door and opened it, waving Duncan inside. "I'll have my daughter Betsy bring up a pitcher of water and cloth. The bedding's been aired out and the room swept. Here's your key. Eggford is usually a safe village, not much crime with Lord Ross in residence, but the fair does see more people in our village, so lock the door."

"Thank you. How much for a meal?"

"Stew and bread is ha'penny," Abe said as he started back down the stairs.

Duncan McDuff closed and locked the door. He walked over and pressed down on the bed's mattress. It wasn't too soft, so he'd sleep well. A knock on the door startled him before he remembered Betsy was bringing up a pitcher. Opening the door, he stood silently while she entered and set the pitcher and cloth on a table near the bed.

"The chamber pot is in that cubby near the hearth. You'll need to empty it yerself because I don't. There's a privy hole down the hall and behind the door. Please close the door when you're done so vermin don't come in. Oh, my dad says if you want to eat, you best come now. Stew's nearly gone."

With that message, she left. Duncan took his travel bag and put it in the cupboard near the bed before he left the room, making certain to lock the door behind him.

FORTY

Percy swept Aisha up and carried her to their bed after bathing her. "I do love an early morning fuck, and this morning's oil is honeysuckle. When I lick your puss, the scent gives me such an appetite."

Aisha giggled. "Do you recall which bottle?"

"Of course, Isha. You lie there and let me have my way with your body."

He went to the cabinet filled with oils, instruments of pleasure, and erotic books Aisha had collected while owner of the Cock & Oyster. They'd made use of a few of the more adventurous books as inspiration. Searching among the oil bottles, he found the one he wanted.

When he didn't return immediately to bed, Aisha lifted her head to peer at him. "What are you doing, Percy?"

He finished warming a porcelain bowl with hot water and dried it before pouring oil into the dish. Moving to the bed, he set the bowl on the side table. "On your belly, my lady. I prefer to begin with your delicious bottom."

Aisha turned onto her stomach and cooed when warm

hands began to rub oil onto her shoulders. "You do realize these aren't my arse."

As he rubbed, Percy talked. "I thought I'd start here and work my way downward. Do you recall the first time we made love, Isha? It was a joy I never expected to receive in my lifetime. Your skin bewitched me with its purity of color, a brown so exquisite no dye-maker could achieve its hue."

His hands smoothed oil on her back, fingers gently kneading her flesh. "Your bum was as soft as lamb's wool...don't you dare laugh, Aisha Howard!"

"Lamb's wool? Is that what you thought of my arse?" Aisha sputtered. "Why have you never told me this before?"

"Embarrassment," he mumbled. "At the time, I was befuddled, and it was the first thought that came to mind. Also, there are few things as soft as lamb's wool, my love."

"I do love you with all my heart, Percy Elwen Howard."

Silence reigned as he smoothed oil over his wife's buttocks and legs. The soft moans escaping beyond the pillow where Aisha's head rested bespoke her rising need. Percy slowly ran a finger along the crack of her arse, and a smile creased his lips when Aisha's hips lifted. Not one to deny his wife her pleasures, he stroked and teased the hole until her incoherent pleas accompanied the twitch of her bottom.

Running his hands along the back of her legs to her feet, he performed the same ministrations he'd given her arse. "Turn over to your back, Isha."

He dipped his fingers into the bowl and rubbed oil onto his palms, then smoothed it onto her breasts. "So firm, so luscious, and all mine," he murmured, leaning down to suck a nipple into hardness.

"I had no idea how perfectly even your coloring would be that day we first met, though I did wonder. You have no idea how much pleasurable joy staring at your naked body gives me."

He kissed her belly as his hand moved between her thighs and parted them. "However, it was your sweet puss that enthralled and took my soul captive for all eternity."

His tongue traced a sensuous path along her inner thigh, halting before it came in contact with her fleshy pearl. Percy adjusted his body so that his forehead touched her stomach. He remained motionless, his eyes closed as he took in the treasure he'd been gifted.

A shiver rippled down his spine when the memory of her kidnapping flooded his mind. The fortnight without Aisha had been the most heart-wrenching days of his life, and he'd nearly lost her.

"Percy, he didn't succeed," Aisha said, sensing the emotions rocking her husband. "My puss is weeping for affection; may she please know thy inclination? Is it to lick until her honeysuckle sweetness flows, or dwell on what never happened?"

His teeth nipped her bud. "Do not chide me for dwelling on the potential, Lady Ross. Had Farquhar succeeded, I would have lost you forever."

"And I you," she said soothingly. "He failed and died by his own foolishness. If I am to leave this world, I promise, Percy Elwen Howard, Lord Ross, I shall take you with me in a riotous conflagration of blissful ejaculation."

Percy pushed all thoughts of Farquhar from his mind and set about pleasuring his wife and his hunger for her body. "Ah, fuck," he murmured when he dragged his tongue along her slit. "You taste so good."

The faint quiver of her flesh against his lips goaded his cock into rampant hardness and he rubbed it against the bedcover. With each stroke of his tongue, the taste of honeysuckle and

Aisha's juices invaded his senses, spurring him to lap up the creamy liquid before it left her cunny.

"Percy!"

His hands gripped her hips, lifting her legs over his shoulders, and he tongued her fiercely before a finger teased its way into the tight sphincter of her arse. Aisha bucked against his mouth, his tongue captured by the clinch of her lower lips.

'Oh Percy, yes!"

With a final "Oh!" she screamed, and her juices flowed like honey across his tongue. When her body ceased its quivering, he moved until he was over her, his cock pressed against her wetness. He pushed into her with a single stroke. "Ah, sweet Isha, never has my rod and staff felt such bliss."

She lifted lust-heavy eyelids and stared at him, a seductive smile on her lips. Taking her bottom lip between her teeth, she tugged and released before her thighs captured his hips. "Do not move, Percy. I wish to try something I read."

Aisha lightly clenched his erection, then relaxed her hold on his hips. Her feet rested against his thighs, and he wondered what mystical form of sex play she was about. He closed his eyes and let his mind follow the push-pull of her inner muscles on his flesh.

The feeling was faint, nearly imperceptible, but as powerful a sensation on his cock as a storm battering a ship at sea. Pressure built inside him, a tightness desperate to escape its prison. His hips flinched, and all sensation ceased. "Isha," he stammered.

"You must remain still, beloved," she whispered. "Otherwise, I cannot tell if what I'm about works."

"It's working," he gasped.

"Be strong, my sweet Percy."

Once his body relaxed against hers, her muscles held him as gently as one would hold a songbird. After a few seconds, the pulsations returned, firmer and more intense. He needed to thrust into her, to drive home to heaven, yet his body refused, held by invisible bands.

Preoccupied with his desire, Percy's mind took several seconds to recognize the subtle signs of Aisha's pending release —the hesitant breaths, the faint taps of her heels against his thighs, and the near-stranglehold her cunny had on his cock.

There wasn't any movement of her body except for the muscles inside her privy parts, and even that was so slight Percy wasn't certain they moved at all. "Oh, sweet Jesu, Aisha. I need relief."

"In a moment, Percy, my love, in a moment," she cooed.

He wasn't sure how much longer he could remain motionless. He'd never been drawn so bow-tight when they made love, and if he snapped...

The quiver came ever so subtly like a feather on a gentle breeze, moving directionless and with ever greater force. His cock was painfully erect, ready to explode. Aisha's feet slid down the sides of his legs, her hips arching and her puss gripping him. Then she moved, and his release shot forth with the force of a cannonball. "Isha!" he roared.

The wet heat of her as she bathed him with her liquid triggered a second quake, and Percy nearly wept from the pleasure. She squeezed her thighs, and he shuddered, drained and happy.

They laid in each other's arms for some time until Aisha wiggled her legs. "I need to piss, Percy. And take another bath since the ladies want to visit Eggford."

"No."

"No?"

"I'm comfortable, my rod and staff is comfortable, and I have no desire to go into Eggford."

Aisha slapped his arse. "No one has invited you to join us,

my lord. This is a lady's outing to the fair. You'll have to entertain yourself being lord of the manor or dispensing justice somewhere in the county until it's time to attend the performance."

"Abandoned by my wife," he groaned as he eased his body from hers. "Lord Ashedon is due to arrive before noon. I believe Lady Ashedon is to accompany him, and I'm sure she will be disappointed to discover your absence."

"Banish whatever thoughts are swirling in that handsome head of yours, Lord Ross. I intend to enjoy today's festivities. Please have Silas escort them to the back parlor, and make certain the windows are open."

Percy laughed. "He's already aware of what to do, including covering the chairs with tarpaulin and then linen cloth. I'll inform the Ashedons the chairs are being redone to explain the matter. I will join you and the ladies once I'm done, and try not to get into trouble before I arrive."

Aisha rose from the bed and strode into the privy closet. When she entered the bathing room, it was chilly, and she hurriedly stoked the still-warm coals in hearth before laying several pieces of wood on top. Once the fire was going, she swung a kettle with water over the flames before going to fill the tub with water from a large cask. The idea had been Silas's design to save the staff several trips up the stairs. Every bedroom had a similar cask.

"Will you come wash my back, husband?"

"With pleasure, dear wife."

FORTY-ONE

Aisha and Percy strolled into the dining room to find their guests already seated. Silas escorted Aisha to her chair. Percy peered at the man, who shrugged. "She is the lady of the house."

Percy plopped onto his chair. "When did I become invisible?"

Silas inclined his head. "You haven't, my lord. Lady Ross has brought order to our household and therefore we defer to her."

Ahmara cackled. "I adore you, Silas."

"Thank you, Lady Howard."

She tsked him. "You do realize I'm no longer a lady of the manor."

"You will always be so," Silas replied as he placed a cup of atay next to her plate.

"Here, here," Robert chimed in. "Wine, please, Silas."

Ahmara looked at her husband and shook her head. Robert shrugged. "Sweeting, I had atay before we made passionate love this morning. I need to fortify my blood."

The blushes that colored Ahmara's cheeks evoked hoots from the Cock & Oyster women. Bella grinned mischievously. "Are you having wine as well, Cousin Percy?"

"Bella!"

"What, Isha? I heard you screaming in pleasure through the walls," Bella retorted. "If you don't wish your affairs to be public, you need to silence both yourself and your husband."

"And with that declaration," Silas intoned, "I shall leave you to serve yourselves breakfast."

"Coward," Percy mumbled as he lifted his atay cup and sipped.

"Will you be joining us this morning, Lord Ross?" Hannah asked.

Percy shook his head. "Alas, I must mediate a dispute between Lord Ashedon and one of his neighbors. Since Ashedon plans to attend the fair, I insisted that he and the neighbor attend me this morning. I will join you for the performance later today."

"What is the dispute, nephew?"

Percy's sigh was long and pained. "His neighbor's dog has slain a few of Ashedon's chickens who wander on the neighbor's land. Ashedon wants the dog killed and payment for the loss of the hens."

"How are the hens getting loose? Usually, one creates a locked enclosure," Bella remarked. "To keep them from wandering."

"That doesn't work with Walter," Aisha drawled.

"Walter? Who's Walter?"

"My husband's wandering cock," Aisha replied and waited for the laughter to die. "A very handsome rooster, I must admit. Walter has impregnated quite a few hens in the vicinity. He's also taken up with Ermegarde, a lovely cow of questionable taste, Hannah."

A ruckus in the hallway drew everyone's attention. Before Percy could rise to see what it was about, the door was flung open and an inebriated William Shakespeare staggered into the dining room.

"Forgive me, my lord. He was most persistent," Silas gritted out.

Aisha smiled at him. "We'll handle it, Silas. Do have Martha make you a cup of atay."

He nodded and closed the door. Aisha rose from her chair and went to Shakespeare. "Would you care to join us for breakfast, Will?"

"No," he grumbled. "I'm here to speak to Bella."

Aisha took his arm and gently led him to the table, then seated him next to Ahmara before she went to the side table and prepared him a plate of food. Setting it before him, she smiled. "Please breakfast with us, Will. We're to attend our village's midsummer fair, and I'd prefer not to have you carted off because of hunger and drunkenness."

She returned to her chair and resumed her stories of Walter's escapades, knowing Ahmara had Shakespeare well in hand. Talk soon turned to the fair's entertainment, and Percy informed Shakespeare the local thespians had adapted his Pyramus and Thisbe for the day's performance.

"Do they have talent?" Shakespeare slurred. "Or will the theatrics resemble my rude mechanicals?"

Percy stiffened on his chair, his gaze stern. "They are men whose theatrical efforts raise funds for poor widows and orphans in and near our village."

He sipped the nearly cold atay before he said, "Your arrival was precipitous and unexpected. You show up reeking of wine and demanding to address my cousin by virtue of marriage. Would you present yourself to Her Majesty in such a manner?"

Shakespeare shook his head. "I would not."

"Then do not treat her adjudicator for this county so poorly. If your intent is to bring turmoil into our home and community, disrespect Lady Ross's kindness, and presume to act the lord of the manor with your demands, I will not have it, and Eggford, though small, does have a jail where I can house you until you stand trial. 'Tis your choice, Master Shakespeare."

Percy stood. "Ladies, enjoy your day at the fair." His gaze settled on his wife. "Are you certain I can't tempt you to aid me with my negotiations?"

Aisha rose and went to him. Placing a loving kiss on his cheek, she grinned. "There are negotiations I will undertake, my lord, later. This morning I fear you must bear the burden alone."

Once Percy left the dining room, Aisha turned her attention to Shakespeare. "I assume you brought fresh garments with you, Will?" At his nod, she went to a bell pull. When Silas stepped into the room, she said, "Please show Master Shakespeare to a room and arranged for a bath."

Her attention back on Will, she said, "We leave in an hour if you care to join us, Will. Otherwise, you may bathe and sleep off your wine."

He pushed away from the table and started toward Silas. "Before you leave," Aisha said, "I do believe you owe the ladies an apology for the rude disruption of our breakfast, William."

Shakespeare eyed her, recalling before she became Lady Ross, she was Ellen Chapman and not a woman to toy with—if one wanted to emerge unscathed from the encounter. "Forgive me, ladies. Perhaps you'll allow me to join you and to purchase each of you a trinket to atone for my ill-mannered behavior."

"Go bathe, Will," Bella chided. "You stink of the road."

FORTY-TWO

JESSUP BROUGHT the carriage around to the front of the manor. Once the ladies were settled inside, he directed Shakespeare to the space beside him. "You ready to depart, Lady Ross?"

"We are, Jessup."

The road was smooth, and Aisha used the short ride to Eggford village green to explain the intricacies of the coach's interior design. The muffled words and laughter caused Shakespeare to tap on the panel. Aisha slid it open. "Yes, Jessup?"

""'T'weren't me, my lady. Was Master Shakespeare who was a-knocking."

"Yes, Will?"

He leaned his head so that his face was visible in the small opening. "Is everything well among you?"

"Of course," Aisha said. "The ladies are admiring the interior my husband had done for my comfort. Is there anything else?"

"No," he mumbled and turned to face forward.

She closed the wood panel before leaning toward Bella. "I

do believe it's time to end your affair with the man," she said in a whisper. "I worry he'll become overly possessive if you don't, and he is married, Bella."

"I've said as much, Ellen," Hannah intruded. "He should be with his wife and children instead of chasing Bella across the country. Besides, he's become a boring, obnoxious drunk of late. The only kind word one can say is that his writing hasn't yet suffered."

"I did end the affair," Bella groaned. "He refuses to accept that I want nothing to do with him any longer."

Aisha peered at her cousin. "Is there someone else?" At Bella's nod, she pressed, "Does Will know?"

"I believe he suspects, but I refuse to confirm or deny the matter. 'Tis none of his affair. When I turned down Kit Marlowe's proposal to become his wife, I realized it was time to end things with Will." Bella's eyes darkened with irritation. "When I discover who told him I was visiting you, Isha, there will be a debt to pay. I'm sorry for the embarrassment he's brought to your house."

Aisha shrugged. "He's much like some of the men who believe they have a right to the Cock & Oyster and become spoiled little boys when they can't get what they want. I'll send him back to his wife tomorrow, and we shall talk, cousin."

The carriage stopped, and Jessup climbed down and opened the door. He helped each of the ladies to exit while Shakespeare stood sulking near the green. Aisha turned her back to him and said, "Are you well-armed, ladies?" Each one patted a hip and grinned. "Good, then shall we make merry?"

Shakespeare moved to walk on one side of Bella while Eveline took the other side. Aisha squelched her laughter and locked arms with Hannah to stroll the stalls. It wasn't long before several young men joined their company, on the pretense of protecting Lady Ross until Lord Ross's arrival but to engage in flirtations with the courtesans.

When one of the young men approached Bella, Shakespeare's growl of disapproval had the lad begging her father's forgiveness and inquiring whether she was betrothed or wed. Hannah's cackle was the loudest, and even Bella couldn't stifle her giggle before she said, "He isn't my father. Evan, this is Master William Shakespeare and a friend of my family."

"Oh my, forgive me, Master Shakespeare," Evan stammered, "I meant no insult."

"None taken," Shakespeare grumbled.

"Are you aware your Pyramus and Thisbe is the play chosen for this year's entertainment? Masters Willoughby and Tanner wanted to perform *A Midsummer Night's Dream* in its entirety, but there weren't enough players. However, I believe you'll enjoy their performances and the justice they've done to your tragedy."

Much more interested in the beauty walking beside Shakespeare, Evan directed his attention to Bella after masterfully inserting himself between her and Shakespeare. Shakespeare's umbrage rippled across his shoulders, and Aisha's unmuted laughter floated before her.

"Master Shakespeare, come stroll with me," she invited. "I'd like you to meet Cassio and Othello, two of Eggford's finest crafters. Evan and Charles, I assume you will be perfect gentlemen and escort the ladies to the dais without trouble."

"Of course, Lady Ross. We will guard them with our lives," Charles boasted.

Aisha shook her head. "I doubt there will be any need for violence, dear Charles. The Eggford fair is touted to be one of the most peaceful festivals in Somerset."

Shakespeare's frown smoothed, though his jaw remained

clenched as he joined Aisha and Hannah. He offered Aisha his arm, ignoring Hannah.

"Master Shakespeare," Aisha said, accepting his escort. "I've not taken you to task for your rudeness because I prefer to be hospitable. However, you have exceeded the few spoonfuls of tolerance I have for ill-bred white men. Your fame in London may allow others to overlook this type of behavior, but you are not in London."

She halted to speak to one of the stall owners and purchase some oils. With her package in hand, she continued toward the stage area. "I assume my cousin has ended her affair with you."

He flinched at her words and opened his mouth to speak. She waved her hand to silence him. "I am pleased since you are far too advanced in age and married. The rashness that led you to follow her from London I'm willing to lay at the excessive amount of drink you've consumed and your affection for her."

Aisha halted, directing Hannah toward the spot where Bella, Eveline, and the two young men stood. Once she had Shakespeare's ear alone, she abandoned all pretense of affability. "Go home to your wife. To your children. Your life, which you have wasted these past several years with excess, has affected my family and my cousin. Bella is not nor can ever be your wife, and she deserves a life of happiness, not taking care of some old drunken sot."

Shakespeare glared at Aisha before he angrily whirled and strode to the stall serving ale. Aisha shook her head, then joined her cousin and the courtesans, who stood near a canopied dais reserved for Lord and Lady Ross.

Jessup watched her approach, his stoic expression softening when he saw Aisha until a man appeared, reaching for her arm. Jessup moved quickly to intercept, then saw Lord Ross striding rapidly to his wife's aid.

"Remove your fingers before I remove them for you," Aisha

hissed, her dagger poised over the man's gloved hand. He froze and slowly lowered his arm, stepping back out of range of her weapon. He bowed, all the while keeping an eye on her left hand and the large man looming at her back.

"Forgive me, Lady Ross. I didn't mean to trespass."

Aisha eyed him. "You know who I am, but I cannot say the same for you."

"Duncan McDuff," he replied. "I sought you out after overhearing your name near one of the stalls. I need your assistance in finding a killer."

"I thought I asked you not to seek out trouble, Lady Ross," Percy intoned as he took up a protective stance beside his wife. He focused on McDuff, and the man shivered. "'Tis also impertinent and dangerous to approach my wife when I'm not present, McDuff, as I'm sure you've just discovered."

"Forgive me, Lord Ross. I only sought to ask your lady's assistance to speak with you directly."

Percy brushed his lips across Aisha's cheek. "Please put your dagger away, my love. The good folk of Eggford are on edge for fear of your safety."

She slipped her weapon inside her cloak. Percy placed her hand on his forearm. "Shall we go take our seats? The musicians are starting up." He turned his gaze to McDuff. "You may join us, and we can speak after the performers have taken their bows."

FORTY-THREE

Aisha stifled a laugh with her hand when Thisbe ran onto the stage and abruptly halted, stared at Pyramus' cloak and, with a terrified expression, screeched, "But mark, poor knight, What dreadful dole is here!" before kneeling to moan, "O dainty duck! O dear!! Thy mantle good, What, stain'd with blood!"

Thisbe rose and pulled a knife from her skirt. Inhaling deeply, the actor exhaled and, in a tremulous voice, said, "O Fates, come, come, Cut thread and thrum; Quail, crush, conclude, and quell!"

Thisbe elegantly lowered to the stage floor and, with a large sigh, uttered, "I am dead."

Behind her, Aisha heard Shakespeare mutter, "What in damnation did they do to my play?" Percy shushed the man when Pyramus lumbered onto the stage and faltered, seeing Thisbe lying still. He went to her and lifted the actor's head before letting it fall.

"Oww," the actor groaned. "That hurt."

Ignoring him, Pyramus continued with his lines. "O Sisters

Three, Come, come to me, With hands as pale as milk; Lay them in gore, Since you have shore with shears Thisbe's thread of silk."

After a brief tussle with the belt around his waist, Pyramus removed his short sword. "Tongue, not a word. Come, trusty sword; Come, blade, my breast imbrue."

"What Ho! Dead? My beloved daughter Thisbe dead? Have you, wicked boy, slain my only daughter?"

Percy leaned toward Aisha and whispered, "Who is that? I've seen this play several times, and I don't recall this character."

"'Tis Thisbe's father, I believe. You do recall Willoughby did say he and Tanner altered the script somewhat?"

"Somewhat?" Shakespeare gritted. "What they've done is a travesty. If Thisbe's father was to be a character, I would have done so."

Thisbe's father pulled out a sword, and he and Pyramus fought. "Alas, I am mortally wounded," the father moaned. He dropped to his knees and theatrically opened the trapdoor. "Fiends, come for me. I go to join my sweet Thisbe in death," he said as he disappeared from the stage.

"Alas, alas, I have slain my Thisbe's father. There is nothing to do but cut thread and thrum; Quail, crush, conclude, and quell! Farewell cruel world. Remember, Pyramus loved his Thisbe."

Before Pyramus could stab himself, Shakespeare hurriedly staggered past the audience and onto the stage. "What have you done to my play? This isn't what I wrote, and Thisbe's father is not seen. The lovers run away, you boisterous mangler of my words! Where are the Athenians? This is not my play!"

Shakespeare swung his fist at Pyramus, missed, and lost his footing to fall face down on the trapdoor.

Pyramus kicked at Shakespeare's arse. "Who are you?

What do you mean, this isn't the play you wrote? Of course not, you nodcock! This is Master William Shakespeare's tragedy, not some drunkard who stumbled upon a performance."

Suddenly, a bloodcurdling scream came from beneath the stage as someone attempted to jiggle the trapdoor open. "Who's there?"

"It's me, Ned! Andrew, open the door, there's been a murder!"

Willoughby booted Shakespeare out of the way and lifted the door. Ned climbed out, his body trembling. "She's dead. She's dead, and there's blood everywhere!"

"Of course, she's dead, Ned, it is what Master Shakespeare wrote. Thisbe and Pyramus both die."

Ned grabbed Willoughby's arm and dragged him over to the opening. "Not Thisbe, it's Helena McDuff who's dead. She's been murdered!" Realizing what he just said, Ned promptly fainted and landed on top of Shakespeare.

Amid the uproar, Aisha tilted her head and peered at Percy. "Is this the first time there's been an actual murder at the fair?"

"To my knowledge," he groaned. "I suppose I should make my way to the scene of the crime."

"You are the Queen's adjudicator for the county," Aisha said innocently. "Given the crush of people, I believe I'll remain here until you return."

Percy rose and strolled up to the stage. He had several of the more sober-looking men encourage members of the audience to give room. His gaze swept the stage, and he didn't bother to stifle his laughter. Ned and Shakespeare were entangled as the dramatist struggled to push Ned aside while Ned attempted to sit upright.

"Has anyone undertaken to remove the deceased from beneath the stage?"

Willoughby stared at Percy, then stammered, "Oh my, I was so worried about poor Ned I forgot about the Widow Preston— I mean McDuff. Helena."

"Don't you think we should retrieve the body and ascertain what happened, Andrew? Evening approaches, and you are the Constable for Eggford village."

"Yes, my lord."

Willoughby ordered several men to help dismantle part of the stage. Taking Thisbe's mantle, he wrapped it around the deceased and moved her to open grass. Percy sent one of the lads to fetch a wagon, and by the time the vendors had returned to their stalls, the Widow McDuff was on her way to the burial building located behind the carpenter shop.

Percy made his way back to Aisha but was cut off by Duncan McDuff. "Did I hear the name Helena McDuff?"

Percy tilted his head, eyeing the fingers clutching his forearm. Once McDuff released him, he said, "You did, although the deceased was known as Helena Preston before she left the village."

"Do you know how she came by the name McDuff? Did you meet her husband? What can you tell me about her?" McDuff ran his fingers through his hair. "Forgive me, my lord. My brother, Stuart McDuff, died under suspicious circumstances after marrying a widow with the surname of Preston from Eggford. While the estate came to me as his heir, his widow vanished with the silver and monies belonging to my brother. I fear her only reason for marrying Stuart was his wealth, and like the female scorpion stung him until he died. 'Tis the reason I've traveled to Eggford."

Percy peered sympathetically at the man. "Do you know what she looks like? Perhaps you might view the deceased and confirm whether she is the woman you seek?"

"No, I've never met my brother's wife. I was in Scotland,

caring for our land near Dunsmuir, when a letter arrived with details of my brother's marriage and sudden death."

"It's getting late in the evening, McDuff. Where are you lodging?"

"The Eggford Tavern. I intended to remain for a day or two while seeking information."

Percy nodded. "Since the Widow McDuff isn't going anywhere, we can talk in the morning."

"Happily," McDuff replied. "I came seeking answers, and I shan't leave until I have them."

Percy bade the man good evening and brusquely ignored the gawkers trying to question him as he went to Aisha and, his voice soft, said, "Come, my lady. It's been an eventful day, and I am in desperate need of several glasses of wine and a good fuck."

Aisha strode beside him to the carriage, Bella, Hanna, and Eveline, accompanied by their admirers and a wobbly Shakespeare, following. "What did McDuff want?"

"Once we're home, sweet puss. 'Tis not information I want bruited about until I can investigate the circumstances."

"You intend to accept my aid? What a surprise, Percy dear," she said drolly.

"Oh, my disbelieving Isha, on this case I definitely want your help. I fear the Widow McDuff or Preston was very much a charlatan."

"Ooh, do you think she returned to find another husband?"

"I don't know, Isha. Hopefully, we'll uncover the reason for her return and her death."

FORTY-FOUR

Aisha's palm cupped Percy's testicles and gently squeezed as her lips glided down his cock. His groan at the quick tongue flick filled her with satisfaction. She dragged her mouth upward and pulled away. "I love your cock; the thick veins against my tongue when I suck your flesh are especially nice."

Aisha lifted her head and climbed off the bed to test the silk ribbons that had Percy spread-eagle on their bed. When they retired for the night, she'd silently got the ribbons from the cabinet and, with no word between them, he'd laid on the bed and spread his arms and legs to be bound.

In the years of their love, they'd come to understand each other's signs, especially when they made love. There were days or nights where no words were needed, and others where the erotic language of love was such a heady spark they barely made it to their bedroom before taking their pleasure.

Satisfied with the security of her ribbons, Aisha returned to the task she'd set for herself—keeping Percy as hard as possible for as long as he could stand the pressure. Tracing the vein from the tip of his erection to the base of his cock, her tongue scraped the taut skin with feather-like touches. Percy's hips wiggled, but the silk restraints binding him made the movement almost imperceptible.

Her hand left his balls and a finger went to the puckered hole of his arse. She teased him with a circular motion that mimicked her mouth on the head of his erection. The first time her lips encircled his penis, she knew she'd never tire of the taste and feel of him on her tongue and against the back of her throat. The gentle roughness of his flesh, the rhythmic pulse of blood-filled veins, and the unique scent that was Percy Howard delighted her.

"Sweet puss," he moaned, "will you give me release?"

"Not yet, beloved. I intend to make love to you for a bit longer. Do you need a brief cessation?"

"No, woman! I need to ejaculate," he growled.

Aisha laughed as she languidly slid up his body until her lips hovered over his. She pressed soft kisses at the corner of his mouth, on his chin, and his throat before she replied to his demand.

"Oh, my lusty husband, thou canst control thy passion," she murmured. "I wish to toy with thee a bit longer before I take you to paradise. Canst thou bear it?"

While she spoke, Aisha moved until her lower lips lightly pressed against his hardness. "I would caress your cock with my private parts until thou ached with desire, begged to be set aflame with pleasure."

She rubbed against him, the friction of flesh against flesh momentarily stealing her breath. Percy's incoherent mumbling added to the tension building inside her. She slid a finger between them and felt the slickness. Her fingers parted her lips and her free hand gripped his staff, guiding it inside her.

"Oh fuck, Isha!"

A throaty laugh preceded her declaration. "Sweet Percy, that is exactly what I'm about to do."

~

PERCY'S HAND grazed along Aisha's hip. "We have company, sweetheart."

She groaned then mumbled, "Who'd dare to visit so early in the morning?"

Walter Howard's soft crow and gentle peck at her hair evoked a curse, then a giggle. As the rooster settled between her and Percy, Aisha shifted until she sat. Stroking Walter's comb, she greeted him. "Good morning, Walter. I'm not going to ask how you managed to violate our privacy or escape Martha's notice. However, I will ask how Othello's hens and Ermegarde are faring."

As Walter clucked and crowed in response to Aisha, Percy groaned. "Don't encourage him. Can't you have these little talks in the coop? Perhaps take over the feeding of him and the hens so he ceases these visits?"

Walter swung his head in Percy's direction and eyed him dangerously before crowing as loud as possible. The rooster glanced at Aisha before he turned and, with apparent intent, walked across Percy's belly to hop off the bed and strut to the door. The cock shook his feathers, then leapt for the door's handle, his feet pulling it down. The door now ajar, Walter strode out of the room.

"'Tis a sad, sad day when I have to compete with a rooster for my lady's affections."

Aisha leaned over and kissed him. "Never fear, my lord. I much prefer the cock I married to the one who just departed."

Sometime later, Aisha and Percy strolled into the dining room. She smiled to see everyone, even a disgruntled

Shakespeare, seated at the table. She and Percy went to the side table and prepared their breakfast and joined the others. She wasn't surprised when Uncle Robert was the first to speak.

"Had I known there would be a true murder, I would have attended the fair. The last time I attended, the company's performance was interrupted by Squire Wesley's bull."

Robert's face became reflective. "If memory serves, it was the Widow Everett's cow Maude who stirred such extraordinary passion in Wesley's bull that he broke free of his pen to seek his lady love. The entire village chased after the bull. However, by the time Wesley caught up with him, the bull had mounted Maude, and Sadie was screaming for him to cease."

Ahmara rolled her eyes at her husband. "Robert dear, what does a bull and a cow have to do with the murder of that poor woman yesterday? I'm terribly confused by your tale."

She sipped her atay and directed her gaze to Percy. "My husband means the world to me, but sometimes I cannot fathom the workings of his mind. Is the victim Helena Preston, Percy?"

"According to Ned and Andrew, the deceased is, and she returned to Eggford after her latest husband died, a Stuart McDuff. She was residing with Mistress Simply. We'll know more once I question those who came in contact with the victim."

He glanced at his wife and the other women sitting around the table, who'd been struggling with their amusement the entirety of his uncle's tale. "Isha, I intend to ride to the village. Do you go with me?"

She shook her head. "I shall remain here with our guests."

Ahmara nodded. "You go, Percy, and confirm the deceased is the Preston woman. Robert and I will tell Aisha what we know about Helena Preston."

"Why can't you tell me before I leave? Perhaps the information will help solve the case."

"Because nephew, if it isn't Helena, then there's no point in spreading rumors," his uncle stated. "Now you go and investigate and leave me here with the ladies."

"Yes, uncle." Percy rose from his chair and went to kiss his wife. "I'll return as soon as I can, Isha."

With breakfast at an end, Aisha suggested they go to the small parlor. She was curious to hear what her aunt and Percy's uncle had to say about the dead woman. Once everyone was seated, Aisha frowned. "Where's Bella?"

The door swung open and Bella strolled into the room. "Bidding farewell to Will. Cousin Percy is taking him to Eggford so Will can make his way to London or Stratford."

"Well done, Bella!" Hannah cheered. "Let his wife handle his uncouth manners and drunkenness."

Silas was several steps behind Bella as he rolled in a cart. He placed it next to Aisha. "If you need anything, my lady, please ring for me."

"Is Martha free?" Silas nodded, and Aisha said, "Please ask her to join us."

Once Silas left, she began to fill the cups with atay. "I believe Martha may also have information about the hapless widow."

Martha entered the room, and Robert waved her over to a chair next to Ahmara. Before Aisha could explain why she'd sent for her, Robert launched into an account of what happened. Aisha handed Martha a cup of atay and waited until Robert decided to take a sip of wine to gain control of the conversation.

"Since my lord is off to Eggford to verify the identity of the deceased, we're left to our devices. Aunt Ahmara and Uncle

Robert were about to tell us what they knew of Helena Preston or McDuff."

"Isn't she the woman who seduced old man Preston with the lie of pregnancy?" Martha asked, looking at Ahmara and Robert.

"My word," Robert said. "I'd forgotten that bit. She and her mother, Marjorie Douglas, were both bedding Preston."

"Ewww," Eveline sneered. "I would never fuck someone who bedded my mother!"

Aisha frowned. "What do you know about the pair, Martha? Were they born in Eggford? Douglas is not an English name. Were the women from Scotland?"

"That I can answer, my lady. Marjorie was a distant cousin to Edwina Simply, and when Marjorie's husband died, she and Helena came to live with the only living relative Marjorie had. Squire Simply wasn't too pleased, but he accepted his wife's decision in the matter."

Robert snorted. "Edwina governed that house. Besides, Simply married her when she was but seventeen and he nearly fifty. After she gave him a son and a daughter, he refused her nothing, no matter how distasteful."

"The widower Oliver Preston became enamored of Helena and married her; she and her mother ruled his household with iron gloves. Marjorie died within two years of her daughter's marriage, and Preston followed her to the grave three years after. It was then Helena cast her eye on Ned Turner and Andrew Willoughby, playing them like puppets on a string."

Ahmara tutted. "I remember, and then she upped and skittered away to who knows where, leaving those two at war over her arse."

Robert got up and refilled his wine glass. "Mistress Simply said Helena met a man and married him in London, and that's the last Eggford saw or heard of her. At least until now—if that body is hers."

The door opened, and Percy strolled into the room. All eyes were on him as he came over to kiss Aisha. "Miss me, sweet puss?"

"You haven't been gone long enough for that, Percy Howard. Only an hour or so. What did you find out about the mysterious woman?"

He went to fill a glass with wine and returned to stand beside her chair. "The victim was Helena Preston, and possibly Helena McDuff and the widow of Stuart McDuff. According to Duncan McDuff, his brother married a woman named Helena in Clerkenwell, so I've sent for the marriage records."

"What happened to the husband?" Bella asked.

"Rumor until confirmed, but Stuart McDuff died as a result of his fondness for eels. I've also requested the coroner's records on McDuff's demise."

"A female scorpion," Eveline commented.

Bella cried, "Of course!" while Hannah simultaneously said, "Mate and slay."

Ahmara stared at the trio. "What on earth are you three babbling about?"

"Something I read when the brothel had to close while Lord Ross investigated Lord Tidwell's death," Eveline explained. "Apparently, there are female scorpions who mate and kill the male, sometimes eating them. What if Helena McDuff was such a woman? I've heard stories of women who engaged in such things." She giggled and added, "Although they don't eat their dead husbands as the female scorpion does."

Percy smiled at her. "I do believe, Miss Eveline, you may have provided a clue on Helena's murder."

Eveline's blush earned her the teasing of Hannah and

Bella. Aisha listened to the playful words and smiled. While she had great affection for all of the Cock & Oyster ladies, Hannah and Eveline were dearer to her heart. The pair, along with Randall, had taken Bella under wing and taught her the skills she needed to manage the brothel.

"Percy, Uncle Robert, we are leaving you two to your own devices. The ladies and I will be in the garden. We will see you for dinner."

"I need to have a word with our hen keeper," he replied. "Walter is becoming far too bold with his incursions into our bedroom. Also, wife, I really wish you wouldn't encourage him with your caresses."

Aisha shrugged and rose from her seat. "You're jealous because I know how to please your cock."

Laughter trailing behind her, she and the other ladies strolled out of the parlor.

FORTY-FIVE

"Boil, boil, toil and trouble," said a deep burr.

"Eye of newt, tail of a scorpion," uttered a second voice.

"Cauldron full, she lives no more," hissed a third.

Three heavily cloaked and masked figures emerged from the darkness to gather in the shelter of a group of trees. Late evening fog provided concealment for their clandestine meeting, a small lantern the only source of light. Angus MacBeth, a grizzled Scot, was the first to speak, his voice gruff and his Scottish burr thick. "Did the townspeople confirm the witch's name?"

"Aye," Duncan McDuff replied. "It was Helena Douglas as Preston will confirm. I refuse to give her my brother's name."

"Nor my father's," Clifford Preston spat. "I, for one, am glad she can no longer prey on the hapless."

"How can we be certain, Duncan?" Angus demanded.

McDuff cackled softly. "We can be certain, cousin. One of the town's women, a Mistress Simply, is a kinswoman, and she confirmed the body as the daughter of Marjorie Douglas, her cousin. The two players also knew the witch, for she'd plied her wiles on them before she married my brother. 'Tis a scorpion we've killed for sure."

"Then I'll be heading back to Dunsmuir," MacBeth said. "I came to see justice served, and 'tis done. Thank ye, Preston, for your hospitality and discretion. I'm for home since I've been away from Lady MacBeth and our bairns too long. What of you, McDuff? Will ye be heading back to Scotland?"

"Nay, I'll stay a few days to see what Lord Ross does."

Angus's growl echoed among the trees. "Lord Ross? Percy Howard, Salisbury's man?"

"Aye, he's the laird of Eggford and the Queen's representative for the county."

"What can ye tell us about Ross, Preston?" Angus questioned. "Will he pose a danger to us? Do I need to fix another problem?"

Preston gasped. "No, you return to Scotland since your hand is spotted with the scorpion's blood. Ross is extremely clever, and 'tis better for you to play the ghost in this matter."

"Aye, Angus. Recall Alastair Farquhar's foolishness and how that ended," McDuff agreed. "I'll send word if we need your aid. Go home to my cousin. Introductions have been made betwixt Preston and myself, and Squire Preston has offered me a room while I must remain in Eggford. We'll keep watch over Lord Ross's investigation."

"Aye, then. Fare thee both well," Angus said as he strode back in the direction he'd came. A minute later, the muffled clatter of horse hooves heading north pierced the fog.

Preston and McDuff waited a few minutes before they returned to their horses, mounted, and rode in silence to Preston's house.

PERCY KNOCKED on Clifford Preston's door. He'd sent a note telling the squire he'd would pay him a visit this morning. Fortunately, the Cock & Oyster ladies had extended their visit when Randall and Matthew returned to Islington and decided to join Aisha on a visit to Patience Delbrey and the ladies of the Wandering Eye.

"Good morning, Lord Ross," Preston's servant said as he opened the door.

Percy followed him to Preston's library. Once the door closed behind him, Preston rose to greet him and offered him a chair. Sitting, Percy smiled. "I won't keep you long, Squire. I have a few questions, and I wondered if I could find the answers with you since your father was married to Helena Douglas, although it appears that was only one of her names."

"Of course, my lord. May I offer you a glass of wine?"

"None, thank you. Were you aware your father was Mistress Helena's third husband?"

Preston gaped at Percy. "Third? Her mother declared she was never wed, and virginal when my father married Helena. He was deeply infatuated with her, you know."

Percy arched an eyebrow, and a sardonic smile crossed his lips. "No, I wasn't aware of your father's affections."

"Three husbands, you say?"

"Apparently, Mistress Helena's first two husbands were minor lords in Scotland, Banquo McBain and Seamus MacBeth. Both men died within two years of marrying Helena."

"How old was she? My father believed she was twenty years of age. Were there children?"

"The information I've received doesn't indicate offspring," Percy responded. "What the men had in common was prosperity and a rather unexpected demise. How did your father die, Preston?"

"I wasn't here, my lord. I'd traveled to Manchester to visit my aunt who was ailing. I received word of my father's death and rushed home. Sadly, he was buried before I arrived." Preston stared at him. "Do you suspect foul play?"

"Since it's been two years since his death, I can only speculate, but I do believe Mistress Helena may have had a hand in all three men's deaths. Her death, unfortunately, puts paid to that speculation. However, I do have to ask whether you were involved in her murder."

"No, my lord. While I despised her and her mother's avaricious natures, once my father's estate was settled and Helena proved not to be with child, I gave her what my father bequeathed in his will and sent her on her way. I had no idea what became of her until the day you summoned me to identify her remains. My hands are spotless in her death even if her actions are like those of a female scorpion."

Percy stood. "Thank you for indulging my questions, Squire."

"I'm sorry Helena's life ended so tragically, though if what you've revealed about her past is true, then I am not surprised by the outcome."

Preston escorted him to the door and stood watching while he mounted his horse. As he rode away, Percy found the man's scrutiny unusual. He was also puzzled by the absence of curiosity about Helena's other husbands, as well as Preston's calling her a female scorpion—a description Duncan McDuff also used, and baffling since the two men allegedly met for the first time over her corpse.

Too many pieces missing, yet the scorpion reference wasn't happenstance. Both men knew more than they revealed even if they weren't Helena's murderers, and the connection was Scotland.

FORTY-SIX

Percy descended the stairs and went to the small parlor. The room had become the favorite gathering place for the women. As he neared the door, he heard Ahmara's cackle and hesitated before he knocked. Did he want to ask Aisha about scorpions and Scotsmen with the other women in the room?

"I know you're hovering, Percy Elwen Howard," Aisha declared. "Come in, we promise not to bite."

Bella's gaze flicked between her cousin and Percy once he entered the room. "How did you know Cousin Percy was there, Isha? I didn't hear footsteps or a knock."

"A ripple in the air, Bella," she laughed.

Aisha rose and went to pour her husband a glass of wine as he drew up a chair and sat. She handed it to him and resumed her seat. "Well, my lord? What conundrum are you trying to resolve that requires my logical mind?"

Ahmara snorted. "You and logic in the same breath? You have joyfully joined Percy in solving murders, kidnappings, and all type of nefarious doings. There's nothing logical in that, Aisha Resonne Howard."

"My kidnapping wasn't entirely my doing, Aunt," she huffed. "Farquhar's quest for revenge didn't succeed because I was perfectly logical. He called me a guest and I made him treat me like one. Another day in my company, he would have delivered me to Percy and paid him to boot."

Laughter erupted, and Percy added, "Even so, you can't find fault in what your aunt says, my lady. You have been quite busy in my affairs."

She stuck her tongue out, and he leaned over and kissed her cheek. "I do need your help. Four husbands, four deaths. Except for Preston the others were Scottish gentry, no two husbands died in the same manner, and yet everyone is dead, including Helena."

"Female scorpion," the ladies said simultaneously.

"Interesting that all of you spoke at once. A twist I hadn't mentioned is Preston and McDuff used precisely those words to describe her."

"There you have it," Aisha said. "The motive—a father and a brother murdered by the same woman. Revenge." She tapped her chin. "Which man killed her?"

Hannah pursed her lips, then grinned. "McDuff. His brother was the most recent husband to suffer the scorpion's sting."

"True," Aisha agreed. "However, Preston's father was a victim as well. Both men have motive, and Preston the means to hide the body beneath the stage."

The door opened and Robert strolled in, wine glass in hand. "What cruelty to Shakespeare's comedy despite his abominable behavior to Isabelle. Besides, no one dies in *A Midsummer Night's Dream*."

"Come sit next to me, Robert dearest," Ahmara said, patting the space beside her. "The players weren't performing the entire play, just the play within the play. The Pyramus and Thisbe bit, and in that, the lovers die by their own hands."

"Ah, Romeo and Juliet again. What foolishness, though Shakespeare's verse is quite fetching. The lovers met secretly; why didn't they carry forward rather than kill themselves? Although I do understand the Pyramus and Thisbe mishap, but Romeo and Juliet..." he snorted. "He married her. Should have taken her to Mantua since she was his wife."

Robert kissed his wife before he said, "I would never leave my sweet Mara behind. Where I go, she goes, and where she goes, I go."

"Percy, my love?"

"Yes, Isha?"

"Did you examine Helena's body?"

Percy grimaced before he said, "The only woman's body I'd examine is my wife's. The funeral man did at my behest."

"How was she murdered?"

"She was strangled, and it appears she struggled with her attacker. Her body bore bruises and cuts, though those may have come from the force used to push her past the trapdoor and out of the way of the actors. It's why there was blood."

"What a horrible way to die," Eveline said softly.

Aisha smiled when Hannah wrapped an arm around Eveline's shoulder. "Percy, do you think McDuff and Preston committed the murder? They joined together for revenge?"

Percy nodded. "I don't have a means to prove it, Isha. McDuff did not leave his room at the tavern, and Preston had the Ashedons visiting for the night."

"Then there was a third person involved. It would be useful to know how long she'd lain beneath the stage," Aisha muttered more to herself than to Percy. "If she were placed there at night, foxes and other creatures would have found her. So she had to be murdered and put beneath the trapdoor before sunrise when very few people are stirring."

She tapped her chin. "Who in Eggford is about before dawn? Aha!"

Everyone gazed at her expectantly as she grinned at Percy. "Stephen Coleman."

"You're brilliant, my lady." Percy set his glass on a nearby table and pulled Aisha onto his lap. He kissed her until she was breathless. "Sweet puss, I want to take you upstairs and throw your skirt over your head and devour your cunny," he whispered against her lips.

"Percy, who the hell is Stephen Coleman?" Robert demanded. "Put my niece down and let's solve this mystery. There's a dead woman who cries for justice."

"No more wine, Robert, my love," Ahmara said. "It's scrambled your reason. Dead people don't cry."

"Are you sending for Stephen now, Percy?" Aisha inquired breathlessly.

He shook his head. "'Tis too late in the day. I'll have Jessup fetch him in the morning. Stephen will be more at ease with him and you. To answer your question, Uncle, Stephen is an orphan, abandoned by his brother after their parents died and left at the door of the Eggford stables."

"That is horrible," Bella hissed. "Where is the brother? Did someone take a crop to his arse?"

Aisha chuckled at her cousin's fierceness. "Sadly no, Bella. The brother disappeared so the village folk adopted Stephen. He's very good with animals and very shy with people. His speech is slow and careful, and he only allows a few people to touch him."

"Your cousin being one," Percy chimed in.

"I couldn't stand the smell. 'Tis bad enough he carries the odor of the stables but the lack of bathing was far too much."

Ahmara knew how fierce her niece was about the topic. "How did you resolve the issue, Isha?"

"He and Jessup had become close because of their love of horses. I had Jessup bring him to the house, and I gifted Stephen with a soap made just for him, along with clean trousers and shirts."

"He's worshiped Lady Ross since that day. She's the only one who can get him to bathe," Percy remarked. "Which, beloved, is why I want you to speak to him about the victim. If he saw anything unusual."

Aisha grinned. "I knew you'd need my help, Lord Ross."

"Always, Lady Ross. Always."

AISHA SAT in Martha's kitchen, drinking atay and chatting with the older woman, when the back door to the manor opened. Jessup's voice, a husky sound, carried in the passage. He stepped into the kitchen, a freshly bathed Stephen at his heels. Jessup turned to the lad. "I'm going to leave you with my lady and Mistress Martha. I'll come fetch you when you're done."

"Good morning, Stephen," Aisha smiled. "Come sit with me. Mistress Martha made sweet buns this morning, and I'm about to have some. Would you like one?"

Stephen sat opposite her. "If you'd like to share."

His deep voice wasn't hesitant as he spoke—a sign of his comfort in her presence and Aisha pushed a plate in front of him with several buns on it. Stephen's grin was heartwarming. As he ate, she sipped her atay. When he'd devoured two buns, she began.

"You know about the woman found beneath the stage some time ago." He nodded and she continued. "Lord Ross and I wondered if you might have seen or heard something the morning of the performance. Strangers talking, perhaps."

Stephen nodded once more before picking up a third bun.

"Would you like to tell me what you saw or heard, Stephen? It's very important."

He put the half-eaten bun back on the plate and drank milk from the cup Martha had set in front of him. A worried look crossed his face as his eyes met Aisha's gaze. "There were two of them, the man and the woman. They were arguing because the big man wanted her to go with him and she didn't want to."

"Was the man from Eggford?"

He shook his head. "No, my lady, because his words were hard to understand. The woman broke free and ran toward the stage, but the man caught her and knocked her to the ground because he was bigger and faster. She wasn't moving and the sun was coming up and I ran to the stables to fetch Master Fletcher. When we got to the stage, they were gone."

"Did you see the man's face? His garments or anything that might tell us where he was from?"

"No, my lady. Wasn't enough light to see except maybe he wore a fur cloak because it was cold in the morning. His voice was different, like Master Burns but not kind."

"Thank you, Stephen. I think you may have helped Lord Ross solve a murder," Aisha said warmly as she stood.

Surprise colored his face, and Stephen's grin exploded. "I did? I helped Lord Ross?"

"Yes, you did."

Stephen bounded up from the bench and grabbed the last bun. "I need to tell Jessup and Master Fletcher." He whirled and grabbed Aisha in a tight hug. "I helped Lord Ross! Thank you, my lady."

Aisha and Martha watched him race out to the stables,

their eyes teary. "It's the first time he's hugged me, Martha," Aisha stammered.

"We all love you, Lady Aisha. All of Eggford. Well, except Simply and the widows. They'll not get beyond the fact Lord Ross fell in love with you and you've made him, and us, so happy."

Aisha hugged Martha and left the kitchen in search of Percy. She found him in the library. "Good morning, beloved."

He looked up and smiled. There was so much love in his eyes she felt hers starting to water again. Closing the door behind her, she strolled over to his desk and sat on her favorite chair.

"Behind the emotions in your beautiful brown eyes, I see satisfaction. Your conversation with Stephen went well?"

"It did, and he gave me a hug," she said. "I was surprised, although I think it had to do with my telling him he helped you solve Helena's murder."

"Yes, but I don't think I'd get a hug."

"Of course not, you're not as lovely and kind as I am, husband. Stephen did witness an altercation between a man and a woman. The woman attempted to flee, and the man caught her. Stephen left to go tell Fletcher, but when they returned, there was no one there."

"Did Stephen see the man's face or perhaps a horse he may have ridden?"

Aisha shook her head. "It was just before sunrise and there wasn't enough light. He did hear the man speak and said he sounded like Burns, which makes the killer a Scot."

"McDuff had to be involved," Percy gritted. "I suspect the second Scot was kin to MacBeth and Helena Douglas's murder was a revenge killing, Isha. And I doubt Preston is innocent in the matter as well."

"Do you plan to interrogate Preston or McDuff further?"

Percy rose from his chair and walked around to where she sat. He offered her his hand. "I don't think so, puss. McDuff has left Eggford. I'll report my suspicions to Salisbury and leave the matter in his hands. He or Her Majesty will have to decide whether it's worth pursuing the Queen's justice for a woman who murdered three, maybe four husbands."

"'Tis interesting, my love." At his cocked eyebrow, she tilted her head and peered at him. "The Tidwell case and this one are similar. Three women who killed their husbands or betrothed for wealth, yet to my knowledge, only one is dead. What is the difference?"

Percy tugged her up from the chair. "The difference is Ellen Chapman's kind heart. Come, I'd like to walk in the garden with my wife, maybe taste her cunny before supper."

"You aren't worried 'twill spoil your appetite?"

"Nay, love, it staves off the evening's hunger for pleasure."

"Such pretty words, Lord Ross."

"Why thank you, Lady Ross."

EPILOGUE

Dᴜɴsᴍᴜɪʀ, Scotland

NIGHT HUNG over the valley as Angus MacBeth strode into his stronghold. The stone walls were a welcome sight as he turned toward the stable. Leaving his horse in the hands of one of the lads, he tugged his fur cloak and strode toward the front door. The warmth of his house brought a tired smile to his face as he closed the door on the cold air and the end of his journey. His wife came rushing downstairs and flung herself into his arms, kissing his cheeks, then his lips. "You're home."

"Aye, told you to look for me in ten days."

His wife studied his weary face and ran her fingers along his reddish beard. "Is it done, Angus?"

He kissed her forehead. "Aye, my lady. I have done the deed. Didst thou not hear the noise of her screams as she rode the winged creature into hell?"

Lady MacBeth removed his thick fur coat and tossed it on a nearby chair. "The morning winds did howl and methought I heard a woman's voice pleading as the fates did cackle. Then all was quiet, and I believed it was nothing more than a dream."

"The she-scorpion is dead and will sting no more mates. Scotland is rid of her poison, forever."

"What of her mother? Does she still live?"

"Nay, she died some years back. I don't think anyone will care that Helena Douglas is on her way to hell to join her mother," he spat. "Now, no more talk of your wicked mam and sister, Hermia. Tell me how the sheep-shearing went and the health of our children."

"I will, but first let me feed you and get you a whisky," she replied, stroking his chest.

Her eyes narrowed, and she rubbed at a spot on his jerkin. His hand closed over hers. "What is it, wife?"

"A spot of dried blood. Out, out, damn spot," she muttered, her palm rubbing vigorously at the stain. "Out."

Our revels now are ended.

WILLIAM SHAKESPEARE

ABOUT THE AUTHOR

Elysabeth is the author of historical, paranormal, and contemporary romances and irreverent cozy mysteries. She loves writing about excluded Black histories, women with daggers, and the people who love them. In an alternative persona, she is a Shakespearean. While she enjoys writing the complexity of happily ever afters, she admits to writing characters who are dangerous when it comes to those they love, although she's not shy about sprinkling sexy sweetness where she can.

www.elysabethgrace.com

ALSO BY ELYSABETH GRACE

<u>The Daughters of Saria Series</u>

Fate's Match

Fate's Kiss

Fate's Consort

Fate's Promise

Fate's Guardians, A companion novella

<u>Midsummer Sisters</u>

For Your Heart Only

One Chance Only

<u>The Resonne Family</u>

Elizabethan Mischief

A Heart's Gift